The Unbearable Inspector Oberlin

Book five

of

The Cassie Black Trilogy

TAMMIE PAINTER

Yes, book five, because trilogies (like sourdough starters) refuse to be tamed.

The Unbearable Inspector Oberlin
Book Five of The Cassie Black Trilogy

Copyright © 2024 by Tammie Painter, All Rights Reserved

Daisy Dog Media supports copyright. Copyright fuels and encourages creativity, free speech, and legal commerce. Thank you for purchasing an authorized copy of this book and supporting the hard work of the author. To comply with copyright law you agree to not reproduce, scan, distribute, or upload any part of this work in any form without permission from the author.

This book is a work of fiction. Names, characters, places, and incidents either are the product of the author's imagination or are used fictitiously. Any resemblance to persons, living or dead, business establishments, events, or locales is entirely coincidental. This story was concocted entirely with human creativity; no generative AI was used in its creation.

You may contact the author by email at
Tammie@tammiepainter.com

Daisy Dog Media
Portland, Oregon 97222, USA

First Edition, October 2024
also available as an ebook

ALSO BY TAMMIE PAINTER

The Undead Mr Tenpenny: Cassie Black #1
The Uncanny Raven Winston: Cassie Black #2
The Untangled Cassie Black: Cassie Black #3
The Unusual Mayor Marheart, Cassie Black #4
The Unbearable Inspector Oberlin, Cassie Black #5
The Unexpected Mr Hopkins, Cassie Black #6
The Unwanted Inheritance of the Bookman Brothers
Hoard It All Before (A Circus of Unusual Creatures Mystery)
Tipping the Scales (A Circus of Unusual Creatures Mystery)
Fangs A Million (A Circus of Unusual Creatures Mystery)
Beast or Famine (A Circus of Unusual Creatures Mystery)
The Great Escape: 15 Tales of Humor, Myth, and Magic
Domna: A Serialized Novel of Osteria (Six-Part Series)
The Trials of Hercules: Book One of the Osteria Chronicles
The Voyage of Heroes: Book Two of the Osteria Chronicles
The Maze of Minos: Book Three of the Osteria Chronicles
The Bonds of Osteria: Book Four of the Osteria Chronicles
The Battle of Ares: Book Five of the Osteria Chronicles
The Return of Odysseus: Book Six of the Osteria Chronicles
13th Hour: Tales from Light to Midnight

WHAT READERS ARE SAYING...

ABOUT THE UNDEAD MR TENPENNY...

"...a clever, hilarious romp through a new magical universe..."

—Sarah Angleton, author of *Gentleman of Misfortune*

"Wow and wow again! I absolutely loved this book! You get such a feel for the characters and the story is so fast paced you don't want to put it down."

—Goodreads Reviewer

"Man oh man, did I love this book!"

—Jonathan Pongratz, author of *Reaper*

"...suffused with dark humor and witty dialogue, of the sort that Painter excels at..."

—Berthold Gambrel, author of *Vespasian Moon's Fabulous Autumn Carnival*

"...a fun and entertaining read. Great wit too."

—Carrie Rubin, author of *The Bone Curse*

ABOUT THE UNCANNY RAVEN WINSTON...

"More, please!"

—*Goodreads Reviewer*

"...quirky with a capital Q, and I mean that in the best way! ...I laughed out loud several times while reading this..."

—*Bookbub Reviewer*

"Magic, mayhem, mystery, it's all here."

—*Bookbub Reviewer*

ABOUT THE UNTANGLED CASSIE BLACK...

"...a great ending to a truly delightful ride."

—*Bookbub Reviewer*

"...super captivating! If you love magical hijinks, punny witticisms, and crazy adventure, then this is the series for you!"

—*Bookbub Reviewer*

"A truly satisfying end to a charming, funny, action-filled trilogy."

—*Goodreads Reviewer*

"If you are curious, you'll find the puzzles around you. If you are determined, you will solve them."

—Erno Rubik

THE
UNBEARABLE
INSPECTOR
OBERLIN

ANOTHER QUICK NOTE BEFORE WE BEGIN

A little wasp-, math-, and alligator-filled warning before we jump into this story...

This is the second book in The Cassie Black Trilogy 2.0. And since I find it's always good to start a book off with a dollop of mathematical confusion, it's also the fifth book in The Cassie Black Trilogy 1.0.

Anyway...

The Cassie Black Trilogy 2.0 is very much a traditional trilogy, meaning that the entire story takes place over the course of three books.

Which means if you don't read Book Four (*The Unusual Mayor Marheart*) before this one, you're going to feel very, very, *very* lost.

Now, I know getting lost can be a great way to discover new places and people, but it can also leave you stranded in a pit of ravenous alligators that you might escape... only to find yourself smacking face first into a wasp nest occupied by wasps who have just won the Angriest Wasps of the Year Award.

So, really, unless you are both an alligator wrangler and a wasp whisperer, please spend some time with **The Unusual Mayor Marheart** before you jump into this book.

And if you have already read *The Unusual Mayor Marheart*, I'm so glad to see you back! Now, let's get cracking on Cassie's misadventures with *The Unbearable Inspector Oberlin*.

PROLOGUE
LOCK HER UP

Cassie Black: A Dangerous, Despicable Fiend

She's been kicked out of the Academy for cheating. She's been running an unlicensed detective agency. She very likely obtains clients for that agency by stealing their treasures and tricking them into hiring her. She then pesters those innocent people about paying up while refusing to hand over the items she 'found.' She's worse than a thug from an organized crime ring.

Yes, I'm talking about Cassie Black.

But even when she's not coercing and conning clients, she's behaving like a child who spews insults and throws tantrums, as she recently did with our own Mayor Marheart. At least the mayor was wise enough to fire this childish scoundrel on the spot.

That said, my readers will be glad to know they no longer need to worry about Miss Black's predatory and infantile ways, because rumor has it that yesterday she failed to get her detective's license.

All I can say is, what a relief!

It is my hope that any day now she'll be closing up that agency of hers and leaving Rosaria for good.

We'll all be able to rest easier once she does. After all, how can we ever feel safe with someone in our midst who's been caught on camera at the scene of not just one, but TWO vicious attacks: Clive Coppersmith a few days ago, and our dear Winnifred Oberlin just yesterday.

As if the despicable attacks aren't bad enough, not only are Mr Coppersmith's and Mrs Oberlin's valuables still in Miss Black's possession (suspicious? I say yes), but two more of Miss Black's clients have disappeared.

And those clients?

Her own parents!

Think about this a moment. Miss Black is a detective who has a dwindling number of clients; and with bills to pay, she must be getting desperate for money.

What's my point, you might ask?

Well, as my readers might know, Chloe and Simon Starling not only have a couple of nice pieces of real estate in Rosaria, but they've also received a substantial amount of back pay from HeadQuarters as recompense for the time they were in the Mauvais's clutches.

Think about it. A fair amount of money? Enviably located property? And only one person who might inherit both? Again, one's suspicions don't have to wander too far.

With Miss Black's previous rule-breaking behavior in both the Norm and Magic worlds she has already proven her propensity for questionable behavior and flexible ethics. So, it's hard not to worry about the fate of her clients. Even the ones she's related to.

But it's not my role here to cast stones. All I can say is, for a 'detective', for a person supposedly on the side of the law, Cassie Black sure seems to be at the epicenter of a lot of criminal coincidences.

Personally, I wouldn't be surprised to see Miss Black under arrest before the year, perhaps even the month, is out. In fact, for the safety of us all, I hope Inspector Oberlin has her behind bars sooner rather than later.

I leave you with this to ponder, my friends: Why did Clive Coppersmith and Winnifred Oberlin have to die? Where are Chloe and Simon Starling? Was Mel Faegan, who has also recently gone missing, a client of hers? And which of us is her next victim?

Should Cassie Black be scrutinized more closely? Should she be locked up? I say YES. Whole-heartedly.

Because Cassie Black is no friend of ours. She's not wanted in Rosaria. And she never will be.

CHAPTER ONE
UNWANTED VISITORS

A light tapping inside my closet door disturbed what was turning into an Olympic-level sulk. Seriously, we're talking silver medal moping. And if I was ever going to get the gold, I needed practice. Which is why I ignored the tapping to wallow in the many sources of my foul mood.

First, as my admirer at the *Herald* had delighted in pointing out in this morning's opinion section, there was my ever-worsening client problem. Two had been murdered and another one, Mayor Matilda Marheart, had fired me.

Which meant that my only remaining client was a very persnickety Bookworm whose missing book I did find, but he refused to sign off on a job done simply because the book was missing a couple of pages. The mind boggles.

Of course, Dr Runa Dunwiddle was also still a client, but so far, I'd been too distracted by slanderous newspaper articles, squawking desk calendars, and slapstick-loving office chairs to sort out what had happened to her magic samples and her antique bone saw that were stolen when her clinic was broken into a few days ago.

Luckily, so far, she's not annoyed with me for neglecting her case, because at this point she might be the only person in Rosaria — MagicLand, to you and me — who isn't.

Second, as noted ever so eloquently by the *Herald*, my parents are missing.

Again.

I mean, I know I'm not the most organized person in the world, but it's hard to believe that even I could misplace two people twice in one lifetime.

Yesterday, as soon as Fiona had pointed out that my parents' missed appointments with Runa might mean something more than them being too busy eating pastries to go to the doctor, I'd tried calling them. I tried texting them. And when the calls went to voice mail and the texts remained unanswered, I remembered their phone sitting on their bathroom counter. The spot they'd left it when they'd—

What? Left it behind as they often did when they went out? Hadn't been able to get to it when they'd been parent-napped from their own home? I didn't know.

All I knew was that, after rushing to my parents' house straight from Mrs Oberlin's, I'd discovered their phone still on the counter but found no clue as to their whereabouts. And even though I'd taken the phone with me, I'd stubbornly (and illogically, I'll admit) been calling their number nearly every waking hour, if only to hear their voices on their voice mail message.

Third, over the past few weeks, hundreds of other Magics around the world had gone missing without a trace. No one, not even Olivia at Magic HQ, knows if they're alive or dead. This sounds like the perfect case for a clever and wily detective who has already proven her mettle at finding un-findable people, right?

Wrong.

See, HQ insists I have to have a detective's license to undertake official cases, even though you'd think a missing Magics emergency would be the exact time to bend the rules.

But Magic bureaucracy has no room for that sort of thing.

To get that license I only needed a single satisfied client to slap their signature on my application form. Which, with the client issues I've just noted, proved much harder than expected and the application's due date went whooshing by faster than Tinkerbell when she's pumped full of pixie dust.

After some groveling on my part, Olivia at HQ had practically handed me my license on a platter. But my stupid need to prove myself left me abandoning any sense of logic and turning down what I now realize was a very generous offer that probably won't be repeated until at least the next millennium.

There's more, but that gives you the general idea of why, when I crawled out of bed this morning — which, for anyone keeping track, puts us at barely fourteen hours after discovering Winnifred Oberlin dying in her driveway — I'd decided the best course of action would be to hole up in the apartment and mumble curses at myself over several cups of the strongest English Breakfast tea known to man.

It's also why I was still ignoring that insistent tapping from inside my closet and mentally begging the tapper to go away.

But, as privacy seems to be something that happens to other people in MagicLand, my closet door eased open anyway.

"Ah, you are home," said Mr Tenpenny as he stood on the threshold of the portal to MagicLand at the back of my closet.

"What are you doing here?" I grumbled.

"Sometimes I think it's not your magic that needed training, but your manners. May I come in?" He glanced down at a jumble of shoes. "Rather, *can* I come in without risk to life and limb?"

Knowing I couldn't tell him to buzz off without feeling even worse about myself, I made a reluctant be-my-guest gesture. With a sweeping motion of his hands, he cleared a narrow path through my closet like Moses parting the Red Converse Sea.

The moment Mr T stepped into my apartment, an overwhelming feeling of frumpiness added to my already low mood. Even though it was late afternoon, I hadn't bothered to change or to brush my hair, while everything about Busby Tenpenny was neat and crisp. Crisp suit. Crisp collar on a starched shirt. Crisp part in his steely grey hair. And a crisply folded pocket square in his breast pocket. Although, the yellow smiley faces on the silky accessory did offset some of its crispy formality.

Pablo, perhaps feeling frumpy himself, gave a pitiable mewl from the confines of his carrier.

"Is he in jail?" asked Mr T as he squatted down to poke his fingers through the bars and tickle Pablo under the chin.

"Alastair insists Pablo has to be caged if he's going to be in the apartment."

Did I forget to mention that Alastair's mad at both me and Pablo? Me, because after I'd made a statement to the police regarding the death of Clive Coppersmith, they'd dragged Penley Tremaine from Tremaine's Toy Emporium in for questioning.

Once released (without any charges being leveled against him, mind you), Tremaine canceled Alastair's most lucrative contract and refused to carry any of Alastair's handcrafted, very in-demand collectible toy timers. With my inability to keep my clients alive long enough for them to pay for my work, that lost contract meant our only source of income was some mysterious commission Alastair's been working on night and day.

Which leads us to why he's furious with Pablo. With the worst of bad timing, right after Tremaine fired Alastair, Pablo snuck into Alastair's workroom and launched a fatal attack on his nearly completed commission. Then, when Alastair went to pick up one of the broken pieces, Pablo swatted at him, leaving four rows of scratch marks across Alastair's cheek.

"He thinks Pablo is dangerous," I said, after explaining the feline follies to Mr T in a very rambling, out-of-sorts manner. "So, yes, Pablo's now confined to kitty jail."

"He's always seemed perfectly tame to me. Perhaps you should have Runa look him over when she has a moment."

Ignoring my non-committal noise, Mr T tilted his head toward Pablo's tiny prison cell. "May I?" I nodded, more out of curiosity than anything else. "Or perhaps you'd like to learn this spell. It's quite handy, especially when you find yourself in a cramped hotel room."

"Better not," I said. Because in addition to the multitude of misfortunes mentioned above, sometime last week my magic suddenly decided it didn't want to behave. Which means any spell I cast could either be fifty times stronger than intended or do nothing at all. With Dr Dunwiddle having no idea of what was causing this or how to fix it, I'd not only been put on magic suspension, but also had a trace put on my magic that would alert HQ if I so much as performed a Cooling Charm on an over-hot cup of tea.

"That problem's still acting up?" asked Mr Tenpenny. "I thought you—"

"Runa's seeing to it," I said curtly.

"Good. I don't want you to be concerned, but this isn't typical. Especially for someone with your magical strength."

"Yeah, that's really reassuring. So, the spell...?" I gestured to the carrier.

"Best get him out first. It's not dangerous magic, but you never know how it might affect a feline. If Alastair's annoyed with him now, he'd hardly approve of a puma-sized Pablo. Now you behave, young man," Busby said as he reached in and lifted Pablo from the carrier. Rather than bolt for freedom, Pablo eased into the crook of Mr T's left arm, purring loudly and gazing at the posh Brit like a damsel who's just been rescued by the handsomest knight in the realm.

Mr Tenpenny gave a slight twist of his right hand while making an expansive sweeping motion with his arm. He peered inside the carrier, and a self-satisfied smile lifted his thin lips.

"That should do nicely." Then to Pablo he said, "Shall we give it a test run?"

Keeping his hands against Pablo's sides to point him forward, Mr T set Pablo down outside the cage's door.

"I wouldn't—" I warned, not wanting my cat's claws to turn Mr Tenpenny's Saville Row attire into something so ragged it would be better suited to the wardrobe department of a zombie movie.

Pablo loathed his carrier. He'd once had a near-death experience in its close confines, so getting him into the thing now required brute force and a high threshold for pain. Not to mention dealing with Morelli's complaints about what form of animal cruelty I was inflicting on the poor beast.

But my warning came to an abrupt halt when Pablo glanced inside the carrier, then gazed up to Mr T with — I'm not kidding — a look of appreciative awe in his green eyes. Without unsheathing a single claw, Pablo leapt into the carrier.

"Did you do a BrainSweeping Charm on him?"

"Not at all. Just a simple Expansion Spell. Have a look." He stepped aside. Hesitantly, I crouched down to peer in.

I've seen and been through too much in my formative years to normally be a person filled with child-like wonder, but magic could still astound me. You'd think I'd get used to doors opening onto entirely different cities, trolls healing broken bones with only their touch, and tea kettles serving as video call conduits. But this? This had my mouth gaping.

Inside Pablo's cage, which from the outside measures maybe one foot across by three feet long by one foot tall, was a cat's paradise of armchairs to sprawl across, boxes to lounge in, leafy trees to climb and scratch, a catnip garden to roll in, sunny spots to bask in, and birds to swat at (hologram birds, of course, don't freak out and call the Audubon Society on me). All in a garden that stretched at least thirty feet deep and twenty feet wide.

"You can go in if you'd like to spend time with him," said Mr Tenpenny. "But remember to apply a Marshmallow Charm to yourself first to avoid a rather uncomfortable squeeze through the carrier's opening."

Which would be great advice if I could do magic. Well, I could do magic, just not reliably. With my power off kilter, a Marshmallow Charm on myself could either permanently turn me into a pile of squishy sugar, or backfire and make me as rigid as a block of marble. If I wanted time with Pablo, I was going to have to coax him out. Although, seeing how pleased he was to wiggle his butt and pounce after a glittery sparrow, I doubted even an entire bag of Kitty Crunch Cat Treats would lure him to my side.

"Now, as to why I'm here," Busby began after I'd finished making various sputtering sounds to show how stupidly impressed I was by his magic.

"It wasn't just to remodel my cat carrier?"

"Hardly," he said coolly, the crisp façade having returned.

Despite the late summer heat warming the apartment, my cheeks went cold. I'd been fearing this visit.

See, Busby Tenpenny was the case manager for my detective's license. I could go into details, but this catch-up is already getting lengthier than I intended. To sum things up, as already noted, I didn't get my license application done by the deadline Busby had set, so I'd gone to HQ for help. Olivia Whalen had granted me that help in the form of a two-week extension to solve a case and get a client to sign my application form.

Clearly, by going to Olivia, I'd gone over Mr T's head. Even with my social IQ being shallower than a rain puddle in Death Valley, I know that's a big faux pas if you want to keep your higher ups happy. And right now, Mr T did not look happy.

"So, you're here to...?" I prodded tentatively.

But before Mr T could answer, someone began pounding on my front door in a very invading-troops-armed-with-a-battering-ram manner.

"Black!"

I suddenly wondered if, even without performing a Marshmallow Charm, I had the shoulder flexibility to squeeze into Pablo's cage.

CHAPTER TWO
A TENPENNY ESCORT

"Black!" Morelli shouted again as he continued hammering on the door.

Mr Tenpenny raised a questioning eyebrow, and Pablo ran over to sit in front of the door, making the mewling meow-bark thing he does when greeting a visitor.

"I better see what he wants before he breaks the door down and makes me pay for the damage." I went over and nudged Pablo aside. Then, timing it with the knocking, I whipped open the door. Morelli's fist, finding no door where one was supposed to be, continued its momentum and caused him to stagger forward a pace.

Morelli, with dark and heavy circles under his eyes, glowered at me in a way he hadn't done in months.

"What did you say to Matilda?"

"We agreed to terminate our contract together," I replied pragmatically.

From the corner of my eye, I could see Busby, who stoutly refused to read the *Herald*, do a double take at this news.

Morelli's hands went up like he wanted to strangle me. Then, as if some unseen force was pushing them down, he lowered his arms.

"You're just lucky I've never been released from that promise to protect you," he grumbled, his hands now unwillingly pinned to his side. "How could you be so rude to her? I thought you needed clients."

"Yeah, well, I don't need clients who think they're the only clients in the universe, and who talk down to me like I'm a moronic two-year-old."

This brought Morelli up short. He was likely still at that stage of a relationship where he thought Matilda could do no wrong. I'd never been like that with Alastair. Almost from day one, I was more than willing to assume he had sided with an evil wizard, assisted that evil wizard in his plans to destroy the world, and kidnapped four-year-old me from the safety of MagicLand.

"Well, that's not how she tells it," Morelli huffed. He looked awful. And that's not just me taking a dig at my half-troll landlord. He had the appearance of someone who's had a really rough night and an even rougher morning.

"I'm sure she doesn't."

"I recommended you to her. Did you have to go off and be all, all… all *Cassie* on her?" After a very put-upon sigh, he said, "I'll see what I can do to get her to give you another chance."

"Please don't."

"Then don't expect help from me in the future," he snapped.

"I won't," I snapped back. Again, I owed Morelli a lot, but the past couple of days had been about as delightful as an appendectomy performed without anesthesia. I'd lost my stamina for playing nice.

Morelli turned to march down the stairs, stomping with harsh, ground-jarring footsteps. And this from the guy who was always on *my* case about being noisy on the stairwell? I shut the door, and Pablo growled low in his throat.

"You tell him, boy."

I went over to the table and took two deep swigs of tea. Which by then had gone disgustingly tepid. Mr Tenpenny was staring at me.

"Did you really have bad words with the mayor?"

I shrugged. I didn't want to talk about it. I suppose neither Matilda nor I had been at our best in that conversation.

"You've got to learn a little customer service, Cassie." I didn't appreciate the critical tone in Mr T's voice, but, having run out of scones and cookies several hours ago, I couldn't muster the energy for an argument. "These aren't dead people you're working with now."

"The dead were so much easier," I muttered.

"Were they?" he asked wryly.

He had a point. It was working with the dead — some of whom, like him, turned out to be not-quite-as-dead-as-you'd-expect — that had gotten me tangled up with an incredibly powerful Magic trying to drain me of my power to turn me into a lobotomized catatonic who could serve as his rechargeable magical battery while he took over the world.

I'm sure you can relate.

"If you even think of lecturing me about this, I will turn your hair permanently orange," I threatened half-heartedly. "And trust me, with your coloring, it won't be a good look. Also, with the state of my magic, your hair might just end up plaid. Do you want plaid hair?" Busby gave an acquiescent tip of his head, as if dropping the Matilda matter. For now. "So, back to my question. You're here because…?"

"You need an escort."

My belly flipped, lurched, then made a stab at the pole vault. With my magic in disarray, I needed someone with reliable power to take me, to *escort* me, through long-distance portals. You know, like the one from MagicLand to Magic HQ.

And why would I be hauled off to HQ? Again, please refer to the *Herald's* latest article. Two dead clients? Two mysteriously missing parents? No matter how you try to spin it, that's some bad math.

Olivia had let these facts slide when I'd met with her yesterday, but if Mr Tenpenny was peeved at me for going over his head, he might have made sure she was well aware of the various crimes I was at the center of.

"How long will we be gone?" I asked, my nerves taking up a shovel and speedily digging out a very large pit in my stomach. "Do I need to pack a bag?"

"Bag? No, although a gift might be in order."

Now this was too much! Olivia could call up cake, tea— hell, entire four-course meals with the flick of a finger (thanks to the hard-working pixies at the Tower of London). She couldn't seriously expect me to bring her a gift at such a time.

"And you really ought to change," said Mr T, scanning the outfit I'd been too mopey to change out of that morning. "I know casual is quite the thing for young people today, but I think something dressier than Snoopy pajamas is more appropriate for a party, don't you agree?"

"Party?" I said, completely baffled. I mean, I know I sometimes have trouble figuring out the logic of Magics, but this was taking it to a whole new level.

Busby's fingers barely grazed his blazer at the spot where an inner pocket would be. A cream-colored piece of cardstock appeared between his fingers. Having received one myself, I instantly recognized it.

"Mr Wood's retirement party," he said. "You haven't forgotten, have you?"

Disbelief rendering me mute, I stared at Mr T. Maybe something was wrong with his mind. After all, he *had* died twice in only a matter of a few weeks. Surely, that sort of thing has to cause some lingering effects.

"You can't expect me to go to that," I said once I found my voice. "Not with everything—"

"Yes, with everything." His gaze darted to the newspaper, open to the most recent anti-Cassie article — sorry, 'opinion piece' — and its accompanying photo of me looking down grimly at Mrs Oberlin. "That, this business with Alastair, your cases. You need a break. Now, go get yourself suitably attired, and we'll pop in for a bit to offer up our felicitations."

When I didn't move, he added, "You can't not go. It would be rude. And," he said after a pause, "I have something to discuss with you on the way."

A statement which had my nerves swapping their shovels for a backhoe to more thoroughly scrape out that pit of worry in my gut.

CHAPTER THREE
SNORT 'TIL YOU GAG

Still convinced Mr Tenpenny had lost it and that perhaps he, not Pablo, was the one who needed examined by Runa, I went into the bedroom and changed into a black skirt and a red V-neck t-shirt. As I tried to tame my hair, I could hear the *clank clank clank* of metal being hammered in the workroom below. Call me petty, but I might have wished for Alastair to hit his thumb with the hammer as punishment for being such a jerk to Pablo.

"Better," Mr T declared when I stepped out. "Shall we?" He held out his arm, and I took it, feeling more awkward than a buffalo on rollerblades. On our way down the apartment's stairs, Mr T spotted the garden gnome on duty at the workroom door and gave me a quizzical glance.

"I'm apparently a threat to the secret workings of whatever is going on in the man cave and must be kept out at all times."

"Given how clumsy you can be, I might almost understand." Mr Tenpenny nodded to the gnome. "Hello, Guildenstern."

"How do, Busby?" The gnome directed a disgruntled snort my way. Probably because, even after seeing them day in and day out for the past few weeks, I still couldn't tell which of the twin gnomes was Rosencrantz and which was Guildenstern. I'd kind of been hoping they hadn't noticed.

I suppose I should have asked Mr T how he could tell the difference, but I was still too lost in a daze of bewilderment over his expecting me to function at a party with all that was going on.

"I'll need to speak to you and your brother later," Mr T told the gnome.

"HQ business, sir?"

"I'd rather not say."

Busby darted his eyes to me and gave the tiniest shake of his head, as if I wouldn't notice. I let it slide, filing it away in the Questions to Ask Later part of my brain.

The moment we stepped out of the building's main door and onto the streets of Real Portland, Mr Tenpenny's nose wrinkled. I couldn't blame him. The odor of vehicle exhaust from the congested traffic was a sharp contrast after the clean air of MagicLand; and the thick smell of stale frying oil from the nearby food carts couldn't compare to the tempting aroma of Spellbound's fresh-baked bread.

With Mr T making forgettable small talk, we walked the five blocks to Wood's Funeral Home. When we got there, the parking lot was packed with cars.

"It's good we didn't drive," my escort commented as peals of laughter bubbled out from the small building. And although that's not a sound you normally hear at a funeral home, that's not what gave me pause.

"I can't do this," I said and stopped walking, pulling my arm from Busby's. "I can't go in there with laughing, happy people when my parents could be dead. It's ridiculous we're here at all. We should be looking for them, not going in to eat cake and drink whisky."

"There's whisky?" Mr T asked keenly.

"Just an assumption. It's Mr Wood's favorite tipple. But that's not my point. It's just like before. You're not taking the absence of my parents seriously. What is it with you Magics?"

Rather than answer, Busby scanned the area until he spotted a park bench. The same one I'd sat on with Mr Boswick back when I thought I was handling the Zombie Apocalypse like a pro.

"Let's talk," he said, guiding me toward the bench with a gentle press of his hand against the middle of my back. Once there, a pair of pigeons strutted before us like models trying out for a spot on the catwalk. "You understand the Confidentiality Spell. How it works?"

I did. It was a spell put on a group of people who agreed to share a secret, and it bound them by magic law to never reveal that secret. If any of the group did spill the beans, that secret-spiller faced immediate punishment, which could range from a mild censure to a full extraction — a process that sucks your magic from you and leaves your brain useless for anything more than breathing and sitting upright. Just not both at the same time.

However, the Confidentiality Spell can be broken if someone who *isn't* a party to the agreement guesses the secret correctly. And, well, since rules were made to be smashed apart, some Magics could loophole their way around the agreement with the ease of an obstacle course champion.

"A Confidentiality Spell exists between myself and your parents," Mr T stated, annunciating each word carefully as if being very cautious about not saying too much.

"And how is that relevant or helpful?"

"It's relevant because we added a contingency to the secrecy agreement that you be included if specific circumstances required it. Olivia said we should wait for you to obtain your license, but as the circumstances have come to pass, I believe you should be brought into the group now. At least partially."

I sat up straighter as all the cookies, scones, and tepid tea from earlier threatened to make a reappearance. I didn't want to hear this. What exactly triggered the contingency? Their deaths, or just them going missing? Either way, I knew it would be terrible news, and I really didn't think I could handle any more of that sort of thing until well into the next decade.

I didn't realize I was shaking my head, trying to fend off the bad tidings, until Mr Tenpenny said, "Don't shake your head. This is something you need to know, otherwise it will drive you to distraction."

Distraction? Distraction!? My parents were missing, possibly dead, and he thought I might be a little distracted?

"Being in on a secret," he continued, "is a nuisance, to say the least. You have to always watch what you say. The punishment for this one isn't too severe, and we can expand the group if necessary. Actually," he said, more to himself than me, "yes, I do believe it will be necessary to keep others from making more of this situation than it is—"

"Mr T, if you don't get to the point, there's a baseball bat not far from here, and I'm not afraid to use it."

"Right, yes. Your parents aren't missing."

Like a punch to the gut, all the air seemed to rush from my body. My head spun.

"So they're dead," I said, the words barely audible.

"Dead? No, of course not," he blustered, like this was the stupidest conclusion anyone could come to. "You are quite the pessimist, aren't you? No, your parents are on a mission for HQ. A mission under my command."

"Mission?" I stammered, utterly bewildered. Besides Olivia telling me, *assuring* me, that it would be deplorable to ever put my parents back into the field again after what they'd already faced, without regular transfusions of magic, my parents couldn't maintain the necessary strength to do any sort of active duty. Unless, of course, that duty was to order cinnamon rolls from every bakery in town and conduct a rigorous taste test. "But they're not supposed to do anything—"

Busby fluttered his hand dismissively. "Yes, yes, I know. They aren't supposed to do anything but gather information and do consultations until they've fully recuperated. I'm well aware of Olivia's objections and Runa's precautions. But, in truth, that's what they're doing: gathering information we will later consult."

"Gathering information *in the field*," I stated, unable to believe Mr Never Bend the Rules could be such a rule contortionist. "That's a far cry from doing a few Google searches from the comfort of their own home."

"A technicality," he said with a dismissive shrug. "Why are you looking at me like that?"

"Because I find it amazing that you can make a pretzel out of HQ's own stipulations and Runa's advice for your little mission, but yet you can't twist a few rules to waive the requirement for my detective license. A license you keep saying is so important, so urgent, for me to obtain."

"You've had this explained to you. That requirement is a piece of bureaucratic magic put in place by someone other than myself."

I don't know if it was simply the relief of learning that my parents were still alive, but something allowed realization to finally dawn on me.

"You can't figure out how to undo it, can you?" At the sight of Mr T's cheeks flushing crimson, I laugh-snorted so hard I nearly gagged. "And you've tried, haven't you? That's what Olivia meant about HQ's recent stabs at changing it. Here I thought you were just a stickler for paperwork, but the truth is you've been beaten by someone else's spell. Come on," I nudged him with my elbow, "cheer a girl up and tell me how many times you've tried."

"We're well overdue for this party." Mr Tenpenny stood and fastidiously adjusted his pocket square. "There's fashionably late, and then there's just rude."

"Ten times?" I teased as I stepped past the pigeons. "Twenty times?"

"I may not be able to undo the license requirements, but I'll have you know I'm quite adept at a variation of the Silencing Spell that you would never be able to reverse."

I grinned as we approached the funeral home's doors. My parents were okay (even if they might be in danger), I'd finally found a chink in Mr Tenpenny's magical armor, and I was about to get cake. At least the day was turning out a little better than it had started.

CHAPTER FOUR
CAVIAR POO

The crowd inside Mr Wood's was nearly impossible to get through as people milled about, questioning each other about how they knew my former boss, how they hoped he posted pictures of his trip to the Cotswolds, and how he seemed more full of life than they could ever remember.

That "full of life" thing would more correctly be "full of magic." See, Mr Wood had recently gotten into a little scuffle that had left his body riddled with life-threatening injuries. He'd been lucky to have survived. But he *had* survived. And he'd done so in record time thanks to Morelli pumping several rounds of magic into the system of his live-in patient.

Typically, when you give a Norm magic it'll do what it needs to do, but it won't stick around for long. Their cells just don't know what to do with that kind of power. But somehow Morelli's repeated doses of magic did stick, and Mr Wood found himself able to fetch his pain meds and fix himself a B.L.T. with little more than a well-intentioned twist of the wrist.

Much to Morelli's dismay when he found his bacon stash depleted.

That had been months ago, but Mr Wood's magic was still holding tight. I wasn't sure what spells my former boss could conjure, or if he even realized he might still be able to swish and flick his way out of a jam, but the power given to him had invigorated him with new life. So much so that he'd decided to retire early and zip off to the Cotswolds for a trek through quaint villages and idyllic landscapes.

"I don't see him anywhere," said Mr Tenpenny, whose height and perfect posture allowed him to see over the heads of most of the party's attendees, about two-thirds of whom had already lost several inches due to age.

"One guess as to where he is," I said before heading straight to the funeral home's kitchenette. "I knew it."

The round man at the table had been about to bite into a substantial sandwich from which pieces of lettuce, a hunk of tomato, and strips of bacon poked out. At the sight of me, he leapt out of the chair. He really was feeling spry, because before I could avoid it, he had me wrapped in a hug. A one-armed hug, that is. The other hand still clutched his B.L.T.

"Cassie! You made it. I was beginning to wonder."

"I made sure she got here," said Mr Tenpenny. "Thank you for the invitation, Nino."

"I thought it only appropriate I invite the first dead person I'd ever spoken to. Or, at least, the first one who spoke back," Mr Wood added with a warm chuckle.

"Why aren't you out there?" I asked, knowing Mr Wood loved being amongst people, especially living ones.

"I was absolutely starving. Don't get me wrong, Daisy is a stellar employee—" I bristled at his compliment of the person who had replaced me. I mean, just because she didn't raise the dead and hadn't nearly cost him his family business, was that any reason to sing her praises? Hardly. "But she has terrible taste in food. Everything out there is—" and here Mr Wood, the guy who'd seen real live zombies, shuddered then whispered as if he dare not speak the word too loudly "—*vegan*."

"No!" I said in mock horror.

"Yes. Not even a bacon bit. Even the cheese is... well, I mean, why is it so shiny? Is it made of wax?"

"Wait," I said, realizing there might indeed be a crime against party snacks going on here. "The cake?"

"Was my contribution," Mr Tenpenny assured me. "One of Gwendolyn's. Plenty of eggs. Covered in buttercream."

"Oh, thank Gandalf," I sighed.

Mr Wood sat back down at the table and pointed to his sandwich. "Want one?"

We declined, but told him to eat up.

"When do you leave for your trip?" asked Mr T. "I've never been to the Cotswolds, but I hear they're very... cute." Busby spoke the word as if it were a foul term that should never be used to describe anything British.

"It does look like a fairy tale, doesn't it?"

"It's been known to have its problems in the past, but I believe wealthy incomers might have routed out any lingering miscreants."

"That's a relief. Wouldn't want any graffiti messing up my photos. And as for your question, I leave tomorrow evening."

"So soon?" I asked in surprise. I didn't recall him telling me exactly when his tour started, but I'd assumed his departure date would be at least a month from now. "Don't you have to...?" I fluttered my hand vaguely at the kitchenette, which showed no signs of being in the process of packing up.

"Exciting, isn't it? It's been a bit of a whirlwind, but they had a few vacant spots and offered a last-minute special, so how was I to resist that? I'll have plenty of time to wrap things up here when I return, and then I'll put the old business up for sale. Suppose I'll have to find a new place to live too," he added, since he currently lived in the apartment above the funeral home. I briefly wondered if Morelli might want his old roommate back. "But those are chores for later. For now, the party, followed by suitcase packing, of course. Oh, and sorry to put you on the spot, Cassie, but would you be able to drive me to the airport? We can use my car, of course. I'm feeling good, but I don't think I'm quite spry enough to ride on your bicycle's handlebars."

Mr Wood chuckled at his own joke, then asked Mr T about the proper way to order drinks in a British pub and whether or not they had B.L.T.s in England. While Mr Wood swooned over Busby's explanation of sausage rolls and bacon butties, I went to the kitchenette's window to see if any cake was within easy grabbing distance.

The moment I poked my head out, a smiling face with flawless skin appeared.

"Cassie, you're here!" enthused Daisy — job stealer, Magic, and Tobey's girlfriend. Or maybe fiancée. I still wasn't sure if he'd proposed to her or not.

"I am," I said flatly, because for some reason perky people always bumped up my inner grump level by at least a factor of six. "Where's the cake?"

"Oh, you don't want that. So unhealthy. Here, have this." She held out a plate on which were thin, pale crackers topped with unappealing, dull-brown orbs that looked suspiciously like little poo balls. "Vegan caviar, made with..."

If you want the recipe for vegan caviar, go ahead and look it up, because I tuned her out as my eyes scanned the reception area for the cake.

"It hasn't been brought out yet," Daisy said with a resigned sigh, as if finally accepting she wasn't going to sell me on any poo pellet canapés. "I was just coming to get it."

"Daisy?" called Mr. Wood. "Would you mind stepping in here?"

"I was just getting ready to, Nino," she said brightly. An instant later, she swept through the door to join us, her Barbie-blonde ponytail swishing in time to her steps with an annoying amount of frivolity. "Cake time?"

"In a moment. I wanted to apologize again for leaving you in the lurch like this. I just... well, the tour I wanted to do wasn't being offered again until next spring, and I know it's been short notice for you. I'd also appreciate some help tidying up when I get back, if you're available. You'll get a severance package either way, of course."

"Yes, that's... I mean, thanks," Daisy said, her toothpaste-model smile wobbling. I couldn't help but grin at her discomfort. And yes, I know, it's terrible of me to be so critical of her and to have quite as much schadenfreude as I did just then, but Circe's sainted aunt, she drove me bonkers. It should be illegal to be that blonde and that perky at the same time.

"Might I make a proposal for your next career move?" Mr Tenpenny interjected.

"Sewer cleaner?" I suggested.

"You're so funny, Cassie," Daisy giggled. Where was her off button? She had to have one, right?

"Not quite what I had in mind," Mr T said, a scolding note in his voice as he shot me a be-nice look. "I think you would make an excellent assistant for Cassie."

Daisy gave a yelp of delight and began clapping her hands excitedly, even as I blurted, "Why would you ever think that?"

"Because I've seen the state of your agency. You could use an assistant, even if only to organize things." He had a point. The agency had gone from alphabetized order to hurricane aftermath in only a week of me actually having work to do. "You also still have Wordsworth's missing book case to sort out, preferably as soon as possible. And as they say, two heads are better than one."

Not when one of those heads is full of more air than a balloon in the Macy's Day Parade.

"In case you've forgotten," I said, "my clients are finding it difficult to stay alive, which means I'm earning zero dollars per hour. How exactly am I going to afford an assistant?"

Daisy babbled something about volunteering, but Mr T said, "I can make arrangements for that."

"I have no choice in this, do I?"

"It will be good for you." So would vegan poo pellets, but I wasn't about to invite those into my life. "Now, shall we indulge in this cake?"

Daisy reluctantly agreed, but only after a last-ditch attempt to swap out Gwendolyn's creation with something from the vegan bakery just down the street. As Mr T gathered up a stack of small paper plates, I reached for a knife to cut the cake. But right before I could grasp the handle, Daisy threw her arms around me and gave an enthusiastic squeeze.

"Partners! Can you believe it? It's going to be so exciting. You don't have a name for the agency yet, do you? Because I was thinking we could call it the Witch Clue Agency. Get it? Witch Clue. Which clue."

If only I'd gotten to the knife sooner.

CHAPTER FIVE
BAND NAMES

I ate more cake than is healthy for a human. A Norm human, that is. For Magics, sugar is top-notch fuel. Which is why, as party-goers lingered over coffee and lemonade, I wondered if perhaps my cake indulgence might be just the thing to jolt my magic back into shape. Especially since I'd just spilled half a cup of tea on the kitchenette's counter.

I aimed a Drying Spell at my mess. Curiously, the few drops of ruby-brown liquid merged together. They then expanded, and suddenly tea was waterfalling off the edge of the countertop with a Niagara-like gusto. Luckily, Busby walked in just then.

"Does this sort of thing happen every time you cast spells?" Mr T asked, arching an eyebrow at the kitchenette's new water feature. Or, rather, tea feature.

"Nah, I just get a bit wild at parties."

"I can imagine," he said wryly, then evaporated all the liquid with a confident snap of his fingers.

"Was that just good timing on your part," I asked, "or do you have magic spidey senses?"

"HQ texted to tell me I should make sure the spell you were attempting wasn't causing problems," he said.

Ever since Dr Dunwiddle had been required to put a trace on my magic, I'd been curious about how it worked. I'd even tried a few very safe spells to test it out; and while the results had been strange (I'm still trying to figure out how to get the pillow unstuck from my ceiling), there'd been no visits from the authorities.

I asked Mr T about this — leaving out the pillow thing, of course — and he told me only troublesome, dangerous, or property-damaging spells set off the trace and called in the guards.

"Now, if you're done with these raucous party games," said Mr T, "I believe Mr Wood was about to deliver a toast with some very fine single malt."

It was well past six in the evening before the last of the revelers offered up their good wishes to Mr Wood for his trip and his retirement.

"Won't you take some of this food home with you?" he begged each person as they slipped purse straps over their shoulders or pulled car keys out of their pockets. While the cake platter, a large bowl of mixed nuts, and the container of chips and salsa now stood empty, nearly all the trays of Daisy's hors d'oeuvres were still well-stocked.

Every pleading comment from Mr Wood was met with exaggerated stomach patting and complaints of being unable to eat another bite as his guests nearly crushed each other to get out the door before a doggie bag of vegan selections could be forced into their hands.

Undaunted by, or perhaps oblivious to, her party food faux pas, Daisy packed up the remaining snacks, including the poo pellets and the unnaturally shiny 'cheese' slices, saying how much Tobey would enjoy them and that he'd gotten quite fond of plant-based treats.

Mr Tenpenny and I exchanged a glance. But why be skeptical? I mean, Tobey was a man in love, and who knows what he might do to make Daisy happy? Still, I'd seen firsthand the very *non-veggie* burgers and chicken tenders he devoured on his lunch breaks from the Academy.

When time came for me to bid Mr Wood a *bon voyage* it was all very awkward, with plenty of mumbling on my part and attempted hugs on his part. In the end, I made him promise to send me a postcard.

"Just a postcard? Daisy's already roped me into texting her a photo every day of my journey."

Of course she had.

A few farewell embraces and handshakes were exchanged, with me dodging another squeeze from Daisy. It's not as if I wouldn't be seeing her soon, since we agreed (okay, she and Mr T agreed) that she would start in a couple days.

As Busby and I walked back to my apartment building, I asked him about the secret mission my parents were on.

"It's a secret," he replied unhelpfully.

"But you said I was included in it."

"Partially included, yes. Included only to the extent of knowing they are on an HQ-sanctioned mission and not in danger. I'm hoping that will be enough information to keep you from worrying and going off on some mad hunt for them," he said, adding heavy meaning to the words.

"At least tell me what it's regarding. I mean, if I manage to get my license and you bring me in on whatever this mission is, then you're going to have to brief me at some point. I'm just being efficient."

"I've seen where your efficiency leads. Typically to you nursing several broken bones." He remained quiet a moment, then said, "But you're right. You deserve some information."

I nearly gave a Daisy-like yelp of delight.

"We have concerns about the vampires. That they are planning an uprising in the very near future."

This wasn't news to me. Back when he was speaking to me, Alastair had brought up HQ's thoughts on this vampire uprising. Runa had mentioned it as well, but both she and Alastair seemed very dubious about the logic behind these worries.

"How *near* is this near future?" I asked.

"Our guess is that it will happen in about thirteen days, on the anniversary of the signing of the Vampire Tolerance Act."

The cake suddenly dropped like a lead sinker in my belly. When Olivia had advised me it would be best if I could get my license within the next two weeks, I had an inkling there was some significance behind the deadline. But could there really be a war coming to MagicLand, to all the Magic communities, so soon?

"To what purpose?" I asked. "Don't vampires live alongside us now?" Not that I'd ever seen a vampire in MagicLand, but I'd noticed a striking lack of diversity in Portland's Magic community.

"They do, but they feel they're not being treated equally. Complaints have been registered that the terms of the Vampire Tolerance Act, while it ensured the vampires' fair treatment, excluded them from some aspects of the very magical communities they were trying to assimilate with. It made them different by its very existence. Which I can see their point in that regard."

"Complaints I can understand, but what makes you think that's leading to an uprising?"

"You obviously know about Magics across several communities going missing."

"Sure. But Rosaria's only lost one, right?"

Mr T nodded solemnly. "Mel Faegan. And we've only lost one *so far*. Other communities — Galway, for example — have been nearly wiped out so many Magics have gone missing."

Okay, this *was* news to me. But I suppose I shouldn't have been surprised that the *Herald* hadn't been telling the full story. They were too busy publishing anti-Cassie nonsense.

"It's abduction, plain and simple," Mr T continued as we waited at a crosswalk, "and it was a tactic used by the vampires during their previous uprising. A way to put us on edge, to keep us afraid."

"Were any of the taken Magics killed? Hurt?"

"Nothing but minor injuries, but the victims did provide the vampires considerable negotiating power. I believe it did more damage to those of us who weren't taken. We were constantly on the alert, looking for danger around every corner since we never knew who would be next or even how they were abducting us without a trace of evidence."

Alastair had also mentioned this similarity to the vampires' past actions, but his opinion was that the vampires were too smart, too clever to recycle old tactics. Could someone else be stealing pages from the Vampire Playbook? Which I then realized would be an excellent band name.

"This time, though," Mr Tenpenny said distractedly, as if so lost in his own thoughts that he'd forgotten I was there, "something new is happening, something we didn't see before."

"What?" I asked. I shouldn't have. I should have just let him muse out loud to see if he dropped any clues or gossip that might be useful. But the moment I stirred Busby's attention and he realized I was still there, he resolutely leveled his chin and straightened his shoulders.

"It's nothing you need to know just yet," he replied, as the light changed and we continued on our way. "But I can tell you

HQ is quite troubled that there have been no demands from the vampires regarding the missing Magics. We have no idea how many more communities they plan to hit, what their aim is, or if our people are alive or not."

"What if these disappearances aren't the vampires?" I said, trying my hand at the whole optimism thing. "Maybe it's some serial killer who thinks he's a vampire. That'd be good, wouldn't it?"

"Your definition of the bright side of things is rather disturbing. However, I do agree that it's odd. The frequency of the disappearances and the number of Magics being taken certainly doesn't match the vampires' actions last time. Although that might simply be me hoping this isn't leading somewhere. For now, though, HQ's focus is on why the Magics are going missing, where they might be, and who's behind it."

"And they've come up with…?"

"Not much. Theories, many of them based on suspicion, have been bandied about, especially after a handful of representatives of the vampire community contacted Olivia to give their thoughts regarding the kidnappings." Mr T let out a heart-weary exhale. "By Morgana, I do hope they turn out to only be kidnappings. If the vampires start killing Magics…"

I wasn't the top scholar of Magic history, but I did know that part of the Vampire Tolerance Act required vampires to not hunt or kill living creatures, human or otherwise. Still, I couldn't help but agree with Alastair and Runa that there seemed to be a lot of assuming going on.

"Contacting Olivia, though? Why is that suspicious? It sounds more like they're trying to help."

"It could also be a trick to send us on a fool's errand or to lead us into a trap. That would be similar to what they did in the past. It was those deeds that brought about a prejudice against them, and why we eventually had to create laws to curtail them. We should never have stripped them of their power, though," he said, almost as an afterthought.

"Their power? You mean they're not Magic?"

"They can do some simple spells, of course. We didn't extract them or anything like that. But grander spells, say a Mirage Hex, are impossible for most of them."

"Most? Why not all?"

"Because whether human, elf, or vampire, royals are treated differently." Vampire Royalty? Vampire freaking Royalty! Seriously, is there any way to get paid for coming up with band names? "But all have to abide by certain rules. You're aware of the part of the vampire stories which says they can't enter a building without being asked?" I said I did. "That's only been true since the very first of the vampire laws went into effect a few centuries ago. It was a way to protect our homes from them, and even the Tolerance Act didn't clear it from the books.

"It's rather degrading, in my opinion. And theirs as well. Which is why we think they're preparing to force our hands to grant them their full power once again. From the notes Olivia has compiled, she believes some sort of ritual is being planned, perhaps involving the missing Magics."

Vampire Rituals, although another amazing band name, did not stir up warm and fuzzy thoughts.

"So just prevent the ritual," I said.

"We hadn't thought of that," Mr Tenpenny said with an uncharacteristic amount of sarcasm. "Unfortunately, we don't know how. We don't even know which ritual it might be, what it requires, or what the cost might be to us. Banna may have known, but we lost that knowledge when we lost her."

"That's what Olivia's had Fiona researching, isn't it?"

"It is. Uncovering anything that might suit their needs and

what it might entail is Fiona's main goal. And Alastair's as well. He's looking into other aspects of an uprising, including a great deal of background work that should help us, so try not to be too hard on him for his absences lately. It's for the greater good."

"His treatment of Pablo isn't, though. I can still be mad at him for that."

"True. But until we get some additional information on the ritual, we can't know what to watch for. And we can't know how to stop it," he added, his brow troublingly furrowed as we turned onto the final block to my place.

"Why not just talk to the vampires? Maybe there's been a misunderstanding."

"Have you ever tried to have a meeting with a vampire?"

"Can't say that's something that's ever come up, no."

"They can be very pushy, very moody, very stubborn." Busby then scrutinized me from the corner of his eye, an amused grin on his lips. "If I didn't know you were Simon and Chloe's daughter, I might wonder if you didn't have vampire genes in you. You are quite pale. Any cravings for blood?" he teased.

"Maybe if laced with enough sugar."

We'd reached my building by now. The usual gang of scruffy kids were loitering in the parking lot of the neighboring abandoned business and kicking a faded soccer ball between themselves. I entered the code to get in and held the door for Mr Tenpenny.

The door hadn't even closed behind me before Morelli poked his head out of his ground-floor apartment, crochet hook in hand. The bandage was gone, but I could still see faint marks from where Morelli's pet goldfish, Gary, had decided his owner's fingers were tastier than fish flakes.

"Keep it down, Black," Morelli grumbled, even though the only noise had been a *whoop* from the kids outside. "I've had a long day."

And with that, he stepped back in and shoved the door closed.

"Is he always in such a foul mood?" Busby asked.

"Foul mood? That was him being gracious and friendly."

"Well, do cut him some slack. He's probably had a tough twenty-four hours."

A statement I didn't comment on because I really didn't want to know what trolls, especially Morelli, might get up to when they wanted to cut loose.

Once upstairs, Mr Tenpenny peered into the cat carrier and smiled at his handiwork. I looked over his shoulder to see Pablo flat out on his back in a bed of catnip, a beam of evening sunshine glinting off his orange fur.

"I'll have a chat with Alastair, shall I?" Busby offered. "I'm sure nothing's wrong with your Pablo. At least I hope not."

And because vaguely worrying sentences were his way of ending a conversation, Mr T slipped out to go back downstairs. I watched Pablo for a few moments, thinking of his recent bouts of biting and scratching Alastair, who he'd always adored, and Morelli's goldfish attack. Could vampirism infect our pets? Would this uprising involve a snapping, swatting, and snarling army of parakeets, pugs, and pampered Persians?

And if so, how many Magics would record it in the hopes of going viral on social media?

CHAPTER SIX
A DINNER DATE

Despite Mr Tenpenny's assurances that all would be well between me and Alastair, we barely spoke during dinner that evening. After giving up on my clumsy attempts at small talk, I was left in bitter silence to ponder how Tobey's evening meal of poo pellets and shiny cheese was going.

Showing he was wise beyond his nine lives, Pablo remained inside his carrier throughout the meal. Can't blame him for that, really. I had half a mind to climb in myself.

Once the plates had been cleared, Alastair told me he was going back downstairs to work on his commission. Or at least I think that's what he said, since it was spoken in a very terse mumble as he was closing the door behind him.

Not wanting to dwell on what was going on between us, I worked on making good on my promise to help Tobey with his second stab at passing the Academy Exams. Especially as I'd been partially responsible for him failing his first attempt at the rigorous test a few days ago.

I don't know if it's because I was concentrating so hard on not thinking about Alastair, or my parents, or getting my license, but I managed to come up with a practice quiz that was jam-packed with some real brain teasers on police procedure, laws pertaining to the use of magical force, and the various protocols

Tobey would need to follow most often as a detective. Not only would it tax his knowledge, but it also cleared my head so thoroughly that I fell easily asleep for the first time in days.

The next morning, I woke early, and the only sign of Alastair was a squeal downstairs that could have been the cutting of metal or Morelli using a bandsaw to trim his toenails.

Once I'd wolfed down a quick-as-you-can breakfast and before I dashed to the bedroom to throw on a publicly acceptable outfit, I placed a dish of food outside of Pablo's carrier. When I came back out, the dish was empty, and he was back inside his new playhouse, distracted with tackling a particularly fat holographic mouse. I latched and hoisted the carrier by its handle, went through my closet portal to MagicLand, and was behind my desk at the agency before most of the citizens of Rosaria had started sipping their first cups of coffee.

My hand had finally regained feeling (I should have asked Mr T to include a Lighten the Load Spell on the carrier) when the bell above the agency's door cheeped. From somewhere deep inside his carrier, Pablo replied with a lazy meow.

"How was dinner?" I asked, grinning knowingly at Tobey.

"It was an experience, that's for sure."

"She really fed you the leftover platters? Tell me you didn't eat the vegan caviar."

"It was just overly salted lentils, and it was pretty good. Especially after Daisy left the kitchen and I added some bacon crumbles to it. Still, there are just some things you shouldn't do with almond milk. She wants to make me a vegan soufflé this weekend. How is that even possible?" We spent the next few minutes trying to figure it out, but couldn't. "I feel bad, but I'm almost glad for the dinner I've got to go to tonight."

I arched an eyebrow in a request for more information.

"Matilda's invited Inspector Oberlin for a meal, and apparently, without Winnifred around, he's decided I should be his plus one."

"That sounds utterly miserable," I said. Inspector Oberlin detested me (the feeling was mutual), and I wasn't sure Matilda Marheart had any better opinion of me after my little temper tantrum a couple days ago. A meal with both of them would be about as pleasant as swapping out my toilet paper for a roll of two-ply sandpaper. "But, seriously, Oberlin's wife just died. How can he even think of going to soirées?" Says the person who allowed herself to be dragged to a retirement party when she thought her parents had been kidnapped.

"Died?" Tobey asked incredulously, like I was the sort of person who got their news from very biased sources that hadn't grasped the concept of fact-checking.

"Yeah, died. I saw the body being taken away."

"No, Winnifred's not dead. I mean, she's certainly seen better days, but they think she might pull through. Eventually."

"Not dead?" I said dumbly, wondering where she was and if she was able to hold a pen so she could sign her contract. After all, I had found her brooch. If she could just sign off on a job well done, I could get my detective's license without facing the impossible task of hunting down another copy of Wordsworth's book.

"How do you not know this?" Tobey snarked. "They said she was taken directly to the Tower's medical ward after she was attacked. Morelli and Chester spent most of that night and the next day stabilizing her. Divided the work up into shifts, but it still took a lot out of them." Which suddenly put Morelli's grumpy mood yesterday into perspective. "They got her to a point where it was safe for the medics to put her in a magically induced coma. They say it'll allow her to heal more easily."

A coma. So I supposed it would be rude to go in and ask them to wake her up for just a quick sec so she could sign on the dotted line. But really, it wouldn't hurt to ask, would it?

"Okay, so he's not grieving, but he should at least be by his wife's bedside," I said critically. Tobey, a mouth full of his ham-and-egg breakfast sandwich, merely gave a what-can-you-do shrug in response. "Okay, the whole bad-husband thing aside, I thought he couldn't stand the mayor. And she him. Why are they arranging dinner dates?"

Tobey swallowed the last bite of his very non-vegan meal, then said, "Why she invited him, who knows? Probably just politics. As to why Oberlin accepted, he does always advise us to keep our enemies close."

"You think they're enemies? It's not just animosity because Oberlin's a sore loser?" Matilda Marheart had narrowly beaten the Inspector in Rosaria's recent mayoral campaign.

Just then, Pablo emerged from his cage, looking rather dazed to be in the real world. But the confusion didn't last long as he jumped onto my desk, sprawled out, and instantly fell asleep. I guess chasing holograms and rolling in beds of catnip is tough work.

"Who knows why anyone does anything? But look," Tobey began, as he stroked Pablo's belly, "I just wanted to thank you for taking on Daisy as an assistant. She's been miserable ever since she found out she was losing her job at Mr Wood's."

"I didn't know she came with a miserable setting. And it wasn't exactly my idea. Your grandfather volunteered her services. Which is no way to repay someone who brought you back from the dead."

"Well, she's over the moon and can't wait to start. She was telling me some ideas she had for the agency—"

"Stop right there. No ideas. She's an assistant. She can take calls, file..." I glanced at the mess on my desk "...well, things. But no ideas. No changes. I don't even know how I'm going to keep this place open, for Maleficent's sake."

"You might brainstorm with her." Tobey held up a hand to stop my retort. "And before any smart comments come out of your mouth, yes, she does have a brain. She's great. You'll love her."

"*You* love her. I'll work my way up to a mild tolerance. I can't promise anything more. So, when's your next exam?" And yes, that was me deftly changing the subject.

"Four days."

That wasn't too terrible. I told him I'd come up with some real doozies the night before, and he was keen to grab a seat and start working on the sixty questions I'd thought would be demanding, challenging, formidable.

It took him less than twenty minutes to complete the entire thing.

Like I've said, Tobey Tenpenny knows his stuff. He knows the history, the rules, and even the statutes on the legal books. In a casual setting, that is. In an exam room, he chokes up and barely understands which end of the pencil to use. Unless I figured out a way to get Tobey over his fear of test taking, it wouldn't matter if we had four days or four months, he'd freeze the minute a test booklet was in front of him. Which gave me an idea.

"Does Busby have any old test booklets?"

"I can't cheat off those. Besides, his would be from HQ, not from the Academy, and they'd be well over seventy years old. The questions now would be completely different than what they would have been back then."

"No, not to copy off of, but if we could duplicate blanks of them, then add in some questions Oberlin might ask, you could practice taking a test with an actual test booklet. It'd be like muscle memory training. You learn how to take a test, how to fill in the blanks without any pressure, then by the time test day arrives, by the time you have an actual test booklet in front of you, you'll go right into question-answering mode."

Tobey pondered this a moment, then began nodding his head. "That's actually not a bad idea. I'll see if he still has any."

"Or you could just ask Oberlin for a test booklet."

"You really think he'd say yes to that?"

"He's taking you on a dinner date. Who knows what he might do to win your affection."

"Very funny, Cass," Tobey said as he unwrapped another breakfast sandwich. Sausage this time.

"I'm just saying, you're Oberlin's pet student. He wants you to pass, and he might do what he can to move that along."

"He could just not give me the test and graduate me on merit."

"And Wordsworth could have just approved the job I did for him so I could get my detective's license. But you know how these people love their rules and protocols."

"Just be glad there's not a Magic DMV."

"Believe me, if Magics flew brooms, there would be. And it would be a nightmare."

Tobey agreed, and we spent the next fifteen minutes coming up with various quandaries about the registration of flying carpets (where would you put the number plate?), the parallel parking portion of the test to get your broom rider's license, and whether magic cars (if they existed, mind you) would run on fairy farts or unicorn spit.

Tobey glanced up at the wall clock. "Classes are about to start," he said then stood and scratched Pablo behind the ears. Pablo purred slightly louder — which seemed to be all the energy he was willing to muster. "I'll check about the test booklets tonight. In the meantime, be nice to Daisy."

"As if I'd be anything but."

CHAPTER SEVEN
TROLL PROTECTION SCHEME

Soon after Tobey left, something on my desk began squeaking wearily, like a lab mouse that's had an exhausting day of maze running. It took me a moment to realize the sound was coming from my calendar.

This blasted innovation in magical office supplies was enchanted to squeal and squawk and endlessly chastise you about procrastination and tardiness. But a few soakings of tea, some heavy-handed smacks, and a couple instances of Pablo using it as a scratching board had finally broken it. Apparently, mine wasn't the industrial strength model.

After about twenty seconds of the half-hearted grunts reminding me it was time to get over to Dr Dunwiddle's, the calendar gave up with a drawn-out groan. I knew exactly how it felt.

While I appreciated Runa's concern, these daily sample draws were getting tedious, especially as she was no closer to figuring out the wobbly nature of my magic. But, since her clinic was only a couple blocks away from the agency, and since she handed out lollipops after each visit, it wasn't the worst of inconveniences.

With the *Herald's* recent rhetoric against me, my reception in MagicLand had been deteriorating by the day. And, I'm no psychic here, but I was pretty sure a pair of clients meeting bad ends wasn't exactly going to help. Which is why I kept my chin tucked deep into my collar as I race-walked the short distance from the agency to the clinic.

At the sight of Runa's now-repaired window, I chided myself for my utter failure to do any work on her Case of the Vanishing Vials and Swiped Saw. Here was a problem any detective worth her magnifying glass should be able to solve. Not only would it get me the signature I so desperately needed for my application, but it would also give me the perfect chance to gloat over cracking a case that Inspector Oberlin had refused to look into.

With every muscle in my body tensed, I took a deep, fortifying breath and pushed open the door to the clinic, fully prepared for the catty whispers and wicked sneers I'd come to expect.

But when I stepped into the robin egg blue interior of the pharmacy that fronted the clinic, no one was gossiping at the cashier's counter and no one was sneering at me from behind the circular rack of greeting cards. In fact, the entire place was eerily silent.

It's not that the place was empty. Three of the waiting room chairs were occupied — one by Mrs Kawasara, her head tipped down as if sleeping, and two by a pair of women who, the last time I'd seen them, had been giving me the stink eye. Now, they sat rigidly upright, lips sealed, and eyes staring forward with catatonic stillness. It was better than their critical sniping, but not much.

The door to Runa's exam room opened, and a patient emerged with Runa by his side. She plucked a tube of something from the pharmacy shelves for him, and when he paid, she whispered, "It won't be like this forever."

"Promise?"

"It's just a temporary precaution."

Which had me coming up with all manner of wickedly contagious diseases the little man might have. And which is why I gave him a wide berth as he hurried past me to get to the door.

Runa tipped me a nod of greeting, then waved me back toward the exam room. The *confined* exam room where the little man's cooties might still be floating around. I was about to object, to offer my place to the kind ladies who had been waiting so patiently. But before I could say anything, Morelli poked his head out from the room and called, "Next!"

Mrs Kawasara began to stir from her nap, but Runa jerked her hand out. The woman's head instantly dipped again as she fell back into sleep.

"I'll see Cassie now," Runa told Morelli firmly.

"But she hasn't—"

"She'll only take a moment," Runa insisted.

"This isn't how you run a medical clinic," he told her. "Now, if this was a triage situation, you could take Cassie before the others, but since this is clearly not an emergency—"

"She only needs a sample taken. It'll take two minutes, then you can get back to your schedule," said Runa, clearly exasperated with Morelli's demanding punctuality. Which was saying a lot since Runa sticks more closely to her agenda than an atomic clock.

I stepped past Morelli, then eased myself onto the exam table, doing my best not to rustle the paper covering. You could practically push against the uncomfortable tension crowding the small space. Even Runa's normally curious and perky glasses had tucked themselves into a far corner.

"I'll be safe enough seeing this patient alone, Eugene," Runa said when it seemed my landlord wasn't going to leave.

"No guarantee of that. She's really good at causing trouble."

"We'll need the files for the next group of patients. Why don't you get those ready?"

When Morelli stepped out, Runa gave an audible sigh of relief and her glasses zipped back over to her, diving into her breast pocket as if seeking safety.

"Job shadowing?" I asked as Dr Dunwiddle placed a collection vial on my arm.

"Hardly," she said. "Apparently, he's here for my own protection."

"I'm sure the break-in was just a theft. Nothing to feel threatened over."

"Not until I asked you to find those stolen samples and my saw. Now, since I'm a client of yours, Olivia is worried that I'm at risk of being next on the hit list."

"You could fire me," I offered. "You wouldn't be the first."

"I'd have to go through the work of breaking a magical contract, and believe me, I'd rather take my chances against a murderer than waste my time wading through that administrative mire."

To be fair, Olivia had good reason for her concern, since Clive and Winnifred had been attacked soon after I'd solved their cases. While I appreciated Runa hiring me, and it would be a huge win if I found her stolen items, it was impossible to know if that would put her at risk. Although, I had solved Lola's case, and she was still in perfect health. But she was also the only client who had recovered her lost treasure and who had paid me for my work.

So, other than not getting their items back and not paying me, was there some connection between Mr Coppersmith and Mrs Oberlin that led to their attacks? I'd also found my mom's pendant (and promptly lost it), so were my parents truly safe? And would Runa be in danger if I ever made time to work her case? Perhaps it would be best for her to slog through the paperwork to break—

"Wait, magic contracts can't be broken?" I blurted, realization having just smacked me upside the head. "Even if I've been fired?"

Runa's glasses, which had been hovering in front of her eyes as she noted a couple things on my chart, zipped over and gave me what I was pretty sure could be called a Spectacle Scowl.

"What have you done, Black?"

I explained to her about Mayor Marheart, about how I'd been in a foul mood when she'd been pestering me as if she were the most important person in all of MagicLand and we should all bow to her whims.

"Long story short," I concluded, "words were exchanged, and I'm not exactly sure if I quit first or if she fired me first, but either way, I'm pretty sure Matilda's no longer my client."

"Not unless you've gone through the official channels to get the contract cancelled," Runa said as she removed the vial and stuck a blank label on it.

"Great," I huffed.

"Be nice to her, okay? She's not that bad."

"First Morelli, now you," I complained. "What sort of sway does she have over you people? Because, honestly, the woman is a nightmare to work with." After a pause while Runa searched for a pen, I said, "So, your saw and the samples…?"

"I doubt you'll be able to find either of them," Dr D said, half-distracted by her glasses repeatedly nudging her cheek then zipping over to the pen next to the exam room's sink.

"Thanks for the vote of confidence."

"Not what I meant, and you know it. I only mean that I'm sure whoever broke into this place has already used the samples and sold the saw. They certainly aren't going to keep the things around as tokens for the Runa & Cassie Fan Club."

"They might," I said, feigning indignation. "I know it doesn't make up for neglecting your case, but I really have been meaning to look into it. It's just with everything… well, it's no excuse."

"No, it's not." Because Runa Dunwiddle does not mince words.

"Which is why I should get moving on it. Do you have any information about the saw that could help?"

"I really don't know that much about it. Like I told you, it was a gift from a patient. I don't know what I was thinking putting it in the window. That handle's sparkle didn't come from cut glass; those were real gemstones. But like they always say, you never expect something like that to happen here. Doesn't matter where *here* is. Could be a kleptomaniac ward, and people just never expect it."

"Who was the patient? Or are you allowed to tell me that?"

"I'm allowed, as long as you don't ask me what he was seeing me for. Name was John Stagman. Long story short, I was just finishing up my residency at the medical ward at HQ, he had a problem no one seemed able to fix, I looked into it, tried a few things, came up with a solution, and he was over the moon with gratitude. Nowadays, it's a routine procedure, so I can't believe no one figured it out before me, but there you go. Sometimes it takes new eyes to solve a problem.

"I told him the saw was too much, but he said it was a family heirloom just collecting dust, and that he'd love for a real doctor to have it. And now it's gone. Annoying, but not the end of the world," she added stoically. "Still, I wouldn't mind if you found it."

The way she said this (and the tsk-tsk motion her glasses executed) made me feel like an utter heel for not digging into her case sooner. As she said, the samples were probably long gone, but that saw was too unique to get rid of easily.

"You said someone might have used the samples. What would they use them for?" I asked out of curiosity.

"Hit of magic, would be my guess. You're a strong Magic, and a fair number of people know that. Someone takes your samples, then gives themselves a little boost when time calls for it. It's not unheard of, especially when students are cramming for final exams. Of course, when I brought this up to Oberlin, he couldn't be bothered with it. Just anti-Retro-Hex-vaxxers or a stupid prank, he told me. Prank or not, Olivia's worried there might be a pattern."

"Pattern?"

"You know," Runa said apologetically, "with your clients. Clive, Winnifred, your parents."

I nearly blurted that my parents were fine (I hoped) just to ease the concern on Dr D's face, but I caught myself at the last moment. Mr T was right, you had to be careful with these Confidentiality Spells, and I really hoped Runa was one of the people he planned to expand this particular secret's circle to.

"And so she made Morelli promise to protect you?" Because trolls, even half-trolls like Morelli, guard their charges with a fierce loyalty. A promise of protection was a promise they were bound to keep, whether they wanted to or not.

"Not a promise. Not yet. But she asked him to keep an eye on me, and he's taking his job seriously. Too seriously. His medical training keeps him from being completely useless, but he got that training in the military. Procedure, organization, efficiency," she said, rolling her eyes, her glasses mimicking the gesture before settling just above her forehead. "If you thought I was strict with schedules, he's downright obsessive. One man was thirty seconds late, and Morelli nearly cursed him."

"Did he do that to the ladies in the waiting room?"

Runa nodded. "His idea to keep the appointments on time.

Said if patients were up shopping and chatting when their appointment time came, it took at least twenty-seven seconds for them to cut short their conversations or to step away from their browsing. And twenty-seven seconds adds up over the course of the day," she said, mocking Morelli's baritone. "He claims it's better to put them under a Pause Charm so they don't cause any hiccups in the schedule. I honestly don't know how long I can put up with it. And," she added, glancing at her watch, "it's barely been two hours."

Runa slid the sample vial into a rack, then attached another vial to my arm. Clearly, she was drawing out this reprieve as long as humanly possible, since I knew very well that both samples could have been taken at the same time.

"Is HQ doing anything about finding your parents?" Dr D asked. "I'm concerned about them. Simon and Chloe need regular infusions. I'm afraid to think what might happen if their magic levels drop below the threshold level again."

The same thought had been going through my head.

After being drained almost entirely by the Mauvais, my parents had been receiving transfusions of magic. The magic wasn't taking as strongly or as quickly as Runa would have liked, but their power had been showing improvement recently. And the only way to keep that improvement on the right track was with regular doses of donated magic.

Which begged the questions of how far their magic levels could fall before they were too low to recover; and, with their power fading every minute, how much longer would they be able to magically defend themselves? I'd kind of been hoping these worries were nothing more than my usual glass-is-half-empty attitude, but hearing Runa express the same concern wiped out most of the relief I'd felt at Mr T's news that my parents weren't truly missing.

"I—" I began. But what to say to calm Runa's concern? I was under a Confidentiality Spell regarding my parents' whereabouts, but I couldn't have Runa worrying about them. I mean, she had to deal with Morelli, and wasn't that bad enough? "I've heard it's not too concerning."

"Not too concerning?" Runa snapped as she removed the sample from my arm and began filling out a label for it, practically mashing the pen's tip as she wrote. "They haven't fully recovered. If they're being kept captive, if they're being harmed in any way, it could be a huge setback. And then you'll probably end up doing something stupid like going after them."

Which was Runa's way of saying she cared. Very slowly, with my eyes locked on hers, I said, "It's nothing to worry about."

Before Runa could comment, there was a single, heavy thump on the door. Both of us flinched, and Runa scowled at the door.

"Black, time's up!" Morelli bellowed.

I jumped off the exam table and wished Dr Dunwiddle good luck. She was in such a foul mood I didn't bother asking her for my lollipop.

CHAPTER EIGHT
UNEXPECTED INTEL

I tried to make my escape, but before I could reach the clinic's exit, Morelli grunted, "Black, you stay put."

I turned, fully ready to give my landlord my most impatient stare, but he was too busy ushering Runa's next patient toward the exam room door. This was Mrs Kawasara, an amateur gardener who seemed to have a special talent for accidentally growing poisonous plants. Which obviously meant Morelli wasn't letting her anywhere near Dr Dunwiddle on her own. "Do not enter that room until I come back," he ordered her, leaving the dazed woman staring dumbly at the doorjamb.

It was only when Mrs K mumbled her acquiescence that I noticed her lips were so swollen, she could barely move them.

I couldn't help but give Morelli a questioning look, my curiosity overwhelming my irritation.

"Thought it was a good idea to biggie size her blueberries with a Swelling Spell. I tell you, some people should simply not be allowed around plants."

His eyes darted to Mrs Kawasara, as if double-checking that she was staying put.

"Are you sure Runa'll be safe in that exam room on her own?" I teased. "I mean, some of those cotton swabs could be up to no good."

"Security's no joking matter, Black," Morelli grumbled. "You, of all people, should appreciate what having a troll around can do."

Which was a fair point. Although neither of us had been aware of it at the time, when I'd moved into Morelli's building, the promise to protect me he'd made over two decades ago had kicked in. Part of this unwitting protection meant a lot of him harassing me about overdue rent, contraband cats, and minor scuffs on the stairwell, but I suppose that was better than an evil wizard dragging me off to aid in his world domination goals.

"Look," Morelli said, barely meeting my eye, "I just thought I should apologize for snapping at you yesterday."

"Wait, have you been possessed by the ghost of Miss Manners?" I asked, arching an eyebrow at him. I mean, come on. Morelli? Apologizing? That's not how he functioned.

"No, and I don't have a lot of time to play the banter game. I just wanted to tell you that I think some of my people might have found something you're after. And I really can't say anything more than that at the moment, so don't bother asking."

"Is it a copy of Wordsworth's book?" I asked anyway.

From the corner of my eye, I saw Mrs Kawasara take a shuffling step forward. "Ma'am," Morelli said with a voice that was full of warning. Her forward foot tucked behind the ankle of her other leg, as if hiding it from any scorn Morelli might deliver. Morelli gave her one more look before turning his attention back to me.

"I thought you already found that thing," he said.

"I did," I replied, surprised Morelli had been keeping track of my cases with everything else he'd been roped into doing. I supposed I should start giving him more credit. "But a couple pages were missing, so Wordsworth didn't consider the job done.

So, now I get to find him another copy, and I have no idea where one might be." During this last sentence, Morelli began grinning and raising his eyebrows in a way that sparked a wildfire of hope in me. "Are you kidding? You're kidding, aren't you? Torment Cassie for how she acted toward Matilda?"

"I can't verify it's still there because I'm not allowed into certain systems, but a copy used to be at the British Library."

"And you know about this how?"

"I know because my team helped put the first layer of protective enchantments on it. Part of my duties in the M.A.G.E. was security, remember? And not just people security."

"Why didn't you bring this up before? What happened to us being Cagney and Lacey?"

"One, I've been busy, in case you didn't notice. Two, like I said, I thought you'd found it. And three, I don't exactly keep a mental tally of everything I've done in my career, but when I was at the Tower helping Winnifred, something kept picking at my brain."

"Troll worms?"

"If it was, I probably caught 'em from you. Hold on a sec," Morelli flapped his hand at the two women in the waiting chairs. They both yawned and shifted their torsos, never once breaking their catatonic stares at the far wall. "Keeps them from stiffening up," he explained. "Anyway, so when I finally got some rest yesterday, I checked over my notebooks, and there it was: British Library — *The British Wizard's Guide to* blah blah blah — Protection Enchantments."

"You wouldn't happen to be able to tell me how to get around those enchantments, would you?"

"Sorry, no. They always send in a second team to double the protections in these situations."

From the exam room, I saw Runa's glasses peer out, then

zip back in. Half a second later I caught the scent of freshly brewed coffee as Runa took advantage of Morelli's unexpected delay.

"You're sure you're not messing with me?" I asked. "Send Cassie on a wild goose chase because she made your girlfriend mad?"

"Believe me, when I mess with you, it'll be much cleverer than telling you about some book."

"Okay, but the British Library is huge. Any chance of pinpointing the location?"

"I ain't privy to that information." Morelli shrugged, as if trying to look like he didn't care, which only made it obvious how disgruntled he really was over not being savvy to HQ's secrets.

Fumbling over several words of gratitude, I thanked Morelli, unable to believe this troll-sized stroke of luck.

"Yeah, yeah, you're welcome." Morelli glanced toward the exam room. Mrs Kawasara's lips were now pushing up against her nostrils. "I gotta get her seen to before her whole face is nothing but lips. Just remember, you didn't hear nothing about that book from me; and, since I know how you can blunder about things, I won't say nothing about who might be behind it if I hear of any trouble at the British Library. Got it?"

I nodded, but Morelli was already rushing Mrs Kawasara into the exam room.

CHAPTER NINE
SWEET-TALKING CYBERCRIME

A sudden surge of hope and dismay raced through me as Morelli ushered Mrs K into the exam room. His information was helpful — and, frankly, surprising — but I wasn't sure what good it would do me. I mean, even if I could find one book amongst the British Library's enormous collection, I couldn't exactly saunter in, flash my Multnomah County library card, and check the book out with no plans of ever returning it.

Once back to the agency, I immediately tried a search on the British Library's website for Wordsworth's book. My excitement died a slow and agonizing death when the search — and many, *many* variations on it — came up empty.

Of course, it had been silly of me to assume the book was still there. It had been ages since Morelli had been in M.A.G.E., and by now the British Library's copy could have been discarded, it could have been sold off, or it could have crumbled to dust.

My hope of an easy solution dashed, I didn't know what to do next. Which meant the best course of action was to have a snack. After all, the brain runs on glucose, right? And the perfect fuel for that were the remaining few of Lola's coconut-almond cookies I still had stashed in my safe.

Squatting down behind my desk, I let out a sigh as I turned the safe's dial. It might be stressful knowing my magic-deprived parents were off on some secret mission, but the one up side was that I wouldn't have to hide my sweets from my dad until they returned. I just hope they *did* return.

At the back of my safe, I spotted the dwindling packet of cookies. When I grabbed it, Clive's sack of marbles tumbled out, and then Winnifred's brooch came along for the ride.

I stared at my clients' found items. With Clive dead, what should I do with his treasure? I supposed I could give the marbles to Tremaine as a peace offering, but he'd probably throw them at me and accuse me of bribery. As for Mrs O's brooch, I guess I'd just have to wait for her to recover. And who knows how long that might take.

I was just returning the things to the safe when my phone rang. I'd left it on my desk, so I leapt up from my squat to answer it. I instantly regretted it when my head swam from the hasty action.

"Hello?" I answered, as I sat down. Or tried to. I could have sworn the chair from hell had been right in line with my backside until that very backside landed hard on the floor. And call me crazy, but I'm pretty sure I heard something that sounded very much like laughter coming from the chair's stuffing.

"Is everything alright?" my caller asked, his deep, pleasant voice sounding truly concerned.

"Yep," I said, reorienting my phone, scowling at the chair, and deciding the safest place to sit was cross-legged on the floor beside my desk. "Just a little issue with my office furniture."

"Office furniture...?" the man asked uncertainly, but then wisely decided to get his call under way. "Am I speaking with Cassie Black?"

"Yes," I said warily. I mean, the guy might sound nice, but that didn't mean he wasn't part of the anti-Cassie League that had been swarming the streets of MagicLand lately.

"Oh, terrific. This is Pascal Torres, from the Oregon Historical Society. You called me a few days ago."

"But I didn't leave a message," I said, not adding that the receptionist had been in too much of a hurry to clock out for the day for me to leave my name and number. Just because I was plummeting toward career failure didn't mean I had to take everyone else down with me. "How did you—?"

"We have our ways. Working with Rosaria has provided my office with some special benefits. Which is good since our current receptionist is the niece of the director, and she seems to think phone etiquette is beneath her. Now, was there something I could help with?"

"Well—" I began, then realized this man might have no idea who I was. "I'm a detective. Or, well, I'm trying to be. Might not be one much longer. Anyway, I'd originally called to ask about a jewel one of my clients had asked me to find, but since she's fired me…"

"I'm sorry to hear that."

"Don't be, it might be for the best. And it turns out I might not be fired."

"Yes, well…" he said, sounding as confused as I felt. "In that case, perhaps I should learn about this jewel. If nothing else, I'm always curious to delve into more of the magic side of Portland's history."

"It's not exactly Portland history, though," I said, already feeling like I was striking out on my second lead of the day. "Or, at least, I don't think it is."

"Maybe you should explain a bit, and we can go from there," he suggested in a way that had me telling him all I knew about Matilda's jewel. Which wasn't much.

I told him that it fit into the lid of a box that was in the mayor's possession, that my own research kept pointing to

Elizabeth I owning it at some point, that William Boncoeur was either the jeweler or the box's craftsman, maybe both, and that, while the box was still around, the jewel hadn't been seen in over five hundred years.

"That does make it more difficult, but I'll see what I can find. I've dug up some rare objects with less information than what you've given me."

"Rare objects? You wouldn't happen to have any skill at finding rare books, would you?" I asked, because why not?

"Indeed, I do. Not to toot my own historical horn, but I've found some very obscure titles for a few collections. Anything in particular?"

"*The British Wizard's Guide to Magical Creatures, Untoward Spells, and Enchanted Objects of the Tudor and Stuart Eras.*"

"Doesn't exactly roll off the tongue, does it? Is this another item you've been hired to find?"

"No. I mean, yes. It went missing, but I found it, but now I have to find it again at the British Library. Sorry, I'm making no sense."

"Not entirely, no."

Collecting my whirring thoughts, I explained to Mr Torres about Wordsworth's book, about how a copy had turned up at Bookman's Bookshop, but a couple missing pages meant Wordsworth wouldn't allow it back into the sacred realm of his library at the Tower of London.

"The Society does have an extensive collection of books in our storage areas. And we digitize anything that has been in our hands, whether outright purchased or only on loan."

My heart jumped in my chest. A copy of the pages wouldn't be the perfect solution since Wordsworth insisted he wouldn't accept a pasted together copy of his book. But maybe, just maybe, if I could get Olivia to put some pressure on him...

"Give me a moment," Mr Torres said, and I heard the clacking of a keyboard. After a few moments, the sound stopped. "No, sorry, that one's never been in our collection, so we don't have a digital copy." Again, optimism. Stupid. Pointless. More evil than my office chair. "Hold on, did you say something about the British Library?"

I told him what Morelli had told me, and again, the clickity-clackity sound of typing came through from Mr Torres's side.

"If you're searching the British Library's site, I already tried that."

"No, that won't give you anything," he said distractedly, "but if you hack into the back end of their catalog..."

"I'm sorry, did you say 'hack'?" I mean, this was a guy who worked in a history museum, and who sounded like a highly polished and respectable fellow. Not exactly the sort of person you'd associate with cybercrime.

"Magically hack," Mr Torres commented, as if this was something he did every day. "Learned it from one of your people. Doesn't take any actual magic, obviously. It just requires speaking nicely."

"To who?"

"To the website, of course. Government sites are so used to being cursed and grumbled at, that when you do treat them nicely, they will practically trip over their electronic feet to do whatever you ask."

Good to know.

Mr Torres then began telling someone how lovely their cache was looking, saying how gorgeous its JavaScript had been applied, and very coyly asking if it had done something new with its HTML code.

"There we are," Mr Torres said triumphantly. "You are so kind. I can't believe you haven't won any awards for your usability." I really hoped he was saying this to the computer and not to me. "Yes, of course I'll search you again. No, I don't tell all the domains that." In a whisper, he said, "Sorry, they can be so needy sometimes, but I'm pretty sure I've got a location for you."

I jotted down the numbers and letters Mr Torres read out, then offered up many rounds of thanks. It still didn't put me any closer to actually getting the book or knowing how to sneak it out if I did, but it at least gave me the sense of accomplishing something other than eating cookies and watching cat videos.

"It was my pleasure. Things can be quite slow here, so I'm always glad for a new challenge. And I wasn't kidding about that jewel. Let me dig into a few more resources and, if it's alright, I'll call you back with anything I uncover. Again, only if it's okay with you. I'd hate to butt in, but the summer tedium has set in here and you'd truly be saving me from dying of boredom."

Trying not to shout with glee, I told him it would be more than alright. He then gave me his direct line. "Just so you can avoid the wicked gate keeper in the future."

I'd just finished writing down the number and thanking Mr Torres once again when a slim, dark-haired, mahogany-skinned man stepped into the agency. In his hand he carried a hamper with a scrollwork *F & M* on the side. The beast within my belly let out a Pavlovian growl.

"Please tell me that's not full of your dirty laundry," I said as Pablo, who'd been lounging in an empty cardboard box, perked up at the sound of Rafi's entry, stretched like a rubber doll, then trotted over and stared expectantly at the basket.

"Not this time, no," Rafi replied, then began pulling out tiny tea sandwiches on crustless white bread, thick sandwiches on hearty brown bread, jars of mustard, bowls of cut fruit, salad, an entire carrot cake, and a platter of cupcakes that probably turned other cupcakes green with envy. You know, if there were such things as sentient cupcakes. Which would be more than a little disturbing.

"You should really come by more often," I told him.

"I should have just come straight here." I gave him a questioning look, my mouth now too full of the world's sprightliest spring greens tossed in a perfectly piquant balsamic vinaigrette to speak. "I went by your place before here to check in with Alastair, and the guard gnome wouldn't even let me through the door. Ah well, his loss," he said as he slathered some spicy brown mustard on a ham-and-cheese sandwich, after having removed the ham and tossing it to Pablo.

"I'd say I could give him a message for you, but we're not speaking," I said as I reached for an egg-and-cress tea sandwich. "Unless grunts of displeasure count as speaking, that is."

"Trouble in paradise?"

"He's decided Pablo is a vicious psychopath."

Pablo, at that moment, was pawing at the air. Which either meant he was begging for more ham, or he was having catnip-induced hallucinations of hologram butterflies. Or perhaps both.

"Clearly, his aggression levels are at an all-time high," Rafi said wryly. "But let Alastair sulk; it's actually you I wanted to talk to. I have an idea for Wordsworth's book."

"I have news on that front." I told him what Morelli had told me, but when I showed Rafi my notes from Pascal Torres... well, the impressed smile that took over his face was quite the ego boost.

"The Oregon Historical Society, of course! For a Norm, Pascal is an absolute genius when it comes to researching magical objects. How did I not think of him?"

I shrugged. "You've probably been pre-occupied with things

other than helping me do my job."

"True. Although, Sebastian has been looking into things, and maybe it's his whole guardian spirit thing, but he swears a copy of— well, whatever that thing's title is —isn't far."

"*Not far* as in somewhere in the Western Hemisphere, or *not far* as in within the Portland metro area?"

"I think the second one. I'm having some gnomes scout around for it. But that really doesn't matter now, since this," Rafi tapped my notes with his fork, "solves the whole I-have-no-idea-where-the-book-is aspect of my plan for wrapping up Wordsworth's case."

Before Rafi could tell me of his brilliant — and hopefully cunning — plan, the bell at my door tweeted someone's arrival. I perked up, stupidly hoping it was a client with a case that could be solved in three minutes or less. I then groaned at the sight of the person skipping in, a pink cardboard banker's box hovering alongside her.

CHAPTER TEN
STEALING... TEMPORARILY

"Cassie!" squealed Daisy as she and her bubbly demeanor flounced toward my desk. "Oh, are you having a picnic? What fun! Although, it will be hard to get used to eating at my desk, given that my previous desk used to be covered in dead people."

"You aren't scheduled to start until tomorrow." Which was my way of saying, *You may go away now.*

"I know, but I wanted to get a feel for the place. And I figured I'd bring in some personal items so I can be all ready to go first thing tomorrow morning. Ooh, are those cupcakes?"

She reached for one, but I slipped my hand in under hers to block the attempted cupcake thievery.

"They're not vegan. Sorry." I was so *not* sorry.

"That's okay. I've created a charm that, if I do it over a food item that has animal products in it, a baby animal is born somewhere in the world. It's kind of like carbon offsets."

"Wouldn't the baby animal be born anyway?" Rafi asked. "I assume you aren't forcing mother animals to endure an entire gestation period *and* birth in a single instant."

Daisy's face went slack. "Oh my golly, I never thought of that. I—" Even under her makeup, her face went a little green. "I ate yogurt for breakfast this morning. Some poor cow has just— Oh dear."

"I'll help you work on it," offered Rafi, who had an uncanny knack for crafting new spells and charms. Probably hexes, too. I might have to hire him to come up with a Bubbly-Bright Bursting Hex for my new assistant.

"That'd be spectacular," Daisy cheered, recovering from her existential crisis rather quickly. She waved her box over. "I'm just going to put these on… well, I don't know. Cassie, where will my desk be?"

With only a single client during the first two weeks I'd been in business, I'd had plenty of time to explore every inch of the agency. During that exploration, I'd discovered one of the bookshelves nearest the window (and farthest from my desk, Gandalf be praised) had a hidden leaf that folded out to make a desktop. I went over and showed it to her.

"And here, take this. I insist," I said, rolling the evil chair over for her.

"You're too nice, Cassie." Thankfully, by now Daisy had the box in her hands, because I could see her arms twitching, longing to reach out for a hug.

I returned to my own desk and promptly ate a cupcake — okay, *two* cupcakes — before Daisy abandoned her vegan ways and gave in to the spongy bliss.

"You were saying," I asked Rafi through a mouthful of vanilla frosting. "Your idea? Will it get Wordsworth to sign off on a job done?"

"I don't see how he can refuse. Once you get the British Library's copy, that is."

"And how do we do that? Wait, do you have a library card there?" I'd been joking earlier about walking in and checking it out, but what if we could? Then we'd just… Why did I not like the sly way Rafi was looking at me? "We're stealing it, aren't we?"

"Stealing?" asked Daisy worriedly. "I shouldn't be hearing this. After all, I'm not-quite engaged to an almost-police detective. If I aided and abetted any type of criminal behavior, he'd never forgive me."

If he forgave her for the party leftovers she fed him last night, he'd forgive her anything.

"You'd only be stealing it for a little while," Rafi said, then took a large bite of carrot cake.

"Isn't that called borrowing?" I asked, even though I probably should have been questioning why he kept saying *you* and not *we*.

"It would be if the Library allowed books for Magics to be checked out. It's not, so it's stealing. But only temporarily."

"So we steal the book, and…?"

Daisy, as if trying to ensure she heard nothing incriminating, began humming to herself.

"Then we take it to Bookman's," replied Rafi.

"This wouldn't be for any self-serving reasons, would it?" I asked, since even someone with the social skills of a mosquito couldn't have missed the spark between Rafi and Sebastian, the clerk at Bookman's Bookshop.

"Maybe a little, but just be glad for those self-serving reasons since it was thinking about Sebastian and his special skills that gave me the idea."

"Idea to what? Steal books?"

"*Temporarily*," he emphasized. "You liberate the book, then we take the pages that are missing and add them to Wordsworth's copy."

The humming came to an abrupt halt.

"Stealing *and* defacing a book?" Daisy scolded. Her eyes

narrowed, and she planted her hands firmly on her slim hips. It was a look that left no doubt that, if she and Tobey had kids, they'd be very well behaved children who knew to never anger their mother. "You will do no such thing. Books are precious, and they do not exist to be taken apart and rearranged at your whim."

Which kind of surprised me, since I thought the only books Daisy would care about were the ones that contained mostly pictures and featured a single, easy-for-a-toddler-to-pronounce word on each page.

"The pages aren't going to be torn out and used to line a bird cage," I told her. Then, thinking I better confirm this, I asked Rafi, "Are they?"

"Not this time, no. It's more along the lines of copying and pasting."

Daisy gave a sigh of relief.

"Let me get this clear," I said. "You want to temporarily borrow the British Library's book, copy the pages, and then what? Paste them into Wordsworth's copy?" Rafi nodded, his mouth now too full of cantaloupe to speak. "But that gets us nowhere since Wordsworth's already said he won't accept a pasted-together copy of the book. Why can't we just give him the British Library's copy and leave them the one that's taking up half the space in my safe?"

"Besides coming up with a way to explain to Wordsworth where you got the copy that will very likely have some sort of British Library identifier attached to it?"

"Minor detail," I said petulantly, then swiped the frosting off the nearest cupcake.

"It's all very simple, especially now that you know where the book is. You get the British Library's copy, we take it to Sebastian, and he can perform a Duplex Spell over the missing pages. Duplexing, not defacing," he said to Daisy, who was paying rapt attention despite her concerns for her relationship. To me, he said, "Sebastian then uses his little demi-god skills to work the duplicated pages into the binding of Wordsworth's book."

"He'll know," I asserted. "We're talking about a guy who knew a book was missing from his collection because the library 'weighed' differently. He'd probably sniff the book and know it contained non-original pages."

"No, Rafi's right," Daisy piped up, I guess assuming we wanted to hear her thoughts on the matter. "This Wordsworth won't be able to tell the difference. My grandmother was an avid cookbook collector, and she was super strict about the condition of her books. One time, she let my mom borrow one of her most prized cookbooks, and I... well, I sort of tore out all the rabbit recipes. I just couldn't bear the thought of all those fluffy bunnies being stewed, broiled, and fricasseed.

"My mom almost died when she saw what I'd done, so she hurried the book to Bookman's. Sebastian did the Duplex thingie over a new copy he had in stock, then worked the copied pages into Grandma's damaged book. My grandma scrutinized every page when we returned it to her, but it totally passed her eagle-eyed inspection, so I'm sure your Wordsworth won't complain."

"I can pretty much guarantee he'll complain," I said. "There's no way we'll get this by him."

"Not if you used your human magic to do the repair," Rafi said. "As a guardian spirit whose speciality is protecting books, giving them new life, Sebastian has a certain flair for flawless repairs. You've seen yourself what he did for *The Enchanted History of the Portland Community* after you tried to kill it."

I had. After its time in Sebastian's recovery ward, the book now showed zero signs of the damage I'd done to it. I'd also seen how Sebastian's magic could transform a tattered, secondhand paperback into something that looked brand new, straight from the publisher. Rafi told me that was simply the magic of a reader finding a new story to enjoy, but I'd certainly never seen that happen with any of the overpriced used books at Powell's.

"Wait," Daisy said. "Couldn't you just do a Duplex Spell over the pages you need while you're *at* the library? No stealing, no defacing. Doesn't that sound better?"

She had a good point. Damn it.

"It does," said Rafi, "but there's the little issue of no magic other than protective spells being allowed on the books while they're in the Library. A security measure on top of security measures. Try any sort of spell or hex and..." He thought a moment. "Yes, I believe they have the Backwards Backfire Charm in place at the moment. Anything you do to the book, even a Lighten the Load Spell, will fire back on you and do the opposite of what you intended."

"So a Duplex Spell on the book...?" asked Daisy.

"Would hit you. But instead of duplicating you, it would snap you out of existence."

"That wouldn't be good," Daisy said, her ponytail sagging dejectedly.

"Which is why you need to get it out of there," stated Rafi. "Assuming, of course, that the book itself doesn't have protections on it that remain in place even once it's out of the Library."

I really wasn't liking how vague Rafi was about the exact details of his brilliant plan, but it was the only plan we had. I was about to ask about the timing of all this, when Rafi glanced at his phone and announced, "So, it's just coming up to ten a.m. here, and the security staff have a shift change at six-thirty p.m. there. What do you say? No time like the present, right? Just give me a ring as soon as you're back, and I'll help you get the book to Bookman's."

"Wait, you're not going with me?" I asked. See, I knew there was something to all those *yous*!

"They would recognize me in a heartbeat, and I'm not exactly allowed in that section of the Library," Rafi said off-handedly.

"Why? What did you do?" I teased.

"Nothing. It's just the way it is since I'm not a Magic. I mean, I am. An elf Magic, though. Not a human Magic. We caused a fair bit of mischief in the past, mostly due to our talent with spell craft. As if it's our fault human Magics can't figure out how to undo the spells we used to come up with. Remind me to tell you about that Roanoke Colony fiasco sometime.

"Anyway, these days, living amongst you humans means we need to keep our ear tips clean. Sometimes," he said wryly, "Magics help us maintain that cleanliness by not allowing us access to enchanted items, including certain books."

"They can't do that," Daisy said. "It's not like you're a vampire or anything."

"Don't worry. It's mainly just the underground levels of the British Library and a few areas of the British Museum. Security's a little tighter there for us."

"Tighter than the Tower?" I asked, hardly believing this magical segregation existed.

"Let's just say Olivia, being what she is, makes allowances for non-human Magics within the Tower. There, I'm allowed to look at whatever old book is on the shelves and to play with even the most cursed magical objects." I recalled the mess in Rafi's office and wondered what exactly might be hidden in those piles of boxes and bins. "So, you, Miss Black, will have to go in and get the book on your own."

"I can't."

"Come on, now," he cajoled. "Self-confidence is key."

"No, I mean, I can't get myself through long-distance portals. My magic, remember? It's not behaving."

"Not behaving in what way?" asked Daisy.

As briefly and flippantly as possible, I explained to her my little problem.

"When did you say this first started?" Rafi asked. I'd told him before, but he was on such a donut high at the time his magic was likely buzzing too loudly for all the words to sink in.

"I think sometime when I was working Mr Coppersmith's case."

"Interesting," Rafi said, then went silent. After a moment, he clapped his hands together once and said, "We'll explore that later. Right now, the only trouble is getting you through a portal and into the Library."

"The *only* trouble? You mean besides traveling to London without the use of my magic, managing to locate and steal something without getting caught, then making the return trip with a priceless book that weighs at least twenty pounds?"

Temporarily stealing a rare book from a high-security library suddenly sounded very difficult. I couldn't wait to be done with this case. Then maybe I could tackle some easy ones. You know, like finding Amelia Earhart or tracking down Big Foot.

"Sure, besides that," Rafi said with a casual shrug.

"I could take Cassie through," Daisy volunteered.

"Brilliant," cheered Rafi. "See, Cassie, she's proving to be an asset already."

I would have shot Rafi a withering glare, but I was too busy squinting away from Daisy's blindingly bright smile.

"And we're going now?" she asked, bouncing on her toes excitedly.

"Can't see why you shouldn't," said Rafi.

"Yeah, let's get this over with," I grumbled, recalling those lovely, bygone days when teamwork wasn't part of my business plan.

CHAPTER ELEVEN
CORRIGAN'S COURIER

When Rafi suggested we use the international portal at Corrigan's Courier, even the ever-upbeat Daisy groaned.

"She has a point," I said, even though I hated agreeing with my bubbly new colleague.

While it would deliver us directly into the underground area of the British Library, this particular portal was designed for the transport of packages, not people. Which meant, once you performed the contortions needed to squeeze yourself through the slot, you found yourself getting tossed and tumbled around more vigorously than a package stamped 'fragile' that's in the hands of the world's most disgruntled postal carrier.

"Yes, it's a tad uncomfortable," Rafi said, as he typed something on his phone, "but Corrine's portal is the only one in Rosaria that won't track you as it sends you right where you need to go." A message pinged through and, after reading it, Rafi slid his phone into his pocket. "Now, unless you'd like to waste more time complaining, we need to get moving if you're going to take advantage of that downtime in security the Library's shift change will provide."

Although still full of doubts about this plan and reluctant to stuff myself into a magical mail slot for the second time in my life, I had been meaning to ask Corrine about the shipping of

Wordsworth's book. It was her own courier service that had transported the books he'd sent to and from his Bookworm convention. But when his box of books arrived back at the Tower's library, one had been missing. And I needed to figure out who might have taken it.

So, two birds, one stone, and all that.

At Corrigan's Courier, clerks were busy attending to the late morning, pre-lunchtime rush. As they took collection receipts from customers, the rows of cubbies on the rear wall slid and shifted so that the instant the clerk turned around, he or she was eye to eye with the very item that needed picked up.

At another counter, clerks took packages people needed to ship, and rather than wait for the correct cubby (a form of portal) to slide down to them, the clerk would simply fling the package into one of the moving slots with better accuracy than a basketball all-star.

"How do they know the package is going into the right slot?" I asked Corrine once she'd bustled over to greet us.

"Training," Corrine said, smoothing back a loose strand of her flaming red hair. "Takes years, but any clerk worth their salt will memorize small details of the cubbies. One to New York might have a scuff mark on the front. One to Paris might have a chip out of a corner. Honestly, I don't know how they manage it. I can barely remember my own phone number. Speaking of, Rafi texted and said you needed a quick trip to—" She darted her eyes around, as if anyone could overhear us with all the rustling, stamping, flinging, and other postal activities going on. "Well, somewhere. Come on back."

Once to the back room, we approached the familiar, oversized slot. My body tensed as if preparing itself for the upcoming aches and pains.

"It opens in a few minutes," she said.

"I thought portals were fully open now," said Daisy, since, until recently, international portals had been strictly regulated and only ran at certain times due to fears regarding the Mauvais.

"Oh, things are much less rigid now. We don't have the strict schedule we did when all that trouble was going on in the spring, but," Corrine gently patted the wall near the portal's slot, "Old Bessy still needs a bit of rest between runs." I was about to take advantage of the delay and ask Corrine about her handling of Wordsworth's book, but she barreled on, "Are you going to the town hall today? I never miss one. Always good for gossip."

Although I'd seen them announced in the *Herald*, I'd never been to a town hall. The *Herald's* editor organized them, and that alone was enough to keep me away, but I also didn't have much community spirit lately. Hard to when most of your community is glaring and glowering at you and assuming the worst about your business tactics.

"I've been to a few," said Daisy, covering my silence.

"Oh, you really must go to this one. I hear it's going to be a doozy."

"We'll be there," Daisy said, then hooked her arm in mine. Hold on. We? Had Mr Tenpenny put some sort of Buddy System Clause in her hiring contract? Then again, maybe Daisy needed someone to walk with her so she didn't get lost.

From within the wall came a clattering and rumbling. The noise distracted Daisy enough for me to extract my arm from her grip.

"That'll be Bessy waking up. Any minute now."

"Corrine," I began, seeing my chance to get my questions answered, "do you remember the recent Magics International Library Consortium Conference?"

Corrine's crimson cheeks paled. "I do. Why do you ask?"

"You handled the transport of Wordsworth's books, didn't you?"

"Look, I've explained all this to Olivia. I saw to that shipment personally. Wordsworth and I both had a copy of his list of books, and we each checked everything off to ensure it was all in the box. I watched the books being loaded, and I monitored while Wordsworth sealed up the crate. I even put some extra protections on it at his insistence. It was secure," she added defensively.

"So, how could one book have gone missing by the time the crate arrived at the Tower without any sign of damage?" Corrine looked worried, so I rushed to say, "I'm not accusing or casting blame; I'm just curious to get your thoughts. I mean, was anyone hanging around who shouldn't have been?"

"Well, no one really stands out, but Mayor Marheart was very interested. At the time, she was either just elected or maybe election day was approaching. I don't recall exactly, but she went to the conference — to any local event, really — to show her interest in the workings of Rosaria.

"But that doesn't mean she did anything. How could she, with all those protections? In fact, I thought it quite good of her. No other elected official had ever shown that much curiosity in how this community functions. You know, the day-to-day stuff that keeps everything running and often goes unnoticed? More people in charge should be doing that. Then maybe they'd understand a bit more of people's everyday lives. I was happy she won. Figured she'd do a good job."

The mail slot made a clanking noise that had the distinct sound of something in need of a tune-up.

"And you sent it from here?" I asked.

"No, it went straight from the conference. Temporary portals had been set up especially for the attendees to transfer their goods directly to and from the venue." The mail slot pinged, then let out a loud clunk that sounded like a dump truck backing into a metal door. "Ah good, Bessy's ready. Now, I don't know what Rafi's got you doing, but I didn't see a thing."

I later learned that, along with his text asking to use the portal, Rafi had promised Corrine a Spellbound gift certificate in a very large denomination if she kept silent about our unsanctioned trip. Which goes to show the power sweets have over Magics.

We might need an intervention.

CHAPTER TWELVE
A TRIP TO THE LIBRARY

Okay, I know I'm at risk of repeating myself, but let me just reiterate that, while Corrine's portal was convenient for our purposes, traveling through it was about as smooth as driving a car with square wheels over a deeply rutted road.

And yet somehow, when we emerged, every single hair on Daisy's head was still in perfect place, her clothes hadn't shifted one bit, and her makeup looked even fresher than it had when we'd entered the portal.

Meanwhile, I felt like a mangled teddy bear that'd been tossed around in a stone-filled tumble washer, emerged from the washer even more dirty and decrepit than it had gone in, and would probably be destined for the donation box before the day was done.

I immediately scanned the room, but Rafi's timing had been right and there were no security or other staff on duty. We were in one of the many subterranean levels of the British Library, and if we were normal law-abiding patrons, we could have taken the elevator up to the main level, put in a request for what we needed, then parked ourselves in the comfort of one of the study areas while we waited for the conveyor system that was trundling along behind us to deliver our book right to us.

But doing things the law-abiding way — well, law-abiding

until we got up and walked out with the book — would leave a very obvious paper trail.

Plus, ignoring the fact that the Library probably had strict security on their centuries-old books, the thing weighed at least as much as a small toddler. We'd be struggling just to get it out the door, and if we didn't want anyone to notice, we'd have to put the entire staff under some sort of Confounding Charm. And I just knew Daisy would object to that plan.

Once I'd straightened my shirt that had somehow twisted around backwards and chased down my shoe that had ended up on the conveyor belt, I found Daisy standing at the threshold to the room and staring down a sterile corridor that was glaringly lit with fluorescent bulbs and lined with stark white moveable shelving.

"I always pictured this place looking a little less like a morgue, and more... well, impressive," she said despondently.

"These are just the lower levels. The upstairs is nice. You can come back and play tourist some other time. For now, let's go find this thing."

"Hold on." She grabbed my arm to stop me moving forward, then tilted her chin upward and glanced toward the ceiling. Only then did I notice the camera she'd spotted. Luckily, we were standing out of its field of view. Daisy lifted her hand, fingers poised as if ready to snap them. Realizing what she was about to do, I clapped my hands over hers.

"Remember what Rafi said?" I whispered. "Any spells will backfire."

Please don't take that above comment as my sudden concern for Daisy's safety. It was for mine. See, if Daisy tried to darken cameras that were enchanted with a Backwards Backfire Charm, it might make her teeth and hair even brighter than they already were. Losing my vision to an over-dazzley Daisy was not a risk I wanted to take. Plus, I doubted Pablo would make a good seeing-eye cat.

"Only if you use magic *on the books.*" She gave me a will-you-let-me-get-on-with-this look. I released her hand and shielded my eyes. Daisy snapped her fingers. When I dared to look, the tiny green light at the side of the camera had gone out. "Motion Detector Putter Outer Charm," she explained. "The camera will come back on as soon as we leave the room. When we come back in, it'll shut off again. I'll do the same for any other cameras we encounter, okay?"

Was it wrong of me to hate that she was proving so useful on her very first day of work? Especially considering it wasn't even her official first day.

As we made our way through the underground corridors and storage areas, Daisy chatted and revealed that, while she had proved her love of books by scolding me for wanting to steal one, she'd never been to a library. Ever.

"You're kidding," I said, dumbfounded.

"Nope, never understood the point of them. If I wanted a book or movie or magazine, my parents just bought them for me."

My mind boggled. If my library card had been an airline credit card, I would have racked up enough miles to fly to Jupiter and back by the time I was eight. I'd been taking advantage of libraries for so long that I could step into any one of them and, like a homing pigeon, immediately locate the fiction section, never make a wrong turn to whichever non-fiction topic I needed, and hone in on the DVDs faster than a greyhound after a fake bunny.

This innate library knowledge also meant I could hold on to my title as Queen of the Introverts by never having to ask for the location of something on the shelves or interact with any staff until I had to check out. Even then, I worked very hard to uphold the library's please-remain-quiet policies.

Which is why, with just the few numbers and letters Mr Torres had given me, I made only one wrong turn on our way to find Copy Number Two of Wordsworth's book.

Like the other spaces we'd passed through, this one had horribly bright lighting, a cheap plastic chair so a security guard could rest without getting too comfortable, a wall-mounted fire extinguisher near the entryway, and two lengthy columns of row after row of moveable shelves — those floor-to-ceiling monstrosities that can be shifted back and forth with a simple turn of a handle.

Feeling like a pirate at the helm of his ship, I cranked the handle of the shelving unit the book should have been on, according to Mr Torres's notes. These shelves really were a marvel, because without a lick of resistance, the whole thing — which was loaded down with books on every shelf and had to weigh several hundred pounds — slid easily along the floor to reveal its contents. With Daisy standing guard, I slipped into the gap I'd made and, given that it was the largest one on the shelf, found the massive book in less than thirty seconds.

And if you're thinking all this seems too easy, so was I. But why does that have to be a bad thing?

Not good enough for you? Okay, I do have scrawny arms, and the book was really heavy. I grunted with the effort. I staggered back and nearly toppled over from the weight as I heaved the book from its shelf. There, the protagonist suffered. Happy now?

The moment I had the book cradled in my arms, my fingers tingled. This really was a magic book. Wordsworth's hadn't created that sensation, which gave me hope that this one was intact. When I returned to Daisy, she was nervously pacing by the entryway, her gaze darting up and down the length of the room, over her shoulder, over my shoulder, and beyond the entryway into the corridor. The mere sight of her frantic attention ratcheted up my already-escalated anxiety.

Just as a thought occurred to me, an automated robo-vacuum whirred by. Daisy nearly yelped, only stopping herself by slapping a hand over her mouth. I would have volunteered to do the slapping, but my hands were full of book. Maybe next time.

"Can we go now?" she asked, shuffling her feet like a five-year-old who needs to pee.

"No, one sec." I set the book down on the plastic chair and started to lift the cover.

Daisy whacked my hand. The cover snapped shut, the sound echoing through the storage space. "What are you doing? This is no time for reading. Let's just get out of here. I don't like this."

"I'm not lugging this thing back until I know it's got the pages we need."

"Okay, actually, that's not a bad idea. Just hurry. I swear that vacuum thingie was eyeing me up."

Given that I thought my office chair had it in for me, I wasn't in any position to go all snarky over this statement.

I re-opened the cover, vaguely noting that this one was of blue leather whereas Wordsworth's had been green. I then hefted the first billion pages (or so it seemed) to get to the final third of the book.

After Wordsworth had kicked my detective license dreams to the curb with his complaints about the missing pages, I'd repeatedly opened Wordsworth's copy of *The British Wizard's Guide* to that minuscule, soul-crushing gap. This was during the hour or so Rafi had commiserated with me, and I don't know if I was making sure the pages really were gone, or if I hoped new ones would spontaneously emerge from the tattered remnants in the binding. Either way, this pointless behavior meant I knew exactly which pages I needed to double-check were indeed in the book in front of me.

I flicked through a few dozen more pages, scanning the numbers at the bottom center of each until I got close to the spot I needed. Something bright flickered. A bulb on the fritz, I assumed.

I'd nearly reached the pages I was after. Barely breathing, I turned the page. My heart staggered over itself at the sight of the numbers at the bottom. So far, they were all in sequence. Afraid of causing any damage, I gingerly held the edge of the page, ready to turn it to see if those two pesky pages were there.

The bulb, or whatever, flickered again. I ignored Daisy asking if I'd seen that and peeled back the page.

Was it my wonky magic? Was it a protection hex on the book? Was it just my ever-horrible Cassie luck? I don't know. All I know is that Daisy nearly deafened me with her shriek when the book erupted into flames.

I smacked the flames, pounding at them with desperate force. Other than sending impact pain through my palms and up to my shoulder, it did no good. This was a magic blaze that wasn't going to pay any attention to the laws of physics.

I hefted the back cover and slammed the book shut. Again, stupid magic meant that cutting off the fire's oxygen did nothing. Licks of violet flames were now shooting out the sides of the book, but not the binding or the cover, which I still had enough sense to wonder at.

"Do something," I hissed at Daisy, afraid that if I tried to magically douse the fire, I'd not only alert HQ to my presence here, but also flood half of London.

The command jarred some sense into Daisy, who went running for the nearest exit. Okay, not exactly Employee of the Month behavior. But then she dashed back over, fire extinguisher at the ready. She aimed the nozzle, pressed the trigger, and coated the book in a thick layer of fire-retardant foam. As my heart jack-hammered at a rate of ten thousand beats a second, the foam quickly dissipated.

The book was ruined. The foam had pulled off the pages' golden gilt edging and had left the cover cracked and crinkled. Even if we could do a Duplex Spell in here, the section that contained the pages I needed were charred worse than a campfire marshmallow. So much for Daisy's stance against defacing books.

Because Alastair says I'm too pessimistic, I would like to add here that I did see one good side of all this: The magic flames hadn't produced any smoke, so no fire alarms were blaring, and none of the overhead sprinklers were spewing water on us.

See, I can do optimism.

"What do we do now?" asked Daisy.

"Put this away and get out of here would be my suggestion."

"But that's—" she paused, tilting her head in the way of a dog picking up an ultrasonic sound "—a very good idea. Hurry."

Adrenaline giving me superhuman strength and speed, I rushed the bedraggled book to its shelf, crammed it back where it belonged, then spun the crank to cover up the evidence as best I could.

"Let's go," Daisy hiss-whispered. "Someone's coming."

"How do you—?" But before I could finish the question, Daisy had grabbed my hand. In addition to her other annoyingly perfect qualities, she also had an excellent sense of direction, because despite all the turns we'd made to get to the room, she hurried us back to the portal without a single misstep.

Once we reached it, she tightened her grip on my hand and practically hurled us through the opening. Before the portal whisked us away, I heard someone asking if they'd just seen something, and someone else wondering who had burnt their dinner.

CHAPTER THIRTEEN
DEAR CITIZENS OF ROSARIA

When we came back through the Corrigan's Courier portal, Corrine was there, pacing excitedly, her fiery red hair bobbing with each step.

"Oh good, you made it in time," she said as Daisy crawled out of the mail slot and brushed down her skirt.

"In time for what?" I asked.

"The town hall. Starts in five minutes. I was just about to leave, but I heard you were on your way."

"Heard?"

"You curse like a sailor."

Daisy snickered, and my cheeks burnt with embarrassment. I'd never given any thought to a portal not being soundproofed.

I didn't want to waste time on some town hall where everyone would likely spend an hour griping without accomplishing anything. Thanks to my problematic trip to the library, I now needed to find the third copy of Wordsworth's book. I also needed to find out why the second one had burst into flames in my hands and to give Rafi a piece of my mind over his not-so brilliant plan.

"Sorry, but I don't—" I began, but Daisy cut off my protest.

"Cassie, we promised." We? I don't remember *we* making this promise. "You can't go back on a promise. It's very rude, and Corrine's done us a big favor."

Which was true. And who knows, maybe hearing some of the gossip blazing around MagicLand would help me dodge some of it. Sighing resignedly, I agreed to go.

"Come on, then," Corrine said. "We should make it just in time."

Grabbing hold of my arm, Corrine pulled me through the courier shop's customer area that was now empty. I assumed the clerks were either at the town hall or taking their lunch break. But even without any of the workers tending to them, the mail and parcel cubbies were moving along, shifting upward, sideways, or downward as packages and letters popped into existence from wherever they'd been sent.

Corrine practically dragged me out the door, and I could have sworn I heard the click of a photo being taken. But seeing no sign of the lanky photographer who'd been dogging my every clumsy step, I figured it was just the door latching shut behind us.

Corrine truly was a force of nature, and as Daisy jogged beside us, I found myself being swept along the streets of MagicLand until I saw we were heading straight toward—

I ground my heels into the pavement, forcing Corrine to stop.

"Here? It's being held here? I can't go in there."

"Just because you were kicked out of classes doesn't mean you can't ever go into the Academy," Daisy assured me.

"Yes, what if you were arrested?" Corrine teased.

"But why here?"

"It's one of the few places in Rosaria that has room for this many people. Now come on, we'll sit toward the back if it'll make you happy."

What would make me happy is not going in at all and getting

about my business, but in we went.

The main classroom of the Academy has seating in a half moon arrangement that rises up in theater-style rows, with the back row being the highest, and the front row being the lowest. During my classes, there had only been five rows of seats, but to accommodate what seemed to be half of MagicLand, another twenty rows had been magically added.

At the bottom of the room was the "stage" of the theater, where Oberlin (or whoever was speaking) would stand at a lectern. Behind this were a series of chalkboards with chalk that was enchanted to jot down anything important the speaker had to say. In Oberlin's case, the chalk had had very little to do.

Currently on the chalkboard were three bulleted points I assumed were the topics of this meeting: missing Magics, murdered Magics, and Mayor Matilda Marheart.

"There's Tobey!" Daisy exclaimed when she saw him standing near the front row. She began waving excitedly when he turned and caught sight of us. "Can I take a break?"

An odd request since, technically, she hadn't even clocked in yet.

"Take the rest of the day off, if you like."

"You are the best boss, Cassie. Thanks."

I dodged the hug she tried to throw around me by dropping into the nearest empty seat I could find. Corrine sat down next to me, but it was my other seat neighbor who sneered, "Boss? You've got to be kidding."

"I should have known by the flies circling these seats that you were nearby."

"Cute, Black," said Morelli. Runa and Fiona greeted us as they sidled over to two seats a couple rows in front of us. Morelli wrinkled his nose. "Why do you smell like a campfire gone wrong? You trying to cover up your magic?"

The Unbearable Inspector Oberlin

All Magics have a scent to their power, which varies depending on who's doing the smelling. Only people up to no good try to cover up this aroma with perfumes, colognes, and, in some cases, smoke, usually of the cigarette variety.

"What do I smell like to you?" I asked, because not only did I want to dodge my landlord's incriminating question, but I was always curious to know what my magic smelled like to others.

"Trouble," Morelli quipped. I stared at him until he finally gave in. "Fine. You've got a sort of lilac thing going on." I quirked my lips in disappointment. Alastair told me I smelled like lilies, and Runa had mentioned honeysuckle. Which is nice, but for some reason I keep hoping I'll come across someone who says I smell like donuts. Taking a stab at small talk, Morelli asked, "You get a lot of detecting done this morning?"

"I was just in London following up on a hot lead." Which was not a lie.

"Really? Any luck?"

"No, just smoke and ashes."

Morelli gave me a puzzled look, like he was about to ask what I meant, when Oberlin waddled up to the lectern and, using a Voice Amplification Charm, called for our attention.

"Thank you for coming," he said once the crowd quieted down. "I'm sure our speaker needs no introduction, so I'm simply going to turn the stage over to him. I back his comments, all of them, so please take what he says to heart, my dear citizens of Rosaria."

I tensed at the phrasing. Those were the exact words my admirer from the *Herald* often used to address his readers. I'd long suspected Oberlin of having a hand in the anti-Cassie nonsense, and here was proof from the mouth of the Walrus himself.

Oberlin made a sweeping gesture to the side, and a man dressed in terracotta colored slacks, a pale blue polo shirt, and pink slippers stepped over to the lectern.

"Who is he?" I asked Morelli.

"Leo Flourish," he whispered. "The *Herald's* editor."

Which would explain the slippers. About a week ago, Runa Dunwiddle had asked the editor to stop printing articles that were upsetting her patients. He refused, citing journalistic integrity or some other gibberish that really meant, *"That's the exact sort of thing that sells papers, so of course we're going to keep printing it."*

Having gotten nowhere by asking nicely, Runa had put a Leftie-Rightie Curse on the editor, which meant none of his shoes would fit his feet properly. He'd either have to bear the awkward shoes and walk funny, or as he had done, hope that sporting slippers in public suddenly became a hot trend.

"Ladies and gentlemen," Mr Flourish began, "I believe I speak for us all when I say we are more than a little concerned about the recent crime spree in our community, and in the Magic world as a whole. Especially now that Clive Coppersmith, a longtime member of our community and a kind man we all loved and cherished has been murdered in his own home."

That was rich. Mr Coppersmith had been a lonely old man who hung out in the Wandering Wizard Pub just to pretend he had company coming by to visit him. Had anyone in this room besides Tobey ever stopped by Clive's apartment or his barstool to chat with him, to see how he was doing?

"And then the dear wife of our Inspector Oberlin, fighting for her life in her own garden. Does she have any hope of recovery from her now-critical condition? Even the medics can't help her at this point, and we may lose her. A tragedy in the making," he said with a dramatic shake of his head.

"Tobey told me Winnifred was okay thanks to you?" I whispered to Morelli, who was scowling so intensely I worried his brow might become permanently furrowed. "As in not dying."

"Nearly was. They'd almost given up on her. Then, at the last minute, Runa found a trace of Winnifred's magic was still charged up a bit. We got her to the Tower's medical ward, and Chester and I stabilized her. She's not on the brink of death like this guy's implying. She just needs time to heal."

"Are these just random acts?" Mr Flourish was saying. "Or are they part of a bigger picture of Magic crime? You've read the stories. You know about the Magics who have gone missing lately. Many of them from small communities like ours, as if we're easy targets."

This was a complete exaggeration since the Galway community, a very sizable one from what I understood, had lost so many people it was teetering on the brink of extinction.

"And maybe we are easy targets," Leo continued. "Because maybe our leadership isn't what we need it to be and won't bother to fight for us."

At this, my seat jerked. I looked down to see Morelli's meaty hand gripping our shared arm rest. If he clenched his fingers any harder, the lacquered wood might crumble into dust.

Just then, my phone buzzed with an incoming message, startling me so hard I had to bite back a yelp. It was Rafi.

> *Strange news coming from BL. You get what you need?*

In an indignant flurry, I texted back.

> *Did I get what I need?! If I needed a heart attack, then yes, I got exactly what I needed!*

I then, trying to use vague terms in case any librarians came after me, explained what had happened... and blamed him entirely for not giving his plan a little more forethought before sending me into the fiery fray.

"It's my opinion," the editor went on as I waited for a response, "that with leadership such as that, we need to prepare to defend ourselves, because we are clearly under some sort of attack. Our very way of life is under assault." Morelli groaned and muttered something about *this guy*. "Mayor Marheart, would you care to comment? Because I don't think you're taking any of this seriously. Otherwise, wouldn't you have addressed us by now instead of merely playing the part of a leader?"

A small section of the audience hooted and cheered Mr Flourish's comments with worrying glee. But there were plenty of others in the crowd clearly not in line with what Mr Flourish was spewing — Fiona and Runa included, as evidenced by their stiff postures and their arms crossed over their chests.

"This is a bunch of hooey," Corrine muttered to me. "It's not any one person's fault what's happening. Oh, good, here's the mayor. She'll sort them out."

Another message from Rafi buzzed through:

> *Oops. I really really really didn't know. Sorry. A million times sorry. I promise I'll figure out a way to make it up to you.*

As I texted back that the apology gift better be grandiose, Fiona whispered something to Runa, who lifted her hands in a *who knows?* gesture. She then cupped her hand near Fiona's ear and said something that was impossible to hear over the murmuring speculation swelling through the crowd.

Meanwhile, Matilda was stepping down from the fourth row to the lecture floor, moving with elegant strides on her red heels. Although she appeared paler than normal, I had to give her credit. I'd have been out the door the minute anyone started calling for people to act up against me. Morelli leaned forward with interest as Matilda took her place behind the lectern.

CHAPTER FOURTEEN
A FEMINIST TROLL

"People of Rosaria," Matilda began in a clear, unwavering voice, "I promise you, I am paying attention to these incidents, and I am acting on them in the best way I know how." This was exactly the right thing to say, but unfortunately, Matilda seemed to be in political mode so the words came out false, rehearsed, meaningless. "I am certain, and I do mean certain, that the matters we're facing will come to an end soon. I give you my word that the safety of Rosaria, of all of our communities, is my top priority."

"Your top priority two weeks ago was the size of shop signs on Main Street," someone jeered.

"What's your background?" someone else called.

Matilda flinched, but quickly recovered.

"I assure you that I have the experience to address these matters," she replied coolly.

"Not what I meant, and you know it."

I didn't know what exactly this heckler was going on about, but a flood of Matilda-based memories came to me as the accusations continued to snap through the auditorium.

There was, of course, Winnifred's final action. The M she'd drawn in the dirt. Had it just been random scrabbling as she lost her strength, or had she been trying to spell out the name of her would-be killer? At my parents' place... Someone slim and tall had attacked me, then Matilda was there when I came to, hovering over me. Or had she been there all along? She'd also been spotted near both Mr Coppersmith's and Mrs Oberlin's homes before their attacks. And even though Corrine thought it a good thing, I couldn't help but think it suspicious that Mayor Marheart had shown special interest in Wordsworth's crate.

Down on the stage, Matilda's sleek jaw twitched, and I kind of wanted to see the political façade crack, to see her lash out and tell these people to shut up, but she merely settled her shoulders and said, "I am your mayor, and I assure you, taking matters into your own hands will only cause more trouble. Please remain calm and do your best to go about your daily lives."

Then, with the small section of detractors shouting insults and questions and complaints at her (none of which were clear, since they were all yelling at once), Matilda left the stage, striding without any haste and appearing even more poised than usual.

Leo soon resumed his spot at the lectern, and Matilda, now looking exceptionally pale in the auditorium's low light, moved toward the nearest exit. Carrying herself with forced confidence, she gave Oberlin a curt nod as she passed by him.

Rather than returning her greeting, he glowered at the mayor with pure hatred. I'd honestly thought Oberlin reserved such looks of vile detest just for me, which left me wondering again why he'd gone to Matilda's for dinner. I mean, there was keeping your enemies close, and then there was just downright inconsistently odd behavior. I'd have pondered this matter longer if someone wasn't elbowing me and hissing at me to move.

"I better go see how she's doing," said Morelli, standing to leave just as Runa and Fiona were doing the same. I figured it was as good a time as any to make my escape, so I eased my way out of the classroom with Morelli breathing down my neck and complaining that I was in his way.

"What are you doing, Black? I don't need you tagging along."

"She knows something." I didn't want to go into my many misgivings about Matilda, since, one, Morelli would just poo-poo them; and, two, I needed time to fully formulate what they might mean. Choosing my words carefully, I told him, "You heard what she said. 'Experience to address these matters.' It's like she knows what's happening. Or she's part of what's happening."

Runa, who we'd caught up to by now, jerked her head around and gave me a disapproving look. And we'd been getting along so well.

"Don't go there, Black," Morelli grumbled. "Matilda's good for this community. People just can't see that. You know what I bet it is?"

"This should be interesting."

"Those men in there — because, if you noticed, it was all men doing the shouting and hectoring — they're afraid of a woman being in power. They can't handle the fact that she might actually be competent at what she does, so instead they try to stir up some dirt on her."

"Are you a feminist, or do you just have the world's worst crush?"

"Could be both. But what I'm saying is, Matilda's a great lady. She might have her secrets, but she's the—" He cut his words off, like someone who's nearly said too much.

"But she's the…?" I prodded as we followed Runa and Fiona out of the Academy. As soon as we descended the entry steps, Matilda came around from, I assume, one of the building's rear exits.

"There's nothing to be worried about with her," Morelli

stated, his gaze trained on the mayor. "And maybe you ought to work with her a little, ask her more about that jewel, rather than going around chasing after smoke and ashes, or whatever that was supposed to mean."

"Why aren't you guarding Runa?" I asked as I saw Dr Dunwiddle picking up the pace and heading straight for the mayor. An uncomfortable prickle crawled up my spine. My clients were having trouble staying alive, or at least conscious. I'd assumed it was only clients whose items I'd found, but what if any client was fair game?

"Fiona's pulling duty right now," Morelli said, tipping his chin to indicate the strawberry-blonde schoolteacher who was muttering something to herself as she stood politely out of eavesdropping distance from Matilda and Runa.

"Why is she talking to herself?" I asked worriedly. Fiona had been working hard and had seemed to be handling it okay, but could the strain be proving to be too much?

"Protective Hex. She's good at them. Used to be able to safeguard her entire classroom when the Mauvais's people wanted to get to them and teach their own nasty curriculum."

Matilda nodded to whatever Runa had said, then Runa touched the mayor's arm in a reassuring way that seemed very un-Runa-like. She then rejoined Fiona, and the two walked off in the opposite direction the mayor had gone.

"Now, if you don't mind, I'm going to go talk to Matilda. Don't follow me."

Although my mind was racing with curiosity about the mayor, I didn't follow him. Mainly because there are some things I just don't want to see. Morelli being romantic is high on that list. But also because I wanted nothing more than to collect Pablo from the agency, then go home and wash the burnt book smell off my skin.

CHAPTER FIFTEEN
CURIOSITY KILLED THE...

I'd just gotten back to the agency and was making sure Pablo was in his carrier when my phone rang.

"Hello, Cassie?" I instantly recognized the warm tones of Mr Torres from the Oregon Historical Society. "Is this a bad time?"

It seemed any time was a bad time for me lately, but as that exact moment wasn't a complete dumpster fire, I said, "No, things are okay. How are you?"

"Good, except..." he hesitated "...well, I hate to be the bearer of bad tidings, but have you heard about what happened at the British Library?"

Apparently, gossip spread like wildfire not only amongst Magics, but also to anyone associated with Magics.

"I have. Just my luck, right?"

"Ah, so you weren't able to locate your book before it happened? Such a shame. But you said there was a third copy?"

"Somewhere in the world there is a third copy, yes. Or possibly the universe." I supposed I really should clarify that with Sebastian rather than relying on Rafi's guesses.

"Don't fret over it; I'll keep poking around to see if I can't stumble upon it."

I gave a half-hearted thanks, but my low spirits didn't seem to put any sort of damper on his cheery mood.

"Now, I know it's only been a few hours since we last spoke," he said, sounding like a kid who's just been told the rest of the school day is going to be spent eating cake and playing outside, "but I simply can't stop thinking about that jewel of yours. Perhaps it's a case of curiosity killed the historian, but I really feel I could do something with this. I hope I'm not coming across as too over-eager."

He was, but his enthusiasm was providing light at the end of my dark and winding tunnel of potential failure.

"No, actually, that's good news."

Okay, *good* here was a relative term. If Matilda's contract couldn't be cancelled without a great deal of bureaucratic wrangling, then she was still my client. Trouble was, she had suspicious circumstances sprouting up around her like dandelions in springtime.

But, since no new clients were lining up at my door, and since I still needed that stupid form signed for my license application, I couldn't simply turn my back on the mayor's case. There was just the small problem of having about as many ideas on how to solve her case as I had ideas on how to really make a go of nuclear fusion.

"Good news? Does that mean your client didn't fire you?"

"Not officially," I said uncertainly. "I think she'd like to, but apparently she can't. Sorry, that makes no sense, not even to me. Either way, I'll still be glad for anything you can uncover."

"Well, I didn't get a chance to dig too deeply into things, but you gave the name of William Boncoeur, yes?" I said I had. "The very moment you said it, that name struck me as familiar, but I've yet to pinpoint *why* it seems familiar. Don't you just hate that?" I did. In fact, it seemed like that was how my brain functioned ninety percent of the time. "It'll drive me mad if I don't sort it out this evening, but I believe it could be the start of something very exciting indeed."

"Historically exciting?" I teased. Because seriously, this guy was way more keyed up about some possibly-dead-end research than might be healthy. I guess he hadn't been kidding about things being rather slow in the realms of Oregon History.

"Quite."

"I wouldn't want to waste your time..." I said, even though he seemed perfectly happy to fritter away his time. If he could use his historian super powers to uncover anything about Matilda's stupid jewel, it'd be— I didn't know what exactly it would be, but I was hoping 'immensely helpful' would fit the bill.

"No, no, not at all. And it wouldn't be just for your case. I have a feeling it can add to the history I'm working on of Rosaria's founding."

"How's that?" I asked, wondering if this guy had been sniffing too much vellum since, from what I understood, Mayor Marheart had only recently moved to MagicLand. It seemed pretty far-fetched that her jewel could be tied to Rosaria's history.

"The jewel once belonged to Queen Elizabeth I. You've figured out that much, of course. As you know, many of the original founders of the magic communities in the United States were descendants of courtiers of Elizabeth." I wanted to tell him that I did know something of this from a comment Fiona had made, and that I'd like to hear more about it, but Mr Torres needed no encouragement to continue. "And Rosaria got her fair share of those descendants when it was established. You also got another batch of descendants from Queen Anne's court. Can't blame them for wanting to come here. The weather is quite pleasant.

"Anyway, it may simply be my wishful thinking since this topic would make for an excellent paper that'd really knock the socks off of some of your own historians—" I assumed he meant

Magic historians, not my own personal cadre of history buffs "—but I feel there has to be some sort of tie between the Boncoeur Jewel and Rosaria's history. And like I said, that name is so peskily familiar. You really don't mind indulging a historian's whims by letting me dig into this?"

"Dig away, by all means." I paused, suddenly realizing that most people didn't work for free, no matter how enjoyable they found that work. "What do you normally charge for this type of research?"

"Oh, not to worry. Like I said earlier, very little to do here at the moment. And since I'll be doing this during working hours, I'm technically getting paid for it. Also, Rosaria is a very generous donator to the Society, and a fair portion of that goes toward my salary for this exact purpose. I'm like your personal, on-call historian. Now, if you come up with anything, do keep me in the loop. You never know what small tidbit could be the key to piecing everything together."

"The only other thing I know is that my client has the box now, but it was at the British Museum for a time." I tried to recall the date that had been on the yellowed newspaper I'd seen. "It would have been the late 1970s, I think, but by then it no longer had the jewel."

Through the phone I could hear the sound of a pencil scratching notes on paper. Mr Torres muttered a few words as he wrote, before saying, "That might be helpful. Or it might not. You just never know with history. I'll let you get back to your day, Miss Black. In the meantime, thank you for alleviating my boredom."

We said our goodbyes, and as I packed up my cat, I felt for the first time like I might actually get somewhere with Matilda's case. Which, with my luck, probably meant she'd just finalized the paperwork to officially fire me.

CHAPTER SIXTEEN
TROLL-SIZED CONTACTS

Once home, I resolved to get to the bottom of things with Alastair. After checking if he was in the apartment, I went downstairs to the workroom. As ever, one of the garden gnomes was on duty at the door. The moment Rosencrantz-possibly-Guildenstern saw me, he jerked to rigid attention. Even his hat stood taller as he kept his eyes fixed on me.

"Can't go in there, mum."

"Can you at least tell him I'd like to see him?"

"Which one'd that be, then? The troll or the human?"

"The human, please."

"Step back. Can't have you peeking in at stuff you shouldn't see, can I?"

"What would I see? Morelli working on his ballet routine?"

"That information, it's on a need-to-know basis, innit?" He waited, staring at me with his black eyes. I rolled my own eyes and took a step back. He still didn't move, so I took another until I was back at the bottom of the stairwell. He gave a sharp nod. "That'll do. Stay put, and I'll fetch the human."

When he went into the workroom, I took a seat on the bottom step and wondered if all crimes could be prevented by placing garden gnomes on duty across all of MagicLand. Which would be terribly quaint and Instagram-able, but how secure were they? I mean, was there a distraction they couldn't resist? Could they be bribed with a new hat or beard wax or—

The workroom door clicked open.

And instead of the human I wanted to speak to, out stepped Morelli. At least he wasn't in a pink tutu and pointe shoes. Small favors, right?

"You're not Alastair," I said.

"Your detective skills get better every day, Black. Oberlin better fear for his job with you around."

"Did Alastair send you out here so he wouldn't have to speak to me himself? I mean, it's a cat scratch, and he's acting like Pablo came after him with a flaming pitchfork."

"That's for you two to sort out. And no, he didn't send me out here. He's just..."

"Busy?"

"Something like that, yeah. You got good timing, though. I was going to come by in just a bit with some news." Despite myself, I arched an eyebrow, curious to know what this might be about. Morelli glanced past my shoulder to see Guildenstern-possibly-Rosencrantz watching us with interest. "Maybe outside?"

I agreed, and we exited the building through its main door, which put us in the front garden Morelli had added when we'd renovated the building. To Norm eyes the building still looked like a wrecking ball would be the best thing for it, and the front patch of lawn (to put it generously) looked like the before picture for a weed killer ad.

But that was merely a Mirage Hex surrounding the building. In reality, that patch of lawn had been transformed into a pottage garden that wouldn't have looked out of place on the grounds of a chateau. A very tiny chateau, since it was only the width of the building, but that didn't stop it from currently bursting with tomatoes, peppers, and basil, along with several flowers that Morelli said were natural bug repellants — because if anyone was going to know about being repellant, it was Morelli. At the corner of the garden, under a plum tree on whose branches a few fruits still dangled, were two high-end lawn chairs, decorated with crocheted cushions. We each took a seat. Morelli grunting with relief.

"Rough afternoon of crocheting?"

"More like a frantic afternoon of crocheting. I've hardly had any time for my own projects after taking care of Winnifred and then being put on Runa duty. Hope Fiona is managing okay with that limp of hers, because I swear Dunwiddle must have some special charm on her shoes to keep going like she does."

I thought of the shoes Olivia had given Runa. The ones Runa said were unbearably uncomfortable when I'd first seen her in them. Had she actually taken my advice and charmed them into comfort?

Just then, the usual gang of kids who liked to play kickball in the empty lot next to the apartment building rushed in, shouting and laughing and throwing a ball back and forth as they chased each other to their makeshift playing field. One of them, the tallest boy, caught Morelli's eye and raised his eyebrows. Morelli shook his head, and the kid turned back to his game and deftly stole the ball from an unsuspecting playmate.

"What was that about?"

"What was what about?" Morelli said, suspiciously innocent.

"Never mind. Anyway, I'm sure you didn't want to talk to me about Runa's footwear choices. Wait," I said, thinking of the last time he wanted to speak with me, "you didn't find the location of the other copy of Wordsworth's book, did you?"

"No, sorry. You heard what happened to the British Library one, didn't you? Sucks you couldn't have gotten to it before—" I must have been making some sort of I-am-so-guilty face, because Morelli exclaimed, "Smoke and ashes! You did get to it, didn't you?"

"Yeah. It kind of burnt up when I opened it."

"Ah, so that was the other protection spell they put on it," Morelli said, apparently glad to have that question sorted.

"Don't tell anyone, okay. Only Daisy knows. And wait, protection spell? Those flames weren't just my bad luck?"

"I mean, they could be. But it was likely a charm that told the book it was better to self-destruct than to allow someone with evil intentions to read it."

"I didn't have evil intentions. I just wanted to steal it for a while."

I expected Morelli to say that, to a book, that would be an evil intention. Instead, he thought a moment before saying, "You're right. It does seem a little extreme. I'm not versed in them myself, but I do know objects can be enchanted to defend themselves if they detect something untoward going on with the person handling them."

"Untoward? What? Did the book think I was trying to make a pass at it?"

"Not like that. Like someone in possession of something that could cause harm. Say it's a book of potions. If it has a recipe in there that could wipe out an entire community, and the book senses the person trying to read it has recently touched one of the key ingredients to that potion, the book can be charmed to destroy itself rather than risk endangering people. It's pretty advanced. Not used much, because as you can imagine, it takes a lot of nit-picky spell crafting, but it's not completely unheard of. Obviously."

"But I don't have any plans to use the book. I just want to get the damn thing to Wordsworth."

"Maybe the book just didn't like you. Which I could understand. Anyway, this news. My contacts, they found something, and it's headed your way. You didn't hear anything about it from me, though. Just like I didn't hear anything about you being in the British Library during a certain conflagration. Got it?"

"Got it," I said doubtfully, unsure exactly what kind of underworld stuff Morelli was getting me into. "But I really don't think—"

"I know you don't think. Now, my sources said they'd—"

"Who are these sources?" I interrupted.

"Yeah, because I'm going to tell you that. Let's just say, trolls may be big, but we're often ignored. He says the place he works for—"

"As a security troll?"

Morelli considered this, as if deciding whether his answer would give away too much. After a moment, he nodded. "Yeah, a security troll. Good at his job, so don't go getting him in trouble."

"I don't even know who he is."

"Right. Anyway, he came across a jewel. It doesn't exactly fit your description, but he senses something on it, and, like I said, he's sending it your way."

"Wait, he stole it?" I blurted. I mean, I know I'd planned to steal a gigantic book from the British Library, but only temporarily. It certainly wasn't the same as being the recipient of stolen items — no, a stolen *jewel!* I was about to be the recipient of a *highly valuable* stolen item. Oberlin was going to have a field day with that. "But why would he do that? You just said it didn't even match the description of Matilda's jewel."

"Yeah, but Mattie's jewel is old, right? It could have been altered a bit, cut into a different shape that was more in fashion, or whatever. If it's not the right one, then we'll just figure out how to get it back where it belongs. Assuming no one notices it's missing before then."

"And if they do?"

"You worry too much. He put a Replacement Hex on the display case." Morelli cut off his words, perhaps realizing he'd revealed more than he'd intended.

"And a Replacement Hex does what, exactly?"

"It makes a sort of hologram of the item appear while it's away. Although, he's not very good at them," Morelli added. "Still, we should be okay."

"*We*? I didn't steal it. I didn't ask to be a part of your crime ring."

"Stop worrying. If any questions are asked, I'll back you up."

"I'll need that in writing." Morelli chuckled as if I was joking. I wasn't joking, but before I could let him know that, my phone rang. Morelli arched an eyebrow in an are-you-going-to-get-that manner.

"Chip chip cheery-oh," Mr Wood chortled when I answered the call. "Are you ready to get me to the airport?"

Honestly, what with the book burning and the town hall and Mr Torres's news and Morelli's 'sources', I'd completely forgotten about my promise to be Mr Wood's chauffeur.

"I'll be there in a jiffy," I said, unintentionally throwing a whole lot of perky bubbly-ness into my words.

Merlin's blighted beard! Could Daisy-ness be contagious?

Before I left, I asked Morelli if we couldn't just send Mr Wood through one of MagicLand's Portland-London portals. But he said unless Mr Wood had been added to a roster HQ kept, taking a Norm (even a Norm who'd been able to hold on to his donated magic) through a portal would set off alarm bells and very likely shut down that portal for at least a week.

It killed my idea of making things more convenient for my

former boss, but maybe it was for the best. After all, from the way he'd been going on about his airline's meals, movies, and free drinks, one would think Mr Wood was looking as forward to the amenities of his trans-Atlantic flight almost as much as he was the vacation itself.

I don't know whether it was excitement over his trip or if it was nerves, but from the time we left the funeral home's parking lot to the time I pulled into PDX's Departures drop-off area, Mr Wood prattled on without stop. What about? Mostly just rhetorical questions about who he'd meet, what kind of hiking boots everyone would be wearing, if the weather would behave, and various other quandaries about his tour.

To tell the truth, I was glad the questions were rhetorical and that he seemed happy to yammer on to the void, because I was too lost in my own thoughts to make much conversation.

Something was simmering right at the surface of my mind. Images kept flashing through my head — books, jewels, crochet hooks, marbles, cat carriers, Oberlin's sneer, Matilda at the town hall. But they refused to connect or coalesce.

Then again, I was attempting to speculate while also trying to avoid plowing down the pedestrians who stepped out in front of my moving vehicle as I searched for an open drop-off spot, and while half-listening to my passenger wonder what his first meal would be.

After saying some awkward goodbyes, Mr Wood wheeled his suitcase toward the airport's revolving door. He hadn't even reached it before he found someone new to talk to, and I had a feeling Mr Wood's seat companion wasn't going to get a minute of sleep on the red-eye flight.

Once I'd closed the trunk and gotten back in the car, I noticed

Mr Wood had left his newspaper on the passenger's seat. I considered texting him to see if he wanted to collect it, but a security guy was already yelling at me about waiting at the curb too long. Ah well, at least the airport was full of shops with better reading material.

As I waited for an opening in the parade of traffic moving at a snail's pace through the drop-off area, I glanced at the page the paper had been left open to. At top left was a fluff piece about an irreplaceable item that had supposedly been stolen from the Portland Art Museum.

Quick glances as I inched the car forward told me that when the curator was called over to verify what had been taken, the item was right where it should be. I was just reading the quote from the curator about guards sometimes playing practical jokes on him when a honk startled me back to the task at hand.

I merged in between a massive SUV and a Mini-Cooper and drove home, wondering what exactly Morelli's contact was sending my way.

CHAPTER SEVENTEEN
THE AMOEBA COUPLE

The next morning, just as I was trying to get myself and Pablo's bulky carrier through my closet portal, a text pinged through my phone. Half-hoping it was Mr Torres messaging to say he'd solved all of my cases and would be glad for me to take full credit, I grabbed for my phone faster than I normally would have at that hour. I sneered and then sighed when the home screen showed the text was only from Matilda Marheart.

The phone was locked, hiding the message, but once I tapped in my passcode, I wasn't sure how to feel about what the mayor had sent: *Please come see me today. Whenever you have time. We have things to discuss.*

There were no grumpy face or happy face emojis, not even a thumbs up to imply in what sort of tone I should read the message. Was it, *Come see me today so we can exchange more angry words*? Or was it, *Come see me today because I've realized you're the best detective ever, and we should find a way to work amicably together*?

I opted not to respond. If asked, I could tell her I never received it, or that Pablo had stepped on the phone and deleted her text before I'd read it. I crammed the phone back into my pocket, then lugged Pablo and his carrier (and myself, obviously) through my portal and to the agency.

I'd barely gotten a cup of tea made (because, priorities) before the bell above the agency's door chirped. Wedged in the threshold was a giggling couple, arms firmly wrapped around each other. They both refused to let go, which meant the only way they could fit through the doorway was to enter sideways. Which only increased the amount of inane giggling. Pablo turned his back on them and crawled into his carrier. Lucky little furball.

"Cassie, look who I brought," said Daisy, as if I could miss my six-foot-something cousin who was currently conjoined to her.

Still needing far more caffeine to kick in before I could function as a human capable of speech, I fluttered my hand in Tobey's general direction. Then something Runa had said struck me. Someone had taken my samples from her clinic and someone might have wanted to use those samples to give themselves a boost before a big test.

Now, don't get me wrong. I didn't think Tobey, despite his desperation to prove himself, had taken those samples. But Inspector Oberlin? He'd completely written off Dr Dunwiddle's break-in as nothing more than troublemakers making trouble. Was that because he would do anything to make sure his favorite pupil passed his second Exam attempt with flying colors? After all, it wouldn't be hard to slip an unsuspecting Tobey a hit of magic in a hearty handshake or chummy pat on the back.

I considered that last practice quiz I'd made for Tobey, the one he'd aced in record time yesterday morning. Sure, he knew his stuff, but I'd made those sixty questions as tough as possible, and it should have taken him far longer than a mere twenty minutes to answer them.

Tobey went through a long process of extricating himself from Daisy. This involved so many declarations of "love you," "love you more," and "love you to infinity" that I thought it might be lunchtime before the two completed their amoeba-like separation. Lunchtime a month from now, to be precise.

Finally, Daisy went to her desk, which she'd magically expanded and had decorated with a vase of magenta flowers and several colorfully framed photos of her and Tobey.

Tobey, his face now serious (if you ignored the lipstick smear on his left cheek), came over to my desk and sat down in one of my guest chairs.

"Don't you have class to get to?" I asked as I stretched up my arms and sucked in a deep inhale, trying to surreptitiously sneak a sniff of my cousin. But Tobey didn't carry any scent other than his magic's usual soapy-clean aroma. Still, as the day of his Exams drew closer, I planned to take every chance I could to sniff my cousin.

Which sounds far more unhinged than it should.

"Oberlin had a few things to attend to and couldn't get a guest lecturer in," Tobey explained, "so he gave us a late start today. Anyway, can we schedule another study session? That last one, I don't know, it just really gave me a boost of confidence."

Yes, there would definitely be cousin-sniffing over the next few days.

"Did you ask Busby about the test booklets?"

"Haven't had time, but tonight. Wait, no, maybe tomorrow?" He glanced over to Daisy, who was wiggling her fingers over a label maker that was struggling to keep up with whatever she was enchanting it to type. "We have a date tonight. Celebrating the first time we ate pizza together, if I remember right."

"You can keep track of that, but you can't pass a simple exam on statutes and forensics?" Tobey shrugged and blushed in such a sappy way that made me... well, it made me want to swat Alastair upside the head until he remembered he used to be that way about me. "Fine," I conceded. "I'm not sure what my schedule's like over the next couple of days, so any study session might be spur of the moment, but we'll definitely do one the evening before your test. Sound good?"

The moment Tobey agreed, my tea-stained and mustard-smeared calendar filled in the box for the day before Tobey's Exams with '*Steady toe bees*' in faint blue letters. Honestly, I think I was going to have to put the poor thing out of its misery.

"Look," said Tobey, half-whispering, "you know how I told you Oberlin and I were invited to Matilda's for dinner last night?" I nodded. "I think I saw something."

"Wait, did an angry mob show up," I asked, visualizing flaming torches and pitchforks, "then drag Oberlin away, never to be seen again?"

"No, nothing like that. What in the world goes on in your brain?"

"You don't want to know. So what did you see?"

"Do you have a picture of your mom's pendant?"

Making no comment about this weird reply, I pulled the photo my mom had given me from under my calendar. See, I may not *look* organized, but I know where everything is. Okay, most things. Tobey scrutinized the picture for a moment, then sat back with a self-satisfied smirk on his face.

"This," he said, tapping the photo, "was at Matilda's."

"What? You're sure it was this one?" I remembered Fiona saying HQ once gave out the pendants to top-tier recruits. Had Matilda once worked for HQ? A question that also brought to mind what the town hall attendees had shouted yesterday. What had they meant about Matilda's background? Something to look up as soon as I needed a bit of nosy procrastination.

"I'm more than certain," replied Tobey.

"But what does that mean?" I asked as worry blazed through me like a bolt of lightning.

Since getting sucked into the whole Magic thing, I'd involved myself more than once in matters that I was supposed to keep well out of. Namely, going after the Mauvais when I knew he wanted to turn me into a human battery and tracking down my parents when it seemed no one else was doing a thing for them.

This habit of mine to jump feet first into a pool of trouble would be an excellent reason for Mr Tenpenny to lie about my parents being off on a secret mission when he truly had no idea where they'd gone. I mean, what sense did it make that they were off gathering intel — or whatever they were doing — when it had been orders direct from HQ telling my parents they weren't allowed to do any field work until Runa gave them a clean bill of magical and physical health? They'd been improving, but Simon and Chloe Starling were hardly pictures of vitality, and they were certainly not the people you would send in to chase down the bad guys.

"I don't know," Tobey said, distracting me from my angst. "But I do know she played off my interest in it."

"What do you mean? And hold on, was the pendant just out in the open? Like hanging from a philodendron or something?"

"Not a philodendron, no. It was hooked over the frame of a mirror. The reflection of the jewel caught the setting sun, otherwise I don't think I'd have noticed it. I said something about the pendant being a nice sun catcher, but Matilda merely said she didn't know what else to do with it, then quickly returned to talking to Oberlin. I don't even know why I was there. Apparently, it wasn't Inspector Oberlin wanting me as his guest, but Matilda insisting he bring me along. Still, I felt like a third wheel the whole night."

"You don't think there's something between—?"

Before I could almost feel bad for Morelli, Tobey cut me off. "No, no, nothing like that. Just like, well, for so much animosity between them, they both acted like it was all water under the bridge, like they were old friends catching up. I pretty much sat there the whole night drinking her wine. Not that I'm complaining. It was a really nice Bordeaux."

"Still made you smell like a bum when you stopped by to kiss me good night, though," Daisy commented with a mock scowl.

"You didn't seem to complain."

"Please," I insisted. "Just stop right there before I have to vomit on your shoes."

"Did you want me to bring the pendant thing up to Oberlin?" Tobey asked.

"Can't see any point in that. He dismissed Runa's break-in, he dismissed my attack at my parents' place, and he'll probably just dismiss this as well. Besides," I said, thinking of the mayor's message, "I might go by to talk to Matilda today, anyway."

"Don't do anything rash, Cass."

"When have I ever done that?"

"Pretty much every day since I met you."

CHAPTER EIGHTEEN
PIANO PERILS

Tobey had barely been gone fifteen minutes before, from my assistant's desk, came a heavy sigh. And then another, heavier this time. Was the air in her head leaking out?

Figuring she was just moping over being separated from Tobey, I tried to ignore the noise while also trying to sort out how to organize my day. Replying to Matilda was high on the list. Possibly even going to Matilda's. And then what? Sometimes I really did miss the days where my biggest decision was whether to apply Fawn's Fancy or Ivory Tower foundation on the dead person spread out before me.

Daisy sighed again.

"Everything okay?" I asked, hoping that, like a parakeet, if I gave her some attention she'd shut up.

"Sorry?"

"You. You're sighing. Unless those are some pre-work breathing exercises you're doing over there."

"Was I?" she asked… with a sigh. "I'm just really worried after seeing all that stuff on Fae-book. It's so awful, isn't it?"

"Fae-book?" I asked, hating that Daisy knew about things I didn't.

"The social media platform for Magics. It's a great way to chat with other communities. All kinds of Magics are on there. I've got followers who are elves, trolls, even some werewolves. They are *so* interesting. Did you know, even in human form, they just love a good chunk of rawhide to chew on? Really, you *have* to get on there. Did you want me to set you up? I could be your first follower. Wouldn't that be fun?"

Even if she could boast no other skills, Daisy certainly had a talent for going from being fretful to cheerful in record time.

"Yeah, I think I'll pass," I told her. Given that I had never mastered the art of being social in real life, I rarely bothered with being social online. There were probably abandoned rail stations that were busier than my Norm social media accounts had ever been. "Anyway, what's awful?"

And if she started spouting things about manticores rigging elections, the astounding properties of unicorn snot, and Middle Earth being flat, I didn't care how much Mr Tenpenny wanted me to keep her as an assistant, I was going to have to kick her out of the agency.

"Well, I follow this one account that reports the Norm news. Makes me feel like I'm spying," she said with a twinkle and a giggle. I was becoming more and more convinced that she hadn't been born; she'd been crafted by Mattel. "There's been reports of Norms being attacked in their homes. It's pretty grim."

Daisy tapped a few things on her laptop, then turned it so I could see one of the headlines on the screen.

"That's not unusual. Especially in America."

"Oh, only a few have been in America. Most of them have been in the U.K."

"Still not seeing the newsworthiness of this."

"They say the Norms are being killed in a 'ritualistic manner'." She made air quotes around the last two words.

I sat up straighter. About a week ago, I'd seen a news article about people being killed in a disturbing manner. Were they related to what Daisy's Fae-book conspiracy theory folks had dug up?

"What does 'ritualistic' mean?" I asked. "Like a cult?"

"Dunno. Could be. But it just makes me worry, you know, with these things going on when Mr Wood is over there."

"He's probably safer there than he is here," I said, thinking of the U.S.'s number one status for mass shootings. "Besides, you said these people were attacked in their homes. Mr Wood is in a hotel."

"Not in the Cotswolds. He's in bed-and-breakfasts. He told me all about them. Well, not so much about the beds, mostly about the breakfasts. All those different sausages. It turned my stomach. I hope he sticks to the baked beans on toast."

Because that was going to happen.

"How many of these ritualistic killings did you say there'd been?"

"Let me check." She swept her finger across her screen. "Looks like five here in the U.S., four in the Portland area itself." Which I'll admit was worrying. Luckily, Morelli had a ton of protections on the building. "And, looks like eight in the U.K. Seven of those were around London."

"That's only thirteen people," I said, trying to sound unconcerned, but in the back of my mind I wondered where exactly my parents were conducting this secret mission. Again, assuming they really were on an HQ assignment, if not... well, probably best not to let my mind wander down that dark alley. "Do any of your followers have a clue as to what this ritualistic killing entails?"

"Nope, although there's plenty of speculation that the vampires are behind the murders because they're tired of being told what to do by Magics, and so they're killing Norms just to make a point."

Which, to me, even knowing what I did about Olivia's reports and theories, seemed ridiculous. If the vampires really were going to lash out, if they really wanted to make a point, wouldn't they kill more than thirteen people? Most likely, it was just a pair of nutcase Norms, one local and one Brit, who had read too many Anne Rice novels.

"Oh, and several of the Gorgon Girls — they're members of this far-right thingie — are convinced the liberal media is behind it."

"Of course they are. Any other ideas floating around?" I asked.

"Just some comments from people who say they have to remain anonymous—" because those are always the most reliable of commenters "—who report that despite the murders, there wasn't much blood at the scene. So, maybe it's poisoning?"

"Could be. Either way. There's millions of people in London and plenty of people here. The fact that thirteen random people got killed... it's a wonder that even made the news. I'm sure Mr Wood is fine. I mean, he's probably got a higher chance of a piano falling on his head than falling victim to these supposed ritualistic killers."

Daisy quickly turned a strange shade of green. "Do not say that about Mr Wood."

"What? That he'll be fine?"

"No. The piano thing. Very dangerous those pianos."

I could see Daisy had been adversely affected by Bugs Bunny cartoons at some point in her formative years.

Daisy thumped the screen to close her Fae-book app, puffed out a determined breath, then said, "The only way I'm going to keep myself from fretting is to get to work. So, what are we up to today, boss? Please tell me it's not book burning again. That was *so* traumatizing."

Considering what Tobey had spotted at Matilda's, I was itching to respond to Matilda's text. What had Tobey really seen? Something similar, or the exact pendant my mom had lost, I'd found, and then had lost again? And I'd not just lost it, but I'd lost it after an attack that Matilda had been on the scene of moments later.

"I need to step out for a bit," I said, already tapping out a message on my phone to let Matilda know I was on my way. "But you could stay here and do some research for me, if you like."

Daisy's eyes lit up, as if she really would enjoy the task. I had to give her credit; at least she was an enthusiastic employee. And she'd shown up on time. Now, if she never expected a paycheck, I'd be set.

"What can I do?"

After tugging Matilda's file out from under Pablo, I handed it to Daisy. Even if Mayor Marheart was only inviting me over to officially fire me, something about her having my mom's pendant had stoked my curiosity about this jewel she was so eager to find. Plus, I'd really like to be able to share something with Mr Torres if he called back. Him knowing more about my cases wasn't exactly painting my detective skills in the best light.

"I need you to see if you can find out anything about this jewel. And I mean anything. History. Where it's been. Who owned it. Whatever you can dig up might help."

"And should I work on finding the other copy of that book you're after? There's a third one, right? Maybe that one won't catch on fire. Or does that happen to you often with books?"

"Not with books, no," I said, thinking of the disasters I'd caused in Gwendolyn's kitchen. "But don't you think researching a jewel that hasn't been seen in over five hundred years is enough?"

"Just in case I run out of... what do you call them? Oh yes, *leads*. I hope you don't mind, but I came back here last night and did some studying."

She pointed to the dozens of classic mystery and detective novels on the bookshelf.

"You started one?"

"No, I read them all." To my dumbfounded expression, she added, "I'm a quick reader. It's like I open a book and," she made a sucking noise, "I just mop it all up. I think it's because I've been reading so long. Did I tell you I read my first book at three years old?"

"So did I," I said, then was suddenly hit by a flash of a long-forgotten memory. Me on my dad's knee reading Dr. Suess's *Hop on Pop* out loud to him.

"We are so alike," she enthused, which I was starting to realize was her default mode. "I can't believe it. Was yours *A Tale of Two Cities* as well? Because that would be too weird, wouldn't it?"

"Yeah, weird," I grumbled, then grabbed my satchel and got out the door before I had to reveal my younger self's woefully age-appropriate taste in literature.

CHAPTER NINETEEN
FINDERS KEEPERS

At the mayor's place, I hesitated before knocking. Although I'd gotten better at interacting with humans, I still wasn't keen on confronting people, pestering them with questions, or knocking on their doors. Hell, I barely felt comfortable calling people, even ones I knew. If it can't be done by text or email, it hardly seems worth the effort.

Still, if my agency was going to go anywhere, I had to get out of the office, do the legwork, interact. And maybe pilfer necklaces, if needed.

I'd barely tapped the door before Matilda answered. She arched a precisely plucked eyebrow at me.

"You showed up," she said abruptly. Even face-to-face, I couldn't get a read on her.

"I can always leave if you're planning to tell me off again."

"I apologize for that," she said, a touch of sincere warmth creeping into her voice. "It was a stressful day, and I may have gotten a little pushy."

"And my day hadn't been much better, so I may have been a little defensive."

She smiled, revealing teeth so perfect they belonged in a toothpaste ad. And not the cheap toothpaste, either. The really high-quality stuff that cost more than the pound-size bag of

Pablo's Kitty Crunch Cat Treats.

"Come in?" she offered.

I stepped past her, but before I could do any looking around, Matilda said, "Just to get this out of the way, I would still like you to find my jewel. It's becoming quite important, actually."

"Important in what way?" I asked carefully, since the Garden of Matilda Suspicions was getting repeat doses of MiracleGro.

Was I reading too much into a few coincidences, or was Matilda really up to no good? Could this jewel be part of a weapon? Some sort of concentrator of power that could be inserted into her diabolic contraption so she could zap zap zap her enemies?

I shook my head. I needed to stop binge-reading Alastair's collection of *Action Comics*.

"It's just—" She thought a moment before saying, "I think it can help with certain goals."

Holy hexes, I was right. It was top-grade evil weapon fuel.

"Goals to prove who you are?" I asked, thinking of the town hall heckler mentioning her background, while also picturing her ripping off a form-fitting mask to reveal she was actually the Joker in disguise.

Okay, perhaps I should cut back on the *Batman* comics as well.

"You could say that, yes. It's just very important. Can we leave it at that?"

"Will it cause anyone harm if I find it?"

This is where the mayor should have laughed at Cassie for being foolish and having too active an imagination. Instead, she thought a moment before saying, "No one you care about. Now," she said, her tone forcibly bright and welcoming, "I was just going to have something to drink. Come along, we'll chat in the kitchen."

She turned to go down the hall toward the rear of the house. I started to follow, but just opposite a door that led into a sitting room was the mirror Tobey had mentioned.

Perched on a small, decorative table beneath the mirror were a pair of framed photos. One of Matilda with the Oberlins. The same photo I recalled seeing on the Inspector's desk when he'd kicked me out of the Academy. This time, I noticed Mrs Oberlin was holding a small, dark blue flag with a yellow kangaroo in the center. The second photo was also familiar. It showed the mayor beaming her politician's smile as she stood amongst a row of Bookworms at, according to the banner above them, the recent library conference. Between the two photos was the crochet version of Caliban, Matilda's dragon, that Morelli had made for her.

The pink creature and the photos might have caught my eye, but those weren't what nearly made my heart stop.

Just as Tobey said it had been, my mom's pendant dangled by its chain from one of the curling metal scrolls of the mirror's frame. The morning clouds were still hanging around, so it didn't catch the sun. Which was handy for my purposes, since it made the piece of jewelry less noticeable.

As Matilda stepped through the door at the end of the entry hall, I slipped the chain off the frame and shoved the necklace and pendant deep into the front pocket of my skirt.

Matilda's kitchen was unusually clean for just having had a dinner party the night before. But I supposed, as mayor, she probably had help for that sort of thing.

"Care for some?" she asked as she poured a thick glass of tomato juice. The sight of it turned my stomach. I never understood how anyone could drink the thick liquid, whether plain or in a Bloody Mary, because seriously, even alcohol couldn't cover up the stuff's cloying consistency. I hoped I wasn't grimacing with disgust as I politely declined.

"So, how has the detective work been?" she asked as she settled herself onto a bar stool at an oak kitchen island and invited me to do the same.

"I've gotten an extension for my license application. And I'm hoping your jewel might be the key to getting the signed contract I need for the paperwork." I considered my words a moment before pointedly adding, "Since Mr Coppersmith and Mrs Oberlin are in no state to do any signing."

Did the mayor's eyes dart away momentarily? I couldn't say for sure; it may have just been the noise of kids playing in the yard next door that drew her attention, but she didn't respond to my comment, filling the silence by taking a sip of her drink.

"Anyway, my assistant's looking into it, and Rosaria's contact at the Oregon Historical Society is also onto something," I said, because it sounded way more productive and professional than admitting I had no idea how to go about solving her case. "Did you know there was more than one jewel box made?"

"Was there?" she asked, truly curious. When she'd hired me, Matilda had said the craftsman had only made one of the ornate boxes, but I'd recently found a couple of auction houses that sold boxes that were near matches for hers. The only difference between them and hers was the lack of a depression for a good-sized, heart-shaped jewel. I explained this to her.

"Then perhaps there was only one jewel made," she mused. "Could that be? I know I heard somewhere along the line that there was only one jewel box, that the one I have now is unique. But these family stories get so convoluted. Perhaps that got mixed up with the jewel itself being unique. I do apologize for not knowing more about it."

And yet she had badgered me about not uncovering everything about the jewel with superhuman speed? Some people, am I right?

"Is there anything more you can add to what you know about the jewel's origins, last seen location, who owned it in the past? There's just so little to go on."

"I wish I could give you more information. As I said, it dates from the time of Queen Elizabeth I. She often commissioned jewel work. And I don't know if it's just family conceit, but my ancestor William Boncoeur was reported to be her favorite cutter for these commissions."

"Commissions?" At least this was new. Although it would be really helpful if she'd just cough up all this information in one go rather than making me drag it out of her memory banks bit by bit.

"I didn't mention that?" I shook my head. "Must have slipped my mind. This was many years after she gained the throne. The Crown didn't have extra cash to throw around when she first became queen, but after some wise management, she undid her father's excesses. Maybe not always through the kindest or most ethical means, but England under her rule became a very wealthy nation indeed.

"Some of that wealth she used to reward her courtiers, loyal ones who stuck with her through the thick and thin of the early days of her reign. The gifts she had specially made were symbols of solidarity. And of favoritism, to put it bluntly."

"Robert Dudley?" I asked, since he was one of the few of Elizabeth's courtiers whose name I could recall. "Was he a recipient?"

"Oh, no, not at all. She'd pegged him as a scoundrel long before the gifts were commissioned."

Damn it, at least that would have been a name to start with. Still...

"Do you know if the jewel ever left England? I mean, your family? When did they come to the U.S.? Did they have it when they did? And how did they get it in the first place?" Even as I was bombarding her with questions, I recalled the old newspaper photo I'd seen in my parents' bedroom. "Oh, and how did you end up with the box if it was at the British Museum?"

"My—" Matilda seemed to catch herself, then let out a self-deprecating laugh. "Sorry, I'm terrible at all these great greats. One of my London-based great-great-somethings donated the box to the museum, but I don't know if it still had the jewel then. The box was returned to me, without the jewel, after a friend who worked for the museum pulled some strings. So, yes, the jewel could possibly still be in London." Matilda drank the last of her juice, leaving small chunks clinging to the inside of the glass. "Does any of that help?"

"It might," I told her, while thinking, *Not really,* since she'd hadn't even replied to half the questions I'd asked. I wondered if she didn't know the answers, or if she was being intentionally vague to cover up something that might be incriminating.

I wanted to pry further, make her give me some concrete information, but the longer I sat there with Matilda's eyes fixed on me, the larger the pendant was growing in my pocket. Worried it would start shouting its presence at any second, I slid off the stool. "I should really follow up on things while they're fresh in my mind."

"Sounds like an excellent plan. I'll walk you out."

"No need," I blurted, stepping back so quickly from the stool I nearly knocked it over. "I'm pretty sure finding the door won't tax my sleuthing skills too much."

"Then I'll leave you to it." She stood and held out her hand with its long, manicured nails and perfectly smooth skin. Yeah, she definitely hired help, because those were not the hands of a woman who did her own dishes. I shook it, her touch as cool as ever. "Glad to be your client again, Miss Black."

I felt uncertain about having the mayor as a client again. Or *still*, as the case may be. Something about her — something besides her having my mom's pendant and something besides all the many suspicious connections surrounding her — left me wary.

I rubbed at the back of my neck, trying to scrub away the feeling of someone watching me as I double-timed it out the door and down the walkway.

CHAPTER TWENTY
WALRUS HARASSMENT

I zigged and zagged my way through the quieter streets of MagicLand, avoiding the busier thoroughfares and pondering my next move. Which only filled my head with a billion questions about the pendant in my pocket.

Why was it at Matilda's? Had she stolen it after attacking me? And if so, why would she hang her purloined treasure on a mirror in her entryway for all to see? I supposed she simply could have found it somewhere after the real jewel thief dropped it. But would someone who was bold enough to break into my parents' home and ambush me to get a piece of jewelry really drop it on their way out? I mean, what kind of butterfingers thief were we dealing with here?

Should I report Matilda? It would be the logical thing to do, but the *Herald* was already accusing me of stealing my clients' objects to create work for myself. If I went to Oberlin with this, it might only back up that claim. And, call this self-serving, but if I turned Matilda in for thievery and assault, I'd lose a client at a time when I desperately needed to cling to every client I had — even if that client was a criminal who'd whacked me with a Spark Spell that had scorched my face and nearly blinded me.

My zig-zagging route back to the agency took me past my parents' place. I'd often found myself making this side trip over the past few days. On the surface, I told myself it was to make sure their flowers were watered and their mail collected, but if I'm being honest, I think I kept hoping they might have returned from Mr T's secret mission. If so, I would drag them into Runa's, pump them full of magic transfusions, then scold them for taking off without telling me and insist they never do such a foolish thing again. I mean, someone had to be the adult around here, right?

Unfortunately, there was still no sign of them. The garden flowers were doing well and bursting with colors. The mailbox was brimming with a few postcards, the latest issue of *Vanity Fairy* magazine, and several advertising flyers (because even in MagicLand it would appear you can't escape junk mail).

With the clouds having cleared, the temperature being absurdly pleasant, and me needing a break, I sat down on their stoop to sort through what mail could be tossed and to read the postcards. What? I'm a detective (or attempting to be one). It's my job to be nosy.

I was just struggling to make out the cramped handwriting filling the back of a card from Dublin when a shadow cast over me. A large shadow. Before I'd even looked up, a defensive spell rushed to my fingertips so quickly it's a wonder the postcard didn't go flying off into the ether.

Forcing back the spell for fear of what it might actually do, I shielded my eyes and glanced up. I'm pretty sure I grimaced then groaned because, seriously, who expects a walrus sighting in a sunny garden?

Inspector Oberlin stood there, looming over me and blocking the pathway that curved through the garden from the front gate to the front door. Why he wasn't trying to sort out what had happened to his wife, why he wasn't taking some time off, why someone else, *anyone* else, wasn't working his beat was beyond my comprehension. Even as mad as I was at Alastair for how he was treating Pablo, I'd still be right by his side if he were attacked and in a medically induced coma.

"This is a crime scene, Black," Oberlin snarled. "Kinda suspicious how you always seem to be lurking around places where people end up hurt or missing or dead."

What could I say? I couldn't tell him my parents weren't dead or missing or hurt (I hoped). I couldn't tell him they were only on an assignment for HQ. I couldn't even give any snarky retorts thanks to this stupid Confidentiality Spell.

"My parents are fine," I said tersely.

He smirked at my feeble response. "You would say that. I just find it really strange you being connected with so many crimes. Especially as Rosaria was nearly crime-free before you came here."

Again, this sounded exactly like something my fan at the *Herald* would say, and it further cemented my certainty that Old Walrus Face was behind those opinion pieces. I narrowed my eyes at him, wondering how soon he'd spin this into another of his stellar examples of journalism.

"I'm doing more than you are."

He chortled at that. "Yeah, I'm well aware you're 'doing' something I'm not. Don't think you haven't been observed coming by here. People saw you entering Simon and Chloe's home not long before they went missing. And who knows, maybe they're not missing. Maybe they're hiding for fear of what you might do to them. I'd suggest if you know anything about where they are, you tell me now, because at the moment you're pretty high up on my list of suspects for their disappearance." He looked to the sky, tapping his finger on his double chin as if pondering something. "No, you know what? You're the *only* person on my list."

I was about to say something about *his* parents being moronic walruses who probably drowned after they couldn't figure out which side of the ice to rest on. But just then, Lola bustled up to us. Her magic created an instant air of calm (well, as calm as the Inspector and I were going to get around each other).

"Wesley, you are being idiotic, and you know it." Lola was probably the only person in MagicLand who could get away with speaking to the Inspector like that, and I wondered if I couldn't give her a few more choice words to throw at him. "Of course she's here, and of course she's been seen at Simon and Chloe's home. She's concerned for them, and she's their daughter. I know you don't have children, but it's not unheard of for kids to visit their parents when they live only a few blocks apart."

Oberlin dropped a small amount of his accusatory air. "It's still very concerning the Starlings going missing when all this other stuff's been happening."

"Like I said, my parents are fine," I repeated through gritted teeth.

"Just because you repeat it, doesn't make it true," Oberlin quipped, and the look Lola gave him was sour enough to curdle the milk of an entire herd of dairy cattle. Oberlin, perhaps proving he's not a complete moron, took this as a sign to continue on his way and waddled out of the garden.

I thanked Lola, then asked her what she was up to. Because, to be honest, if she wasn't busy I would have liked to follow her home. Even if she made me do chores the rest of the day, it would be worth it to bask in her calming elfin air. And to hopefully get a refill of her coconut-almond cookies.

"I've got an appointment at Runa's. I kept putting off my RetroHex Vaccine, and I better get it before fall settles in. You get yours yet?"

I shook my head no. Unsure if the vaccine was delivered in the Norm jab-and-stab style, I'd been avoiding it.

"Well, come on then. I'm sure she can squeeze us both in. And," she added, patting her wildly colored handbag, "I've got a treat for us afterward."

Sold!

Walking with Lola through MagicLand was an entirely different experience than what I'd been facing lately. Gone were the sneers. Gone were the rude comments. Gone was anyone even noticing me. And I wondered if I couldn't bottle some of Lola's magic to spritz over myself before running any future errands.

At Runa's, the waiting chairs were empty, likely because it was nearly time for Runa's lunch break. But that didn't stop Morelli from interrogating me about what I was doing there.

"You don't have an appointment. You have to make an appointment. Otherwise, the whole schedule will get thrown off."

Runa stepped out from behind the counter, her glasses zipping up from a receipt booklet to tuck themselves into the breast pocket of her jacket.

"Lola has an appointment that has far more time scheduled than needed. Cassie can double up with her. We really don't need to be quite so strict with the timing, Eugene."

"It only takes one person running behind before we're stuck here well past closing time."

"Oh, that's right," I said. "*All in the Family* reruns start at six p.m., don't they?"

"It's actually *Good Times* reruns, but that's not the point."

Runa, Lola, and I exchanged a glance. We were pretty sure that was precisely the point.

"Black needs a sample draw, anyway," said Runa. "Come on back, you two."

Once Dr Dunwiddle had given Lola her vaccine — which turned out not to involve any needles, but was instead administered via a quickly dissolving piece of licorice-flavored candy — Lola went out to the pharmacy area of the clinic to see if there were any new lotions in stock.

I obediently held out my arm before Runa had even finished preparing the sample vials.

"Any change in the last ones?" I asked.

"Still all over the place. Even as they sit over the day, the levels change." To the unspoken question in my eyes, she said, "No, that's not normal. Once removed, a sample should stay at the same level it was when it was taken. It's the damnedest thing. I've sent my reports and a few of the samples off to the medics at HQ to see what they come up with. I have to say, they're pretty excited about such a perplexing problem."

"Great, magical medical anomaly, just what I wanted to be known for."

Runa gave me a reassuring smile and even her glasses emerged from their hiding place to tip their frames encouragingly at me. At least, I think it was meant to be encouraging. Perhaps I should see if Duolingo offers a course on the language of enchanted eyeglasses.

CHAPTER TWENTY-ONE
A WHOLE LOTTA WHATEVER

Happy to be restocked with more of Lola's cookies, I returned to the agency, where Daisy beamed a gleaming smile at me, and Pablo trotted over, meowing the chipper greeting he gives anyone who makes the door's entry bell chirp. When he neared me, though, the fur on his back went up, he did a military-precise about-face, then he marched off to sit in an empty cardboard box, staring at me and vigorously flicking his tail.

Maybe I really did need to have a vet look him over.

"Has he been acting weird while I've been gone?" I asked Daisy as I twirled the dial on the safe.

"No, he's been a total sweetheart. I've never heard a cat purr so much, and he's so affectionate."

Great, even my cat proved unable to resist Daisy's bubbly charm.

I placed the pendant in the safe, bitterly noting how I now had another found item with no client around to sign off for it. Once I'd stashed the cookies in my desk drawer, I slumped into my chair without paying attention to what I was doing. You've seen this play out enough times that I'm sure you can already picture me flailing my arms and thumping down hard onto the wood flooring.

"Oh my golly!" cried Daisy, running over to help me up. "Are

The Unbearable Inspector Oberlin

you alright? Should I call Dr Dunwiddle?"

"I'm pretty sure she can't repair a person's pride. What is this doing here, anyway?" I asked, pointing to the chair.

"I just didn't think it was right you not getting the best chair in the office, so I moved it back."

"No, really. I insist. Me and this chair... we..."

"I understand completely. When I was little, we had a toaster that only ever burnt the toast whenever it was the last slice of bread in the house. Apparently, someone at the factory had hit it with a Petty Hex when they didn't get the raise they expected."

"But that doesn't explain why it only acts up when I try to sit in it."

"That is odd, yes." She beamed a brilliant smile and gave a coy little shrug of her shoulders. "Maybe it just doesn't like you. Have you tried being nice to it? Buying it a pretty cushion or something? Oiling its wheels?" The look I gave her spoke volumes. "Right, well, I'll just put him back at my desk, shall I?"

"You do that."

As Daisy began rearranging the furniture — telling the chair how wonderful it was to have it back as she did so — my phone pinged. I half-expected it to be Matilda again. With her pushy behavior a few days ago, I wouldn't have been surprised to see something along the lines of, *It's been well over an hour, why haven't you found my jewel yet? Also, I've reported you to Oberlin for stealing that pendant I had hanging in my hallway.*

Instead, it was a trio of texts from Mr Wood, each with an accompanying photo. The first was of a tray that contained something that looked like chicken and mashed potatoes drowning in gravy. The message attached to it began with a frowny face emoji and continued with: *There was no ham option!*

Under this was a shot, clearly taken through an airplane window, of what looked like the exterior of a large airport terminal. The accompanying text read: *The eagle has landed. I'm here! In Jolly Old England. Can you believe it?*

He followed that up with a snapshot of a crowded arrivals hall filled with exhausted and/or frantic people. The message this time: *Just got luggage, now must find tour shuttle, then it's off to a jaunty holiday for me.* To punctuate this, he added a thumbs up emoji, the British flag, and a person walking emoji.

I'd just sent my response when Daisy's phone erupted with a tinny muzak version of The Beatles' "Norwegian Wood". She leaned over her phone, then exclaimed, "Nino made it!"

From his box, Pablo purred — probably because he sensed my smug satisfaction that Mr Wood had texted me first.

Because I assumed she couldn't do two things at once, I waited for Daisy to finish what seemed to be a lengthy response to Mr Wood. She looked up from her phone to see me staring at her.

"Sorry, are personal calls not allowed? I was just reminding him to ask about the vegan option for his return flight. Should I not have?"

I had many responses to that, but merely said, "It's fine. Get anywhere with the research this morning?"

I asked this in the sincere hope that she'd come up with something. Because other than pestering Mr Torres for information on Matilda's jewel, searching every pawnshop in Portland for Runa's saw, or scouring every used bookstore in the world for a copy of Wordsworth's book, I wasn't sure what my next steps should be.

"Not really," replied Daisy. "I started focusing on that book you're after and kept hitting dead ends. I can keep trying, though. I've never been one to give up," she added brightly, and I swear the sunlight twinkled off her sparkling white teeth when she flashed one of her go-getter smiles at me.

"No, that's fine. I mean, you can keep looking, but I think we should concentrate on the jewel for now."

"Oh, the jewel," she said flippantly. "It was easy to find stuff out about that."

"And you didn't think to lead with this information?" I asked.

"I always think it's best to tell the bad news first. Get it over with, you know?" When I didn't respond to another of her eye-damaging smiles, she said, "Anyway, it was once owned by Queen Elizabeth—"

"—the First. Yes, I know that. Anything else? Anything more precise?"

Undaunted by my critical tone, Daisy went on. "Well, she gave it to Mary Queen of Scots when Mary was imprisoned in the Tower of London." Her voice trailed off as she approached the end of her sentence. Probably because I was rolling my eyes. This was getting me nowhere. "Oh, did you know that already?"

"I did." It had been one of the few things Matilda had known about the jewel. I was starting to question the supposed time-saving benefits of having an assistant. "Maybe I should have you look into Runa's saw—"

"Wait, no, there's a little more. But you probably already know this, too."

She both looked and sounded utterly dejected. Holy hexes, had I finally broken her?

"No, go ahead. What is it?" I asked encouragingly, and she instantly perked up again. Damn, only temporary damage.

"Well, Elizabeth gave it to Mary as a token of friendship. She thought maybe they could come to terms, like making Mary her heir, that sort of thing. The report I found said Elizabeth didn't know much about the jewel— Sorry, I didn't find out how she came to have it, but I could—"

"Later," I urged, desperate for any new details. "Elizabeth didn't know what about the jewel?"

"That it has some sort of power. Mary, though, she recognized it for what it was. She was a Magic, not a very strong one and not a very smart one, but I suppose she's one of those cases that proves being a Magic doesn't automatically make you a genius." And if you're looking for an example of the pot calling the kettle black, there you go. "Anyway, Mary got it and used it to somehow encourage her supporters to stage a prison break. But Elizabeth found out before anything could go very far. And, well—"

I recalled something about this bit of history when I'd been on a reading binge of historical novels a couple years ago. "Mary was executed soon after, wasn't she?"

"Yep, and that's how Lizzie got her jewel back."

Which sounded like an excellent rom-com title.

"Was that good?" Daisy asked, practically begging for approval. "I thought it was good. Certainly better than all those dead ends. Those are so poopy for morale."

I hated to admit it, but it was good. Still, had the jewel merely been a way for Mary to bribe her supporters, was it a form of symbolic power, or did it possess a Magic's true power? And if it did, what might Elizabeth have gotten up to with that jewel once she took it back?

"Yeah, good job. Maybe you can dig something else up about the jewel itself. Something about how Elizabeth obtained it? Or if anyone knows who had it before her, or after her, or… just, you know, whatever."

"A whole lotta of whatever coming right up," Daisy said as she plucked a pen that was tipped with a puff of pink feathers from the daisy-patterned pen holder on her desk.

CHAPTER TWENTY-TWO
CAMERA ANGLES

Daisy had popped off for lunch, and I was in the kitchenette tackling vital executive decisions such as whether to have peanut butter cookies or chocolate chip cookies or whether I should just sandwich one of each together when my phone rang. Anticipation tingled through me at the sight of the number.

"Cassie?" said a warm, familiar voice.

"Mr Torres? Or is it Dr Torres?"

"Doctor, actually, but call me Pascal. Any breakthroughs with your detective work?"

What did I say to this? That I had a client who I was harboring some serious suspicions about? That I kept failing to make time to inquire after Runa's saw? That I'd just spent the past ten minutes contemplating what filling would go best in my cookie sandwich? Since I wasn't sure how much Dr Torres really wanted to know about my professional or culinary woes, I merely said, "Slowly. As in, glaciers have gotten more done this week than I have."

"Ah, sorry to hear that. But I have news that could help you with the jewel you're after."

"Are you serious?" I stood up straighter. Who knew hope could be so good for your posture?

"Yes, quite serious. Do you remember I told you that something about the Boncoeur Jewel seemed familiar? I finally remembered it's because I'd read about it— oh, I don't know —perhaps five years ago in a paper by Alvin Dodding."

"Wait," I cut in. "Professor Dodding? From the Museum of London?"

"You've heard of him?" Dr Torres asked, excitement punctuating his words.

"I met him a few months ago. He's... well, he's a character, that's for sure."

"I can't believe you've met him. I should have recognized the name of the jewel straight away. Professor Dodding, is... well, I —" Dr Torres made the sound of someone trying not to let their hero worship run away with their senses. "Ever since I became associated with Magics, I've read all of his papers. I have to say, I was so nervous reaching out to him, but he seems quite nice."

"You contacted him? About the jewel? What did he have to say?"

"Well, I knew I'd be too excited to keep it all in my head, so I asked if we couldn't have a meeting sometime, and he said that would be delightful. Would that be okay with you?"

"That would be more than okay with me," I said, feeling stupid that I hadn't thought of Professor Dodding before.

Alvin Dodding appeared to be about eighty, which, given that Magics aged differently than Norms, meant he had likely lived and breathed well over a century and a half of history. In addition to this, he'd spent a lifetime studying and filling his head with all manner of historical facts. If there was a tidbit of history, especially Magic history, you needed to know, he was your guy.

"Great!" Mr Torres said with unrestrained enthusiasm. "I'll let him know we're coming, then? Will an hour give you enough time to wrap up whatever you're doing and get here? When I was having breakfast this morning," he gushed, "I would never have dreamed that I'd be meeting Professor Dodding this very afternoon. Portals really are the most convenient things, aren't they?"

That's when Reality stepped back around and kicked me in the backside.

"I can't," I told him.

"I know it's short notice, but—"

"No, sorry. I mean, I have time, but I can't get us through a long-distance portal. Little issue with my magic."

"Oh, it's no problem. I have a supply of absorbing capsules. The magic they provide is just enough to get me through the portal HQ set me up with."

"They gave you a portal?' I asked, somewhat surprised they'd let a Norm have access to Magic technology.

"Bit of a hassle to get the approval from some council or other, but Olivia Whalen is quite tenacious. Said it was essential for me to be able to pop over at short notice to the British Museum for research and to attend meetings with HQ's historians. But I also take my greyhound through at least once a week — he just loves a romp on Hampstead Heath."

After a thoughtful pause, he added, "Although, I've never taken a person through before." And let me just say that the concern in his voice wasn't comforting. "Olivia laid out strict rules about taking other Norms through, but I'm sure there'll be no issue getting you through, will there? What's the worst that could happen, right?"

My mind reeling with the irreversible, bone-breaking things that could very much happen, especially with my luck, I hesitantly told him I'd be at the Historical Society within the hour.

* * *

After texting Daisy to ask if she'd babysit Pablo — to which she responded with a series of emojis that I assumed meant she'd be happy to — I hurried back to the apartment from where I could easily ride my bike to the Historical Society.

I'd just snapped on my helmet when my phone rang. I half-expected it to be Dr Torres, telling me he couldn't risk disappearing into a black hole and that maybe we should just video chat with Professor Dodding. Instead, the screen showed it was someone calling from Bookman's Bookshop, which struck me as odd since I didn't remember ever entering the shop's contact info into my phone. But you just never know what magic is capable of until you experience it. Usually as a victim.

"Cassie, it's Sebastian. You know, bookstore guardian spirit, blah blah blah."

"Kind of hard to forget. Wait," I said, optimism kicking in for the second time in under an hour. Sebastian had found Wordsworth's book just a few days ago. Okay, more correctly… someone walloped him with Confounding magic, left the book right on the shop's cashier counter, then walked away. But still, could lightning have struck twice? "You didn't happen to find another copy of Wordsworth's book, did you?"

"Sorry, no such luck." Again, I repeat my stance on the pointlessness of optimism. "I was actually calling because the lady who runs the pharmacy across the street came in looking for some books for her grandkids. She said she didn't have much time for browsing because she had to get back across the street to meet a repairman, so she asked if I could just recommend some to her.

"I did. And then, just to make conversation as I was ringing her up, I asked what needed repaired. Turns out it was her security camera. It had been aimed the wrong way, and it had taken ages to get someone to come out. She said she would have done the adjustment herself, but that would have cancelled the warranty on the cameras. Isn't that the most ridiculous thing you ever heard?"

"It is, but is there a point to this?" I asked. I mean, I didn't want to be rude, but Sebastian and I had only met a couple times, and we didn't exactly have a call-up-and-chat-about-our-days relationship. Or maybe we did. Again, the low social IQ can really be a problem sometimes.

"There is," he said cheekily. "The camera had been pointing at the entry to Bookman's, or rather, a little to the left of our door. Long story short, I asked her how long it had been askew. About a week, she said. Which matches up to when our mysterious guest dropped off your book."

"Tell me you were able to see the footage." My entire body hummed with possibility. Not optimism, mind you. Just possibility.

"I *was* able to, but don't get too excited. Whoever dropped it off never faced the camera directly, and the footage is kind of grainy because of the distance, but I can tell you the person was most likely female, fairly tall with dark hair, and slim in that elegant way royals have. Know what I mean?" I said I did. "I took a screenshot of that bit. Hold on. I'm sending it to you now."

My phone pinged, and the image that came through sent my heart thudding. It certainly wasn't anything that would stand up in court, but the heels on the woman's feet and her confident air were too familiar.

"Match anyone you know?" asked Sebastian.

"It looks like Mayor Marheart."

"Ah, that could be difficult. She's a client of yours, isn't she? And being a politician, well, it's never easy putting them through the wringer, is it?"

"But why would she leave the book with you? Why not just throw it away?"

"I can't even begin to guess, but magic books want to be owned. Unless completely destroyed, it would have found its way to a good home eventually. Maybe she was just saving it the effort."

As I rode the few miles from my building to the Oregon Historical Society, I pondered what Sebastian's news could mean. If Matilda had the book in her possession at some point, was she the one who'd taken the pages from it? Or had she found it somewhere, discarded and already damaged, and merely wanted to get rid of it?

If she had taken the pages, though, what spell did they contain? And more importantly, what did she plan to do with it?

CHAPTER TWENTY-THREE
KINDRED SPIRITS

Once I'd arrived at the Oregon Historical Society, the guy manning the reception desk phoned Dr Torres, then told me he'd be down in just a moment. Other than a quick stop several months ago to deliver a package for Corrigan's Courier, I'd never visited the museum, so I wandered around the entry area where I ended up admiring a large painting of a stag with an impressive rack of antlers. Silhouetted fir trees created a dramatic frame around him as he stood proudly in a stream of sunlight.

I'd just caught the title *Hart of the Forest* and had started to read the info plaque next to the tableau, when a familiar voice said, "Cassie Black?"

I turned toward the speaker. Average height, dark hair that was starting to grey at the temples, and olive-skinned. I recognized him as the contact I'd handed the package off to all those months ago when Corrine quite literally pulled me off the street to fill in for her usual bike courier.

"We've met before," Dr Torres said, with a spark of surprised recognition in his hazel eyes.

"Briefly. I did some work for Corrine a few months ago."

"Ah, yes, of course. You like this one?" he asked, turning to gaze up at the painting. I said I did. "It's one of my absolute favorites. I've been trying to convince them to move it to my office for years now, but so far, no luck."

"You have noticed the misspelling, haven't you?" I asked, tapping the word *Hart* in the painting's title.

"You're not the first to point that out," Pascal chuckled amiably. "*Hart* is an old term for a stag. I keep meaning to look into the origin of the word, but for now, enough art appreciation and linguistic quandaries. Shall we?" he asked, tipping his head toward a corridor that led away from the main desk.

As we passed by the reception area, I caught sight of a wall clock. Only then did I realize, since Portland was nearing two o'clock in the afternoon, it would be almost eleven at night in London. Perhaps in his excitement over meeting his idol, Mr Torres had misunderstood the appointment time.

"Sorry," I said as we passed through a door and started up a staircase, "but are you sure Professor Dodding said in an hour? It's kind of late in London."

Mr Torres glanced at his watch. "I shouldn't think two p.m. is too late."

"But with the time difference, it's going to be past bedtime in the U.K."

"Time difference?" Mr Torres asked as we went through another door and into a hallway that was filled with natural light. I was trying to think of how to explain to him that portals didn't time travel. Which is exactly what we would have to do if he planned to show up to a two o'clock meeting in London when it was already two in the afternoon here. But I couldn't wrap my head around how to put into words the various Einsteinian laws that prevented this before Dr Torres said, "Here we are. My home away from home."

The office was a historical jumble. Books and maps were scattered across the desk, nearly burying a framed photo of Dr Torres and a blonde-haired man, both in tuxedos and top hats and holding up their left hands to show off what I assumed were new wedding rings. On the blonde man's shoulder perched some sort of hawk, looking nearly as proud as the two men.

Behind the desk, woven baskets, arrowheads, and other Pacific Northwest artifacts were piled on shelves alongside modern trinkets such as old street signs, black-and-white Rose Festival photos, and menus from restaurants that had closed down decades ago but whose names would still be familiar to long-time Portland residents.

"Stuff to be processed," Dr Torres explained. "It never ends. I would tidy up, but then I'm afraid I'd never be able to find anything."

This guy and I might just be kindred spirits.

Using a key he'd had in an inner pocket of his waistcoat, Dr Torres unlocked a wall cabinet, then let out an exclamation of delight before saying, "There you are!" to something inside. He turned and held up a slim, metal tube about the length of my index finger. "My husband's falcon whistle," he said with an indulgent smile as he placed it on his desk near the framed photo. "I swear our vows should have included, 'and do you promise to locate each other's misplaced treasures."

Dr Torres then retuned to the cabinet and pulled out a small glass jar. Inside were about a dozen tablets. You might mistake them for cold capsules... if you ignored the fact that they were glowing purple, signaling they were full of magic.

"Who exactly gives you those?" I asked.

"Usually Busby Tenpenny. I let him know when I'm running low, and he does the paperwork of getting me new ones. As to whose magic it is, I've never thought to ask."

"Well, as long as they work. And your portal?"

"Just through there." Dr Torres pointed to a coat closet.

"And that goes directly to the Museum of London?" I asked,

thinking that and the whole no-time-difference thing was a bit too convenient.

"Today, yes. Or near enough, at least. Once we arranged our meeting, Professor Dodding put in a work order for the portal to be shifted to somewhere nearby. By default, it goes to the British Museum's storage areas, but I can put in requests for it to drop me off elsewhere. It's very handy." He must have seen my look. "Is all this not normal?"

"Not that I've seen. Most portals in Mag— in Rosaria have a fixed destination and have to honor the time difference. Yours, I don't know, it must be a sort of temporary portal," I mused, curious as to why more of our portals weren't like this. But, then again, since portals have to be registered with HQ (the legal ones, anyway; the illegal ones, not so much), I imagine the paperwork to make every portal send you wherever you wanted and to break a few laws of relativity to get you there would be a bureaucratic nightmare that HQ would only make worse, because that's what Magics seemed to do with bureaucracy. Still, I'd have to ask Morelli if he knew anything about these things.

"We should get going. I'd hate to be late," said Dr Torres, sounding excitedly nervous. He held up the jar of absorbing capsules. "Ready?"

I said I was. Dr Torres then took a capsule in one hand and clasped my hand with the other.

"Forgive the mess," he said, as we stepped into the closet, then waded past several boxes of file folders, antique linens, and a few pairs of running shoes to get to the back.

Yep, definitely kindred spirits.

After the strange sensation of whizzing across thousands of miles in less than a minute, Dr Torres pushed open a heavy door that creaked and squealed on its rusty hinges.

I expected blinding daylight after the darkness of the portal, but we emerged onto a deeply shadowed alley that was barely wide enough for two people to stand shoulder to shoulder. I could see why HQ chose the spot for a portal. Most tourists would avoid it, fearing for their safety, and it was far too damp and cold even in late summer for any homeless person to choose for their camp.

"Where are we?" I asked, then glanced up. I nearly staggered back — more from awed surprise than my usual clumsiness. "Is that—?"

"St. Paul's," Dr Torres said, his voice full of wonder. "My, it is... looming, isn't it? Let's get into some sunshine and get our bearings. If we go the right way from here, it should be just a short walk north to the Museum of London."

Once we emerged from the alleyway, we were bombarded with Londoners trying to go about their day amongst the crowds of tourists and tour groups. I couldn't help but stare up once more, gawking at the soaring dome.

"Tallest building in London from 1710 — the year it was completed — to 1963," stated Dr Torres, allowing me a few more moments to admire the massive domed building while he glanced up and down the street. Soon enough, as if he had the full contents of the *London A to Z* stored in his head, he pointed. "That's the street there. Ready?"

Ten minutes later, we were in the lobby area of the Museum of London, with Dr Torres fidgeting and me wondering if we had time to pop into the cafe for some cake.

CHAPTER TWENTY-FOUR
A DATE WITH DODDING

"If it isn't Cassie Black," said a raspy yet cheerful voice that belonged to a small, elderly man — his hair so wispy it seemed to be following rules it was making up as it went along.

"Professor Dodding," I said and felt genuinely glad to see him. He had an infectiously welcoming air about him, was inspiringly energetic despite his age, and was engagingly interesting even as he lectured to you about whatever historical facts were flitting through his head.

"So good to see you. Now, tell the truth, have you been missing me?" Alvin Dodding also seemed to derive great pleasure from teasing me about finding him irresistible. "No, I won't make you confess. We'll keep it our little secret," he said with a wink, then turned his attention to the man shifting on his feet next to me. "And you must be Dr Pascal Torres."

Pascal stuck out his hand, and the two shook. Actually, Dr Torres seemed to be shaking all over. Who knew there could be historian fan boys. "Such a pleasure to meet you, sir."

"Pishposh with the *Sir* business. I'm Alvin to you. Now, it seems you wanted a quick history lesson?" When we said we did, he replied, "Then I'll try my best to keep my old mind focused on the subject at hand. Shall we, then?"

We followed him up to his office, with Professor Dodding

taking the steps two, sometimes three, at a time. When Pascal stopped in mid-stride and gaped at the old man's nimble manner, I told him it was just a Floating Charm Dodding worked on himself to take the strain off his aging joints. "And, because it's fun, I imagine," I added.

Dodding's office was just as I remembered it, with one wall filled floor-to-ceiling with books, while another wall was nearly all window and looked out on a portion of London's old Roman wall. Dr Torres immediately went over to admire it, and Professor Dodding delighted in telling him about the extent of the excavations.

"Now, what is it you'd like to cover?" Dodding asked as he settled down into his desk chair. His well-behaved chair, I noted grumpily.

"Well, as I said," Dr Torres began, his voice trembling slightly, "Cassie here has been hired to find a jewel you've written extensively on, and we were hoping you could shed some more light on it. Not that your paper wasn't thorough and fascinating," Dr Torres rushed to say. "Just you know…"

"Hearing it from the historical horse's mouth is better?"

"Something like that. And Cassie could ask questions," he said eagerly, as if I didn't know full well he was going to be the one bombarding the professor with his enthusiastic inquiries. "Questions about the Boncoeur Jewel," he babbled. "Or anything really."

"Ah yes," Dodding smiled indulgently at what seemed to be his Number One fan, "the Boncoeur Jewel. That paper was a while ago, and I didn't have time to re-read it before your arrival, so let me think."

After several moments' pondering, Dodding's lips twitched to one side and he looked utterly perplexed.

"If you don't know or remember," I said, "that's okay, we can talk about—"

"I'm only teasing you again." Dodding chuckled his dry, old man's laugh, his eyes gleaming impishly. "You young people are so quick to think anyone over thirty-five is a doddering old fool. It makes you such easy targets for my antics." Taking a paperback from his desk, he fidgeted with it as if needing to give his hands something to do as he started in on the jewel's story.

"According to legend — and by that I mean there are no verifiable physical records, just plenty of corroborating stories — the Boncoeur Jewel originally came from the Carpathian Mountains. You'll have heard of them from our Bram Stoker." I wasn't sure if he meant *our* as in a fellow Irishman or *our* as in a fellow Magic, but he continued on before I could ask. "It would be a rare find since those mountains aren't exactly known for their gemstones, which is likely why the king wanted it for himself."

"But plenty of evidence I've come across has the jewel once belonging to Queen Elizabeth," I said. "How did it get from Eastern Europe to England?"

"Patience, my dear. I'm getting there. What you must also know is that this jewel, once it was cut, gained a troubling amount of power, and I don't mean symbolic power."

I thought of my recent conversation with Matilda. Her vagueness about why it was important she get the jewel. Goosebumps sprouted along my arms.

"Was the jewel first cut in the Carpathians," Dr Torres asked, "or in England?"

"In the Carpathians. By a skilled craftsman. A gorgeous job by all accounts, but the king decided he didn't want to pay the craftsman. So, rather than dealing with invoices or debt collectors, the king simply imprisoned the jeweler in the castle's darkest dungeon. Which, I imagine, was very dark indeed, since this king didn't lean toward the do-gooder end of the ruling spectrum.

"The craftsman was furious over the king's betrayal, but he hid it well. Which is why, right before he was imprisoned, the craftsman's request to see the jewel one last time was not dismissed. The king — for whatever reason, maybe just to humor the man — granted the favor.

"But the king was unaware the craftsman was a Magic — I'm unsure of what variety, though, possibly elf, definitely not human, according to my research — and while the jewel was in his hands, the craftsman filled it with power. Whether that was on purpose or simply his indignant fury pushing a large dose of anger-tainted magic into the jewel, I can't say."

"It had to be accidental," I said, and noticed Dr Torres nodding in agreement.

"Why do you say that?" asked Dodding, truly curious.

"Because why would you fill something with power if you're going to return it to your enemy? I would have filled it with something that could destroy the king. Or at least give him permanent diarrhea."

"One would almost think you've heard this tale before," commented Dr Torres.

"Have you?" asked Dodding. I shook my head. "Well, you've nailed it on the head, my dear. Most royals tended to have a drop of magic in them back then, and the king noticed his magic felt out of sorts the next time he handled the jewel. He couldn't admit this to anyone, so rather than question it or address the odd occurrence, he immediately put the treasure away until he could discover what it all meant.

"But one night his wife found the jewel. Thinking it was a gift her husband had hidden for her to find, she took it, playing with it for quite some time as she posed with it and imagined it as part of a necklace, a crown, a cloak pin. As the queen preened with the jewel, it pulled away her power. *All* of her power. And all of her vitality, as well. The king entered his wife's bedchamber that night to find her dead."

"Oh, wasn't there something about the wife?" interrupted Dr Torres.

"Indeed, there was. She was a vampire. This was back when people didn't care about such things, and actually, for royalty, it was a matter of prestige to be wed to a vampire. But that's neither here nor there, because what it boils down to is that the jewel ended up filled with both the craftsman's vengeful magic *and* the wife's vampire magic. Which is quite a powerful combination indeed."

"And the jewel's journey to Elizabeth I?" Dr Torres prodded.

"Oh, that. Yes, it's a bit convoluted, but let me see if my silly old mind can get it all straight." But rather than continue, Professor Dodding opened a desk drawer and pulled out a chocolate bar about half the size of an average laptop. "Care to partake? I always keep this drawer full of them," he said as he started to unwrap the massive treat.

As they say, when in Rome, or at least near a Roman wall…

I expected Dodding to break me off a piece. Instead, he pulled out another bar, just as large as the first, and passed it to me, then handed another one to Dr Torres. I figured Dr Torres might want to stash his away like a holy relic, so I gave him half of mine.

"Now, where was I? Ah yes, the jewel. The wife. Vampire, we've established that. She had family. Her youngest niece, or some relation like that, had served as her lady's maid. One day, the girl skipped town with the jewel in hand. By this time, due to the king's grief and the loss of most of his magic, the realm was quickly falling into ruin. So whether she took it because she knew what it was, or whether she took it to make up for the wages she hadn't been paid, I can't say.

"Still, as the girl was the only household member besides the king with access to the jewel's case, it wasn't exactly the crime of the century, and she was pursued. After all, the king needed that jewel if he ever hoped to regain his power. However, with the jewel having robbed him of his drop of magic, and with the weight of grief upon him, he soon began feeling the effects of his true age. Poor Norms, I don't know how they do it. Regardless, the pursuit wasn't as vigorous as it would have been if he was in full health."

"Was the girl a Magic or a vampire?" asked Dr Torres. "If she was, how did the jewel not steal her power?"

Dodding, a smear of chocolate on his chin, shrugged. "I can't know everything. Maybe she was an Untrained. Maybe it was full. Maybe it saw no need to take vengeance on the girl. Maybe, as happens with us all, the youthful passion within the jewel dissipated over time, and it became less aggressive. Who can say with these pesky magical objects? They do what they want when they want to do it.

"Anyhow, I won't bear you down with all the dates and the exact journeys — that's in the paper if you care to read it. But the niece ended up in Luxembourg where she entered the household of a very powerful Magic named Jacquetta. Jacquetta had a daughter, Elizabeth — not the one you're thinking of, but Elizabeth Woodville, who inherited the jewel from Jacquetta.

"The Woodville woman gave birth to a whole brood of children, including a daughter, also named Elizabeth — they weren't terribly creative with baby names back then, I'm afraid. This Elizabeth's first son died, and the second son unexpectedly became king. Henry VIII. You may have heard of him," the professor joked. "And then we finally get to the Elizabeth you're so curious about."

"So she inherited the jewel?" I asked through a mouthful of chocolate.

"She did. Unfortunately, she didn't realize what she had in her hands until she gave it away to her cousin, Mary Queen of Scots, perhaps as a guilt gift for imprisoning her in the Tower. But Mary, who had a fair bit more magic than Elizabeth, immediately sensed what she'd been given. She used the power to raise a rebellion and nearly escaped. That's when Elizabeth chopped off her cousin's head and took the jewel back for herself. Only fitting, really.

"By this point in English history, most royals had almost no magic left in them, but Elizabeth was keen to make the most of what she had, so she began working with John Dee. You've heard of him?"

I nodded. John Dee was the queen's astronomer for many years. He adored dabbling in magic and alchemy, but I'd always thought that was just a charlatan's trick to gain a position in the Elizabethan Court.

"Was he a Magic?" I asked.

"One of the original founders of HQ, in fact," replied Professor Dodding. "With his guidance, Lizzie was able to tap into the jewel's power, which had most definitely shifted by this time, *mellowed* one might say. But Dee was able to sense that the jewel retained a portion of the powerful fury and revenge the craftsman had imbued it with. He may have even discovered how to access that power. Which would be a very handy discovery for someone serving a queen who'd spent a fair bit of time struggling to keep her detractors at bay."

"Sorry, Professor," interrupted Dr Torres, "but I've always been unclear where the name *Boncoeur Jewel* comes in."

"My client seemed to think William Boncoeur was the original cutter of the jewel," I added.

"No, no, he was Elizabeth's favorite jeweler, so wouldn't have been alive when the jewel was originally cut. Boncoeur was another of Elizabeth's Magics — she seemed to be able to surround herself with them, from astronomers to maids, to courtiers. Like a Magic magnet, that woman was.

"He did set the jewel into a box of his making, however. He designed several, but only crafted one that could hold the Tudor family jewels." Dodding grinned cheekily, and Dr Torres blushed. "The box became known as the Boncoeur Box, and as such, the jewel took on his name as well. Unfortunately, we have almost no information on where he came from. We do know he joined James I's court when James inherited the throne, and he got into some trouble with Matthew Hopkins — a very anti-Magic fellow who King James kept around. But after that, he simply vanishes from the records."

"Any idea what happened to the jewel after Elizabeth? Could James have inherited it?" Dr Torres asked, and for a brief, hope-filled moment I imagined Professor Dodding knowing the exact path the jewel had taken throughout its existence, where it had been, where it had gone, whose hands it had passed through, and most importantly, where it had ended up.

"That, unfortunately, is where my research dries up."

Why?! Why do I keep falling into the optimism trap? Is it some sort of optimism pheromone? Optimism blindness? Is there a cure?

"The boxes have found their way to collectors," Dodding continued. "The one that held the Boncoeur Jewel was on display at the British Museum for a time, but as for the jewel... well, of course, some prophecies began circulating around before it ever went missing. We Magics do love our prophecies and curses."

"And this one said...?" I asked.

"Sadly, that's not my area of expertise, but I'm sure one of

Olivia's people will dig it up at some point, if they haven't already." Dodding took a bite of chocolate. After nearly swooning with pleasure, he asked, "Does any of this help?"

Although I told him it did, I wasn't sure that was entirely true. It was intriguing and filled in some of jewel's story, but it told me nothing about where the jewel had gone. Nor did it get me any closer to putting the jewel into Matilda's hands and obtaining my detective's license.

"If you had to speculate," Dr Torres asked conversationally, "what could someone do with the jewel?"

"Most likely they'd just put it on display somewhere, but I imagine you wanted a more 'magical' answer?" Pascal nodded, and Professor Dodding pondered this a moment. "Given the jewel's past, I'd say it might give them power over an enemy they truly despised."

Suddenly, the chocolate that had been so perfectly creamy and rich tasted like cardboard. Why exactly did Matilda want this jewel so badly? Was she plotting something? Did she have someone in mind she wanted to use it against? Or was she just a woman collecting family treasures to display in her curio?

My throat dry with worry, I thanked Dodding for his time and was about to say farewell, but he wasn't ready to let us go just yet. He snapped his fingers and, from a side cabinet, pulled out three large mugs of hot chocolate topped with about five inches of whipped cream.

As we sipped (all three of us ending up with whipped cream up our noses), Dr Torres answered Professor Dodding's questions about his own research into the history of the Portland community. Meanwhile, my mind drifted to the possibilities of what Matilda might do with the jewel if she had it. I didn't know who her worst enemies might be, but I reminded myself to speak very nicely to her the next time she called.

CHAPTER TWENTY-FIVE
A-BOMB AFTERMATH

Once back to Portland, Dr Torres offered to take me on a guided tour of the Oregon Historical Museum. I knew I shouldn't waste the time, but he'd really done me a favor and, like a little kid showing off his room, he seemed quite eager to take me around the place, so I agreed.

The museum isn't terribly big, I mean, we're not talking about a stroll through the Louvre here, so our tour of the public areas only ate up about an hour. But when Pascal asked if I wanted to visit the behind-the-scenes areas, I made my excuses about needing to get back to work, promising that it would give me a good reason to come back again soon.

Just as I was about to leave, Dr Torres dashed over to the reception desk and nabbed something from a small holder.

"Here you go," he said, handing me a postcard. On it was a copy of the *Hart of the Forest* painting with the OHS logo embossed at the bottom right. "A little souvenir."

I thanked him, told him I'd be back, and when I stepped outside, was happily surprised to see my bike hadn't been stolen off the rack.

* * *

When I arrived back at the agency, the door was unlocked and I cursed Daisy for not locking it when she left for whatever tooth-brightening errand she was on. Then again, she was used to living in MagicLand, where people rarely bothered with locks since a quick bit of *alohomora* could get you past most of them.

And just so you know, we don't actually use the Harry Potter version of the Unlocking Spell. Rumor has it that Mr Tenpenny banned it.

I was coming up with the exact reprimand I would give Daisy when I pushed open the door and froze in place in the threshold. The agency was a mess. And this is *me* saying it was a mess; that's how bad it was.

At a quick glance from my spot at the door, nothing appeared to be broken, but files were scattered everywhere and drawers had been pulled out and upended.

My jack-hammering heart then leapt into my throat. Where was Pablo? I frantically darted my gaze back and forth across the agency's A-bomb aftermath, worried about stepping in and destroying any evidence.

Finally, I spotted Pablo's carrier. I'd missed it before because in front of the carrier, from which Pablo was warily peering out, was the evil office chair. Almost as if it had been protecting—

I shook the thought off as ridiculous. But at the same time told myself I really should be nicer to the thing.

"Welcome back, Cassie," bubbled Daisy from behind me. A bag of groceries in her hand, she came to an abrupt halt by my side. "Oh my."

Tobey, who must have been done with classes for the day, and who was also carrying a bag, glanced past Daisy. "Wow, Cass, I know you're great at making messes, but you've really outdone yourself this time."

"What are you talking about?" I snapped. "I didn't do this. I've been broken into, Mr Future Police Detective."

"Ooh, sweetie, do your police thing," Daisy said excitedly.

"I'm not really qualified. I mean, I'm allowed to take statements, but—"

"Just do it so I don't have to call in Oberlin," I told him. "Who knows, maybe he'll give you extra credit for it."

Using spells we'd both learned during our mentorship with Mr Tenpenny, Tobey checked the door and a few surfaces for fingerprints and for traces of magic, but the only matches were mine and Daisy's. He then used a Clue Collecting Charm to check over the agency for anything my unwanted visitor might have dropped or left behind, but he found nothing.

"Come on in and have a look, Cass. See if there's anything missing."

It was hard to tell if any books or files had been taken since about half of them were on the floor, but my main concern was the safe. It wasn't in its place behind my desk and, while it was heavy, a simple Lighten the Load Spell would make short work of stealing it. After shoving aside several empty Spellbound bags and unused napkins, I found a mint tin on the floor. It looked very much like the one Busby had given me a— Great Galloping Galadriel, had it only been a little over a week ago?

"Tobey, do you know anything about magic safes?" I asked, as Daisy began magically tidying up her desk and repairing the cracked glass of her framed pictures.

"What about them?"

"Can they sense danger or disguise themselves?" Tobey strode over to me, and I pointed at the mint tin.

"That's one of Grandad's. He gave me one, too. And yeah, a Danger Detection and Deception Charm is one of the features he put on them. It'll either make itself too heavy to be picked up — I think he uses a Deadweight Hex for that — or it can become something nobody would be interested in stealing. Not sure exactly, but I think he does that with a Lackluster Letdown Spell. Makes it so even if they do open it, all they'll see are stale mints."

"Any idea how to get it back to normal so I can check?" I asked as Daisy, now done with her desk, skipped with the grocery bags into the kitchenette. "What is she doing with those?"

"Said you had too many non-vegan snacks in there," he whispered, "so she's remedying that."

"Does this remedy involve caviar poo or shiny cheese?"

Tobey merely shrugged apologetically. "Anyway, the safe. It should be magicked to recognize you. Just touching your finger to it should do the trick."

Tentatively, I touched the lid of the tin with my index finger. It shimmied a little, and I jerked my hand back. Twenty seconds later, it had expanded back into a full-size safe. I unlocked it and checked inside. The marbles, the brooch, and my mom's pendant were all there, sitting on top of Wordsworth's book.

"Nothing's missing," I said.

Tobey was noting this on the sheet of printer paper he'd been making his report on, when Daisy emerged from the kitchen with a worried look on her face.

"You're not going to like this," she told me. Other than being invaded by vegan nibbles, I couldn't think of what could be worse than losing my clients' (even the dead and comatose ones) treasures. Daisy swallowed, then said, "They've broken the kettle and taken all your tea."

"Those bastards!" I turned to Tobey. "Do they hang people in MagicLand? I mean, this is a crime against caffeinated humanity. How am I supposed to work— no, *exist* without tea?"

Daisy put a consoling hand on my arm. "I can start cleaning up. Why don't you go to the store? A little tea-centric retail therapy might do you good."

I hate to admit it, but Daisy was right. Shopping really was a mood booster. Especially since she had insisted on letting me use her credit card. At the Tea Tattler Tea Shop, I bought a new kettle and every type of black tea on offer, as well as a dozen tins of proper (aka "butter-rich") teatime biscuits. On my way back, I picked up a little something from the Enchanted Abode home goods boutique.

When I returned to the agency, Daisy was sitting on the floor sifting through some scraps of paper, and books were magically slotting themselves back onto the shelves, but most of the filing and paperwork was still in disarray. Or, at least, I think it was. It might have been like that when I'd left to meet up with Dr Torres.

I dropped the tea things off in the kitchenette, then hurriedly threw the cushion from the Enchanted Abode onto the evil chair, muttering a quick *thank you*.

"Cassie, did you ever notice this?" Daisy asked as I read over the copy of the report Tobey had left.

I looked around. There was a whole lot of stuff to notice, quite a lot of it on the floor, so I asked her for a bit of clarification.

"This receipt." She held it out for me to look at. "From a pawnshop?"

"It's from when Rafi and I picked up Mrs O's brooch. Just file it in the folder for the Oberlin case."

"Oh, okay, but it's just kind of weird, the person who brought the brooch into the pawnshop," she said, staring at the receipt like a parakeet who's just discovered another bird in the mirror and doesn't quite know what to make of it.

"It's just a fake address. From *The Simpsons*."

"I recognized that, but the signature. I mean, it's a fake name, but the writing is kind of distinct." She brought it over to me and pointed to the final letter. "That little zigzag thingie. That's what Mayor Marheart does when she signs forms. I've seen it on a few of the commendations Tobey's gotten."

Wait. Tobey had gotten commendations from the mayor? For what? Test bungling? Best hair on a future detective? But before I could ask any of this, Daisy was digging out Mayor Marheart's folder. She flipped it open, found the hiring agreement, then pointed to the signature at the bottom. Nothing matched what was on the receipt. Except the little zigzag.

"But what does this mean?" I asked. "Why did she have the brooch? And why did she take it to a pawnshop? Is she a kleptomaniac who's also into decluttering?"

Daisy shrugged. "Dunno. We could ask. Want me to call her?"

"No, definitely not. Not yet, anyway," I said. One, because I needed to mull over how this information fit into everything else swirling around the mayor lately. And two, because I'd already experienced firsthand the angry mobs you could stir up in MagicLand if you accused people of crimes they hadn't committed.

CHAPTER TWENTY-SIX
EARLY MORNING MUSINGS

My mind reeling with half-formed theories, partially linked connections, and thoroughly discomforting break-ins, I got too little sleep that night, and woke up far earlier than normal the next morning. Even in the dazed state my brain is usually in before my first cup of tea, I noted Alastair's side of the bed was already empty, and the apartment was silent except for the muffled thumps and thwacks of Pablo playing inside his carrier.

On the kitchen counter, Alastair had left a copy of the *Herald*. Why he'd not taken it with him, I didn't know. I hoped he'd just forgotten it in his haste to get to the workroom before I woke up. *Hoped*, because the other option was that it contained a whopper of an opinion piece about me, and he'd left it out to rub my status of Undesirable Number One into the gaping wounds of our struggling relationship.

Clearly, with thoughts like these, I needed to hash this out with him, but I knew it was best to wait until my brain was functioning less foggily.

As soon as I started dishing up some yogurt, Pablo emerged from his carrier looking quite pleased with his morning workout. While he sat on the table trying to steal bites of my breakfast, I found myself lazily flipping through the *Herald*.

The front page was filled with a report on the missing

Magics. No one else had disappeared from Rosaria, but other communities such as York, Toulouse, Auckland, and Oslo had lost several people in the past week.

Perhaps as a way to add poignancy to the news of the missing Magics, the *Herald* had filled most of the rest of the front page with personal stories of the lives and achievements of the Magics who'd most recently gone missing from other Oregon communities like Eugene, Salem, and Seaside.

For Magics who had gone missing from communities further afield, the paper had begun to include a list of all their names. This took the form of a callout box with the world's Magic communities listed alphabetically. Next to the community's name was the current tally of the missing, and under this, dozens of names in small print. It did exactly as intended and truly hammered in the point of just how many were gone. I was so staggered by the numbers that Pablo nearly managed to get a nibble of my yogurt.

And yet only one person had gone missing from Rosaria. Perhaps, despite my many concerns about her, Mayor Marheart really was doing her job.

Speaking of, the only other front-page news item was a full summary of the town hall. Apparently, things got quite heated after I'd left, with demands to recall Mayor Marheart and put Inspector Oberlin in her place. Not wanting to ruin my appetite, I didn't bother to read the rest of the article.

When I turned the page, I noticed an easy-to-miss paragraph in the lower corner briefly mentioning there'd been a fire in the British Library but that, so far, the source of the fire hadn't been found. I made a note to myself to pester Morelli further about the protection spells on the book. I mean, protecting something by completely destroying it? Didn't sound like the most efficient use of magic to me.

Other than some spots reserved for advertising, most of the *Herald's* interior was a continuation of the personal stories from page one. There were also statements from spokespeople from various communities, all saying how the situation needed to be addressed with care and urgency, but that they didn't want to point fingers. Then, by the end of their interviews, they'd be pointing fingers right at the vampire community.

So it wasn't a surprise to see an article on page four about the rise in hate crimes against vampires, even ones who had been long-standing pillars of their communities.

Perhaps thinking it would drive the vampires out of their communities, some menacing Magics had gone so far as to blockade the blood infusion cafes that had been set up for the vampires. Which seemed like a really stupid move, because what did they think the vamps were going to eat if they couldn't get the lab-created, nutritionally balanced blood treats that ranged from double-O espresso shots to AB-positive ice cream? And, of course, the blood sausages served with plasma sauce.

With the missing Magics giving the paper a new focus, I almost thought a day might pass without them publishing anything negative about me.

But, when I turned to the opinion section, centered at the top of the right-hand page was a picture of yours truly outside of Corrigan's Courier. Corrine was pulling me by the arm, my clothes and hair were in disarray from the courier portal, and my face was contorted in irritation and annoyance. It looked for all the world like Corrine had been forcibly escorting me out of her business.

There was no accompanying article, but there was a caption: *Let's celebrate Corrine Corrigan as she refuses to fall for the manipulative tactics of Cassie Black, the detective who apparently can't even find a comb for her hair!*

I set the paper aside. It wasn't the most complimentary photo, but the insults were becoming stale.

Needing something sweet, I pushed my almost-empty yogurt dish over to Pablo, who immediately stuck his face in it and began lapping up the leftovers. Over a thick slice of jam crostata, I considered the *Herald's* photo, then let my mind wander over other photos I'd seen lately. And the connections I made didn't sit well with the swirling storm of thoughts I'd been having about Matilda Marheart.

Clive Coppersmith had had a photo from his marble conference that showed Matilda had been there. Sure, Tremaine had ended up with the stolen marbles, but what if that was only because he'd gotten to them before the mayor had? Unaware the marbles were already missing, she'd then gone looking for them at Clive's place, and…

The memory of Clive's unmoving feet brought a lump to my throat.

Then there was the picture of Matilda at Wordsworth's library conference from where his book had gone missing. Corrine herself had said the mayor had been interested in Wordsworth's crate of books before it had been sent off. Could Matilda have overheard what protective spells were on the crate and undone them? Or had she Confounded one of Corrine's employees to get them to open the box for her? I didn't know why she would want the book, but I left the motivation aspect of the crime for later because a flash of another photo had just come to me.

Mrs Oberlin had been convinced she'd lost her brooch during a party at the Canberra community. It was just a guess, but I'd bet my knock-off Doc Marten's that the photo I'd seen in Matilda's entryway had been from that very party. Could Matilda have attacked Mrs O because she wanted the brooch? Or had Winnifred suspected her of taking it, and so Matilda struck first before Winnifred could report her? But then why had Mayor Marheart taken the thing to a pawnshop? Had she left it there to ditch the evidence? Then when she went back to find it had already been purchased, she'd assumed it was back in Winnifred's hands? Or was Matilda just a very indecisive criminal?

As for Runa's saw... Well, I had seen Matilda with a bandaged hand the very morning the clinic had been robbed. Was the injury from broken glass? Of course, she'd also been first on the scene at my parents' place when the pendant had re-lost itself and I'd had my face seared with an attack spell. And let's not forget her dogged demands I find a jewel that might (or might not) give her power against anyone who would defy her.

Which are all thoughts you don't want to have about your client when that client had been pretty gracious about not firing you. I ate the last crumbs of the crostata and filed my theories away. For now.

As I finished up my morning routine and packed Pablo into his carrier, all was quiet in the workroom, so I assumed Alastair was working on the super secret HQ research. Although I was fully awake now, I had no idea how to break through the Wall of Grump he had erected, and my efforts at small talk lately did nothing but annoy him further.

I knew I needed to speak to him, but, call me a big delaying-the-inevitable chicken, I decided now was not the time. Which is why I stopped in my tracks when I entered MagicLand and saw Alastair and Fiona standing confrontationally face-to-face on her wrap-around porch.

Fiona's house, as you might remember, is right next to the nondescript door that serves as the portal from Rosaria to my apartment. So I had a clear line of sight of Alastair stabbing at a piece of paper like it had offended him, and Fiona's brows pulling into a knot of concern.

I managed to get my portal door shut without a sound, but just then, Pablo let out an enthusiastic meow and I felt him jumping after something inside the carrier.

Both Fiona and Alastair turned toward the sound, then immediately stopped speaking when they saw me. Fiona's eyes darted to Alastair with an expression that clearly said, *Go talk to her*, but he didn't budge. Instead, he shook his head and, in the morning quiet, I heard him say, "I can't. Not yet." To which Fiona murmured something, but my ears weren't as attuned to her voice as they were to his.

I couldn't just stand there staring at them, and neither of them were beckoning me over, so I turned on my heel and, with Pablo's carrier in hand, I marched off toward the agency.

After dwelling on Alastair's behavior for several blocks, my mind gave up on trying to figure him out and drifted again to my worrisome client and what I'd learned from Professor Dodding. With so many aspects of the jewel centering on the Elizabethan Court, my best course of action (okay, the only one I could come up with) was a return trip to London. Specifically to the Tower.

Which would mean finding someone to escort me through the London-Portland portal; and, given we'd only just met, I didn't want to pester Dr Torres again so soon.

I was sure Runa would love to go see Olivia, but that would involve taking Morelli too. Although, perhaps he would appreciate seeing I was trying to make progress on Matilda's case.

Once I got to the agency, I unlatched Pablo's carrier, and he immediately trotted over and jumped into the evil office chair, curling up against the new cushion and purring with utter contentment.

I checked my phone for the time. Fiona, unless she was still dealing with Alastair, would be starting classes soon, as would Lola. Gwendolyn would be preparing for her busiest time of the day. And Corrine had told me before that she didn't like traveling.

I supposed I could ask Daisy when she got in, but I hadn't had enough sleep or caffeine to spend the next couple of hours with her effervescent personality. Actually, I doubted there was enough sleep or caffeine in the world for that.

Which narrowed down my choices to Tobey, who was likely already heading to the Academy for the day, and Mr Tenpenny.

Mr Tenpenny it was.

CHAPTER TWENTY-SEVEN
BUTLER CHARMS

I texted Mr Tenpenny to ask if he was free. And, since I wasn't sure how to handle another Alastair sighting, to make sure Mr T wasn't at Fiona's.

As a show of how stuck in their ways they were, neither Busby nor Fiona had yet to fully move into the other's home, and were instead doing a weird one-night here, two-nights there sort of thing. I wondered if this would change, if Mr T would finally move in with Fiona full-time, when Tobey and Daisy got married. Or would Tobey move in with Daisy? It struck me that I had no clue where my assistant lived. Probably in a full-size Barbie Dream House, if I had to guess.

As I waited for Mr T to reply, a chill scratched along my arms when I took in how clean the agency now was. Not that I have anything against cleanliness (regardless of what people might think), but it was discomforting to know that the tidy desks, the perfect rows of books, and the organized files were the end result of someone sneaking in and searching for something. But what? And, more importantly, who? Or maybe those were equally important. I'd have to sort that out later.

Busby responded that he was at his home and to come by whenever I was ready. Since I was more than ready, I left a quick note telling Daisy I'd be away for a few hours, then headed out, making triple sure the locks were engaged.

At Mr T's place, I knocked on the side kitchen door that was the only entrance to his Real Portland house from MagicLand. A face appeared in the door's window. And I don't mean a face attached to a human body. It was like something from a fairy tale mirror with the image floating eerily within the glass.

I considered asking who was the fairest of them all as the disembodied head of Mr Tenpenny came into focus. His hair was combed into place, but shaving cream covered half his face.

"Ah, come in, Cassie. I'm just finishing up," the floating head said as he pulled a straight razor along his foamy cheek.

The door then unlocked itself, and I stepped into the Tenpenny kitchen with its rustic oak dining table and, as I knew from experience, well-stocked fridge. I peered inside. Too early for one of Tobey's IPAs, but it wasn't too early for one of the cups of organic, small-batch skyr, which was, according to the label, handcrafted by a family of Icelandic elves.

Then came the task of trying to find a spoon in an unfamiliar kitchen. I'd already opened three drawers before Mr T appeared, looking as crisp and fresh as a head of iceberg lettuce.

"It's that one." He pointed to the drawer nearest the sink. "I see you've helped yourself. Have you come by solely to raid my pantry?"

"You didn't give me time to raid the pantry. And what's with the floating head at the window?" I gestured to the kitchen door with my spoon.

"Ah, that. One of Rafi's ideas I'm testing out for him. Haven't come up with a name for it yet, but it's quite handy when you can't get to the door, but also don't want the person knocking to leave."

"Butler Charm?" I suggested.

"Not a bad idea. I'll share it with him," said Mr T as he got his own cup of skyr. "Now, to what do I owe the pleasure of this visit?"

"Funny you should mention Rafi. Would you want to go bounce spell names off him? Like, right now?"

"What's this about, Cassie? You are focusing on Wordsworth's book, aren't you?"

"Focusing, sure. But I'm still on the Marheart case, and I've got an idea I want to check out. Her signature is just as good as Wordsworth's for my license application," I said when Mr T gave me a look of disapproval.

"It is, but I'm somewhat uncomfortable with you turning your attention to Matilda's case. Concerns have been raised about her past and about her plans for Rosaria."

I probably should have, but I didn't want to bring up my own suspicions about Matilda to Busby. Not yet anyway. First, I was afraid he'd tell me to abandon her case altogether, and I was growing too curious by this point to do that.

Second, I really wasn't sure how valid my suspicions were. Were they just a bunch of coincidences, or could they truly mean something? Either way, I needed a little more thinking time to cobble the ideas and theories into something that made sense before I voiced them to another person.

Instead, I conversationally said, "You think there's something behind what the hecklers at the town hall were going on about?"

"It's being looked into." He paused a moment, taking a few pensive bites of his elvish skyr. "You know, perhaps your searching for this jewel would be for the best. The inquiries you'll have to make can only add to our knowledge of whether she's a person of concern or not. And you can do so without being fully brought in on this matter by HQ."

"Wait, do you think she's involved with the missing Magics thing?"

"No, of course not. Matilda's an upstanding member of our community. Sometimes, though, I do wonder about her true aims for seeking such a position."

"So, will you take me to London?"

"As Olivia has been pressing me for a meeting anyway, it would be my pleasure. But you can go there on your own now," Mr T said as he sent a message to, I assume, Olivia. "With us no longer having to worry about the Mauvais, any Magic is allowed to travel as he or she wishes between magic communities."

"Yeah, good to know, but I can't. My magic levels, remember?"

"Ah, yes. My apologies. Portal travel is such second nature I forget we need reliable magic to be able to do it. It's not getting better?"

"Runa tells me the levels are still all over the place. And you saw what happened at Mr Wood's with my Drying Spell."

Mr T quirked his lips. "It certainly is a matter of concern. You're not working too hard, are you? Undertaking too much stress?"

I thought of Alastair, of the articles, of having to keep Pablo locked away when he was home (not that he minded his new feline wonderland), of floundering under cases that seemed impossible and could literally make or break my career. But something prickled along the magic in my cells that none of these were the root of my problem. After all, I had no trouble tapping into my magic when I kept rousing the dead and had an evil wizard chasing after me, so why should a few everyday worries bog me down so much?

Besides, I'd already resolved to let the professionals

figure out my Magic Gone Berserk problem since I've never been terribly good at self-diagnosis. Just as an example, I once convinced myself I had bone cancer when it was nothing more than an ingrown toenail.

"I'm sure she'll come up with something," I said. "I'm probably not eating enough sugar."

"Since I've seen your parents' tab at Spellbound, and since I know a fair portion of those purchases end up in your hands, I highly doubt sugar deprivation is the issue." Busby's phone pinged and he gave the screen a quick glance. "Olivia says now would be fine. So, if you're ready, no time like the present. We'll use the portal near Lola's, if that suits you."

"Better than Corrine's courier slot," I said. This had been how Mr T and I had first traveled to HQ. But after my fiery trip the other day, I had no desire to appear in the British Library again so soon. Or ever.

"Not an option, anyway. It's been temporarily closed down. Quite a pain for getting the packages one is expecting," he said peevishly.

Rather than respond, I paid very careful attention to getting every last microgram of skyr out of the cup.

Busby Tenpenny might be in his eleventh decade, but he's no frail old codger. He appears and carries himself like a man at least five decades younger. Which is why I felt no need to tuck my chin into my collar or throw a Mirage Hex over my face when we turned from his street onto Main Street.

For the most part, I'd avoided this busy thoroughfare since the accusatory sneers, snide looks, and cruel comments were all things I could do without. But with Mr T at my side, people kept their sniping to themselves, and one of the catty ladies from Runa's clinic even tipped her chin to Busby in greeting. I narrowed my eyes at the butt-kissing bully.

"I paid a visit to Pascal Torres," I said, and Mr T asked how the historian was doing. "He's great, but he had a portal that went wherever he wanted without any time difference. Why can't you get something like that?"

"Pascal is a special situation. We need him to be able to do his work, but as you know, a Norm cannot enter Rosaria without a Magic's assistance. As he would prefer to maintain his dignity by not having one of us hold his hand every time he needs to travel, we gave him a special dispensation to use a unique form of portal."

"But the time difference? And why can't you just install those unique forms of portals everywhere?"

"The time difference, I'll admit, is a new and quite enviable feature. But believe me when I say there is only so much tinkering you can do with physics before it starts fighting back. You might ask Rafi about the Roanoke Incident sometime." Frustratingly, Mr T didn't elaborate. "As for installing the Go Anywhere Portals elsewhere, it would be a great undertaking both in regards to budget and security. If portals start going faulty, then we will consider replacing them with the newer Go Anywhere Portals, but in the meantime we will simply have to be patient."

"How long do portals last?"

"Typically, about two to three hundred years. The Rosaria ones still have plenty of life left in them," he said, resigned regret adding a bitter note to the words.

When we reached it, Lola's street was filled with the sound of drums. Not a rhythmic sound, mind you. Just quite literally the sound of various types of percussion instruments being thumped and whacked as joyfully as possible.

"I see Bunny is still learning his instrument," said Mr T as he twirled his index finger near his ear. Busby wasn't indicating that Bunny was a bit loopy, as I first thought; he was executing a form of a Stoppering Hex on himself. He then did the same to my ears, and it turned out to be a brilliant spell that blocked out the drumming, but still allowed me to hear voices and other sounds with near-perfect clarity. I lifted my brows to Mr Tenpenny, asking a silent question.

"Yet another of Rafi's inventions. The charm puts a filter on unwanted noises. How it figures out what those noises are, I've no idea. Still, I can't imagine why they haven't put a Silencing Spell around Bunny's house."

"It don't work," said an elderly woman whose thick, black earmuffs made her look like a Hispanic Princess Leia. "We put it on, and a few minutes later, it's gone. Bunny's got some special magic in his bones, that's all we can figure."

"Too bad someone can't steal his drums," I said.

"Don't think we haven't tried." The woman walked away, shaking her head then jutting her hand, with fingers twisted, toward Bunny's house.

"Inconvenience Curse," Mr T said, by way of explanation. "Causes lost keys, missing socks, and perhaps—" a crack came from inside Bunny's house, and Mr Tenpenny smiled "—a broken drumstick. Let's go through before he finds a new one."

Compared to Corrine's portal, which felt like being jostled around in a dune buggy with flat tires, the portal at the end of Lola's street was like riding in a top-of-the-line Mercedes. Moments after entering, we stepped out to a dark, stone-walled space that smelled of damp and age.

My eyes hadn't yet adjusted to the low torchlight before Busby found himself under attack.

CHAPTER TWENTY-EIGHT
CASSIE SUPER SPY

Massive arms swooped around Mr Tenpenny, who, even as the air was forced from his lungs, bore the invasion of personal space with pure British stoicism.

"Busby!"

"Chester," Mr T grunted, "this is no way to greet people. We've discussed this, remember?"

Chester, the troll who guards HQ better than a pack of Rottweilers, dropped his arms. Mr T staggered under the sudden freedom, then brushed down his suit jacket and re-centered his pocket square — a dark blue one dotted with cartoon corgis wearing tiny crowns.

"Sorry, I just get so happy to see familiar faces. And Mr Cassie!" He raised his arms. I tensed and sucked in a lungful of air, readying myself for the crush. But Chester caught himself, lowered his arms, then held out a hand the size of a serving platter. I shook it. He gripped tightly enough to leave bruises, but thanks to Chester being a troll, the bruises instantly healed under his magic.

"Pleased to see you are…" Chester scrunched up his face, his bulbous nose twitching as he searched for what he was meant to say. His eyes lit up, he smoothed down his wiry red hair, then he continued, "…hail and hearty. Welcome once again to the Tower."

"That was very good, Chester," said Mr T as we moved through the dank corridors beneath the White Tower.

"Rafi's been working with me. He thinks if I get good at my talking, I could be an—" again, the pause to find the rest of the rehearsed sentence he was after "—an integral part of the Tower's work."

"You already are an integral part, Chester," Busby said reassuringly.

Just then, Chester stomped one of his snowshoe-sized feet against the stony ground. The thud was instantly followed by the briefest squeak, then nothing. I shuddered. See, trolls take promises very seriously, but Chester took his vow to guard the Tower against *any* intruder to a whole new level. Not only did he take great pride in keeping out most two-legged fiends, but he also derived an unhealthy level of job satisfaction as he thwarted any four-legged invaders he came across.

"That's what I said, but Rafi told me I could do more. Work more on the administrative side of things."

"Is that what you want?" asked Mr T as we started up a spiral staircase. My legs instantly began complaining. Couldn't blame them, really, since in those two weeks when I'd been 'requested' to stay at HQ, they'd hauled me up more stairs than a team of tower runners (those bizarre people who race up floor after floor of tall buildings) climbs in an entire season of training.

"I like helping. But rat stomping is more fun than office busy work stuff."

Truer words were never spoken.

We came out on a familiar hallway. Or at least it seemed familiar. The halls within the Tower of London's White Tower, where Magic HQ operated from, all look the same. I wasn't sure if this was to confuse trespassers, or if British Magics simply lacked creativity when it came to interior design.

"Here we are," Busby said when we reached a door made of thick hunks of oak.

I suddenly felt nervous and unsure about this. I mean, wouldn't someone have seen Matilda's jewel if it was sitting out in plain sight for tourists to gawk at? Did I really need to remind Olivia that my sleuthing skills were basically just wild guesses and dumb luck? Especially since it was well within her power to withdraw my application extension and send me off to sweep out the dungeon for the rest of my days. And I'd have to do so with an actual broom since I couldn't even manage a proper Shoving Spell anymore.

Mind racing with how Pablo would take to a life in the bowels of the Tower, I found myself being guided into Olivia's vast office space. As a room in a Norman castle, it had walls built of thick stone with only a trio of tall, narrow windows for natural light. But the walls were mostly covered in tapestries to soften the space, and Olivia must have enchanted the windows, because the interior of the office was as filled with warm, late afternoon sunlight as a room with vast picture windows.

Olivia had been at her desk when we entered, but upon seeing Busby, she stood and strode over to greet him, the glass beads at the end of her braids clinking gently as she moved.

"Busby, so good of you to drop by." She air-kissed him on one cheek, then turned to me and, already aware of my preferred form of greeting, held out her hand. "And Cassie. Back so soon?"

"Working on a case," I said lamely. I mean, obviously she didn't think I came here to see the sights and nab a few Baker Street fridge magnets.

Olivia stepped back around behind her desk and gestured for us to sit. At the snap of her fingers, a tea tray appeared, complete with scones and biscuits and cream and jam and all manner of mouth-watering delights. After pouring out three cups of tea, she asked what she could do for me.

"You remember that jewel of Mayor Marheart's—"

"I thought you were fired from that case," Olivia cut in.

"Magic contract," I said.

Olivia nodded sagely, then said, "I'm sorry, but I've been a bit overwhelmed with— well, it seems with everything. I'd be glad to ask some people to look into it, but you do know after all this time, it could be anywhere."

"It could, but it was here at some point. At the Tower of London, I mean." I briefly summarized Elizabeth I's connection to the jewel. "I know it's a long shot, but I'd like to check over the Crown Jewels, if you don't mind."

"I highly doubt it's there, and even if it were, were you expecting to simply walk out of here with it?"

This brought me up short, because, stupidly, I hadn't thought that far ahead. Even though I had wild visions of finding the heart-shaped jewel resting on a velvet cushion and glittering under perfectly staged lights, the folks at the Historic Royal Palaces offices certainly weren't going to let me pay the cashier a few pounds, hand me a receipt, and allow me to walk out with it like I'd done at the pawnshop with Winnifred's brooch.

I fumbled out a few sounds. Not words, mind you. Just random vocalizations meant to convey my stupidity and lack of forethought.

"Let's see how you get along," said Olivia. "If you find what you're after, perhaps we can work something out. The monarchy aren't prone to argue with us over their sparkly things these days, so don't fret until you've found it."

As I enjoyed the treats on offer, Mr T asked, "How's the research been going?"

"It's getting nowhere. I see evidence of—" she paused, then looked between me and Mr T.

"She's been told a few things," he said.

"Good. It'll be even better once we can get her fully on board. Where are you thinking of putting her?"

Because this is what happens when I go to HQ. They talk about me like I'm not there. But I was used to it by now, so I took a sip of my tea. Then played off the pain as the scorching brew scalded my lips.

"The undercover team might suit her," said Mr Tenpenny.

Undercover team? Wait, what team was this? Did he mean like an actual HQ spy? Luckily, I had plenty of black clothes to sneak around under cover of darkness, hunting down my quarry, ferrying out—

"Cassie!" snapped Mr T.

"Sorry, what?"

"I asked you if you wanted milk in your tea."

At least Cassie Super Spy hadn't missed out on anything important.

"Um, sure. It'll cool it down a bit," I said.

"Speaking of cooling things down," said Olivia, "did you hear about the British Library?"

"What about it?" Mr Tenpenny asked.

"They had a fire."

I choked on my tea. Or rather, *luckily* I choked on my tea, since coughing and gasping for air hid the guilty look on my face.

"Sorry, still too hot," I sputtered.

Mr T circled his finger over my cup to cool the liquid a notch. Unfortunately, the tea had actually been at the perfect temperature for drinking and was now unappealing lukewarm.

"You were saying?" he asked, not without a she-never-changes shake of his head.

"A fire in the lower storage areas."

"Ah yes, I did hear about that. Much damage?"

"No, quite contained, in fact. But it's why we had to close down Corrine's portal access. Wanted to keep things sealed off while we made sure nothing more sinister was going on. They tell me only minor damage occurred, but they'll be reviewing the footage to see what might have happened. The techs should have the security recordings to me any time now."

"Was the fire in our section?"

My belly tensed. Magics had their own section? Why had no one told me this? Oh, probably because they didn't expect me to break in and try to steal a magic book.

"With as tight-lipped as they're being, I have a feeling it was. I can't get any information from them yet, but I'll be speaking with the head librarian soon."

I sipped my cold tea as I wondered, if a third copy of the book was found, could Sebastian Duplex the whole thing to make a new copy? I could then sneak back into the Library to replace—

"Wait, did you say footage?" I blurted. I should have known not to trust Daisy and her stupid Motion Detector Putter Outer Charm. Belatedly realizing my outburst might give me away, I asked, "Can the cameras capture everything down there? I mean, with the shelves? It could be difficult to see who the culprit is. Was." I shut up and focused again on my tepid tea before I dug myself a hole deeper than the Tower's swimming pool.

"They take security seriously," said Olivia, "so I'm sure they'll sort it out. Probably making more of this than it really is. It could have just been a mouse chewing on a wire, for all we know."

"When are the techs meeting with you?" asked Busby.

"They'll be calling within the hour, which will give us a bit of time to discuss this vampire situation. I know Runa disagrees, but more details have come to light regarding our current problem, and I have to say it's getting critical." I knew better than to ask what this meant, but don't think it didn't send my mind racing. Were the details from my parents? Were they okay? When were they coming back? Again, all questions I was sure Olivia and Busby wouldn't answer, so I kept them to myself.

"As for you, Cassie," Olivia said, brushing crumbs from her fingers, "let's get you to the Crown Jewels. I expect you'd like a little crowd control?"

"That would be helpful, yes." The jewels are one of the top attractions within the Tower, so, even this late in the day, the display room would be wall-to-wall human.

Olivia tapped the side of the teapot with her index finger. There was a crackling sound like static on an old television, then a familiar voice asked, "Yes, mum?"

"Nigel, yes, I was wondering if you could arrange to have the Jewel House cleared out?"

I got up to stand behind Olivia. There, on the side of the Tealephone, was Nigel, Yeoman Warder (aka "Beefeater") and former ghost. Yet another person who owed their new lease on life to me. I waved.

Nigel's face stiffened as he tried to bite back a smile. It had taken many hours of me tutoring him so he could pass his exam to become a Yeoman Warder for the Tower, his lifelong — and death-long — dream.

The Yeoman Warders are not only responsible for guarding the Tower but also have the duty of leading tour groups around the historic landmark and wowing their guests with the past antics of English kings and queens. And for that you need an exacting and extensive knowledge of Tower history.

When I met him, Nigel knew a fair bit of this history, just not exactly in chronological order. Or with the right people cast in key roles. For example, Nigel once thought Henry V wasn't named because he was the fifth king of that name, but because that's the size of whisky bottle he preferred.

"Miss Black, very good to see you," Nigel said, nearly chuckling at the formal airs he was putting on.

"Nigel, you're a Yeoman Warder," said Olivia, "not a palace guard. You don't have to be so serious."

"Oh good, it does get painful being so rigid. I don't know how those chaps on watch do it."

"Well, I want you to tell those chaps on duty at the Jewel House that we need the room for, say, twenty minutes. You just come up with the diversion; they'll take care of clearing out the crowds."

"Very good, mum." Nigel's hand shot up to his forehead in a sharp salute, and I swear I heard his heels click together.

"Again, Nigel, I don't need to be saluted."

"Right. Just felt the thing to do. I'll be off now."

The teapot's side went back to being nothing more than a shiny surface.

"We'll give him a few minutes, then head down there. Prepare for disgruntled tourists."

Disgruntled tourists? I mentally scoffed. They'd be like a basket of sleepy kittens compared to what I'd been putting up with on the streets of MagicLand.

CHAPTER TWENTY-NINE
CLOSED FOR POLISHING

"How are you progressing with Wordsworth's case?" asked Olivia as we started down the stairs. We'd left Busby in Olivia's office going over some reports she'd had ready for him. "If you'd like, I could ask if the British Library has a copy of that book of his when I speak to my contact later."

"No," I said far too quickly. "I mean, you've got enough on your plate, and I've already got my assistant looking into things. I was actually thinking," I continued, hoping to sway Olivia from bringing up that specific book to this contact of hers, "maybe one from a private collection might be easier to work with."

"Work with?"

I explained Rafi's Duplex-then-Sebastian-fix idea. Olivia nodded with approval. "He is one elf who can think outside the box. Although this persistent notion of his to make Chester some sort of secretary..." She shook her head admonishingly. "I just can't fathom it. HQ have made great strides at being more inclusive, and all manner of people have unexpectedly risen higher in the ranks than I'd have ever imagined, but a troll doing administration? Typing up a spreadsheet? Answering telephone calls and emails?"

"He'd probably run a great slideshow presentation on pest control, though," I said as we exited the White Tower. We then maneuvered through the crowds of bewildered tourists and exasperated tour guides as we made our way to the building where the sparkly things lived.

The English Crown Jewels are displayed in the Waterloo Barracks. This is also where Wordsworth's library soars behind an interior door that, to most eyes, appears to be nothing more than a service access panel.

I glanced up, trying to discern any difference in the building's exterior to accommodate the several new floors of shelf space the Bookworm had been given as a reward for hiring me. But I saw no change in the grand, two-story structure.

Standing tall and proud, Nigel was waiting for us near the guarded entry to the Jewel House. For a moment, I couldn't figure out what was different about him. Then, as he strode over to us, it hit me.

When I'd first met the now-living-and-breathing Nigel, he'd been a ghost. This meant that, although his legs made all the motions of walking, his feet never truly touched the ground. Now, Nigel's shoes were making contact with the pavement and clicking against the stony surface with every step.

Olivia had been right about the angry tourists. A gaggle of people complained and grumbled at the *Closed for Polishing* sign Nigel had just tacked onto the main door. Luckily, most of the vilest complaints were being directed toward the hired tour guides who were trying, and for the most part failing, to appease their clients.

"Don't see why they can't do that later," grumbled a woman with a Boston accent.

"It's very routine," Nigel said affably once he'd escorted us to the door. "We need to make sure they sparkle just for you.

So, two times a day, we close the display for a little buff and grind."

Olivia shook her head, but a few of the less furious tourists tittered at Nigel's unintended innuendo.

"I 'ave never encountered 'zis before," complained a tour guide who had a French accent and a beak of a nose.

"Really?" asked Nigel in astounded wonder. "That must be excellent timing on your part. But I'm afraid your luck has run amok today. May I present our workers." He then made a sweeping gesture toward me and Olivia, as if we were the objects the people had come to see.

Olivia, a black satchel like a medicine bag having appeared in her hand somewhere along the way, tipped a greeting then turned toward the door. I kept close by her side, assuming I was meant to look like her assistant.

"Just through here, ladies," Nigel said. The two regimental guards on duty each took one step outward — one to the left, and one to the right — to reveal the entryway they'd been blocking. When Nigel opened it, the whole crowd leaned and stretched forward to try to peer in as Olivia and I slipped through.

"Now, now," Nigel admonished. "No peeking, you rascals. While they're working, why don't I tell you the story of how Queen Elizabeth was once a prisoner here."

The door closed on me and Olivia, and I just hoped Nigel remembered it had been Queen Elizabeth I, not Queen Elizabeth II, who had been imprisoned here. Although, if he had forgotten, it might be entertaining to hear the story he came up with.

After taking a quick glance at the case of jewels nearest the entrance, Olivia excused herself, saying she had to check in on Wordsworth and his new shelves. Meanwhile, I examined every jewel, crown, necklace, and scepter in the room.

There were no heart-shaped jewels, but one case caught my eye. In it was a set of rings arranged in a circle on a cushion of red velvet. Each had a blue sapphire setting surrounded by a dozen tiny diamonds. One ring stood at the center of the circle. It too had a sapphire, but it was at least three times the size of the others.

"Ah, those are my favorites," said Olivia, startling me since I hadn't heard her re-enter the room. "They're called the friendship rings."

"Like Frodo and Gimli and Legolas and all that?"

"Not exactly," she said with a light chuckle. "Sets like these are incredibly rare since they require cutting a larger jewel into smaller jewels without wasting any of the original jewel. A task that demands a great deal of skill. We're pretty sure only a Magic could have done it, but that might just be Magic arrogance, which our Norm historians often criticize us for."

"Seems a waste of a big sparkly thing," I commented, then pointed behind me to a crown with a massive diamond that instantly drew the eye. "I mean, it does kill the bling factor a bit."

"Which was the point. It showed the friends were all on equal footing, all equally valuable to the monarch, who would have worn that center ring."

"When were these made?" I asked, not seeing any information on them. In fact, most of the displays had little more than a sentence or two about the items. I suppose not having to read kept the tourists moving at a steady pace through the popular exhibit.

"I'd have to double-check, but I believe this set dates from Henry VIII's time. He loved rewarding his favorites. He also loved snatching away that favoritism in the harshest of ways. This was also when medieval legends were still swirling around, and people thought if you split a jewel you diminished its power."

"Wouldn't someone like Henry VIII want all the power he could get?"

"Not if that power could fall into the hands of someone else and be used against him. So, you split the jewel, thereby removing its power. Again, it's all legend, of course," she added as if she didn't believe such tripe. "I'm sure there's some grain of truth to it, but I doubt anything can truly take away an item's power, if it had any to begin with. Magic simply doesn't work like that."

"Can these sets be put back together?" I asked, something nagging at me as I stared at the friendship rings.

"Like Humpty Dumpty?" she said, with a sneer and a stab of irritability in her voice. "Balthazar's bollocks, that fellow was an ass. Always sitting on walls, calling out lewd things to the ladies. He didn't fall, you know? One woman had had enough and pushed him off. And despite what they say, no one ever tried to put him back together again. Sorry, what was the question?" she asked in a calmer tone, seeming to remember herself. "Ah yes, reuniting the jewels. If we're to believe the legends, there used to be spells that could bring the pieces back together, but that magic's been long lost. If it ever existed.

"Now, besides those rings, have you found anything you like?" she asked this as if we were in a jewelry shop, not an ostentatious historical display.

"No, but it's given me something to think about." I could see Olivia wanted more, but the wheels of the notion were still clicking into place, and I couldn't have even described the idea to myself. Instead, I glanced to the door that led to Wordsworth's library and asked, "How is he, then?"

"Let's just say I've put in an order for a pair of gin and tonics when I get back to the office."

"I don't really like gin and tonic," I told her, suddenly thirsty for the bitter hops of an IPA. After all, we were approaching happy hour in London.

"That's good, because they're both for me. You are still working on getting his book, aren't you?" she asked wearily. "I just can't believe, with all the battered and tattered books he has in there, that he's in such a wormy tizzy about one missing a couple pages. Rafi owes us both when this is through." Because it was Rafi who'd convinced Wordsworth to hire me for this literary scavenger hunt. "Now, we really ought to open this back up before any of those tour guides out there gets hurt."

We left the Jewel House, and as soon as the maintenance sign was down, the crowd cheered, formed a queue, and soon began squeezing their way in. Judging from the looks on the tour guides' faces, Olivia wasn't the only one who was in need of liquid solace.

"If you don't need me," I said once we'd gotten past the snaking line of people, "I'd like to see how Nigel's getting on."

"He's doing remarkably well, from what I hear. Be sure to ask him about his tours. I'll have Chester come find you when Busby is ready to leave."

"Did I hear my name?" asked Nigel, striding up to us and looking very much the part in his red and black Beefeater's uniform. He and Olivia exchanged a few pleasantries before she left us, her heels clicking at a rapid pace across the cobblestones, and I couldn't help but smirk at the fact that no one had questioned why a maintenance worker would show up to a job in high-heeled shoes. Or why she no longer carried her bag of tools.

"Come on," Nigel said, hooking his arm in mine. "There's someone who wants to see you."

CHAPTER THIRTY
AVIAN AL CAPONE

"Olivia said to ask about your tours," I said to Nigel as we walked off. "You're doing well, I take it?"

"I most certainly am. Passed my test with flying colors, thanks to you. And the tours," he gushed, "you really ought to stick around for one."

"Don't they go every hour?" I asked, unsure how long Mr T and Olivia would need for their meeting.

"Not these tours," Nigel said as we passed by Lanthorn Tower — one of the round towers that made up the inner wall within the Tower of London complex. "They take place after closing."

This was news indeed. Nigel, a newbie amongst the ranks, leading specialty, after-hours tours? A small sense of pride of being part of his success filled me.

"What's so special about them?"

"They're ghost tours," Nigel said proudly. "Word's really gotten around about them, and I'm booked almost every night."

"Well, there's certainly enough to talk about. All the history here, murdered princes, beheaded queens, tortured traitors. I heard one passage was the most haunted in—"

"No, no, you misunderstand. Not tours *about* ghosts. Tours *for* ghosts. As in, I lead ghosts around the Tower at night and tell them all sorts of interesting facts. Tried doing them during the day, but it's very disconcerting when someone jabs a selfie stick straight through one of your tour members."

"I can imagine."

"Quite. So we switched to night tours, and I simply can't believe their popularity. I've made all manner of new friends. Of course, I get loads of locals glad for something to do — believe me, being dead can be rather boring. I've even made great friends with a ghost couple from Cirencester who say they knew my great-grandfather when he was a teenager."

A couple summers ago, I got sucked into a cozy mystery series set in the Cotswolds, so I knew right where Cirencester was. It made me wonder how Mr Wood was enjoying his trek. And if there'd be a bacon shortage in England by the time he caught his flight home.

"Sounds terrific," I told him as we turned onto a quieter area of the Tower's grounds.

"Oh, it is. And I'm proving quite the international sensation. Just last night I had a ghost all the way from Australia who'd heard of me from his friend in South Africa who'd been recommended to me by a ghost in Canada.

"My previous experience… well, I guess it's given me some special skills at seeing and interacting with our ethereal guests. Here he is," Nigel announced when we reached the raven enclosure. "Usually prefers hanging out with me, but those tetchy tourists back there annoyed him. Winston, come say hello."

Winston, once dead and now officially one of the living and breathing Tower ravens, was the cleverest bird I've ever met and had proved to be quite the ally when I'd gotten tangled up in the whole Mauvais business last spring.

He now appeared to be ruling the roost of the raven enclosure, because as we stood there, another raven swooped in, did what looked like the avian version of a bow, then presented Winston with a purple key ring featuring a glittery crown.

"Quite the lord of the manor," I commented, as Winston hopped out of the cage and onto my shoulder. The weight of him surprised me, and I ran my fingers along his smooth head.

"More like a gang leader. Way things are going, I might have to change his name to Al Capone." I gave him a questioning look. "That key ring's likely a stolen object. Started with just him stealing the items, and he got rather good at it. So much so, he ended up teaching his roommates a thing or two. Now he kicks back while the other ravens target unsuspecting tourists.

"Minute people leave the gift shop with anything that gleams or sparkles, one of his scouts starts following. That person leaves their bag of goodies unattended for more than ten seconds, and the bird snatches up what's inside more quickly than a Dickensian pickpocket. I've yet to figure out how they manage it without the person noticing. Key rings seem to be a particular favorite, but one time a pair of his minions somehow managed a snow globe.

"It's not to say he's all bad," Nigel rambled on. "He is good at finding things. I've even set up a Lost and Found service. Well, mostly just found things that Winston has stolen, but he has managed to find car and house keys people have misplaced, and even an engagement ring when one fellow's nerves got the better of him and he fumbled the ring right down a crack in the stonework halfway through his proposal. Still, I do worry what trouble he might get up to if he ever finds his way into the Jewel House."

I could just imagine the virality of a social media post featuring a raven sporting an emerald necklace he'd just pilfered. This image quickly morphed into Winston using his criminal ways to lead me to Matilda's jewel.

"I might have to hire him," I said. "Then I'd have two bird-brained assistants."

"Pardon?"

"Nothing. Just daydreaming."

Nigel asked what I'd been up to since we'd last met, and I was about to tell him about the agency when a slim, dark-haired woman with a triangular, elfin face approached us.

And I say *approached*, rather than *walked*, not to avoid repeating bland verbs, but because her feet didn't touch the ground. She glided, but with a bounce to her step that gave the impression of walking, like an old habit that wouldn't die.

"Good afternoon, Nigel," she said in a pleasingly soft voice with a slight Eastern European accent.

"Hello, Tilia. You're rather early for tonight's tour, but never mind that. I'd like you to meet my friend, Cassie Black."

Tilia's dark eyes fixed on me with a hot flicker of jealousy.

"Just friends," I said, and the flicker cooled to relief as she offered a shy smile.

"I stop by to see if I could help. See if you need a little—" And here, she let out a haunting call that sent shivers along my spine and made the ravens hunker low into their wing feathers.

Tilia, I guessed, must provide a spooky soundtrack to Nigel's daytime tours. Nigel had once done this for the other Yeoman Warders. It lent a ghostly presence to the spine-tingling stories the tourists craved. Now, it would seem, Nigel was carrying on the tradition, with someone else cast in his former role.

"Maybe tomorrow," Nigel said, pointing to the cloudless sky. "You know sunny days don't work as well for that sort of thing." Tilia's shoulders sagged in disappointment. "But heavy cloud cover is predicted for tomorrow."

Tilia perked up. "I will be there when you are needing me. For now, I will be seeing you tonight."

"Tilia, before you go," I asked, curious about the accent, and why an Eastern European ghost would be haunting the Tower of London, "where are you from?"

"Originally from Wallachia, but I die here," she asserted, pointing emphatically to the ground as if I was challenging her right to be there. "I am a citizen ghost of the land of England for many, *many* centuries now."

"That's great. I didn't—" Before I could explain that I wasn't accusing her of any illegal afterlife immigration, she nodded sharply, then dissipated. Winston clacked his beak as if in farewell. "What was that about?" I asked.

"She had trouble in her homeland and was lucky to make it here. She faced plenty of discrimination during her time in England, but you automatically become a citizen of whatever country you die in, and she takes that seriously. Still, any question of her past or her loyalties makes her a little defensive."

"I noticed. I also noticed how she looked at you."

"Looked?" Nigel blustered. "No, she's far too young for me."

"Nigel, you just heard her. She's hundreds of years old. You're a spring chicken compared to her."

Nigel then did something he'd never have been capable of a few months ago. He blushed.

As we strolled around the Tower's grounds, Nigel and I caught up a bit more. Tourists were just beginning to thin out for the day when Nigel looked around confusedly and twitched his head like someone who's heard the whine of a mosquito and is trying to spot it before it bites them. His face then brightened with comprehension and he touched his fingers to his ear.

"Still can't get used to these ear pieces," he said with a grin. "The buzzing of an incoming message discombobulates me every time." He then gave one quick tap on his ear. "Nigel speaking. Yes. Of course. I'll tell her." He tapped his ear again, then told me, "Olivia says Chester's on his way if you'd like to go meet him outside the White Tower. But promise me you'll come back some evening for one of my tours. You'll just love meeting everyone."

I told him I would, realizing that — with Alastair being little more than a silent non-presence in my life these days — a gaggle of ghosts would be the liveliest company I'd hung out with in several days.

I was nearly to the White Tower when someone called, "Just a moment, Miss Black."

The voice stopped me in my tracks. Then made me want to run straight into the Thames to escape its owner.

"Wordsworth," I said, forcing myself to smile as I turned to face him.

If you knew he wasn't human, the facial features that were a bit too flat and his wormy shape stood out like a giraffe in a herd of pygmy goats. But in a long trench coat, thick, round glasses, and a turtleneck sweater, Wordsworth could pass for a short, stocky, somewhat eccentric person who was adamantly opposed to summer attire.

"Have you gotten anywhere with my book?" he demanded.

"I had a lead, but it didn't exactly pan out."

"Well, I suggest you move on it ASAP. Supposedly the copy at the British Library has burned. Why no one ever informed me a copy was there is beyond my comprehension, but this conflagration could mean something."

"Something?"

Besides my horrible luck?

"That someone looking to do evil is after it. Enchantments were put on it, of course."

Normally, I wouldn't engage Wordsworth in conversation, but as I was really curious to know as much as I could about why the book had gone up in flames, I asked, "What kind of enchantments?"

"Oh, the usual protection charms." He fluttered his hand as if it were hardly worth his time to answer such a mundane question. "Likely one that sensed nefarious objects were in its presence. I can't be certain, since, as I said, no one ever bothered to tell me it was there, but with some of the troubling spells in that book, several layers of protection charms would have been appropriate."

Morelli had said something similar. Which made me wonder what was so horrible about me that would trigger these protection charms. Or maybe I was jumping to self-pitying conclusions. Perhaps the book contained a magical remedy for cat allergies, so it reacted badly when it detected the hundreds of strands of Pablo fur on my clothes.

Wordsworth then let out a heavy sigh, before saying, "If only I could recall where that third copy is. It really should be in my annals of books, but my predecessor— Well, we don't talk about him. An embarrassment to the Bookworm species. Did you know he actually thought we should slim down the collection?" A shudder rippled across Wordsworth's torso.

"Then are you absolutely sure you don't have it? If this predecessor was such a bad record keeper—?"

"*He* may have been, but I know my collection very well. Even the shifting books."

With Wordsworth's odd manner of speech, I thought he said *shitty* books, and couldn't imagine him keeping any distasteful tomes in his precious collection.

"Why are they so bad?"

"They're not bad, per se. Shifting books—" realization struck me as my ears finally caught the word as *shifting*, not *shitty* "—are terribly difficult to classify. Where do you place a historical novel that one day decides to be a gardening guide, or a book on flying cat care that, on a whim, morphs into a three-headed dog training manual? What am I supposed to do about numbering, categorizing, and shelving those?

"I tell you, they are the only books I feel should be banned. At least from my library, anyway. But you've distracted me, allowed me to climb on my soapbox, tried to divert me from the topic at hand." Actually, by now I'd forgotten what the topic at hand was. "When will you look for my book?"

"I'm heading back now," I said vaguely.

"Very good. Don't think that just because Olivia gave you an extension that I'm not in a rush to get my collection back to its proper state. If the Bookworm Board of Directors came by now—" he shook his head as if chastising himself "—the shame would wither me worse than that time my cousin sprawled out on hot pavement during an August heatwave."

And with that, without a goodbye or a tip of his head, he gave a sharp tug on his coat's belt, pushed up his glasses, and waddled off. On his way, he cursed everyone he encountered for not making more productive use of their time, telling them they should be *reading* about history, not standing around staring at it.

Just as Wordsworth waddled away, Chester came jogging up to me.

"Come to collect me?" I asked.

"Yep. And," Chester said as he began scraping his shoes against the ground, "Olivia told me it was time to clean my boots. Doesn't like me bringing... um, *stuff*, into her office."

Yes, I could imagine how tracking in rat guts might ruin the room's aesthetic.

Chester gave one more hearty swipe with each foot and seemed satisfied with a job well done.

"How's the mood up there, by the way?" I asked when we'd reached the door to the White Tower that only Magics can see and access.

"Sir Olivia seems fine. And Mr Sir Tenpenny is…" Chester paused, trying to restrain a grin and failing. "Well, he's very giggly."

Busby Tenpenny giggly? This I had to see.

CHAPTER THIRTY-ONE
A TIPSY TENPENNY

Chester led me up to Olivia's office, where Olivia and Busby were seated on opposite sides of Olivia's sleek desk. A tall glass stood empty in front of Olivia, and I assumed it had once contained the gin and tonic she'd ordered. Her cheeks had darkened with boozy warmth, but she was speaking with perfect clarity to Mr T when Chester and I entered.

Busby, on the other hand, was indeed giggling stupidly at everything she said, and — *gasp!* — his pocket square was askew, its tiny corgis turned every which way. He inexplicably snorted a laugh when Olivia greeted me, thanked Chester, and invited me to take a seat.

"I just got off the phone with my contact from the British Library," she said, then ran her finger up the empty glass. It refilled, and I caught the medicinally floral scent of whatever she was drinking.

"And how did that go?" I asked, despite the knot in my belly.

"It was interesting."

Mr Tenpenny repeated the word with a mocking snicker as he tapped the small shot glass in front of him. It started to refill, but Olivia arched an eyebrow at him, snapped her fingers, and the glass vanished just as Mr T tried to grab it. Undaunted, he tried a few more times, clutching at nothing but air.

"Is he going to be okay?" I asked.

"He only had two drinks, so I doubt there'll be any long-term damage." She was kidding, right? "Anyway, long story short, my contact said the techs can't find any footage of the area where the fire was located."

"Can't find it? As in, someone lost it?"

"Sorry, I misspoke. No, Busby." She swatted at Mr T's hand. He'd been crawling his fingers across the desk toward Olivia's drink. "You've had enough." Olivia returned her attention to me as Mr T slumped back in his chair and sulked. "There is footage, but it's completely blank, just a black screen during the time of the fire. Which is concerning."

"Yes, it is," I said gravely, trying to seem very concerned indeed. "Why is it, exactly?"

"Because it means a Magic was in there. You see, only someone with magic can access that section of the storage facilities. This is troubling because we think—" She paused abruptly, like someone catching themselves before saying too much. She drummed her fingers on the file folder in front of her a moment, then said, "No, I think this is something you should be let in on." And the way she said this made me want to be kept completely in the dark. Ignorance is bliss, and all that. "We think, if there truly is an uprising on the way, that a Magic, a human Magic, might be helping the vampires."

"In what way?"

"I'm not sure exactly, but if one of our own tried to burn down that section of the Library, it stirs up numerous possibilities. Unfortunately, the smell of smoke has obliterated any of the Magic's scent, so it's proving tough to trace. I don't know what made me ask — perhaps it was intuition — but I had my contact check to see if a copy of *The British Wizard's Guide to Magical Creatures, Untoward Spells, and Enchanted Objects of the*

Tudor and Stuart Eras was in that collection."

"Was it?" I asked. Luckily, whatever had been in his drink wasn't your average gin, because otherwise I'm sure Busby would have picked up on the feigned innocence I'd forced into the question.

"I'm afraid so. And it was located in the section where the fire started. In fact, it was only that book that was burnt."

"No!" I exclaimed, in what I thought was a pretty good bit of acting, especially when you're acting in front of an audience that was slightly sloshy and whose BS-spotting senses weren't quite up to snuff.

"Yes. Which means someone else is after the book. And that, I'm sorry to say, adds a new layer of pressure to your finding that third copy. Our only hope right now is that whoever stole Wordsworth's copy and took those two pages did so to safeguard them. But I have to say, it's a rather slim hope."

Mr T was now swaying in his seat and grinning at the ceiling as he waved his pocket square back and forth like a tiny flag for the Corgi Republic.

Personally, whether they were Norm, Magic, vampire, or pixie, I doubted that whoever had taken the book and removed the pages had done so for the public good. But, since I didn't want to throw my messy pessimism all over Olivia's office, I stood up and said, "I really should get back to detecting, then. Ticking time clock, right?"

Olivia flinched at this, her eyes appraising me as if I'd said something I shouldn't have. She then shook it off and asked if I wanted help with Busby, who protested that he could manage just fine, and that he didn't feel one bit 'sozzled.'

The use of such a word being clear proof that he was well and truly sozzled.

The Unbearable Inspector Oberlin

* * *

To ensure Busby didn't brain himself if he tumbled down any of the many stairs on our way back to the portal, Olivia had worked a Marshmallow Charm at the bottom of each landing. Surprisingly, Busby made it down without one faulty step, although I did have to stop him from trying to eat a chunk of the landing at the bottom of the final stairwell.

"Find anything of interest with your… shtuff?" Busby asked as we walked to the portal. Okay, I walked, he staggered.

"I'm not sure." At the portal, while waiting for it to open, Mr T kept swaying. Eventually, he placed his palm against the wall for support. "What were you drinking?"

"Gin and tonic, with a lime twisht."

"And how many of these did you have?"

"Just the two." He indicated the size of his drink with his index finger and thumb, matching the size of the small shot glass I'd seen in front of him on Olivia's desk.

"I didn't know you were such a lightweight."

"Not yoush— yoush— Not usually." He smiled broadly at finally getting the word out. "But that's the thing when you're drinking with a person with banshee blood. They need strong boobs. No, wait, strong *booze*. That's it. Really shtrong. Banshee booze. Crazy stuff. Probably should've just stuck to the one."

Or none at all.

"Wait," I said, grabbing his arm and pulling him back from the portal entry. "You're sure this is okay? I mean, is there any danger of you operating a portal while drunk?"

"Should be fine." Which sounded exactly like the sort of thing you'd hear someone say when you're about to try cliff diving for the first time. "Also, this particular portal only goes to Rosaria. No side branches. Otherwise…" He made a whistling sound while zigging and zagging his hand around like a plane that's just had one wing shot off by the enemy.

Which, as you might guess, did not reassure me one bit.

CHAPTER THIRTY-TWO
INCOMING MESSAGES

Thankfully, Busby was right and his drunkenness had no effect on our journey, but I still thought it best to get him somewhere he'd have someone to look after him until he sobered up.

As we walked away from Lola's street — where Bunny was doing his best to kill a set of cymbals, from the sound of it — Mr Tenpenny sloshingly said, "You know why she's worried, don't you?"

"Who? Lola?"

"No. Olivia. Duh."

Yes, he really said *duh*, which tells you just how far gone he was. And which put me on high alert.

"This isn't going to break any Confidentiality Spells, is it?" I asked warningly. If he spilled the beans on something he shouldn't and ended up having his magic extracted as punishment, I did not want anything to do with it. I mean, just think of what the *Herald* would say if I broke Super Special Agent Busby Tenpenny. Or whatever his exact job title was.

"No, no, just research shtuff. It turns out, the Vampire Tolerance Act has a deadline. Who knew, right? After that, they can do what they want." I considered Olivia's tense reaction when I'd jokingly mentioned the ticking time clock, and her querying look to Fiona when she'd set the new deadline for my license application.

I would have given this deeper thought, but Mr Tenpenny was still babbling, " 'pparently, the signees wanted the act to be revisited at a future date. See how thingsh were going. But it could also mean the vamps can do what they want when that deadline—" he paused mid-sentence to twirl his pocket square "—rollsh around."

"And this deadline is when?"

Mr T counted on his fingers. Well, okay, he tapped his left index finger over the fingers of his right hand several times. So he was either counting, or he was coming up with a new drum beat for Bunny.

"Ten daysh."

"And then all vampire hell breaks loose?"

It sounded too silly to believe. After all, if you're going to stage a coup, you don't exactly set it down in your day planner. At least I don't think you do. Perhaps there was a *Coup Staging for Dummies* book I could consult.

Still, if Olivia's research was showing a connection between the vampires, the end of the Tolerance Act, and all these missing Magics, who was I to second guess her?

"Dunno. Maybe. Maybe not. But there's some signs— Hey, I know this door!" Because by now we'd climbed the steps to Fiona's porch and were standing on her welcome mat. Busby began flapping his pocket square at the knob as if the fluttering corgis might be able to turn it. I rang the bell.

Fiona opened the door to see her husband draped over my shoulder, his pocket square now tucked into the collar of his shirt like a bib at a lobster restaurant.

"What have I married?" she asked with an indulgent shake of the head.

"Someone who can't handle his banshee booze."

"Ah, you've been to see Olivia. Bring him in. I have just what he needs."

"A hangover prevention potion?"

"No, just a large glass of juice, an aspirin, and a bed." Mr T burped wetly. "And perhaps a bucket. Upstairs with him."

Just then, Busby slumped, his head dropped onto my shoulder, and he let out a loud snore.

"Could you...?" I grunted under Busby's drunken weight.

"Yes, sorry I forgot." Fiona flourished her hand, placing a Lighten the Load Spell on Mr T, making it more like supporting a floppy pillow than a full-grown man.

Once she'd gotten Mr T settled, Fiona, saying she had a break between classes, made us tea and a large plate of cookies that we enjoyed in her book-filled living room.

"Now, tell me," Fiona began, her voice brokering no argument, "are you doing okay? And please don't play off the question, because your cases have me worried. I know you can attract trouble without even trying, but with Clive, Winnifred, and then you yourself being attacked, I can't help but be anxious for you. Especially after Tobey told me about the break-in at the agency."

"I think I'm okay, really. It's the *Herald*'s articles causing me more angst than anything else."

"Yes, well, it seems the editor is getting a taste of his own medicine after that piece defending the RetroHex Vaccine he published in yesterday's afternoon edition. Several Inconvenience Curses have been put on him, and he's been suffering under a Leftie-Rightie Curse for at least a week now. I even heard someone put a Marshmallow Charm on his entire house. The walls are absolutely sagging in this summer heat."

I couldn't muster any sympathy, so I nibbled a piece of shortbread instead.

"Before I forget," Fiona said. "Tobey mentioned something about test booklets." I explained to her my idea to beef up Tobey's muscle memory with real test books when we had our next study session. "That's an excellent idea, and I had a feeling that was your plan. I have no idea why he kept them after all these years, but I managed to find a few in one of Busby's boxes."

She got up and collected a stack of five booklets from the drawer in a side table. Handing them to me, she said, "They resisted the Duplex Spell at first, but I finally convinced them I was only using them for practice."

I thanked her, and we chatted about Tobey's test phobia and how he'd do on his second stab at the Exams in a couple days. Then Fiona asked how things had gone at HQ.

Wanting to avoid bringing up anything about Olivia's conversation with her contact at the British Library, I gave Fiona the latest news on my two no-longer-dead friends. "Nigel's really become a hit, and I might have to hire Winston since he seems to be better at finding things than I am."

"I'm sure that's not true," Fiona said, then took a sip of her tea. "What exactly prompted you to go?"

"I thought I might luck out and find Matilda's jewel amongst the Crown Jewels."

"I take it you didn't?"

"No, but I did see a set Olivia called the friendship rings. Split from one—"

"—jewel to make several," Fiona said, her face lighting up. "Yes, I've heard of those. They don't usually have them on display, so that was a lucky sighting."

"Olivia said making them was a rare skill. That a Magic had

to have done the work." Even as I said this I again got that tingling in my brain, but I couldn't exactly sprawl out on Fiona's sofa in the middle of our conversation to have a proper think, so I pushed it aside once more.

"Yes," Fiona said, piling several more cookies onto my plate. "It used to be a more common skill since some objects can be imbued with certain powers. The object is then divided into parts to prevent others from detecting these powers."

"Who do you mean by *others*?"

"Anyone, really. I might be overthinking things, but in my experience, if something's been imbued with power, it's rarely of the good kind. Dividing it, splitting it, would likely weaken the item or render it inert. But brought together again..."

"The object regains its power?" I said, filling in the gap she'd clearly left open for me.

"And supposedly increases it," she added with a dubious grin. "But that could also be nothing more than a craftsman's sales pitch."

Fiona had just lifted her teacup to her lips when the sounds of teenage chatter bounded up from the ground-floor classroom.

"It's time for the sophomores," she said with a heavy sigh before throwing back the rest of her tea. "There never seems to be a long enough gap between their classes." I started to get up, assuming she'd want me to leave, but she said, "No, no, eat your treats. I need to gather up a few things. They've got a practical quiz on Assist Spells, and I honestly don't know if they're ready."

As Fiona bustled around gathering up some test sheets and what looked like a random assortment of nicknacks, I did as she said and ate my cookies. But the mention of Assist Spells — spells that only worked when recited over an object — had shoved Mayor Matilda Marheart to the forefront of my mind.

Matilda had a pressing need to find a jewel she'd never even seen before. Matilda had also, according to Sebastian's footage, taken temporary ownership of Wordsworth's book — a book of troublesome spells from which two pages had been removed.

What was the spell hidden in those missing pages? Was it to ensure every unwanted kitten had a good home, or was it to bring the world under her thumb? My guess was the latter, given how things seemed to play out ever since I'd come to MagicLand.

So, if Matilda had taken the pages, and if I brought her this jewel...

Before I could think much further, my phone pinged a message, then another and another. All from Alastair, and all from the time I'd been at the Tower. I'd had issues with my phone acting up in MagicLand and especially at HQ in the past. I thought the problem had been fixed, but apparently my phone, like my magic, had a mind of its own.

The reasonable part of me wanted to immediately check the messages. The bitter and petulant side of me wanted to delete them without reading a single word.

But reason prevailed and I opened my message app.

I really should have listened to the bitter and petulant side.

CHAPTER THIRTY-THREE
LOVE LETTERS

The first text from Alastair was the exact type of cheery, loving greeting you'd expect from your significant other. If your significant other had suddenly changed into a cat-hating twat, that is.

I told you to keep Pablo in his carrier!!!

Following this was a message from Tobey saying he'd come by when he was done at the Academy for the day to see if I had time for a study session, and not to bother replying because he'd be in classes and would have his phone off.

Alastair's next love-filled missive had been sent three minutes after his first:

Workroom is a mess. Nothing missing. Stuff broken. Commission thankfully hidden from that feline terror.

Then, of course, was the usual thing you type when someone isn't replying to your testy texts:

Hello???!!! Are you reading these?

Finally, there was this, sent just moments ago:

I've made an appointment for Runa to check Pablo over. Be there @ 5pm. Call her if you can't make it.

Some of the fury steaming in me must have escaped through my ears, because Fiona asked, "Bad news?"

"Just Alastair being a jerk."

"He hasn't spoken to you yet?"

"Speak to me? Hardly," I scoffed, then told her about Pablo, about Alastair's ban on him being loose in the apartment, and about the tension between us the past few days — why did it feel like weeks? "And now he thinks Pablo has done something to the workroom. Pablo wasn't even in the apartment. I dropped the carrier off at the agency this morning."

Fiona looked up from the box she was loading her test supplies into, her brows knitted together. Not in anger — although she did agree that Alastair was being overly sensitive, and I wished I could have gotten that in writing — but in the way of someone with an idea that just won't coalesce. A feeling I knew all too well lately.

"What is it?" I asked.

"Nothing." She fluttered her hand as if waving off the question. "No, not nothing. The workroom. If Pablo wasn't at home, it sounds as if someone broke into it and was looking for something."

I thought about yesterday's break-in at the agency and knew Fiona was right. But since Fiona was already fretting over me, I thought it best to play off this double dose of attempted burglary.

"It's probably just Alastair overreacting to Morelli leaving some yarn in the wrong place. That room's got protections up the wazoo, and Morelli has garden gnomes on duty twenty-four seven. And did Alastair even bother to check if Pablo was home? Or does he think Pablo has a portal into the workroom from his cat carrier?"

"It does seem a bit of overkill. Still, you'll take Pablo to Runa? Since the appointment's already made, that is?"

"Might as well. I have to do a sample draw anyway."

"Good." Fiona put a Floating Charm on her box, and it hovered next to her. As we headed down the stairs, she said, "Now, feel free to say no, but I'm sure Busby is out for the count, so if you don't have plans, I'm making more than enough for dinner." A loud, very undignified snore sounded from upstairs. "He really ought to know better than to drink banshee booze. Would six be too early?"

Since my stomach would gladly accept a meal at any hour of the day, I told her six would be great. Before she entered the classroom, Fiona said to bring Runa as well if she didn't have other plans. I told her I would, but really hoped that didn't mean Morelli would be tagging along.

As I stepped out onto Fiona's porch, I was tempted to go home and give Alastair a piece of my mind. We really needed to hash out this... well, whatever you called this thing going on between us. But I also wanted to go into that conversation (okay, argument) backed by the doctor-approved information that Pablo was a perfectly healthy cat with no evil intentions toward Alastair or his precious gears and bolts and doodads. I stared at the portal to my apartment a moment longer, practically daring Alastair to come out and face me.

Unfortunately, it would appear I couldn't summon people with the force of my will, so I made a rude gesture at the door, then turned on my heel and went back to work, where I found Daisy at her desk, coating her nails with a bright pink polish and reading *The Rosaria Book of Statutes*.

"I thought I should familiarize myself with the rules and laws and all that. It's *so* fascinating," she said, without a hint of sarcasm, like she was reading the latest edge-of-your-seat thriller.

"Maybe you should be the one helping Tobey with his test," I told her, as I placed all but one of the test booklets from Fiona in my desk drawer.

"No, he gets upset when I know more than he does. I thought of dumbing down my responses at the Wandering Wizard's Trivia Night to make him feel better, but then I thought, why? If he can't handle a girl being smarter than him, then he's just a big poopy head."

I hate to admit it, but there are those rare few moments when I actually like Daisy.

"Speaking of the poopy head," I said, "Tobey's coming by after class to study. If you want to make use of your statute knowledge, you could help me come up with some test questions."

"That sounds like so much fun. Oh, and we were going to pop by the Wandering Wizard after work if you want to come along."

I did want to come along. Even if it was with Blondie and Tobey, being amongst people who actually spoke to me would be a nice change. A stabbing ache of longing for a chat with my parents hit me. And, if I'm being honest, for one with Alastair as well.

"I can't," I told her, my jaw clenching with irritation. "I've got an appointment, or well, Pablo does. Where is he, anyway?" I asked, suddenly worried that maybe I *had* left Pablo at home today, that he had indeed gotten into and made a mess of the workroom, and that I would have to dish myself up a large piece of humble pie.

"Went in his cage about an hour ago and hasn't been out since."

With a huge sense of relief, I mentally tipped my slice of humble pie into the bin.

As we were working on Tobey's test questions, Daisy said, "So I was thinking—" first time for everything, I supposed "—about that jewel you're looking for. And then I got to thinking about the things from your cases."

Two thoughts in one day? And she didn't blow a brain gasket?

"And you thought what, exactly?"

"Okay, so," she began, her eyes twinkling as she twirled her poof-topped pen, "there's Matilda's jewel, there's your mom's pendant, and then there's Mrs Oberlin's brooch. All those contain red jewels."

"So we're completely disregarding the diamonds and emeralds on Mrs O's brooch, Lola's vacuum, Clive's bag of marbles, Runa's missing saw and samples, and Wordsworth's book?"

"Okay, I know. Cherry-picking data, blah blah blah. But a trio of red jewels…? And three's such a powerful number, it just started nagging me. Anyway, I just wanted to get that out of my head."

Why? Was it crowding out all the air in there?

"It's probably just a dumb idea," she added in that way of someone looking for you to contradict them. I didn't.

Still, as much as I wanted to dismiss her thoughts, they fit too well with some of the disconnected ideas that had been flitting through my own head, both at the Jewel House and in Olivia's office.

As Daisy said, it was cherry-picking facts while ignoring others. But with what Sebastian had sent me, what Corrine had told me, and what I'd observed myself, there was a definite connection between Matilda's and Wordsworth's cases. And very likely my other cases as well.

Daisy and I had just jotted down one final legal-based brain teaser when Tobey showed up. After much cooing and sweet nothings that made me want to gag, I handed Tobey his test booklet. To no one's surprise, Tobey nailed it. He missed a couple questions, but still managed a score that would have him at the top of the class if it had been a real test.

"Feeling confident?" I asked while surreptitiously sniffing my cousin. He still smelled of nothing but his own magic. Could Oberlin be holding on to my samples to dose Tobey up on Exam day?

"Better, yeah. This," Tobey tapped the booklet in front of him, "is a big help. I think I might actually pull it off this time."

"Any quizzes lately?" On one hand, I hoped there had been so Tobey could prove to himself that he could handle a test. But on the other hand, I hoped he hadn't because, if he screwed up, it would demolish Tobey's confidence tree that I'd gotten to sprout so nicely.

"Nope. No tests. He's been busy with the missing Magics stuff, so he hasn't had time to do much more beyond his planned lectures. Which is a relief, I'll admit. We're still on for another of these right before my Exams, right? Please say yes. I'll bribe you with a box of whatever you want from Divination Donuts. The baker's dozen box, perhaps..." he added enticingly.

I was going to work with him anyway, but if he was going to supply me with free dough bombs of my choosing, I wasn't going to argue.

Soon after we'd set up a time for what I hoped would be our final study session, the toy flower on Daisy's desk began singing a song about the work day being done as it shimmied a little dance. Tobey thanked me for the help, and once Daisy tidied up her already tidy desk, the two of them headed out for their evening of being a disgustingly perfect couple. Meanwhile, I had to take my cat to the doctor because my boyfriend thought the creature had it in for him.

I peered in to double-check that Pablo was inside his carrier. He was. Flopped on his side in a beam of sunlight. Yeah, real menace to society there. I latched the cage's door and headed to Runa's.

CHAPTER THIRTY-FOUR
ALWAYS TRUST THE CAT

Since Morelli felt confident that I wasn't at risk of kidnapping or killing Dr Dunwiddle, once I'd waited the three minutes and twenty-four seconds for my exact appointment time to arrive, I was allowed to go into the exam room on my own.

"The partnership going any better?" I asked when Runa closed the exam room door and blew out a sigh of annoyance.

"The best it's been was when he took a two-hour lunch break today. I know it's rude of me to say, he's just following orders from HQ, but I was almost hoping he wasn't coming back."

"He's not really that bad, is he? Overbearing sure, but..."

"Oh, he knows what he's doing, that's for sure. But there's in-the-field care and there's in-clinic care. A patch-up job versus a more comprehensive job. He fails to see that not everything is just a matter of clamping his meaty paws over a troubled body part. Trolls." She shook her head in exasperation. "Then there's this hullabaloo over the RetroHex Vaccine."

I recalled the flyers being pasted up around MagicLand, and even on Runa's own door, criticizing the vaccine and warning of its dangers. There'd even been reports of anti-RetroHexVaxxers harassing people waiting for their annual jabs. Still, it had been days since I'd seen any of the placards around town.

"But I thought things had quieted down?"

"They had somewhat. But with the attacks in Seattle—"

"Wait, what attacks?"

"Don't you read the *Seattle Supernatural Gazette*?" I shook my head. "Well, you should. It's better reporting than the *Herald*. That thing's little more than advertising and gossip these days. Leo's really let those hyperbolic journalists of his go too far. Anyway, the Seattle community was hit hard last night. I think the article said something like sixty percent of the Magics went missing in one fell swoop."

My gut lurched. I didn't know anyone from the Seattle community, but at a mere three-hour drive to the north of Portland, that was hitting a little too close to home for my comfort. Runa might not have appreciated Morelli at that exact moment, but I was suddenly glad for all the protective hexes he had around the apartment building.

"But what's Seattle have to do with the RetroHex Vaccine?"

Runa snatched a sheet off the side counter, held it out for me, then slapped it into my hand when I reached out to take it.

Along with pictures of people who appeared to have fainted, who were struggling to hold on to their bags of groceries, and who were slumped over with fatigue, the notice had a string of tightly packed text.

> *Dear citizens of Rosaria, this is what happens when we trust certain people with our magical health. Weakness. Not just physically, but magically. Is it any coincidence that the Seattle community has been nearly wiped out when they are also the community with one of the highest uptakes of the RetroHex Vaccine? No, it is not.*

Actually, it *was* coincidence, but I doubted the flyer writer would listen to my lecture on causation versus correlation.

> *The vaccine has left our friends, our families, our fellow Magics in Seattle too feeble to defend themselves. I only hope that you took my advice and were not tricked into getting your shot this year. The only reason they want you to have it is to weaken you, to allow you to be made unable to defend yourselves.*
>
> *And if you did take the shot, please stay close to someone who has remained pure. Allow them to protect you, because you won't be able to protect yourself when this wave of terror strikes Rosaria!*

"Bit dramatic, isn't it?" I asked. "If it wasn't so mind-boggling ridiculous, it'd be hilarious." Runa gave a dismissive nod of agreement. I scanned the flyer again. "The wording sounds a lot like my friend at the *Herald*. The 'dear citizens of Rosaria' thing, the over-the-top absurdity. Inspector Oberlin get his shot this year?" I asked casually.

"You think he's the author of those things?" Runa scoffed, then pensively said, "I suppose he could have magicked a pen to interpret his ranting more eloquently."

"So…" I prodded, "did he get his vaccine?"

"Can't say. The Academy has their own clinics for most routine health stuff. He'd have had it done there."

I passed the flyer back to Runa, saying, "Did that make it into the *Herald*?"

"Actually, no. Leo Flourish wrote a special report for the front page. Sympathizing with the Seattle community, but also defending the RetroHex Vaccine. It's quite a bold stance since he's always allowed negative opinion pieces about the shots into the paper. I guess even he has his limits when theories get this ludicrous."

Runa wadded up the flyer and lobbed it into a wastebasket. She then snapped her fingers and a blue flame burst from the bin, dying out as quickly as it had started.

"Still," she went on with a heavy sigh, "I've no doubt that flyer is going to lead to a string of people coming in here to complain about mystery symptoms, blaming them all on the vaccine. Almost makes me glad I've got Morelli out there — don't tell him that, of course. I'm hoping he'll turn the lot of them away. Or scare them off. Either would suit me."

Dr Dunwiddle then jutted her chin toward Pablo's cage. "And now it appears I'm supposed to play veterinarian. Alastair does know Dr Doolally is Rosaria's vet, right?" I shrugged. I honestly didn't know what was going through Alastair's head these days. "If he hadn't been so concerned, I wouldn't have taken this appointment."

"You don't have to take it if you don't want to. He's perfectly fine," I said, as Runa peered through the wire grating of the carrier's door.

"He does look content. Where'd you get this thing, anyway?"

"Mr Tenpenny did it."

"Thought I recognized his expansion work. You should have seen his house when he first moved in. Started out as a seven hundred-square-foot, two-bedroom bungalow. I don't know why he thought he needed such a big place for just him and Tobey, but who am I to judge?"

Runa tapped the carrier three times. The inside changed from Pablo's Dream World to your standard-issue cat carrier. Pablo jerked awake from his nap and let out a mournful cry. "I know, Misery Man. Let's see what's wrong with you."

The instant Dr Dunwiddle unlatched the door, Pablo launched

into her arms and clung to her shoulder for dear life. She extracted his claws from her lab jacket, moved him to the countertop, and began running her hands over his body, palpating the soft areas and stroking the bony ones.

"Do you think this is connected to Gary?" I asked, the thought having just occurred to me. "Morelli's goldfish. Bit him, remember?" Runa smirked and said she did. "Could there be a virus going around? Like magic rabies?"

"No, the RedDwarf Rabies were eradicated before you were born," replied Runa. "Defense, pain, protection, fear, confusion — biting isn't an uncommon response to bad stimuli, even in the gentlest pet. And I can fully understand how Morelli sticking his fingers in where they don't belong could be irksome. Might buy that fish a reward for good service, actually," she muttered, half to herself.

Finished with her poking and prodding, Dr Dunwiddle touched a thermometer to Pablo's ear and, once the reading was ready, said it was normal. Or, at least she thought it was, trying to recall what normal was for a cat. And a peek inside his mouth showed no sign of tooth or throat problems.

"I can do a blood sample, but I'm afraid I'll have to tell Alastair that this cat is perfectly healthy."

"He's not going to like that."

"Maybe Pablo's just jealous of you and Alastair. Or Alastair used a soap the cat didn't like?"

"We use the same soap and shampoo. And Pablo's always liked Alastair up until this recent behavior."

Runa narrowed her eyes at this. "I don't want to say anything bad about Alastair, but, as I've said before, always trust the cat."

"You think there's something up with him?"

"Not necessarily him. Could be someone or something

Alastair's been in contact with."

Suddenly, all the cookies I'd eaten at Fiona's formed into an enormous lead sinker in my belly. Could Pablo be under an evil spell because of me?

If I remembered right, Pablo had nipped at Alastair when I'd had the marbles with me. He'd also growled at the marbles — but then again, they had nearly fallen on him. Still, he had avoided them, and he'd been wary of the safe ever since I'd stashed the brooch and the marbles in it. Were the objects aggravating him in some way? Or was he warning me away from them?

But that made no sense. Pablo had been behaving oddly and Gary had bitten Morelli well before Mr Coppersmith had hired me.

Also, the brooch and the marbles had been locked away in the safe at the agency when Pablo had scratched Alastair. In fact, nearly all of Pablo's 'Alastair attacks' had happened in places where the marbles and brooch had never been. Plus, if the found objects were the source of Pablo's behavior, why had he never attacked me?

Runa threw out some other possibilities that were just as unlikely as the others. Eventually, although I'd run out of ideas, she kept trying, her theories growing more and more far-fetched. When she'd finally run out of medical conjectures, I told her about Fiona's invitation to dinner.

"How can I go with my babysitter?" she complained.

"He can walk you to Fiona's. Then when we're done, we could go next door to my building to fetch him, and he can take you home from there."

"All these missing Magics, and here I've got my very own security troll with me every waking hour. There's others who need guarding more than me. Even if I were at risk, I can handle myself."

"You've told Olivia this?"

"She won't listen. Better safe than sorry, and all that. Why does Fiona want me over? She's not normally one for dinner parties."

"Mr T's sleeping off a bit of day drinking."

Runa arched her eyebrows at that, then she glanced at the clock. "We should probably get going, then. In you get, young man," she said and lifted Pablo to put him in the carrier.

I started to warn her about Pablo's hatred of the thing, how he could fling out his limbs and claws, making it impossible to wrangle him through the door. But at Runa's touch, Pablo went as limp as an overcooked noodle, and she slid him inside gently.

I stared at her. "Did you just melt my cat?"

"No, I'll leave the melting of living creatures to you. Just a little Relaxation Charm I often use on fussy patients." She closed the cage door, then tapped the edge of the carrier three times. Pablo instantly began purring. When I looked inside, the carrier was once again a kitty paradise and Pablo was bounding after an iridescent butterfly.

"Morgana's mammaries, I'd like to join him," Runa grumbled to herself. Then to me, she said, "Let's get a few samples from you while you're here. After which," she added sarcastically, "we can all walk to Fiona's, feeling safe that Morelli is at our side."

CHAPTER THIRTY-FIVE
LEGENDS & CONNECTIONS

Since it felt rude not to, on the walk over we invited Morelli to join us for Fiona's dinner, but he began mumbling something that sounded very much like, "No, going to dinner with… never mind… just dinner. Plans." You could practically feel the heat radiating off his cheeks.

The evening started off awkwardly, mainly because Morelli had insisted on entering Fiona's house and doing a thorough search of the place before telling us to alert him if anything happened.

"*Anything*," he emphasized before leaving.

Soon after, as she was pouring three glasses of pinot grigio, Fiona sneezed. "That was something," she said. "Should we alert him?" Runa and I snorted a laugh, and the tense mood instantly lightened.

"Pascal mentioned that you two went to see Professor Dodding," said Fiona once we'd had our wine and had begun to help her set the table. "He seemed quite excited and couldn't stop going on about finally getting to meet Alvin. It's pretty obvious he enjoyed the meeting, but did you get anything out of it?"

"Besides a chocolate bar the size of my bedroom?" I asked as, from within his carrier, I heard Pablo play-attacking something.

"Besides that, yes."

"He told me a lot about the Boncoeur Jewel, the one Matilda's after. Seems to have quite the legend behind it," I said.

"Really? Did he think it was true, or just a story?"

"Maybe a little of both. You know, started out real, but then morphed into a legend."

"So what did he say?" asked Runa, as she slapped a cloth napkin next to a plate, after having tried and failed to fold it into a swan shape like Fiona had done hers.

I related the story, checking my notepad a few times to make sure I was getting the details right. Although a few of my notes were smeared with chocolate, I believe I managed to recount most of the tale.

"And Dodding thinks whoever owns the jewel would be able to defeat their worst enemy with it?" Runa sneered. Fiona, I noticed, remained rather quiet, occupying herself with fixing the napkin Runa had given up on.

"It was just his idea of what the jewel could be used for."

"But who decides who or what this worst enemy is? And why are you so quiet all the sudden, Fiona?"

"It's just…" she began hesitantly "…Dodding's mention of Matthew Hopkins. It's a bit odd to hear his name come up in that context when it's also come up a few times in my own digging."

"Who's Matthew Hopkins?" I asked.

"He was a witch hunter in the early 1600s. Terrible terrible man. He killed more Magics than I care to think about. Several innocent people, as well. Said it was in the name of a higher power, but I think he was little more than a psychopath." Fiona's cheeks had flushed red with anger. "I know it's not nice of me to say, but I am glad he died young. Now," she said lightly, as if dismissing the subject, "please take a seat, and I'll go get our first course."

"These legends," Runa scoffed as Fiona bustled off to the kitchen. "I bet there was just some cheapskate king who didn't want to pay for some speciality work he'd ordered. And his wife could have died from one of a thousand medieval diseases going around at the time, *not* from some gemstone sucking her magic out of her."

Fiona brought out a bowl of salad large enough to feed three warrens of rabbits, then ducked back into the kitchen to grab some tongs.

"Now, maybe," Runa continued, "just *maybe* that servant girl did steal the jewel. Wouldn't surprise me if this guy was as miserly as he seems. She sells the jewel and it could have reached the English court. But the Boncoeur Jewel could just have easily been any other jewel, and Elizabeth was clever enough to weave an elaborate story around it. Including the whole 'curse my worst enemy' thing."

"I have to agree," said Fiona, finally sitting down with us. She spoke lightly, but there was concern etched across her face. Was it over Mr T? Over how we'd like her cooking? Or was it over the topic at hand? "We Magics do like to spin a tale. Even if the jewel wasn't empowered, Elizabeth I might have feared people would believe it was. Which, in some cases, is a far more dangerous situation. If you look at it that way, it would make sense for her to split it in the hope of diminishing or destroying its power, even if only for show."

Salads eaten, Fiona brought out the main dish. How Busby wasn't woken by the smell of Fiona's homemade gnocchi, served in a butternut sage sauce, was beyond me. And if banshee booze causes you to miss out on such marvelous food, I wanted nothing to do with it. Ever.

"How's the research going?" Runa asked Fiona.

"It seems the more I do, the more convoluted everything gets. I know Olivia wouldn't say so out loud, but it's like she wants me to force the square peg of certain facts into the round hole of what she thinks is going on, and it just doesn't. Almost, but not quite. I'm not speaking ill of her—"

"No, no, don't apologize," Runa said, waving her hand as if dismissing the very notion. "I know she just wants to understand. She wants to see a pattern so she can know what to do next."

"Exactly. And these attacks on the communities, the Norm deaths, they do have similarities to the vampires' previous uprisings, but also not. I just get a little frustrated with trying to figure out what else it could be. Or, if it is the uprising, what they're waiting for. After all, if they're going to strike out, what's the hold up? Sorry, I don't mean to imply that I'm keen for a war, but I simply can't believe they're waiting for the Tolerance Act anniversary. Which is why I keep turning to your cases, Cassie."

"My cases? Why?"

"Call it armchair detecting. Call it procrastinating, but it's a nice diversion from the same tales of vampire lore over and over again. And it's fun making connections even if they are only coincidences."

"I don't do coincidences," Runa stated, then served us all a second helping of the gnocchi.

When we'd gone to HQ so I could grovel for extra time to complete my license application, Fiona had read over my list of clients and the objects they wanted me to find. Even then she seemed to think there was something more to the cases than met the eye.

I hadn't exactly brushed this off, but I was so focused on… well, everything else in my life that I hadn't had much time to let my mind wander over what she might have seen in my cases.

But now, with Daisy pointing out the plethora of red jewels, Matilda's suspicious behavior, and my own nagging thoughts about the friendship rings, I was eager to hear what Fiona had to say.

But instead of telling us her ideas, she asked, "Tell me, Cassie, have you noticed any connections between your cases?"

"Just this afternoon Daisy and I were discussing how the brooch, the pendant, and Matilda's jewel, are all red gemstones. But then there's Lola's vacuum, Wordsworth's book, and Mr Coppersmith's marbles, so it might just be grasping at straws."

"No red marbles?" Fiona prompted.

I thought about the contents of the bag. The array of colors. The swirls and solids that had been mostly blues and greens. But one of those solids had been—

"So, you're really thinking these things are somehow connected?" Runa asked. Fiona, her mouth full of gnocchi, nodded. "To what purpose?"

"Jewel lore," I said. And probably shouldn't have because I'd just taken a large bite of crusty bread.

"Yes, super sleuth, jewelers likely made them," Runa quipped.

I swallowed the lump of bread before speaking. "No. Jewel. Lore. What we were just talking about. Jewels being divided to lessen the original jewel's power. It might just be superstition, but like Fiona said, that wouldn't stop people from doing it, would it?"

"Probably not," Runa commented.

A miserable thought then struck me. "If Matilda's jewel has been divided, that's going to make it a lot harder to find. I'm never going to get my application done," I groaned.

"Well, like we keep saying," said Fiona, "it could all be nothing more than legend and speculation, so let's assume it's still in one piece. I'm sure if you stick to it, you'll be able to find it."

"It would make for a good testimonial on the agency's website, wouldn't it?"

"Not if the jewel is cursed," remarked Runa.

"Wait," I said, lowering my fork. "Do you think there's liability insurance for that?"

"Again," Runa said wryly, "probably not."

As we neared the end of the gnocchi, Fiona mused, "It is interesting, though. There've always been legends around jewels and around the power they contain. I guess it's not difficult to see how people could come to believe something with such beauty, such otherworldly sparkle, might also contain power."

I considered Matilda, her desperation to find her jewel. Did she think it contained power? If so, what did she hope to do with it?

With how defensive Runa was about Matilda, I was wary about mentioning the connections I'd been making between the mayor and pretty much every other case I was involved with.

"Spill it," Runa commanded.

"What?" I asked innocently.

"Whatever's on your mind. You've got that look."

"What look?"

"Abdominal discomfort mixed with the face of a toddler who's just broken Mom's favorite vase."

Fiona examined me and nodded in agreement with Runa's assessment.

"Mayor Marheart," I began cautiously, and saw Runa's face tighten with disapproval. "She's really pushy about me finding the jewel. Which seems weird since she's lived her whole life without it. And, well, I've had other concerns about her, so it kind of makes me wonder why she wants it so bad all the sudden."

Choosing my words very carefully to not annoy Runa, I explained the presence of the mayor being on the scene where the brooch, the marbles, the book, and the pendant had gone missing; her bandaged hand right after the clinic had been broken into; the signature on the pawnshop receipt; and the footage Sebastian had sent.

Even Runa was starting to look less critical (and a touch disappointed) as the evidence stacked up against Mayor Marheart.

"It does make me wonder," Fiona began, "if this jewel truly is a powerful object, does Matilda know what she's after, or is she simply very motivated to acquire a family heirloom?"

"She likely does know," said Mr Tenpenny as he entered the room. "And that's what makes it such a dangerous problem."

CHAPTER THIRTY-SIX
DINNER REVELATIONS

"Busby, what are you doing up?" Fiona scolded.

"More importantly, *should* you be up?" Runa asked with a doctor's critical air as she scanned her patient, who did look rather grey and weathered. Actually, he'd looked healthier as a zombie. "What happened to you?"

"Banshee booze," I said, and Runa nodded knowingly.

"I overheard what you were saying about Mayor Marheart," said Mr T as he took a seat and cut off a hunk of bread from the dwindling loaf. "I believe some of your concerns tie into what HQ has been worried about these past weeks."

"The missing Magics?" I asked.

"That, and more. As has been explained to you, trouble is brewing from a certain sector of the population. HQ fears if we don't contain it, we could be in for tough times, violent times. Worse than what has already begun." Runa scowled, and Mr Tenpenny addressed her when he said, "Nothing should be dismissed at this point. If there is a jewel or any other object that holds power, whether figurative or literal, we need to know why they're after it and what they plan to do with it."

An awkward silence settled over the room, until I blurted, "Mind clarifying that bit of doom and gloom you've just spilled all over the place?"

"Vampires," Runa said, practically spitting the word. "It's the same old prejudice yet again. I remember how it used to be, Busby. You didn't face it over at HQ, where you wouldn't even allow them in, but I was nearly run out of town when I started up my practice. I was one of the few people who saw them trying to better themselves, trying to work *with* us, not against us. But all you wanted to see were the few who stuck to the old ways. Which was hardly any of them," she emphasized when Busby seemed about to interrupt. "A few bad apples. And now I see it starting up again here."

"How do you mean?" asked Mr Tenpenny, truly interested.

"That vamp kid who works for Gwendolyn?" Wait. What? Vamp kid? Oh, okay, so no time for questions. "He came in beat up after some idiots took their prejudices out on him. Cassie, you saw how bad he looked. Bruises. Stitches."

At first I didn't know who she meant, but then recalled him congratulating me for destroying Gwendolyn's monstrous sourdough starter when I'd dropped by the clinic a week or so ago. So there *were* vampires living in MagicLand.

"He did look pretty awful," I agreed.

"And he wouldn't report it because he knows how Oberlin feels about vampires," Runa said acidly. "When are people going to realize they're not our enemy? Where would we be today if they hadn't worked with me to make those sample vials? You prefer to be jabbed and poked every time you need a blood draw or want to make a donation? They're not behind this missing Magics trouble."

"You can't be certain of that," Busby said calmly. Fiona refilled Runa's wine glass. To the brim. It was emptied again as Mr T continued. "They are physically strong by their nature. Although we've put limitations on it, I've no doubt they can still access magic that can equal ours if it came down to a fight. And they have a history of this very thing. Cassie might sometimes jump to odd conclusions, but I do believe her thoughts on Mayor Marheart have merit. If she's up to something..." He trailed off as if unwilling to complete the thought.

"Sorry," I said, feeling like I was missing out on something they all knew, "what's Matilda got to do with the vampires?"

"She is one. From one of the oldest lines, *and*," Runa added defiantly, "from the very family who were the first to assimilate. She's also the first vampire to become the leader of any Magic community. But is she recognized for that? No, she's been dogged with accusations and complaints and suspicions since the day she took office."

"Matilda Marheart? A vampire?" I asked, utterly bewildered by Mr T's revelation. "But I've seen her out and about in the daytime."

"Sunscreen," said Fiona. "Turns out they weren't as sensitive as was previously thought. They just needed a very high SPF."

I considered this. Matilda certainly had the elegant looks and ageless beauty of a vampire. And, wait, had that really been tomato juice she'd been drinking when I stopped by the other day? My disgust for the drink took on a whole new dimension.

"Hold on, can she turn into a bat?" I asked, and the three of them looked at me like I was an idiot. "Just checking."

"And as for why she might want this jewel," Mr T went on, "even if it has no true power it could serve as a rallying point for them. A sign that they have the strength to fight us. That in itself is rather worrying."

"How worrying could it be?" I said. "She has no idea where it is, and all I've been coming up with are tidbits of stories about it. It could be lost at the bottom of the Pacific for all we know."

"Cassie's right." Wait? I was? "Still, I should alert Olivia, let her know what we've discussed." Busby then rubbed his temples. "Tomorrow, though. The world won't end tonight, and I don't think I'm up for another international journey just yet."

"Someone should tell Oberlin," Fiona noted. "Even if there's only the remotest chance Cassie's items are related to the jewel Matilda's after, he should be alerted. And regardless of whether the items she's found are related to the Boncoeur Jewel or not, I'm afraid the footage with the mayor and Wordsworth's book needs to be addressed."

"Oh, he'll love that," sneered Runa. "He's been looking for a way to push Matilda from her position before the votes were ever counted."

"He knew about her?" I asked.

"Of course he knows. He probably keeps tabs on every vampire on the West Coast."

"There's more of them?" I blurted, and Runa scolded my ignorance with a glare. Right. Sore subject.

"Regardless," said Fiona, "Inspector Oberlin won't want to be kept out of the loop."

All eyes turned to me.

"No way. He hates me."

"These have been your cases," said Mr T. "And working with him, showing him you want to help in any way you can, would be a step toward redeeming yourself. Trust me. If you share information with him, he'll see it as a gesture of good faith. As a detective, you always need solid contacts within the police."

"I was hoping Tobey could serve that role."

"Yes, well, he'll need to pass his Exams before that," Busby said with a twist of irritation. "You are helping him, yes?" I said I was. "Well, be sure you do. I still don't understand how he possibly could have failed the first time."

I wanted to point out that Mr T's pressure for Tobey to ace the Exams might be contributing to his test paranoia. But since I wasn't licensed to be a psychologist — okay, I wasn't licensed to be anything — I held my tongue.

* * *

After a dessert of pistachio gelato from the Chimeric Creamery — which Pablo thoroughly enjoyed — we said our goodbyes. Fiona and Mr Tenpenny walked Runa home, while I lugged Pablo's carrier down the porch's steps and crossed the short distance to my portal. On the pavement in front of my door was a folded copy of that day's afternoon edition of the *Herald*. I picked it up, stepped through the portal, and tossed the paper on the table.

From downstairs came the familiar metallic sounds of Alastair at work. I wanted to go down and tell him Pablo had been given a clean bill of health, but knew I'd find it difficult to say anything along those lines without adding plenty of I-told-you-so snarkiness to the words. Besides, I thought peevishly, the gnomes probably wouldn't allow me in. Which begged the question of how anyone could have broken into the workroom?

It also begged the question of, if Matilda had indeed stolen Wordsworth's book and broken into Runa's clinic, was she also the culprit behind the workroom break-in?

It was time for a chat with Morelli. My gut clenched.

Not because I had to go willingly speak to my landlord, but because Morelli really did seem keen on Matilda. If I raised my suspicions about her to him, would he even listen? Did he know she was a vampire? And, if she was on the side of the vampires who had grown to despise Magics, was Morelli in danger of becoming her next snack?

And yes, I did find it odd that I was concerned over Morelli's safety when only a few months ago, I would have gladly sent him off to be gobbled up by a vampire, a werewolf, or even a particularly ravenous sewer rodent of unusual size.

I went downstairs, my fingers crossed that Morelli's date was over and that he hadn't brought her back to his place.

CHAPTER THIRTY-SEVEN
THANK YOU FOR BEING A FRIEND

"Rent's not due. Why're you here?" Morelli said when he answered his door. Glancing past him, I saw the television tuned into an episode of *The Golden Girls*. I also, thankfully, saw no sign of the mayor.

"You could invite me in."

"I could also lick the pavement, but I'm not about to do that anytime soon." I gave him a withering look, and he relented. "Fine. Come in. Just don't make a mess."

Which was a fair statement. Morelli's apartment was much cleaner and cozier than you'd expect if you heard the words 'troll lair'. The front room was decorated with color-coordinated crocheted doilies and cushion covers, the carpet looked recently vacuumed, and the kitchen gleamed. I wondered if maybe I shouldn't hire Morelli to do my housework.

Rather than muss the perfectly plumped couch cushions, I took a seat in one of the chairs at the dining table while Morelli cracked open two bottles of bitter. Surprisingly, one was for me.

I took a sip, then asked, "How was the dinner date?"

Morelli shrugged, downing two large gulps of his beer before saying, "Short." He then picked up a crochet hook onto which was looped some yarn that glimmered under the lamplight, likely some of the shimmer sheep wool he'd recently purchased. When he began working the yarn over the hook, I realized I wasn't going to get anything out of him unless I dragged it out.

"So… how is Matilda?" I asked.

Morelli paused to take a swing of beer, then sulkily said. "Fine, I guess."

"You guess? Trouble in paradise? Is she acting weird?"

"Not weird," Morelli replied, not even noticing that it was kind of a bizarre question for me to ask. "Just busy. Distracted, you know? Like she's got things on her mind."

"And have you asked her what that might be?" I prodded.

"Tried, but she just said it was mayoral duties. Budget things. Probably a real pain, I'd imagine."

"So, the dinner…?"

"I made reservations and everything, but she only popped by for a few minutes. Mostly to say she had to cancel. Then she told me she might have to go to a conference soon, and I suggested making a little getaway out of it. She sort of brushed me off, saying I'd just be bored. You think she's doing that quiet quit thing? I mean, I'm not even sure if we're dating or not, so…"

What was I supposed to say? That his girlfriend was a vampire who might want to bring about the destruction and/or subjugation of all Magics? Because I doubted that would go over well. Also, if she was plotting something, did that include all Magics, or just witches and wizards? Might trolls be off the hit list? I didn't know, but I also hated to see Morelli so deep in the relationship dumps, being pretty far down in them myself.

"Nah," I said encouragingly, "I'm sure she's telling the truth. Just busy. And really, do you think a mayoral conference is being held anywhere worthy of a romantic getaway?"

"Good point."

"Bring up going away together when she gets back, and I'm sure she'll be thrilled to go."

Unless she's busy being Queen of the Vampires and making slaves of us all, I did not say.

"That all you wanted to pester me about?" asked Morelli.

"Not really," I said, remembering Runa mentioning Morelli taking a longer-than-usual lunch break. This seemed a bit strange given how dogged he'd been about guarding her. If he'd been with Matilda at the time of the break-in — which, judging from the time of Alastair's texts, had been right around lunchtime — then she'd obviously be off the hook for the crime. "I was just curious if maybe Matilda met you for lunch today?"

Morelli flinched, but his yarn-crafting fingers didn't miss a beat.

"Why would you ask that?"

"Just wondering." I then muttered under my breath, "About the workroom break-in."

"You aren't just wondering. You think she did it." His hook dropped a loop, and his creation started to unravel. "Now look what you made me do."

I didn't say a word, and after a bit of fumbling that only seemed to be making the problem worse, Morelli gave up trying to fix the mistake and chucked the tangled mess into a basket.

"Look, I only came home to work on these orders." He gestured to a stack of order forms at the edge of the table. "I'd barely gotten here when she dropped by. That's when I asked her to dinner. She agreed. Like I said, she seemed distracted and didn't seem to want to talk much, but she didn't seem in a hurry to leave either, so I figured I deserved a break and I invited her in. We had a couple glasses of midday merlot, and then she left."

"Left? You saw her to the portal and back to MagicLand?"

"Well, no. I— Look, I've been having these long days with Runa, and then trying to keep up on the crochet orders, and well, the wine sort of made me sleepy."

"You fell asleep on your date? You wild and crazy guy," I teased.

"I'm not proud of it. Feel like a right ass over it, actually. Probably why she canceled dinner with me. But I'm sure she wouldn't have gotten up to anything."

"Rosencrantz and Guildenstern can confirm this?"

"They was sort of off duty." Morelli leaned closer, his cheeks blushing as he whispered, "They eavesdrop. So when Matilda showed up, I gave them a couple hours off. Didn't want them hearing me telling her—"

"Please stop. I do *not* want to know about this."

"Nothing like that," he huffed. "Just chatting. I'm sure you wouldn't want people overhearing your lovey-dovey banter with Alastair, would you?"

"Well, since we're barely speaking, that's not a problem I have to worry about."

"Yeah, I've been trying to get out of him what's really bugging him. I know this goes against the whole guys-sticking-together thing, but he really is being a jerk to you."

"Thank you," I said, genuinely touched that Morelli still had my back. "So the gnomes can't confirm Matilda returned to Rosaria right after she left your place?"

Morelli shook his head. "I really didn't expect to fall asleep like that, otherwise I'd have kept them on duty."

"Wait, Matilda didn't pour the wine, did she? Slip you a mickey?"

"'Slip me a mickey?' Do you think she's a 1950s gangster or something? And, no, I opened the bottle. I poured the wine into glasses I'd pulled fresh from the cupboard, and I had my glass in my hand the entire time until I fell asleep. Matilda is not the person who did this, okay?" When I didn't reply, Morelli prodded, "Okay?"

"Yeah, fine."

Morelli seemed to accept this was the best he was going to get out me. He then glanced at the TV, and his eyes lit up. "Oh, this is a good one."

Taking the TV off mute, a singer thanked me for being a friend as Morelli and I settled in to enjoy Blanche, Rose, Dorothy, and Sophia getting up to no good.

CHAPTER THIRTY-EIGHT
HOT NEWS ITEMS

Call me a coward or call me someone who'd already had a long day and wasn't up for a potentially heart-wrenching conversation with her significant other, but I didn't even try to get past Guildenstern-possibly-Rosencrantz when I finally left Morelli's place.

Back at the apartment, I sat down at the table and opened my laptop, knowing I wouldn't be able to sleep unless I got the unwanted task of contacting Oberlin over with. It was one of those ripping-off-the-bandage things — it's gonna hurt more if you approach it slowly, so best get it over with as soon as possible.

When Mr T had suggested I bring my evidence and concerns to Inspector Oberlin, he likely meant I should do it in person. But given my history with the Walrus, I had no desire to stride into his office and announce that I had information he'd failed to put together. Although, it was somewhat tempting.

Instead, I took the easy way out and sent an email, explaining to him I had three potentially powerful objects in my possession; that if they were brought together, trouble might start brewing; and that if we all weren't careful, the combined objects could spell disaster for all Magics. As a postscript, I told him, if he wanted to discuss this, to call my office and set up an appointment with my assistant. I really hoped he didn't take me up on the offer.

As I hit send, Pablo, apparently bored with hologram birds and magical mice, jumped onto the table and started making a play mat out of the copy of the *Herald* I'd left there earlier. This involved him spinning in circles on the paper to make it crinkle, then pushing his paws against it to spread his playground out as much as possible. Any paper in the path of Hurricane Pablo risked utter destruction, so I snatched the postcard from Dr Torres from under the newspaper and slipped it into my satchel.

Two minutes later, Pablo had completed his workout and flopped onto his side. He purred loudly and squinted his eyes in that way that said he was quite pleased with the mess he'd made.

By this point, I should have known it was best to keep my eyes firmly shut when handling the *Herald*. But I'm a junkie for reading, and as I tidied up the papery disaster zone, my word-craving eyeballs scanned the newspaper.

Page one, half in tatters, featured a new list of more missing Magics and offered up additional lamentations for the disaster in Seattle. The page with the opinion section had ended up under the front page and was crammed with letters from readers speculating about who was behind the kidnappings, questioning why HQ wasn't doing anything, and throwing around more 'thoughts' on vampires than I cared to count.

Despite all this, the paper had still made room for an article about me, accompanied by a photo that took up nearly a third of the page. Really, if they were going to devote this much space to me, they should just start calling themselves *The Cassie Chronicles*.

The snapshot was of me with a tight grip around Mr

Tenpenny's waist. It had to have been after Busby had had that banshee booze at HQ, because his face looked pretty darn loopy and I looked pretty darn annoyed to be trying to keep him from tripping over his own feet.

I briefly wondered how the picture had been taken without my notice, then remembered I'd been doing my best to keep an entire human upright, so I was probably a little distracted.

And the article that went with the picture? Well, that was almost entertaining... and enlightening.

Cassie Black, Getting Clients Any Way She Can

It would appear that Miss Black has stooped to new lows in her desperate attempts to obtain clients. It started with her stealing objects to trick people into hiring her. It continued with her coercing even our most valued citizens. And now she's going about drugging people to lure them into her agency.

What else could explain this photo? After all, I've known Busby Tenpenny for years, and I have never seen him tipsy, let alone staggeringly intoxicated as he appears to be in this image.

Since Cassie Black has repeatedly proven that proper procedure, rules, and regulations don't apply to her, the obvious explanation for this photo is that Miss Black has put something in Busby Tenpenny's food or drink. She then very likely ambushed this upstanding member of HQ while in his weakened, inebriated, and highly suggestible state to pressure him — the man who I must remind you is the case manager for her detective license — to approve her application.

Please, dear citizens of Rosaria, take what I say to

heart, and ask yourselves how long we can allow this to continue.

I say entertaining, because I mean, look at this dribble. Drugging people to get them to approve my license application? Sometimes I do wish I was that devious, but the *Herald*'s opinion section was growing sillier than a Saturday morning cartoon.

And I say enlightening, because as I read that final line, I again thought of the town hall. Of how Oberlin had addressed his audience and how he'd told them to take what Leo Flourish said to heart. That much similarity in word choice could not be coincidence. It had to be Walrus Face writing these things.

It almost had me longing for a harpoon.

The next morning there was no sign of Alastair and no yogurt in the fridge, so I headed out even earlier than usual to grab some breakfast items from Spellbound.

As I wrangled Pablo's carrier while also eating one of Spellbound's oven-fresh apricot danishes, I was hit with the hot smell of paper burning and the sharp tang of overheated metal.

When I turned on the next block up from Spellbound, rather than the bright yellow news box that normally stood there, I saw a charred hunk of metal. Its interior was filled with a pile of blackened ashes, some of which floated out and into my face. A voice from inside the news box repeated, "Only one, please. Only one, please. Only one, please." Rather than its previous crisp and admonishing tone, the box's voice was now feeble and wheezy, like that of a woman who's chain-smoked for too many decades.

Plastered on the lamppost nearest the box was a white poster with deep red letters stating, "Editor supports vile vaccine! No more *Herald*!" Another sign, black with white lettering, demanded, "*Herald* in a new editor!"

Well, at least the vitriol was clever.

As I continued on my way to the agency, I came across a few more news boxes, all burnt and all with the same signage posted nearby. I'd like to say I was disturbed by this public protest, and in a way I was. From its quaint streets and small businesses, I'd wanted to imagine MagicLand as being mostly idyllic, and it was a shame to have that vision shattered.

But really, hadn't I known Rosaria had this dark side to it? After all, not long after first coming to MagicLand, I was nearly attacked at the Wandering Wizard for mistakingly using a word I didn't realize was an insult. During my initial magic lessons, I'd learned how Magics might have kicked off the slave trade. And I'd only recently been saved from a violent thug by a pot of geraniums.

But mostly what I felt was a dark satisfaction that the editor, the man who had approved and published all those nasty opinion pieces about me, was finally getting a taste of his own medicine.

CHAPTER THIRTY-NINE
WALRUS LOGIC

Further ruining my concept of the Idyllic Land of Rosaria, when I'd nearly reached the agency, a rumble of commotion was coming from nearby. Specifically, from the direction of Runa's clinic.

Curious as to what the hubbub was about, I changed course and turned onto the next street to see the area around Runa's clinic blocked off with yellow police tape. Several police officers — including Oberlin and Tobey — were milling around and asking people to stay back so they could inspect the scene.

Tobey caught sight of me as he was explaining to a woman that she would just have to get some hand cream from the grocery store for now. Once she'd stormed off complaining of police brutality, he strode over to me.

"What's going on?" I asked.

"Runa's been robbed again." Tobey pointed and only then did I notice one of the square glass panes — the one nearest the handle — of Runa's door had been smashed in. Which was odd since a Magic could have just twiddled his or her fingers over the lock to gain entry.

"They take anything?" I asked. "Do any damage?"

"No real damage other than the windowpane. And as far as Runa can see, there was only one thing taken."

"Let me guess. My samples?"

"Got it on the first try, Sherlock."

Tobey's tone was teasing, but this didn't sit well with me. Two break-ins a week apart when Runa had never had any trouble of that kind before? And both times my samples had been the target. The saw had been stolen in the first incident (and yes, I cursed myself for, yet again, failing to devote any time to Runa's case), but maybe that had just been the thief giving himself a little bonus for a job well done.

"Quick," Tobey hiss-whispered, "here comes Oberlin. Pretend I've been interrogating you."

"Runa locked up last night. I'm certain of it," I was saying to Tobey just as Oberlin and his sour expression reached us. Before the Walrus could say anything to me, I turned on him. "Did you get my email?"

"Some of us," he said scornfully, "have better things to do than sit at a desk perusing our emails. Some of us are out here solving crimes."

"Might be better if you prevented them in the first place, wouldn't it?"

The Inspector's brow furrowed at my remark, and his cheeks turned the red of a sea mammal who's been basking in the sun too long.

"Witnesses tell me you were here last night," he growled. "Gonna deny that?"

"I fully confess to being here at closing, and to leaving with Runa and Morelli. In their company. At the same time," I clarified, just in case he thought I'd lingered around waiting for them to stroll off before I committed the crime of the century.

"Yes, well, this is still very suspicious."

"Crimes usually are," I said in a mocking, singsong voice.

Standing beside Oberlin, Tobey bit his lips as if trying to hold back a laugh.

"I've heard of your little magic problem," Oberlin stated. "That you're not allowed to do any, and that there's a trace on it."

"And...?" I asked, not exactly thrilled that Oberlin had been told of my wonky magic.

"And that door has been broken into by someone who can't do magic. Or," he emphasized, "who knew their magic would be traced."

"And why exactly would I break in and steal my own blood samples?" I asked, truly perplexed by the man's logic. "Last I checked I still have quite a few pints of the stuff in me."

This time, Tobey snorted a laugh. Oberlin shot a dark look at my cousin, who wiped his nose and muttered something about allergies. Oberlin's face softened in sympathy for half a second before he returned to scowling at me.

"You would do such a thing because you know those samples could be used by the police to match your magic to that used at other recent crime scenes."

I actually didn't know this. I knew Magics left a trace of their scent behind when they performed spells and hexes, and that this trace could be detected hours later by sensitive Magics. But were there really magic-sensing tests that could be collected and sent off for analysis in forensic labs like Norms did with DNA from a scrap of hair left at a murder? I wanted to be fascinated, I wanted to run in and ask Runa about this, but I was busy being preoccupied by Oberlin's accusations.

"Either that," Oberlin continued, puffing air through his bristly mustache, "or it's you trying to divert attention from your real crime."

"Oh, and what would that be?" I goaded, wanting to see if he'd start going on about all the madness in the *Herald*'s opinion pieces. One word about me drugging Mr Tenpenny, stealing items just so people would hire me, or harassing clients into doing business with me, and I'd know I had my man.

"Breaking into Alastair Zeller's workroom and vandalizing it."

Surprised by its sheer stupidity, I barked out a laugh at this. "And why would I do that?"

"Revenge," the Inspector said smugly. "I hear he doesn't like your cat. I hear he thinks that creature needs to be restrained rather than just allowed to walk down the street with no leash, no control over it. Which it does."

"Okay, besides your obvious fear of big bad pussy cats, you can't really think I tried to ruin Alastair's stuff because of an argument."

"Just kind of strange that only his side of the workroom had been messed with, don't you think?"

Okay, that was weird. And it was something I hadn't been aware of since Alastair seemed to be doing his best to avoid me. I made a mental note to verify with Morelli what Oberlin had said. I should also have a chat with Rosencrantz or Guildenstern to see if they'd noticed anything around the time of the workroom break-in. And I suppose I *could* talk to Alastair about it. Of course, with the way he'd been lately, there was no guarantee he'd talk back.

"If you think I did this," I gestured to Runa's, "and the workroom job, then you should probably read me my rights before we continue this conversation."

"I don't have enough evidence yet, Black, but believe me, I'll be keeping an eye on you. I'm sure Tenpenny here would appreciate the chance to work on his first search warrant."

"Sir, I—" sputtered Tobey.

"No, Tenpenny, I think you can handle it. None of this self-effacing modesty. It's time you put what you've learned into practice."

"Yes sir," muttered Tobey, who then gave me a sheepishly apologetic half-grin.

Oberlin, meanwhile, returned to the tasks of crowd control and clue gathering and making up lies since he clearly didn't know how to do real detective work.

CHAPTER FORTY
RARE THINGS

Runa was too busy giving statements and organizing a clean-up crew for me to speak with her. I didn't want to stick around and risk having to deal with Oberlin again, so I trudged off to the agency. When I arrived, Daisy was already at her desk, studying another book — this time, a massive collection of Norm statutes.

"Are those really relevant to our work?" I asked as I unlatched Pablo's carrier.

"You never know. Better to be prepared, right? And it might give us ideas for questions for Tobey tomorrow. He's feeling super great about the Exams, but he swears your final study session with him tomorrow morning is going to be the one that really seals the deal on his confidence. He's getting pretty superstitious about it, actually," she added, sounding worried about Tobey putting so much faith in one study session.

But the bubbles of Daisy's demeanor couldn't be held down for long, and all her cheerleader buoyancy was back when she said, "Oh, and a package came for you."

With a waggle of her fingers, she sent a box that was about the size of a ream of paper across the room and landed it in the exact center of my desk. Some people can be such magic show offs, am I right?

Wrapped in plain brown paper, the package had no markings on it except for my name and the agency's address. I stared at it a moment, the pessimistic side of me thinking it might be some sort of prank sent from one of my many detractors.

"Oh my golly," exclaimed Daisy, "I didn't even think." At least she admits it. "Is one of my job duties to process mail? I mean, should I have opened it for you and then typed up a summary of what was inside?"

"No, that would be..." I fought for a word. Weird? Overachieving to a bizarre degree? Ruining my fun of getting to open things? Instead, I simply said, "It would be more than I'd expect. I'm pretty sure I can handle a letter opener."

"Okay, just let me know if that changes, and I'll add it to the job duties description I'm working on. You know, a sort of Standards of Procedure document, just in case someone needs to fill in for me."

The sun seemed to shine just a little bit brighter at this. Maybe Daisy's employment would only be temporary. Maybe she'd quit when she and Tobey got married. My curiosity about this overrode both my interest in the package and my need to get some tea into my system.

"Are you planning to work here permanently? I mean, after you get married?"

"I sure do hope so. Wait. Is this your way of firing me?" she asked, sounding truly distressed. "I knew I should have opened the package for you."

"No, really. Just making conversation."

"Oh, goodie! Because, one career woman to another, I have no interest in being a housewife. I might want a couple days of vacation for our honeymoon, but after that, I am fully ready to be your partner in solving crime." Which was not what I'd signed up for, but I'd smash that magnifying glass over her head when we came to it. "Speaking of, today I'm going to ask Fiona about borrowing *An Enchanted History of the Portland Community* so I can enter my and Tobey's wedding date."

This was a sort of scrapbook for MagicLand. It included historic biographies, important news items, and significant dates and events. It was also the same book I'd broken the spine of a few months ago in a fit of frustration.

"I've never entered anything in there before," Daisy babbled on. "It's so exciting. Of course, my parents noted every time I came in first in all my potion and spell-casting competitions, but that's just what parents do, isn't it? And," she went on, not bothering to come up for air long enough to recall that I'd missed out on the whole proud-parents thing as a kid, "Tobey got to enter his change from an Untrained to a Magic. It wasn't the first of that kind of entry, but it's still newsworthy. Anyway, I really wanted to get to Fiona's before she starts her classes. You don't mind if I run an errand on my break, do you?"

I'd have gladly given her the whole day off just to stop her incessant chatter and blonde-ness from throwing off the agency's feng shui. Assuming it had any to begin with.

"Go right ahead," I told her. "Take all the time you need."

Some sort of *yippee* sound burst out of her. "I'll just shoot Fiona a text and let her know I'm coming. You're the best, Cassie. We make a great team, don't we?"

I made a noncommittal noise, and soon after heard the *whoosh* of a text zipping off into the ether. A couple minutes later, while I was in the kitchenette making tea, Daisy's phone pinged a response.

"So, she says it would be best if I could come by now," said Daisy. "Is that okay? I know I've only put in two hours of work, but she says if I can't get there soon, I'll have to wait until her classes are done with for the day."

I paused in mid-pour, holding the kettle aloft. Two hours? It was barely eight-fifteen in the morning. Did she sleep here? I stand by my earlier comment about her being an overachiever.

"No. Go ahead. Like I said, take your time."

Daisy combed her hair, applied a fresh layer of lip gloss, then snapped her purse shut and headed out with a cheery, "See you later."

Pablo peered out of his carrier.

"Don't worry. It's a blonde-free zone once again," I said, then went to the door to lock it. There'd simply been too many break-ins lately for me to feel comfortable leaving it open.

Once I'd returned to my desk, Pablo trotted over to join me, but just as he was about to leap up, he halted in mid-crouch. His eyes narrowed and he let out a low rumble before hissing in the general direction of my desk.

Although she was the best witch doctor I'd ever met, Runa was no veterinarian and could have easily missed something when she'd examined Pablo. After all, the only true test for rabies was to kill Pablo and chop off his head. Which obviously hadn't happened.

I mentally tallied the few things I knew about rabies. Except toward Alastair and certain newspapers, Pablo hadn't been showing any signs of aggression. He had also just sauntered into the kitchen to lap up some water, so no hydrophobia. Even WebMD would find it hard to convince me he had a raging case of rabies. Even so, I might want to consider an appointment with this Dr Doolally Runa had mentioned.

Pablo soon returned from his drink and sat by the desk, his tail twitching, as I pulled back the tape and pushed aside the package's paper wrapping. Underneath was a gift box. Not one of those Dollar Store boxes you get by the dozen that never seem to assemble correctly, but a sturdy, high-quality one.

I shimmied the lid off and, upon seeing what was inside, my legs went watery. I dropped into my chair. Yes, my chair and not the floor. I suppose even demon chairs need a nap now and then. Either that, or the cushion I'd bought had temporarily tamed it.

My mind raced to Morelli telling me his contact would be sending something my way. And then to the *Oregonian* article I'd seen after dropping off Mr Wood, the one about the supposedly missing museum treasure. The Replacement Hex covered up the gap in the collection, and the curator had dismissed the whole thing as a practical joke. But here was the very item from the article, staring up at me from a nondescript box.

Pablo sat next to his carrier, watching me with wary interest.

"You knew that was in there, didn't you? What's with you and these things?"

Pablo's only response was a slow, knowing blink. And there was something in that sage expression, in my conversation the night before, in the persistent image of the friendship rings that made me consider his behavior toward the other objects I'd found. The urge to find a connection between them, the demanding insistence that there absolutely had to be one, charged through me more intensely than a herd of bargain hunters racing toward a rack of marked-down groceries.

But for now, I turned my attention back to the package. Leaning forward in my chair, I peered into the box again to confirm that there was indeed a glittering tiara inside.

The base of the headpiece was made of some silvery material — sorry, I'm no metal expert. The front of the circlet featured simple yet beautiful filigree twists and spirals to create the outlines of flowers and leaves. In the center of the largest flower was a ruby. Or garnet. Something red and sparkly. Either way, with all my swirling thoughts about gemstone connections and friendship rings, and Daisy's comments about so many red jewels suddenly appearing in my life, the sparkly stood out like a billion-watt beacon in a storm.

I had a brooch, a pendant, and now this. And then there was Mr Coppersmith's red marble that I'd recalled last night. Was this just a seriously weird dose of happenstance or were these all pieces of a puzzle? Had these been cut in the manner of the friendship rings, waiting to be fit back together to make a complete gem? And was that gem the Boncoeur Jewel?

The questions were too tempting and had me on the edge of my temporarily domesticated chair.

My hands shaking with anticipation, I did a rare thing. I actually stopped to consider things before plunging into a potentially dangerous problem.

CHAPTER FORTY-ONE
PUZZLE PIECES

I went over what I'd learned from Professor Dodding, Olivia, and my dinner companions the night before. A jewel with power could be divided, possibly to reduce its power and keep it from being detected. And then the pieces could be brought back together at a later date, possibly to defeat an enemy.

The legends surrounding the Boncoeur Jewel said it once had an unnatural level of power. Matilda wanted, *really* wanted, the Boncoeur Jewel. Matilda was a vampire who'd been at the scene of every location connected to the items currently in my possession. Olivia had said the vampires might be biding their time until they obtained something they didn't have in their previous uprising.

Could the Boncoeur Jewel be that something?

But if the Boncoeur Jewel had been split, how many pieces had it been cut into? Did I already have all the pieces? And if I did, how did they join together? Because even without seeing them side by side, I knew the gems in my safe would only fit together if you broke all the jigsaw-puzzle-solving rules.

My next racing thought nearly sent me tumbling out of my seat without any help from my chair. Wordsworth's missing pages. Granted, it was total speculation, but what if they contained A) a spell that brought the gemstones together, or B) an Assist Spell aided by the Boncoeur Jewel that would give the spell caster unprecedented power?

Okay, I'll admit that by this point I was running a bit wild with trying to force everything going on in my life into a tidy bundle of potential world domination, but it was better than scrolling social media.

So what might happen if I could puzzle together the pieces I had? Would rays start shooting out of them like the Ark of the Covenant in that Indiana Jones movie? Would evil magic seep out and infest me? Well, it wouldn't be the first time. Would I set off the beginning of the end of the world? Again, it wouldn't be the first time.

I figured I'd already been through some tricky situations, so why not take a chance? A careful chance, that is. I wouldn't actually put the pieces together. I'd just arrange them on the desk to see how they fit. Sort of like seeing how South America and Africa fit together on a globe. You didn't need to chop out the Atlantic to know the continental edges matched up nicely.

Under Pablo's watchful stare I retrieved the tiara, the brooch, the pendant, and the marbles from my safe.

I felt terrible pulling the pieces of jewelry apart to get at their gems, but these were all quality items, and if I was careful, they could be put back to rights once I was done. The brooch and the pendant were the easiest. They only required pulling back a few tines before the jewels popped out. The tiara took a little more effort as its jewel had been wrapped with a decorative mesh of fine metalwork, perhaps so it wouldn't fall out if the wearer had a sneezing fit.

The marble, though, had me baffled. It was round, whereas all the other jewels had cut facings, making their edges angular. Was it not part of the puzzle, or did I need to chisel it down to the right shape? I could barely cut a bagel into two equal halves without injuring myself, so I certainly wasn't the person for *that* job. For now, I'd just have to visualize where it might fit.

I set the pieces out, then pushed them around until I noticed a shape possibly forming. The pendant's jewel and the brooch's jewel appeared to form the two upper lobes of a heart. The marble still had me thrown off, so I put it in the center just to have a place for it. The gemstone from the tiara took a bit of turning and shuffling. The fit wasn't so great, but at the right angle, it might form the left edge and bottom point of the heart.

Which, if I'd gotten my puzzle together properly, left the heart with a gap on the right-hand side.

The marble was nowhere near large enough to fill that gap, which meant I needed to find at least one more jewel. Throwing coincidence caution to the wind, I was convinced that jewel would be found in the handle of Runa's bone saw. For the billionth time that week, I cursed myself for not devoting any time to her case.

I wasn't sure whether to be relieved or bothered by the missing piece. Relieved, because this meant the vampires didn't have the totem they were after to take over the world. Bothered, because whoever had stolen Runa's saw might hold our futures in their hands.

And they might not even realize it.

Worried what evil I might call up from the bowels of Hades if the jewels were left too close together, I fixed the gems back into their respective pieces of jewelry, put the marble back in its velvet sack, then placed everything in the safe with plenty of space in between them.

Only then did Pablo relax his rigid stance and roll onto his side. Two seconds later, he was fast asleep.

Sixty seconds after that, he jerked awake, and I jumped out of my skin when someone rattled the door, trying to force it open.

CHAPTER FORTY-TWO
LORD OF THE RING

Don't worry, it wasn't the Mauvais risen from the dead and coming to take me to the fiery depths of hell where all the pastries are stale and sugar-free. Instead, it was Tobey Tenpenny, tugging on the handle then throwing his hands up in a what-the-hell gesture. He then snapped his fingers over the latch and looked mighty pleased with himself when the handle unlocked and the door tweeted open.

"It's still breaking and entering," I told him.

"Why was it locked, anyway? Aren't you open today?"

"Why? Did you have a case you wanted me to solve?"

"No, I'm supposed to be canvassing the area, seeing if anyone saw anything. Of course, no one has, so I figure it's a better use of my time to make sure everything's okay here."

"Well, I kind of had the safety thing covered until a certain future police detective magicked my lock open. Things are okay at Runa's, then?"

"She's pretty annoyed at Inspector Oberlin, and she's going to have Morelli beef up the protection hexes on the clinic, but other than that, she's taking it with a giant grain of salt." He glanced around the agency. "Hey, where's Daisy? Tell me you didn't fire her."

"Not yet. She's off running an errand. Apparently, she's

getting ready to enter your wedding date into the *Enchanted History of the Portland Community*. I didn't know you proposed."

"I haven't, but she's really set on getting married on a specific day."

"She's planning your wedding before you've even proposed?"

"She's very organized like that. And I will propose. I even have the ring ready just in case a romantic moment pops up. But I'm hoping to wait until I pass the Exams tomorrow. You know, a bit of a double celebration."

This seemed like tempting fate, but I was more focused on something else he'd just said.

"You have a ring?"

"Sure. Grandad said I could use the ring he gave Gran when he proposed to her. Said she would want me to have it for the occasion. You think Daisy will care I didn't buy something especially for her?"

I didn't care one lick whether Daisy wanted a newly purchased ring, the Koh-I-Noor, or one of the candy circlets sold at the Sugar Charms Candy Shoppe for her engagement token. Tobey had a family heirloom. All the other items with jewels had been at least a few generations old, passed down through the years. If Tobey's ring was part of the set...

What then? If they joined together would I simply have a long-lost treasure, or would I have in my hands the very item that could give the vampires the strength they needed to thwart us Magics? And if it were the key to their uprising, would it be wrong to ask Matilda to sign my license application form before she made me her magic slave?

"Do you have the ring with you? Can I see it?" I asked, realizing I was counting my crocodiles before they hatched.

"Why? You're not into jewelry."

"Because I've been working with Daisy these past few days, and I think I might be able to tell if she'd like it or not."

"Merlin's balls, you're a terrible liar. But, yeah, I've got it. Like I said, you never know when a romantic moment that's too impossible to resist might pop up."

Which seemed utterly ridiculous. Crime wasn't rampant in MagicLand (well, not until recently), but it did seem like carrying a ring around was begging for a pickpocket to target you. Tobey dug into his front pocket, pulled out the ring, and handed it to me.

"Nice," I said. I was being honest, but even I could hear the dismissive disappointment in my voice. While the rose gold band would go perfectly with Daisy's coloring, and the stone set in that band ring did gleam and catch the eye, the gem was an iridescent opal. Not a ruby. Not a garnet. Not anything that could be remotely construed as a red jewel.

"You don't think she'll like it, do you?" Tobey asked, panic hovering at the edge of the question. "Should I get a new one? A big diamond one like in the ads?"

"It's a gift from you," I assured him. "She'll love it." Just then, a blonde ponytail was perkily swaying past the window (attached to a body, mind you, not just a disembodied ponytail, which would be odd even for MagicLand). "Hurry! Put it away."

Tobey didn't question the command and shoved the ring back into his pocket just as Daisy came skipping through the door, a thick book floating in the air at her side.

"Tobey, you rascal," she said as she signaled for the book to hover over to her desk, "what are you doing here?" She hurried over, stretched up, and kissed Tobey on the cheek. I fought the urge to do my Morelli impression and resisted making any retching noises.

"Just came for a quick study session with Cassie," he lied.

"Oh, that's so fun. I didn't even know you had one planned. But you two ignore me. I'll just be over here, doing a little homework," she said as the book on her desk obediently flopped open to a blank page at the back.

I still wasn't sure how the book worked, but I assumed it somehow kept adding pages and expanding its spine as the community's history went on year after year. Which made me wonder how thick the one for the London community must be by now.

I'd like to say Tobey and I completed an intense and productive study session, that I quizzed him on every legal and police topic I could think of, that by the time he had to leave, he was prepared to ace any test the Academy could throw at him.

But I can't. Because Tobey, while keen on passing the Exams, was even more keen on Daisy and ended up spending more time chatting with her, flirting with her, and giggling with her than he did studying. I tried to get him back in line. I tried to conjure my inner Fiona, but there was no way of breaking through the gooey cloud of love surrounding his brain.

No one can say I didn't try, though.

CHAPTER FORTY-THREE
FAIRY TAGS

"Cassie," began Daisy, who'd been anxiously tapping on and staring at her phone for the entire forty minutes since Tobey had left, "have you heard from Nino?"

"Mr Wood?" I gave my phone a cursory glance just in case some texts had sneaked through. "No, not since he sent the picture of his airplane food and the arrivals hall."

That had been two days ago. Which, now that I thought about it, did seem odd since a few months ago when I'd been a 'guest' at HQ, Mr Wood had sent me photographic evidence of every stage of his crochet journey. If he'd been so eager to share that mundane aspect of his life, surely he would have taken me along on each step of his trip, from snapshots of the tour bus to every sheepdog and thatched roof he passed. I should have had a backlog of texts filled with photos of quaint cottages and pork pies.

"Maybe he's in a dead zone," I said, somewhat concerned, but not terribly worried.

Firstly, Mr Wood was on a group tour, and the companies that run those things tend to do their best not to lose people. Especially since everyone who's present and accounted for at the end might hand over a generous tip. Secondly, Mr Wood had packed at the last minute and could have easily forgotten to grab his charger.

Thirdly, Mr Wood wasn't a tech-idiot, but I had had to show him a few things when he'd upgraded from a flip phone to a smart phone last winter. He might be savvy enough to log onto the Wi-Fi at the airport, but out on the open road, he'd have to rely on cell service. He likely wouldn't have known to purchase an eSIM ahead of time, and I doubted his bargain basement phone plan included international calls and texts.

"You know what it probably is?" I said, and Daisy glanced up from her phone, a hopeful but fretful look in her eyes, like a puppy who doesn't know if it's about to get a treat or a scolding. "I bet he forgot to get a data plan for the U.K."

"That's probably it," Daisy said half-heartedly.

I tried to shake off her unease as silly, but as soon as she wasn't paying attention, I sent a message to Mr Wood. A quarter of an hour later, there was still no response.

Although I tried to convince myself it was nothing to worry about, Daisy's hungry anxiety started to nibble its way into me. After all, even the Cotswolds, a place trying to look like something from another era, had to have a coffee shop with free Wi-Fi Mr Wood could've accessed to stay in touch. The fact that he hadn't…

I chucked this troublesome thought into the bin as soon as it came. After all, Daisy and I weren't his moms, and he wasn't required to check in with us. Wasn't it just possible he was enjoying himself so much and meeting so many new people that he didn't feel the need to text us every five minutes?

"The thing is," Daisy eventually said, almost sounding guilty about something, "and I only did it because I was worried about him being on his own—"

"Did you put some sort of Tracker Hex on him?"

"No," she responded, as if that was a ridiculous notion. "I just had a few Fairy Tags and—"

"Sorry. A what? You mean Air Tags?"

"No," Daisy said, in a very *pshaw* way. "Those things, well, I don't want to speak bad of a company, but they're no match to Fairy Tags. Always reliable, never lose power, and if you put them on your suitcase and the suitcase gets lost, the fairies can fly it home for you or take it to the destination you've told them you'll be at."

Okay, admittedly, that was an impressive piece of tech. Or piece of fairy? Wait. Were Fairy Tags literal fairies glued onto coats, hats, and handbags? Did they get paid overtime? Have a benefits package? Did I want to know the details of how these things worked or what the poor fairies themselves were going through? Probably not.

"And you put one of these on Mr Wood's suitcase?"

Daisy shrugged sheepishly. "Suitcase, wallet, jacket, and well, I can't remember all the places, but I made sure he would have one on him at all times."

"At all times? Even in the shower?" I asked. Rather than answer, Daisy turned her phone to face me, as if I was supposed to understand what the map on her screen was all about. She walked over to give me a better look. On the small screen was a cluster of, at a guess, thirty red dots circulating on the map. "Those are the Fairy Tags?" Daisy said they were. "Is it normal to use that many?"

"I got a discount if I bought them in bulk. Anyway, they're moving, but they're not moving in the Cotswolds." She did the two-finger expand-y thing on the screen, then turned it to face me. "They're in London."

"Sure, that makes sense. The tour probably spends a few days in London, then goes off to the Cotswolds so people don't have to trek through all that quaint-ness while jet-lagged."

Daisy stared at the screen, a skeptical twist to her lips. "I suppose you're right. Most of them do seem to be moving through the heart of the city."

Daisy moped back to her desk, where she switched off her phone and opened her laptop. I could see her screen from where I sat, and on her computer's desktop was a small inset window with the same dot-clustered map that had been on her phone.

Daisy's checking the Fairy Tag map every ten seconds (or so it seemed) and her woeful sighs kept me from being able to concentrate on what to do next with my cases or the items in my safe. It didn't help that something kept niggling at me. Finally, I remembered Mr Wood had given me a brochure for his tour. Was there any chance I'd brought it here the day after he'd told me about his retirement plans?

Trouble was, Daisy had done a really good job at organizing my desk after the break-in. Which meant it would probably be impossible for me to find anything. I mean, if it's not hidden under a Spellbound napkin, how am I supposed to remember where I left it?

Thankfully, while the desk's surface was clean, Daisy had somehow returned my desk drawers to their pre-break-in state of disaster. I sifted through the top drawer and found a bunch of poorly magicked business cards and my now un-alphabetized, non-color-coordinated pens, pencils, and paperclips, but no brochure.

The lower desk drawer, the one meant for file folders, contained a fair number of mangled editions of the *Herald*. I pushed these aside to see, at the very bottom of the drawer, a familiar middle-aged white lady with her trekking poles staring up at me. From the brochure, mind you. I'm not in the habit of stashing tiny hikers in my desk drawers.

With Daisy fixated on her little dots like a cat with a laser toy,

I slipped the brochure from the drawer and hid it in my lap. What would I tell her if I found out the tour really did go directly from the airport to the Cotswolds? And wait, why did I suddenly care about sparing Daisy's feelings? I told myself it was just to avoid dealing with her meltdown as I opened the leaflet as quietly as possible.

On one of the inner tri-fold pages was an itinerary. A huge wave of relief washed over me. The tour did indeed spend a few days in London before they zipped off to the Cotswolds. Then, as I did some mental calculations for the time difference, the wave froze solid.

If the brochure was current, Mr Wood should be on a bus to the Cotswolds right now, if not already cozied up in his first bed-and-breakfast. So why would Mr Wood still be in London? I pictured the dots circling that one area on the map. My jaw tensed and my belly went hollow. Could Mr Wood be lost in London? Could he be wandering aimlessly, begging someone to guide him back to his hotel? Or to the nearest Greggs for a sausage roll?

But that was silly, wasn't it? Mr Wood could still be in London for a dozen reasons. The tour might be waiting for someone who'd gotten delayed; the brochure might be out-of-date; their first stop in the Cotswolds might be experiencing an infestation of anti-tourist protestors, so the group was having to wait things out in London; or the poor fairies on the Fairy Tags might have gone on strike and were whooping it up in the big city.

I was about to tell Daisy my theories when a text pinged through my phone.

I didn't recognize the number, and my gut did a leap of hope. This might finally be Mr Wood texting from a SIM card he'd finally gotten around to purchasing. Or it could be Mr Wood's tour director sending a message to ask for advice on how to pull him away from the food stalls at Borough Market.

Instead of easing my worry, however, when I opened my phone, the message on the screen left me utterly flummoxed.

CHAPTER FORTY-FOUR
TEA WITH LEO

I was so flummoxed, in fact, that I had to read the message four times before I could absorb the meaning of all the words.

Cassie, Leo Flourish here, the editor from the Herald. We need to talk and I would like to meet with you. Spellbound in an hour?

"Editor?" I muttered. "From the *Herald*? Wants to meet with me?"

I then realized that not only was I talking to myself, I was talking to myself solely in questions. Which is a hilarious challenge on certain comedic game shows where everything's made up and the points mean nothing, but isn't a good habit to get into in normal life.

My mind raced with what the message meant. What exactly would Leo Flourish want to talk about? Was he hoping for an exclusive interview regarding my part in all the heinous crimes occurring in MagicLand? Did he need a resource for an article on 'Ten Ways to Coerce Clients'? Or was this to be just a casual chitchat about any of the other things the paper had been accusing me of and mocking me for over the past several weeks?

And was I going to spend the rest of the day thinking in question form?

I ignored the message.

Ten minutes later, my phone pinged again. Same number. Slightly less eloquent message.

> *Sorry. Unclear. Want to apologize. Will pay @ Spellbound.*

Since that last bit is a perfect example of using one's magic words, I immediately texted back that I would meet him there.

Outside of Spellbound, at one of the wrought-iron bistro sets, I saw a wiry man who I recognized from the town hall. When I reached his table, Leo Flourish stood to greet me. Being shorter than your average man, he had to look up to meet my eyes, and his small, inquisitive face reminded me of a mouse. Not a timid one, mind you. One of those mice that will taunt the cat, nab the cheese every time, and prove it's far more clever than feline and human alike.

"I took the liberty of ordering a couple slices of coffee cake and tea for us both. Unless you'd like something else," he rushed to say. "And before you ask, no, the cake isn't from the clearance bin."

Which had been exactly what I'd been thinking.

He gestured to one of the chairs, and as we sat down I couldn't help but notice he was still wearing his pink slippers. Apparently, Runa had yet to lift the Leftie-Rightie Curse she'd placed on him.

"I'm not sure I really want to talk to you. I'm only here because you bribed me," I said, picking up a fork and taking a large bite of the splendidly moist and flavorful cake. I have to admit, he bribed well.

"I can understand that. And straight off the bat, I want to offer up a sincere apology for what has been printed."

Shocked by such straightforward sincerity, my mouth gaped open as the bite of cake I was about to take fell off my fork.

"You see," he began, every bit of his body language now brimming with contrition. "I took some time off. First for a little summer getaway, and then to see to some personal matters that have cropped up. And I'm afraid during these past several weeks, I let someone else make most of the publication decisions. That said, it's no excuse. I wasn't overly taxed with tending to things and should have taken more responsibility for the *Herald*'s contents. I should have also made a wiser choice in choosing a replacement who would be fair in his journalistic decisions."

"But you had to have seen what was being printed. As you said, it's been weeks and nearly every edition has featured some sort of nasty stuff against me. So why apologize only now?"

Mr Flourish's cheeks burned red, and he seemed to have trouble meeting my eye for several moments. Finally, he looked up and said, "You've seen the news boxes? The flyers around town about me for my stance on the RetroHex Vaccine?" I nodded. "I never understood exactly how it felt to have words and vitriol flung at you like that. I realize it doesn't make up for everything, but I am truly sorry."

I'm not the biggest of grudge-bearers, but I wasn't exactly leaping to accept his apology. A few words, even if spoken over cake, didn't make up for weeks of libel, harassment, and attacks. But there was one thing I had to know, and I had a feeling he wasn't in a mood to hide anything.

"Most of the things in the opinion section are anonymous. Did you write them?" Leo had just taken a mouthful of cake, so he merely shook his head. I tried to wait him out, but he clearly wasn't going to give up any information unless I pulled it out of him. "So who wrote them? Who hates me that much that they would write some of those things? Things whose publication you didn't call a stop to." Mr Flourish flinched at my harsh tone.

"Again," he said, swallowing, "I am sorry. I saw them, but no rebuttal to them ever came. If there had been any push back, I would have stopped it. I'd like to think I would, at any rate."

"I was told by close friends that they did complain directly to the paper and that you sent dismissive replies to those complaints."

As I said this I had to work very hard to not look down at the man's slippers. Which is why I didn't miss the genuine confusion on Leo's face.

"I'm afraid the messages never reached me. I did question the pieces, worried the sheer number of them was a bit much, but my replacement told me sales were doing well. So I let it continue. He has been talked to, however, reprimanded, and I'm turning the paper in a new direction. Granted," he said with a defeated shrug, "I don't know if anyone will buy it without the scathing articles, but I don't want the paper to be so..." He rolled his hand. "What's the word I'm after?"

"Sensationalist?"

Full of crap was what I was actually thinking, but that was three words.

"Exactly. I've let it get away from me. All the crazy articles seemed to be what people wanted, and I made the mistake of not questioning it. *The Herald* used to be as respected as *The Preternatural Times*, but easy profits got the better of me. Print journalism isn't immune to its own version of click bait."

"That still doesn't answer my question. Who wrote all that about me?" He paused, as if I'd just asked him to reveal the name of an industry whistleblower. "I deserve to know," I insisted. "And if you're worried about me taking some sort of magical revenge, I can't do any magic without HQ knowing."

Leo Flourish took a deep breath, as if still considering things, then said, "Calder Hackett."

"Wait. Not Oberlin?" I asked, nearly knocking over my tea in my bewilderment.

"Inspector Oberlin?" The editor shook his head and chuckled. "Great Griselda, no. That man can't string four words together, let alone write an entire article.

"Opinion piece," I corrected.

"Yes, opinion piece. And believe me, Wesley Oberlin has tried to write for us, and I've had to stretch my own creative writing skills to keep coming up with polite refusals. He's certainly not someone you want on your bad side." Something I didn't need to be told twice. "If it'll prove I'm sincere about my apology, I could send you a couple of his submissions. They're worth a laugh, if nothing else."

Despite myself, I smiled. The guy did seem truly humbled by the anger being directed toward him and regretted what he had allowed to happen under his watch.

"I think I can live without that. But who's Calder Hackett?" I asked, although the name was slightly familiar. "I've never met anyone by that name."

"Calder, he's..." Leo paused, and for a moment I thought he wasn't going to tell me. Then I realized he didn't need to. I could picture the fury on Mr Hackett's face after I'd had a little magic accident a few months ago.

"He's Pippi's dad, isn't he?"

"Inga," Leo corrected. "And yes, Inga is Calder's daughter."

Inga, known to me as Pippi due to her red braids and gingham fashion choices, had been a classmate of mine when I'd been forced to take lessons with MagicLand's school-age kids —

talk about a blow to your magic ego. One day in Gwendolyn's potions class, I was perfectly willing to let Pippi/Inga do all the work, but then Gwendolyn insisted I had to participate. That participation went a bit awry, and I kind of sort of melted Pippi.

Don't worry. She's fine now, but seeing a pool of Pippi was a frightening experience for me. And I'm sure it was for her parents as well. And it would seem one of those parents wasn't about to forgive and forget.

"He's really written all those articles—?" I began.

"Opinion pieces," Leo said with a grin.

"Whatever. All those because of one mistake that turned out fine. I mean, from what I hear, the girl's remarkably flexible now. She could probably wipe the floor in any gymnastics competition."

"He doesn't see it that way. Feels you should have been punished for what you did. Instead, he sees you getting honors from HQ. It drove him a bit off the deep end."

"And you provided the pool."

"I know. It was wrong. Like I said, I have every intention of turning the paper around. I've seen the errors of my ways and all that." He put down his fork and stuck out his hand. "Truce?"

I left him hanging there a moment, then a longer moment. Finally, I reached out and shook his hand. "Truce."

"And I'll print a retraction as soon as possible."

"Don't bother," I told him.

"But I—"

"Sorry. I mean, don't bother *yet*. If readership for the *Herald* is down right now, what good does a retraction do me? I want sales numbers to be much *much* higher when you do a front-page piece about how I'm not a horrible person. And," I added, really feeling top-notch about my negotiation skills, "I'd also like some free advertising spots for the agency."

Leo held out his hand again, and as we shook on it, he said, "I guarantee. A full-page spread all about the agency, your triumphs, and your talents. And prime advertising spots for at least a month."

Free cake, sincere apologies, and devoted ad space? At least something was finally going right for me this week.

But before I could revel in my feelings of triumph, my phone rang. The caller ID told me it was Tobey, and I was tempted to let it go to voicemail. But, as if the ringing of a phone triggered some sort of journalistic Pavlovian response, Leo Flourish had perked up and now wore a look that said, *"Hurry up and take that call; it could be newsworthy."*

And so, I reluctantly answered.

"Are you at Spellbound? Daisy told me you'd be at Spellbound," Tobey said in a tsunami of words. "You need to finish up. Like now."

"What's happened?" I asked and could only think of my parents. Was there news from HQ? Had something happened to them? Had someone found their bodies?

Before I could start railing against HQ for sending into the field two Magics who had to be running very low on magic by this point, Tobey blurted, "Mel Faegan is back."

CHAPTER FORTY-FIVE
RETURNS POLICY

Who in all of Hogwarts Hallowed Halls was Mel Faegan? I wondered.

I racked my brain, but no Mel Faegans came to mind. Was it a code name for my parents? If so, why had no one told me? And more to the point, why did Tobey know? Also to the point, why had I reverted yet again to thinking entirely in question form?

I made a sound that was meant to imply, *'Oh, that's nice,'* as I took a forkful of my coffee cake.

"You're not interested in this? One of the missing Magics, one of *our* missing Magics, has just suddenly returned, and all you can say is—" And here Tobey did a pretty spot-on impersonation of the sound I'd just made.

"Oh, *that* Mel Faegan." The recollection of his name in the *Herald* slowly seeped into my brain. "Did he say where he's been?"

"Look, you didn't hear this from me," Tobey said, speaking in a brisk whisper, "but if you want to be a real detective, you might want to get to Runa's before the Inspector does. He's out on a call at the moment, but as soon as he's done, he's going to be heading to the clinic to question Mel. So if you want to learn anything, you might want to do it now."

"But what do I want with Mel Faegan? He's not a client of mine, and I'm not allowed to do anything with the missing

Magics cases yet." Not to mention he was no longer a missing Magic.

"Because there are other missing Magics," Tobey said with mounting impatience, "and from what I've heard Grandad say, they're putting you on that the minute you get your license. Gandalf's gonads, why do I have to spell this out to you? You've complained how HQ won't tell you anything about the missing Magics. Well, this is your chance to learn something about them directly. Look, just get to Runa's and check it out, okay?"

"Okay," I said irritably and hung up, drained my tea, then told Leo Flourish I had to go.

"I overheard most of that. In case you hadn't noticed from the front pages of the most recent editions, I'm quite interested in the missing Magics problem. I'd like to go with you. If that's okay, of course."

I nearly told him no. After all, what favors had the *Herald* done me lately? But Leo seemed genuine, like he wanted to turn the paper in a new direction, and proper investigative journalism required in-person reporting.

"It's fine, but if you report a single thing that isn't true, I'll tell Gwendolyn to never serve you again." I then scooped the rest of my cake into a napkin and ate it as we hurried over to Runa's — Leo's slippers slapping against the pavement the whole way.

A crowd had gathered outside the clinic. I don't know why I was surprised, considering how fast gossip spread around MagicLand.

"Anything you can do about this?" I asked Mr Flourish.

He thought a moment, then from a distance about a block over, I heard a muffled version of his own voice shouting, "Another one's come back!"

Dozens of heads whipped in the direction of the cry. Then, like a herd of water buffalo daring to forge a crocodile-infested river, they surged as one to where the voice had come from.

"Ventriloquism Charm mixed with a Sound Distortion Hex," the editor said to my questioning look.

"Nice."

The door to Runa's clinic now showed no signs of the earlier damage done to it, and it was firmly locked. At least the curious mob had been respectful enough not to magic it open. Either that, or Runa had already gotten Morelli to conjure a Locking Spell that couldn't be easily sidestepped.

I rapped on the door's frame. From the exam room, Runa poked her head out, seemed confused that no one other than me and Leo were outside her door, then bustled over to let us in.

As soon as Runa opened the door to us, Morelli emerged from the exam room and asked, "What are you doing here?" Given that he was meant to guard Runa, I wanted to point out that *he* should have been the one answering the door, but I wasn't in the mood for our little verbal games.

"Tobey said I should gather information before Oberlin has a chance to block me."

"That's not a bad idea," Runa said. "Oberlin's not exactly racing to get to the bottom of things lately, and I don't just mean his lack of interest in my recent break-ins. And him?" She jutted her chin toward Leo Flourish.

"Trying to turn a new page," I said.

"Right," said Runa critically, "Come on back. Just be sure to keep out of the way."

"May I join you?" asked another voice, and we all startled like a group of teenagers who have just heard a floorboard creak while sneaking through a supposedly haunted house.

I didn't know how she'd approached without any of us hearing the click of her heels, but Matilda's face showed strained lines of worry as she scanned the clinic. She barely acknowledged Morelli, who was blushing worse than a rosacea victim. "He's still here, isn't he?"

"He is," began Runa, "but I don't think—"

"Come on, Runa—" Morelli began to plead, but Matilda cut him off.

"I know it's unusual, but this whole kerfuffle with the missing Magics has happened during my very first term as mayor, and I want to do all I can for Rosaria. I would like to understand what happened to Mr Faegan. It might help me prevent what's happened in Seattle from happening here."

First off, an astounding number of Magics going missing across the world was a *kerfuffle*? No, Pablo losing Fuzzy Mouse and running in mad circles over its loss was a kerfuffle. Magics being abducted was a serious tragedy. Second, everything she'd said had a forced air to it, like a politician reading from a teleprompter, and it set my teeth on edge. Third, well, there was the whole in-a-small-room-with-a-vampire thing I'd prefer to avoid.

"Very well," agreed Runa, "but if Mel seems overwhelmed by any of this, all of you are going to have to go."

The five of us entered the exam room, and I noticed Leo Flourish pull out a small notepad and pen, as if ready to draft a breaking news article.

On the exam table was a small man who reminded me of what Professor Dodding might have looked like in his younger years. The patient appeared to be about mid-forties with light brown hair that could do with a brushing. He had a cuff around his arm and a stick-on patch slightly off center on his chest. Neither were attached to anything, mind you, but managed to track his blood pressure and heart rate without a single tube or wire sticking out of him. His eyelids fluttered when we entered.

"Mel," said Runa gently, "do you feel up to speaking to someone?"

Mr Faegan fought to open his eyelids, as if they were weighed down by lead sinkers. Runa waved me forward, so I stood next to her and his gaze landed on me. The guy looked like he could sleep for a month, but there was no dullness in his eyes, no glazing over, so I started to ask a few questions.

"How are you feeling?" Figured I'd toss him an easy one.

"Like I've been run over by a truck," he said, his voice weak but clear. "A really big truck that's transporting a herd of elephants."

"Do you know why you feel that way? Can you talk about what happened to you?"

He nodded, but when he opened his mouth, he grimaced and seemed unable to speak. He blinked his eyes several times as if fighting back tears. I glanced to Runa, wondering if I should go on. She tapped her nose and twitched it slightly like a rabbit scenting his surroundings. I took a whiff as she reassured him it would be okay.

Even with my magic off kilter, I'd had no trouble detecting the scent of the Magics around me. My inhale easily picked up a hint of the citrusy fragrance of Runa's power, as well as Morelli's spicy ginger aroma. But Mr Faegan had no scent. I didn't know what his magic should have smelled like, but I doubted it was nervous sweat mixed with dirt, which was the only thing I was picking up from him.

Mr Faegan swallowed hard, shifted his shoulders resolutely, then said, "I think someone took my magic."

"That's impossible," said Morelli. "A draining would have left you unable to speak or to remember anything that happened to you. Perhaps you just feel unwell."

Mr Faegan shook his head. "Dunno about that, but I remember something hurting in my neck, then I couldn't even do a Shoving Spell when I tried to fight back. They seemed so pleased with themselves. I don't know what I'll do, don't know if they'll even let me stay in Ros—"

He broke off as a sob heaved up through his slim chest. See, although MagicLand seems warm and welcoming as long as your name isn't Cassie Black, it has strict rules about not allowing non-Magics in. Tobey had been the rare exception back in the day when he was an Untrained (someone who should be Magic but isn't), since being related to Busby Tenpenny opened certain doors — or portals, as the case may be. If Mel had lost his magic, he might also lose his home in MagicLand.

Mr Faegan apologized for his tears, and I was just about to tell him it was alright, when Matilda stepped forward. All trepidation had vanished from her face. Instead, she looked agitated, angry, ready to strike out at someone.

Since she'd been lingering at the back of our little group, Mr Faegan hadn't seen the mayor before then. But when his eyes locked on hers, his blood pressure and heart rate skyrocketed. He shook his head fretfully and muttered something about, "No, not again." He then clamped his mouth shut, but a frightened keening rose from deep in his throat. He then passed out. From stress or fright or both, I couldn't say.

"Mr Faegan. Mel, are you all right?" asked Runa. She darted her eyes toward the screen with his vitals. They'd lowered from his panicked state, but were still erratic. "This was too much for him," she said, as if admonishing both herself and us. "I'm sorry, but you're going to have to go," she stated firmly. "You've made him remember his trauma too soon. I need to get him stabilized, and I can't do that with all of you in here."

Runa was an excellent doctor, but I knew it wasn't a memory that had set Mr Faegan off. Every part of me wanted to stick around and ask him what about Mayor Marheart had frightened him so badly. Still, I knew better than to press my luck with Runa, so I followed Matilda, Morelli, and Leo out of the room.

Outside, the lookie-loos had gathered again, and they weren't pleased to see we'd somehow been given the privilege of gawking at the patient. Moving toward us through the throngs of people was Tobey Tenpenny.

Matilda pulled up short at the sight of the crowd, and I took the chance to ask, "Why was Mel Faegan so afraid of you?"

"Black," Morelli said, the word so full of warning it caught Tobey by surprise just as he'd reached us.

"No, Eugene, she's right," Leo Flourish insisted. And yes, I was quite literally dumbfounded that the editor from the *Herald* was sticking up for me. "That man in there was mostly stable and speaking coherently. He wanted to tell us what had happened to him. Then he caught sight of Mayor Marheart and nearly gave himself a heart attack. So, Madame Mayor, mind telling us what that was about?"

"I don't know what you mean," Matilda snipped. "The man has obviously had a shock, and his mind is likely addled from his ordeal. I can't speculate on why he reacted as he did. That is for him to explain. Now, if you will please excuse me, I need to reassure these people that Mr Faegan is recovering well and is in capable hands."

The mayor pushed past us, donned a reassuring smile, and began speaking to the crowd, all of whom hung on her every word. Leo stuck around to get the scoop, but I took the chance to make my escape.

CHAPTER FORTY-SIX
VAMPIRE LECTURES

"I'm not sure that was the smartest move," Tobey said, speaking with gentle criticism after we'd moved away from the morbidly curious onlookers and I'd introduced him to Leo.

"You weren't in there," the editor said firmly. "Something clearly happened between those two. And I don't mean they recently sat down to tea and cupcakes." A beeping sound came from his wrist. He glanced at his watch and pulled a look of annoyance. "Look, I have to go. Afternoon edition is about to go out, and if I'm not there, that Hackett will try to squeeze in more of his tripe. Keep me posted, okay?"

I told him I would, and was somewhat glad to see him go. While I appreciated having Leo Flourish on my side, he was an ally I'd have to watch my words around since I didn't know if he was aware of what Matilda Marheart was. Clearly, based on those heckling comments at the town hall, some Rosarians knew her secret, but I doubted the mayor wanted her vampirism confirmed and announced via a boldface headline blasted across the *Herald's* front page.

Also, she had seen me with Leo, so if that headline did appear, and if she thought I'd leaked the story… I shuddered at the image of my blood becoming her bedtime snack.

"Mr Flourish is right," I said, then explained to Tobey what had happened inside the exam room as we strolled aimlessly away from Runa's.

Tobey then revealed that, on the way to the dinner party at the mayor's a few days ago, Inspector Oberlin had spilled the beans about Matilda's heritage. "Then he kept telling me to be on my guard around her. But she didn't behave weird or predatory or anything. She just behaved like a great host."

"She may have been nice to you, but Mr Faegan recognized Matilda. And not in an oh-nice-to-see-you-again way. It was the reaction of someone finding themselves face-to-face with their abductor, abuser, or whatever she was to him. I hate to side with Oberlin on anything, but there's something up with Matilda Marheart. And with her being a vampire… Think about it. His reaction? Something hurting his neck? Drained of his magic? HQ has suspected the vampires are up to something, and Mayor Marheart might be part of it."

Tobey didn't respond. When I looked over to him, he had a strange expression on his face. "Do you need the toilet?"

"No. Just thinking. Oberlin's recent lecture, the one he gave the morning after our dinner with Matilda."

"What? More details on the merits of the Stunning Spell?"

"No, well… okay, maybe a little when he got sidetracked a few times. But I told you about the unit on vampire stuff we had a week ago, right?" I nodded. "Well, the day after our dinner with Matilda, he went over the unit again and was really adamant that we pay careful attention to it."

"You think he knows something's up with her?" I asked.

"Maybe. At first I thought he was just trying to indoctrinate his future police force with his anti-vampire ideas. But with this thing with Mr Faegan…"

I recalled the poster in Oberlin's office. A mugshot of a vampire with the words 'Tolerate But Never Forget' stamped across it. There was also the disgust on his face in the photo on his desk of him, his wife, and the mayor. Which again made me wonder why he'd accepted a dinner invitation from her.

Now, I know this is going to come as a huge surprise, but our aimless strolling had led us straight to Spellbound Patisserie. What can I say? My feet must have some sort of pastry-based homing instinct.

Tobey said he only had about half an hour before he needed to report back to the Academy, but I assured him that was plenty of time to cram some sweets into our mouths — namely, the cookie assortment platter Gwendolyn had recently added to her menu. After all, sorting out the intentions of the undead should always be done with a stack of snickerdoodles in front of you.

Fiona was there when we arrived, sitting at one of the outdoor tables and looking much less harried than she had over the past few weeks. She waved us over, and once Tobey and I had ordered various forms of sugar and caffeine, I filled her in on what had happened at Runa's and Tobey told her about his recent double dose of vampire education from Oberlin.

Fiona pinched her lips at this, but in a neutral voice, she said, "I do hope what he's teaching you is accurate. Wesley can be a bit— Well, you know."

See, I'm not the only one who doesn't think the best of the Inspector.

"It's hard to say," replied Tobey. "I've compared what he's told us to some books Grandad has, and it seems accurate. Although, those books might be outdated."

Thinking of Mel Faegan's missing magical scent, I asked, "Did Oberlin say anything about whether vampires can take our magic? Or do they only want to suck our blood?" I added in my best Bela Lugosi impersonation, which I'll admit is pretty awful.

Tobey took a large bite of his Bakewell tart, then shook his head. "Vampires switched over to synthetic blood a while ago." I didn't know much about the modern-day vampire, but I did know this much. Sort of like Norms' lab-grown meat, the vamps have lab-grown blood. "For special occasions," Tobey continued, "they get bottles of fizzy cow blood, but for their daily drink, it's the synthetic stuff. Some have even grown to prefer it over real blood."

Fiona nodded, as if confirming everything Tobey had just said was correct.

"But you say only some have grown to prefer it," I noted. "That kind of makes it sound like they still consume human blood."

"There are vampire devotees who don't mind donating a little blood to their favorite vampire," said Fiona. "But that's blood we're talking about. Not magic."

As she spoke, I'd been savoring a ginger nut from my cookie assortment, which stirred up the memory of my dad emptying box after box of cookies. I pushed aside my worry for my parents' magic levels, for their safety, and focused on a question that had sprung to mind.

"Magic transfusion works by taking samples from a healthy Magic and donating them to another Magic," I began. "Those samples work by withdrawing blood that contains our power, right?" Fiona nodded. "So why shouldn't a vampire be able to take our magic by drinking our blood? Do either of you know anything about that?"

"That's not my area of expertise," replied Fiona.

"Runa might know," said Tobey.

"Runa might not be terribly helpful with this line of reasoning," said Fiona. "She's one of the vampires' staunchest allies in Rosaria and won't hear a word against them. Plus, she's unlikely to let anyone back into the clinic for a while."

"We could call, though," I suggested.

Fiona touched my arm to stop me when I reached for my phone. "Let's give her a bit to settle Mr Faegan. Now, Cassie, I realize you have many ideas — valid ideas, I might add — swirling around that clever head of yours, but I do agree with Runa on some matters with the vampires. We have treated them quite unfairly. The Vampire Tolerance Act couldn't change long-ingrained prejudices, neither those of Magics nor those of vampires.

"Which is why — although a few vampires have assimilated well to Magic society — many vampires still keep to themselves, remaining in tight-knit circles. Unfortunately, this not only raises red flags for certain less open-minded citizens, but it also keeps the vampires on the fringe and keeps us from truly getting to know them."

"So what if that sticking to the fringes of society has worn thin?" I asked. "What if they're ready to take their place in the world and would do it by stealing our magic and leaving us powerless?"

Just then, a blaring alarm sounded from Tobey's pocket. He dropped his fork and scrambled for his phone. His brow furrowed as he looked at the screen. Pushing his plate aside, he stood up.

"Sorry, gotta go. It's a call out."

"Nothing dangerous, I hope," said Fiona.

"No, just prep for a search-and-seizure situation. Oberlin says it'll be good for me to get some practical experience. Keep me updated, okay?"

We told him we would, and he dashed off, heading up Magical Main Street.

CHAPTER FORTY-SEVEN
FREE REFILLS

"He'll make a good police detective one day," Fiona said, once Tobey was out of sight. "Dedicated, and certainly harder working and more tolerant than Oberlin. That man—" Fiona shook her head. "Cassie, you know I don't normally speak ill of people, but he's rather self-serving, not terribly community-minded, and he can certainly hold a grudge, if you know what I mean." I told her I knew exactly what she meant. "Let's just hope Tobey sails through his Exams tomorrow so he can get his career under way. He says you've really been taxing his knowledge."

"Been trying to, yeah."

"He told me you're doing another round of studying in the morning." Which reminded me that I needed to fill in another test booklet with questions sometime today. "He seems convinced it's going to be the key to acing his Exams tomorrow. It sounds a tad superstitious to me, but you really have done a good job. I've never seen him so confident about a test." I mumbled a thanks, but still doubted that any of my little quizzes were going to cure my cousin's test paranoia.

"Think it's safe to call Runa now?" I said, changing the subject like a gold medalist in subject changing.

"It's worth a try."

I dialed the clinic, and just as I thought it was going to go to voice mail, Runa picked up, "Dr Dunwiddle speaking."

"Runa, quick question."

"I don't have time, Cassie. Mel's just stabilized, and I don't want to leave him alone too long. I'm hoping he might talk to me a little about what happened."

"It'll be really quick."

"Fine," she replied sharply.

"Can vampires suck our magic?"

"Don't you even go there, girl," Runa barked. "Vampires have fought for their rights, for their place in our world, and it's stereotyping them to think they're going around sucking— Wait, did you say magic?"

"Yes. Mr Faegan said he felt something at his neck, which to me sounds like classic vamp behavior. Now he has no magic, or so little we can't scent it on him. So I'm wondering if a vampire can absorb someone's magic by biting them."

"With a vampire's abilities—" Runa mused. "They're natural absorbers, so it could happen. But since they *are* absorbers, they wouldn't need to take someone's blood if they wanted to steal a Magic's power. Just being near us would do the trick. But don't let that little editor friend of yours quote me on anything like that. I fought hard for Vampire rights in my youth—" an image of Runa in bell bottoms and hippie braids popped into my head "—and I won't have the little progress we made ruined by his conjecture. Mind telling me why you're thinking they would want to do this?"

"To take our power. Weaken us so we can't defend ourselves if they staged an uprising against us. Not magically, anyway."

Runa let out a hurricane-force huff of exasperation. "That's fear-mongering and ridiculous. Vampires don't want that. You've been reading too much of the *Herald*."

"Olivia suspects something is up with them. Is she fear-mongering and ridiculous?"

Fiona gave me a maybe-that's-going-a-bit-too-far look, but Runa, sounding deflated, said, "I know. And even when she's shown me the evidence behind her reasoning, I've told her it doesn't fit together. But after today..." She trailed off, and I didn't press her to continue.

Instead, I asked, "Do you think you can restore Mr Faegan's magic?"

"Until I know how it was removed, it's going to be tricky. He's got some relatives in the area, so, assuming they aren't amongst the missing, I'm hoping they can donate some magic that will stick." In the background I heard the sound of boxes falling. "That would be Morelli trying to help with the filing. I gotta go."

With that, Runa hung up.

"I should really get back to the agency," I said, although I had no idea what I'd do once I got there. Given what I'd learned from my puzzle attempt earlier, I supposed finding Runa's saw had climbed to the top of my sleuthing priorities. "At the very least I need to make sure Daisy hasn't gotten lost in the coat closet."

"She's not that dumb and you know it."

"No one that chipper can have all their brain cells intact."

"I'm sure she'll manage on her own for a few more minutes, if you'd like to have a refill." Before I could object, Fiona met my eye and said firmly, "There's one more matter I wanted to discuss with you." She then signaled to the grey-haired server, who, moments later, bustled over with a coffee for Fiona and a cup of wickedly strong black tea for me.

"Refill on those as well?" the woman asked, indicating our empty plates, including Tobey's which I'd picked clean while on the phone with Runa.

"Why not?" agreed Fiona. When I balked, she said, "My treat. For helping Tobey."

The server had just waddled off with our orders when my phone buzzed. Despite the late hour it would be in the U.K., my heart jolted with hope that it was Mr Wood.

But it wasn't him. It was just Daisy. Probably wondering if she should consider color-coordinating her nail varnish with the agency decor. With a sigh I set the phone face down on the table.

"Not who you were hoping for?" Fiona asked, half teasing and half with a touch of concern.

I explained to her about Mr Wood's lack of texting and photo sharing. "I know he's a big boy who can take care of himself, but I can't stop wondering if something really has happened to him."

"He could have lost his phone. Or maybe he forgot to purchase a British adapter for his charger. It really could be nothing." She took a sip of her coffee, then said. "You do have a tendency to jump to negative conclusions, you know."

"That way I'm pleasantly surprised when it turns out not to be the worst," I said, as if this wasn't the obvious way to live your life. "And you're probably right. He did pack in a rush."

"We'll turn you into an optimist yet," she said with a grin. The grin then changed into something more wary. "As for what I had to say, I imagine you've been wondering what Alastair was so worked up about the other day."

Given that Alastair had been worked up most days over the past week, I said, "Which day?"

"When you saw us speaking. You were leaving your apartment. We were on my porch."

"Ah, right." I shrugged and broke off a piece of white chocolate-macadamia cookie. "Sort of blew it off. Maybe we rushed into things. Maybe he regrets it. I honestly can't figure him out, and since I'm not exactly the Love Guru, I've no idea how to approach the question of, 'Do you hate me, or what?'."

"Believe me, he doesn't hate you. He did behave like a child over both the Tremaine contract and Pablo's misbehavior, and Busby gave him quite the talking to about it."

I nearly choked on my cookie at the idea of Mr T standing up for me. "He did?"

Fiona nodded. "Alastair admitted it wasn't your fault, and that he overreacted because he's been under a lot of pressure to get the commission done. Which, I don't understand how it all works, but he seems to keep having setbacks with it."

"Setbacks with orange fur and tabby stripes."

"Yes, I heard about his Pablo Ban. But again, that was probably another overreaction due to stress. He does truly love and care for you. He always has." Which was nice to hear, but I'd rather have heard it from the horse's mouth. Actually, I'd like to hear *anything* from Alastair's mouth. When was the last time we'd spoken? "Just don't give up on him quite yet."

"So, what were you arguing about when I saw you?" I asked, not missing that she hadn't actually addressed the very thing that had led her onto this conversational path.

"Just a matter of contention about the research."

And if you think that reply sounds evasive, well, so did I. And apparently, so did Fiona, because after a pause she said, "Look, I probably should let Alastair tell you this in his own time, but with the way he's bottling everything up lately, I worry that he'll keep letting it fester." This did not sound good. Not at all. "Alastair has found—"

"Cassie, there you are," huffed Lola, who'd just run up to our table and was gasping for breath from the effort. With tears floating in her eyes, she cried, "It's awful, just awful!"

CHAPTER FORTY-EIGHT
THE SOUND OF SILENCE

Fiona immediately got up and eased Lola into the chair I'd grabbed from another table.

"Now," Fiona said soothingly, "take a deep breath before you burst."

"No, there's no time for any of that deep-breathing mumbo jumbo. I was just at the agency trying to find you," she said to me, "but you weren't there, and that lovely Daisy told me you might be here." This was the second time Daisy had tracked me down that day, and I was starting to suspect she'd attached a few leftover Fairy Tags to me. "So I—"

My phone squawked with an incoming call. Lola, already clearly under some strain, startled and gripped dramatically at her bosom. As for me, the sound was so shocking I did the first thing I could to shut it up. Which was to answer it.

"Hello?"

"Cassie, there's a—" Busby began.

"Mr T, I've got Lola here. I can't talk right now."

"How is she?" Mr Tenpenny asked, as if not understanding the meaning of the words, *I can't talk right now*.

"In a near panic," I said impatiently. "Now if—"

"Bunny's gone missing. That's probably why she's there—"

"Stop talking," I told him. "I'm putting you on speakerphone."

Once I did, I asked Lola, "Bunny's gone?"

"The neighborhood's so quiet now," Lola conceded, a reminder that she would find the positive side in even the worst situation.

"Do you know when he went missing?" Busby asked.

"I don't think we noticed exactly. The neighborhood's pretty sure they heard drums around dinnertime last night. But no one's sure exactly when it stopped." Lola paused to stifle a sob. "That's not unusual. I mean, that child has to sleep at some point, and he does respect quiet hours. I guess with people going about their busy days, we just didn't pay the quiet any attention. But we're all so used to complaining about the drumming when we have our neighborly, afternoon chinwag, that the minute we realized we didn't have anything to complain about—"

This time the sob broke through. And because it's Lola, I couldn't help but put a consoling arm around her shaking shoulders.

Mr Tenpenny asked a few more questions, none of which Lola could answer with any precision, but she did confirm that Bunny lived alone. His carer usually came by in the mornings, but today he had an afternoon shift and had shown up at Bunny's a little after the chinwag session began. When the carer came out a few minutes later and told them there were no signs of Bunny, Lola and the carer searched Bunny's place, but there was no Bunny to be found. There was also no sign of struggle, and it appeared the only thing he'd taken with him were his drumsticks.

I probably shouldn't have, but I felt a small stab of sympathy for the kidnappers.

"Can you help?" Lola asked, looking directly at me.

"I..." What could I say? I had cases that still remained unsolved, and I wanted to dive further into the suspicions and theories I had about Matilda. But I couldn't say no to Lola. I mean, it's Lola. I turn into a hugger when I'm around her. That's how powerfully persuasive her soothing magic can be.

"Cassie can't help you with this, Lola," Busby said through the speakerphone.

"I can too," I said, instantly defensive. "I'm actually really good at finding people who've gone missing, as you may recall."

"I'm not implying you're bad at your profession. What I mean to say is that any missing Magics case, which we have to assume this is, is an official case. And as you do not have your license yet, you cannot take this case. Lola, you're still there?"

Lola sniffled then said she was.

"Very good. Now listen. We are taking these missing Magics cases seriously. I'm currently in London, but I'm on my way to the portal and will be to your neighborhood in just a moment. If you'd like to meet me there, I will take statements and make observations personally. Are you okay to get yourself home?"

"I can take her home," offered Fiona.

Mr Tenpenny spoke a few more parting words of encouragement before hanging up.

"There's no reason I can't work this case," I told Fiona while Lola collected herself. "This might not even be a missing Magics case, and the more people looking for Bunny, the better, right?"

"I understand," said Fiona. "But if you go barging over there with Lola right now, Busby will resist. You're not the only one in your family with a stubborn streak. I'll take Lola home and stick around while they gather evidence and ask questions. I can then relay to you what I learn. Because you're absolutely right; people's lives should not be put on the line because of a bit of bureaucracy. After all, even without a detective's license you could 'accidentally' stumble upon a missing person, couldn't you?" she said with a wink.

"Believe me, I can stumble over people without a lick of paperwork," I said, and despite the gravity of Lola's situation, I felt a surge of glee that Fiona had faith in my abilities. And that someone else thought the whole detective's license thing was a bunch of hex-ridden hooey.

"Good, now, I suggest you go back to work. I'll be in touch in a bit."

As Fiona led Lola away, I gathered up the remaining cookies from my plate and slipped them into my satchel. On my way back to the agency, I made a mental list of questions regarding Matilda and Mel, Bunny's disappearance, and possible places to begin looking for Runa's saw.

The more my mental gears whirred and clanked along, the more convinced I became that there was some connection between my cases, the missing Magics, and the vampire uprising. And the more determined I became to find that connection.

I also couldn't help but wonder how my life had gone from solving a simple case of a few lost marbles to wading chest-deep through a swamp of situations that threatened the very existence of the world's magic communities. Seriously, could my life just settle into normalcy for a month or two? Was that too much to ask?

From Main Street and just north of Spellbound, runs Angle Avenue, a side street that — as you might guess — runs at an angle from Magical Main Street. It's not the quickest route from Spellbound to the agency, but it was the least trafficked, which also meant it ran the lowest risk of encountering one of my detractors.

I had just turned onto it when I saw Alastair coming out of a small hardware store called Uncommon Implements. Not having seen Alastair out and about since I'd caught him arguing with Fiona a few days ago, it took me a moment to register the dark-haired, triangular-faced man stepping out from the shop actually was him.

Firmly resolved to untangle this knotty mess going on between us, I marched over to him and blocked his path. He stared at me as if he might get me to shift aside by sheer will. It wasn't exactly the throw-ourselves-into-each-others-arms scene I'd hoped for, but I was still glad to find a tiny spark of attraction in his eyes.

Bolstered by Fiona's words and reassurances running on repeat in my head, I conjured up the courage and grit to say what needed to be said.

CHAPTER FORTY-NINE
NOT THIS AGAIN

"You're being a jerk. A workaholic, cat hating jerk," I stated, as blandly as if listing off a string of long-established facts. "And you need to knock it off."

"Nice to see you, too," he said irritably.

"What is your problem lately?" I said just as irritably. I'll admit that might not have been the best question to ask or tone to use when I was trying to be reasonable. But, seriously, he was being a real pill.

"I've got work to do," he mumbled, then held up the small paper bag he was clutching and tried to step past me. I darted over to stand in front of him. He grimaced and stepped to the left, then the right, with me zipping back and forth to block him. Had there been any onlookers, they might have thought it was a pop-up comedy skit.

"Alastair Zeller," I said, hands on hips, "knock it off. Why are you so mad at me? At Pablo?" Alastair stared at me, then at the pavement. "What? What have I done? Because whatever it is, I can't figure it out, and that's saying a lot because I am a detective."

I added those last words with a hefty dose of dramatic emphasis, but it didn't even earn me a twitch of a smile. Tough crowd.

"Speak," I demanded, "or I will go home right now and start tearing pages out of your comic book collection." Still nothing, and I couldn't help but grunt in frustration. "Why are you so mad at me?"

"I'm not mad at you, alright? I'm afraid of losing you," he blurted, then seemed to regret what he'd said and clammed up again.

"Of losing me?" I asked, completely baffled. "Is this your own lack of self-confidence, or have you developed some ridiculous notion that I might have a fear of commitment?"

"What? No, not losing you like that." Okay, I wanted to ask why not, but since he was almost speaking warmly to me, I didn't interrupt. "As in the 'til-death-do-us-part kind of losing."

"Alastair, I'm a Magic, I'm going to live to a ripe old age unless an evil wizard or a hungry vampire or my own clumsiness does me in sooner. But I *am* going to die one day. Besides, you're older than me, so you'll probably be kicking the proverbial bucket long before I do."

"I don't mean age-related death," he huffed, as if I was the one who was being annoyingly obtuse. "I mean, your death. Soon."

I considered where we were. There were plenty of shops along this street, but at the far end and a block over was Runa's clinic.

"Wait, have you spoken to Dr Dunwiddle? Did something come back with my samples? Do I have Magic cancer?"

"Cassie, I'm being serious."

"So am I. First off, there's the whole patient-confidentiality thing I'd need to address. And second, I can't imagine the prognosis for magic cancer is good. Is there chemo—"

"Cassie! It's not magic cancer. It's my research."

"What about your research? Did you handle some fungal-filled papers that have turned the apartment into a biohazard? Is it in our lungs?"

"Are you really this much of a hypochondriac?" I shrugged and told myself to delete my search history before he saw how deep a rabbit hole of obscure-but-highly-contagious disease I could go down. "The research. There's a prophecy."

I groaned. And not in a good way.

"A prophecy? Seriously?" I scoffed. "I've already seen how those things can go awry, so I'm not really inclined to get worked up over another one. I mean, is it even about me? Because you guys were way off the last time you put too much faith in fortune telling."

"We were close," Alastair said, but at least seemed sheepish about it.

Because of a prophecy Banna made centuries ago, the Mauvais had thought I was his enemy. This meant, in an effort to keep me safe, my life had been a living nightmare from the time I was a toddler up until a few months ago when I met Mr Tenpenny and things became a far worse nightmare for a bit. Problem was, it turned out I wasn't who the prophecy referred to, and that nightmare life should have been lived by someone else all along.

"Let's call it a warning then," Alastair said.

"And what's this warning have to say?"

Alastair pulled a folded slip of paper from the front pocket of his trousers.

"You carry it with you?" I asked incredulously.

"I keep hoping I'll find another meaning to it."

"Let's hear it, then."

Alastair cleared his throat before reciting, "When creatures bring out tooth and claws, magic's end quickly approaches.

When the joining of the heart is near, many friends disappear. Assistance from pages will unite under cages. If captured by hunter, all falls asunder."

Okay, I'll say right here that some of that did send goosebumps up my arms. *Creatures claws?* Did that refer to Pablo? The missing Magics thing had started only a month or so before Matilda hired me to find a heart-shaped jewel that might be broken into pieces waiting to be joined together. Vampires, they were a type of hunter, weren't they? Or had been until they'd been pushed to using certain cafes to get their blood fix. And, I suppose if I wanted to grasp for more straws, there were those pages taken from Wordsworth's book.

Still, it was all incredibly loosey-goosey, and I imagined that if you picked fifty people at random, at least ten of them could find some sort of connection to those words and happenstance events in their own lives.

As if he knew I was about to interrupt to point this out, Alastair silenced me with a glance. His voice shaking, he continued, "The final line reads, Black defeats the dark who see themselves as light, but only by losing life."

That might be vague and grammatically incorrect, but it was also more than a little worrying. Regardless, I couldn't allow Alastair's crushing fear for me to destroy our relationship. I fought down my unease and flippantly said, "That's another of Banna's, isn't it? You know how I recognized it? Because she continues to suck at poetry. Plus, that first line doesn't even rhyme."

"It is one of Banna's, but it's a translation. My translation."

"I suppose you did well with what you had to work with." Alastair folded the paper and returned it to his pocket. I wanted him to throw it away. Far away. "This is what you've been dwelling on?"

"Kind of hard not to. I finished the translation the very day Pablo attacked me. Then I got to thinking about Gary biting Eugene, and that heart-shaped jewel of Matilda's you're after, the missing Magics, and it all fit together too well."

"But why be so angry with me over it?"

"Trust me, any anger you sensed was completely misdirected. Which doesn't make it any better, but…" After a pause he said, "I just became overwhelmed with fear, and I hated that I was so scared of losing you. I think maybe I wanted to push you away so it wouldn't hurt as much if I did lose you. Totally irrational, I know, and the whole time I kept telling myself I should be handling it better, discussing it with you. But I became so desperate to find a counter-prophecy that I—"

"Went off the deep end?"

He shrugged his agreement. "The lack of sleep probably hasn't helped my mood either. And the commission. And the lost contract at Tremaine's. It just all— It seems stupid now not to have talked it out with you straight away. Fiona tried to make me see reason. Reminded me how prophecies are rarely accurate, but I just couldn't shake it."

Considering the line about the joining of the heart and my idea that Matilda's jewel could (almost) be puzzled together from the items in my safe, it was probably good we hadn't been speaking, since I'd have likely mentioned it to him and sent him into an even deeper spiral of angst.

With the hope of pointing out how silly the string of words were, I asked, "What the hell does 'the dark who sees themselves as light' even mean?"

"My best guess is that it means someone who thinks what they're doing is right, but it's actually bad."

I wanted to cast the prophecy off as a bunch of relationship-destroying trollop, but that did kind of make sense. And if

Alastair was right, who did it refer to? The mayor? Oberlin? Both sometimes used their positions of power to twist the truth and brush aside unwanted problems — the break-ins in Oberlin's case, and the missing Magics in Matilda's case. But although Oberlin didn't like me, I doubted he wanted to kill me. Not lately, anyway.

Matilda, however... She could very well have been the person who attacked me at my parents' place. So why had she rushed me straight to Runa's? Was she waiting to do me in until after I'd gotten her jewel back?

Which would be just my sort of luck — I solve a case, I get my license, and then my client kills me.

I wanted to joke with Alastair about what had just run through my head, but if I told him my suspicions about Matilda and her jewel, it would only trouble him further. It was time for me to do my best to close this topic that was driving us apart.

"It's just a bunch of words, Alastair," I said calmly. "Even Nostradamus's predictions are only right if you finagle the facts and strain for coincidences. I survived the bloody Mauvais, for Circe's sake! I doubt any dark-light characters are going to be able to get the jump on me. So, please, stop worrying. Or at least stop misdirecting your worry. It's really annoying."

"We need to get your magic sorted. That's the only way I'll feel you're safe."

"Magic was exactly what put me in danger last time. How about self-defense classes? We liked those, remember?" I was referring to our almost-first kiss that had (or rather, hadn't) happened during one of the defense lessons Alastair had been giving me. I waggled my eyebrows in a wink-wink-nudge-nudge kind of way. This finally got a smile out of him.

"We did." He took my hand, and that familiar spark of magic and love danced across my palm. "You're right about me worrying about this too much. Totally right. One hundred percent right."

"Good. I win. Conversation over. And to make up for it you can cook me dinner. Also, you owe Pablo an apology. I will accept it on his behalf," I added magnanimously.

"And I'm sorry I was a jerk to Pablo. The stress of everything, I guess I overreacted. Is he okay?"

"He's perfectly fine. Get it? Purrrr-fectly?"

Alastair rolled his eyes. "If this is what talking to you entails, I think I'll stay angry. I take it he's fine?"

"Better than fine. Mr T put a charm on his carrier and now he won't leave it."

"Busby or Pablo?" Seeing me grin at this, he asked. "So, have I covered all my apologies?"

"For now."

"I have an idea," said Alastair, looking brighter and livelier than I had seen him in days. "I know you're busy. I know I'm busy. But a few hours away from work wouldn't kill us. What do you say to taking the rest of the day off? Put together a picnic and just hang out somewhere?"

He was right. I was busy. And my head was reeling with theories, suspicions, and, now, prophecy possibilities. But I also knew this was a pretty critical moment that I needed to not screw up. We needed time together, and a few hours wasn't going to doom my career. The time off might actually help clear my head.

"Let's do it," I said, then told him I still needed to pop by the agency to pick up Pablo.

Alastair smiled indulgently as he leaned in to kiss me. And the kiss would have gone on longer if my phone hadn't started ringing. When was I going to learn to silence that damn thing?

CHAPTER FIFTY
A VISIT FROM OBERLIN

My phone was jangling a cheery pop tune that I definitely did not program into it. The screen showed it was Daisy. Again.

I was mere steps away from the agency, and I debated not answering. But in addition to adding a ring tone to my phone, Daisy had also somehow placed a scale on the home screen that rated the call's urgency. It was cranked up to the highest level.

"Sorry, it's my colleague. Can't function without me," I said to Alastair's questioning expression as I took the call. "What's up, Daisy?"

"Cassie, okay, first, Mr Wood's Fairy Tags—" she spoke like the panicked words were racing to escape her mouth "—the ones that were moving? They're not. They just stopped, and I can't get through to him."

Although I needed to learn more about Fairy Tag technology, I was pretty sure this was nothing more than a glitch in the spritely system. I assured her we'd check into it and was about to tell her that was hardly worthy of a Level Ten urgency rating (and to ask how she'd done whatever she did to my phone), but Daisy cut me off.

"Second," she said in an urgent whisper, "you need to get

here. Like now. Something's... well, something's happening, and I don't know how to stop it."

"Is the sink overflowing? Because you just need to turn the tap the other—"

"No, it's Inspector Oberlin. He's going through your things."

"He can't—" I started to say, then realized that he could. Hadn't Tobey just told me the Inspector had wanted him to help with a search-and-seizure? Was this what he'd been called out for when he'd left me and Fiona at Spellbound? Had he known it was to put me through the wringer all along?

As quickly as this thought came, I brushed it aside. Tobey's business-as-usual reaction to that call had been genuine.

My gut was churning, but I couldn't for the life of me think of what Walrus Face thought I was hiding at the agency. Contraband cookies? Purloined paperclips? No, this was just him making my life miserable. "I'm on my way. In the meantime, do me a favor and hit Oberlin with a Stunning Spell."

"Believe me, I've been tempted, but they've put a Shield Spell around my magic."

What kind of gestapo tactics was Oberlin resorting to?

"Sorry," I told Alastair after I'd ended the call, "the picnic might be a little delayed." I told him what was going on at the agency. "I can meet you later at the apartment if you want to get back to your commission."

"I'm not leaving you. This sounds like harassment, plain and simple, and you need a witness. Plus, it's not a picnic, but at least it's doing something together." Which earned him so many good-boyfriend points, I almost wanted to forgive him for his prophecy panic.

* * *

Alastair and I were still two doors away from the agency when Tobey barreled into me, taking me by the arms as if forcing me to listen, to look into his eyes and see he wasn't lying.

"I didn't know anything about this. I swear."

"Of course you didn't. I would never think such a thing," I said innocently.

"You already did think it, didn't you?"

"For like a nanosecond. What's this all about?"

"I'm not sure. I'll go in with you, though. Hey, Alastair."

Alastair greeted Tobey, then seemed about to ask him something when I remembered I had an ally who might just be interested in a little police harassment story.

"While I'm dealing with Oberlin," I told them, "one of you needs to call Leo Flourish at the *Herald*. He'll want in on this."

Alastair agreed to do it, then Tobey and I entered the agency to see Inspector Oberlin digging through my desk drawers.

"Mind telling me what you're doing?" I said more boldly than I felt. If I'm being honest, my legs were feeling pretty shaky, and the mound of cookies in my belly had grown as heavy as if I'd swallowed Mount Everest.

Three heads turned in my direction. Two of them were attached to the broad shoulders of uniformed Rosaria police. The third was Oberlin's, whose hand was now on the latch to my safe.

"Investigating possible criminal activity and a potential coup," Oberlin said smugly.

From the corner of my eye, I could see Alastair, standing in the doorway and holding his phone as if filming what was happening. Or, I hoped, sharing what was happening with Mr Flourish via a video call.

"Coup?" I said, somewhat amused at the thought. "I can

barely organize my calendar. How would I ever organize a coup?"

"It's true, sir. I've seen her calendar," said Daisy.

Oberlin muttered an incantation as he pressed down on the latch to the safe. It didn't work. When he tried again, the safe morphed back into a mint tin. A bit late, but it did prove that the safe sensed the Inspector had no good intentions for wanting into it.

"Open that safe," demanded Oberlin.

I rolled my eyes, but since I knew nothing untoward was in there, I went over and touched my finger to the tin. Then, once the tin had returned to being a safe, I turned the dial to enter the combination for the latch.

The door to the safe swung open. Inside were Mr Coppersmith's marbles, Mrs Oberlin's brooch, my mom's pendant, and the copy of Wordsworth's book he'd refused to take with him after realizing it was damaged. Curiously, the tiara was nowhere to be seen, and I wondered if this was a feature of the safe or if Morelli's contact had put the tiara under some sort of Concealment Charm before sending it to me.

"See," I said as Oberlin squatted down to peer inside, "no Molotov cocktails, no grenades, not even a firecracker. So, how exactly do you think I'm going to stage a coup? Sparkle people into submission?"

Daisy chuckled at that and I warmed to her just a tiny bit.

Oberlin glowered at me like a man who, if he had laser vision, would be using it right then to chop my head off. He reached into his jacket pocket. I half-expected him to pull out a taser, but he didn't need such clumsy, mundane things. He was a Magic and could Stun me anytime he saw fit. He could also do worse, and right then I think he was seriously considering what he could get away with. He then lowered his hand, turned to the safe, and pulled the objects out of it.

"Tenpenny, will you verify what I've just taken possession of?"

Looking guilty and furious at the same time, Tobey stepped forward and did as his boss had demanded.

Then, almost as if this were a staged play and he'd been waiting for that exact moment to create the biggest dramatic effect possible, one of the other officers handed the Inspector a sheet of paper. Oberlin pointed to something at the top of it while asking, "And what do you see on here, Tenpenny?"

Tobey scanned the page, his cheeks blazing and his jaw flicking with tension. "It appears to be an email from Cassie Black," he responded, then quickly met my eyes, his face full of apology. I tipped my head to indicate it was okay. He couldn't be blamed for the Walrus going rabid.

"An email that says," Oberlin stated imperiously, "and I quote, 'I have three potentially powerful objects in my possession. If they're brought together, trouble could start brewing. If we all aren't careful, the combined objects could spell disaster'."

And let me just be clear, he wasn't reciting this in the bland, half-distracted tone I'd written it in. He was reciting it in the manner of someone reading lines for the part of Lead Villain in the latest rendition of *The Two Villains of Verona*. Reading it that way, it sounded incredibly threatening.

"That's not how—"

"Cassie," Daisy cut me off, "you might want to stay quiet until you can get a lawyer."

I really hated that she kept insisting on being right. Alastair was still recording the action, but the look on his face as he stared at Inspector Oberlin was of full-on fury. His eyes then met mine, he strode over and, despite the officers' orders that he stay back, took my hand while keeping his phone's camera trained on the action. "Leo's getting a direct feed," he whispered to me.

"Tenpenny," sneered Oberlin as he pointed to a notepad on my desk, "what else do we have here?"

Tobey again shot me a look that told me he'd rather be anywhere but in the middle of this power play. "They're notes that question if bringing together certain items could result in a jewel that will give whoever has possession of it power over their enemies."

Alastair's hand tensed on mine, his attention now riveted on the objects rather than Oberlin.

"And do you recognize the handwriting, by any chance?" asked the Inspector.

"It's pretty messy, so it's probably Cassie's," replied Tobey the Penmanship Critic.

"So," Oberlin said, fixing me with an accusatory stare, "you seem to know the significance of these objects. Which makes me wonder, when exactly were you going to put your plan into place? And be honest. It'll look better when this goes to court."

"Plan?" I asked, despite Daisy making the zipping motion over her lips.

"Yes, your plan to assemble the Boncoeur Jewel and seize power from other Magics."

"Oberlin, you ought to know I am just not that ambitious. I mean, I can barely remember to do the laundry and feed the cat. Why would I want *more* responsibility?"

And rather than being a smart ass, I really should have been questioning how, and what, he knew about the Boncoeur Jewel.

Stretching logic to its limits, Oberlin said, "You have several gems that don't belong to you in your possession. You also have a book that I believe contains a few banned spells. And, as we are all too familiar, you have been actively seeking out more jewels, as well as the remaining copies of this very book."

"For my clients, you moron. Not for myself."

"Yes," he said slyly, then looked directly into Alastair's camera. "Clients, who I will note, include your own parents, and who have a nasty habit of dying, being injured, or disappearing once you find their items. And the books? One copy damaged, another copy destroyed. Bit too much of a coincidence for me. So, I have to ask myself, what's in that book you don't want other Magics to discover?"

I couldn't believe this. He was being so utterly ridiculous I wanted to slap him, while at the same time I wanted to plead my innocence. I also wanted time to consider what he was implying. Had I been right to see a connection between Wordsworth's book and the jewels I'd found? The prophecy rang in my head: *Assistance from pages*. What was on those missing pages?

"I'm just doing the jobs I was hired to do," I said, trying to sound calm, but my voice shook with anger, with weariness, with the complete absurdity of it all. "I don't want to start a coup. I only want someone's signature on a stupid form so I can get my silly little piece of paper that will show you I'm just as good a detective as anyone from your precious Academy."

I didn't add that a badge would also be nice.

"I doubt anyone ever hired you for anything. Not willingly, anyway. You knew they had what you needed, you stole the items from them, and then you did away with them."

"Runa's still around," said Daisy. When Oberlin shot her a look, she added meekly, her words trailing off toward the end, "The clinic's break-ins. You wouldn't do anything to locate her saw or the stolen samples, so she hired Cassie to find them."

Oberlin huffed. "It's all pointing to you, Black. Thievery, insurrections, murder. But what really gets me is that you would screw over your own parents like this. Betray them. What have you done with them, hmmm?" he asked, leaning in so close I could smell the tuna on his breath.

And that's not a walrus joke. He clearly had a tuna fish sandwich for lunch.

"My own parents?" I retorted, and because I was under about six tons of stress, I nearly blurted out that they were safe and sound and on a mission for HQ. And that HQ hadn't asked him to do it since a walrus like him couldn't solve a crime if one came up and bit him on the butt. Which makes no sense, but like I said, a lot of stress going on right then and my metaphors weren't firing at top speed.

Thankfully, before my mouth could ruin me, Alastair mumbled, "Confidentiality Spell."

"What was that?" barked the Inspector.

Rather than answer him, I said, "You really think I sent packing the very people who I nearly died trying to rescue for a piece of jewelry?"

"Powerful jewelry."

"Jewelry they hired me to find," I asserted. But after that, I gave up. There was nothing I could say that would make him see reason.

"Cassie Black," announced Inspector Oberlin, smirking with triumph, "by the power given me by the community of Rosaria, you are under arrest for the plotting of a seditious act, for intent to restore the vampires to power, and for harboring magical items that could be used for nefarious purposes. Anything you say now—"

"Would probably make your ears bleed, the curses would be so vicious," I growled. Okay, so maybe I hadn't given up just yet.

"Officers," Oberlin droned, "please take note of the criminal's threats toward me."

"What threats?"

"You just said you would curse me."

"As in swearing, as in potty language, as in—"

"Do I need to Stun you?"

I shook my head. I was already stunned enough.

As one officer bagged up the objects from my safe, the other officer pulled Alastair away from me and looped invisible cuffs around my wrists. The Walrus then told Tobey to get me out of his sight.

Tobey. Our study session tomorrow. His Exam results depended on it (or so he thought). I could already hear Mr T blaming me for Tobey's second failure.

"I'll get Grandad on this, Cass," whispered Tobey as he marched me toward the agency's door. "Don't worry."

Worry? I was well beyond worried.

* * *

Does Cassie have a Get Out of Jail Free card up her sleeve? Can she solve her cases from a guarded cell? More importantly, do they serve cake in prison?

Find out in The Unexpected Mr Hopkins, *the conclusion of the Cassie Black Trilogy 2.0!*

BEHIND THE STORY
A SLIM START

Thank you so much for coming along with me on this fifth installment of Cassie getting herself up to no good. And getting into trouble without even trying.

To say this book started out slim is no exaggeration. The only two things I knew I wanted to have happen — the only two things I could picture clearly in my little pea brain — were Wordsworth's book catching on fire in Cassie's hands and Oberlin carting her off to jail. Which, given that one of those happens right toward the start and the other happens at the very end, meant I had a lot of filling in to do.

Although I played with sending Cassie to other locations around the world, I eventually decided to have her return to London because, as Mr Tenpenny says in *The Uncanny Raven Winston,* "It's a rare person, Magic or Norm, who passes up a trip to London." Even if that trip was only in my own mind. And yes, I did have to look that quote up... I'm not clever enough to remember my books.

Or what I had for breakfast, for that matter.

Of course, if I sent Cassie to the Tower, she was going to have to pay Nigel and Winston a visit, and I absolutely loved bringing them back in their now-living forms. Don't worry, although these two play only a small part in this book, they will have a greater role in *The Unexpected Mr Hopkins*.

From the very moment I imagined them, the scenes with Cassie and Daisy became my hands-down favorites to write, and little editing was needed since it was far too easy to imagine Cassie dealing with someone that bubbly.

Beyond the fun, I had the task of moving this second trilogy along, and that meant continuing with everything I'd set up in *The Unusual Mayor Marheart* and what would be happening in *The Unexpected Mr Hopkins* (although that plot line is still VERY hazy). So, I had a lot of plot lines to untangle, situations that needed to happen, clues to drop along Cassie's path, suspicions to beef up, and all the rest.

What I was left with were a bewildering number of scenes with almost no idea what order they should go in. Worse yet? Over a third of them started with "the next morning" even though the entire novel takes place over a mere five days.

I guess I just really like breakfast?

This mess of scenes eventually got transferred onto notecards that I spread out over my kitchen table (after breakfast, of course). It was daunting. There were well over sixty "bits" that needed to be logically sequenced, but Logic refused to behave. I half-considered just shuffling the cards to see what happened — a Choose-Your-Own Cassie Adventure was bandied about for a bit.

It took many passes of shifting, sorting, and stacking (and pushing the cat off the table), to finally get the disorganized madness into an order that mostly made sense, even if I did have to cut a lot of breakfast scenes (many apologies to Divination Donuts).

Anyway, I hope you've enjoyed the result, and I hope you're as excited as me to discover what's really happening with the vampires, with Tobey's test, with Cassie's parents, with the mayor, and with that pesky Oberlin.

For now, though, thanks so much for reading this book. I'd love to stay in touch, so please be sure to sign up for my monthly newsletter at *www.subscribepage.com/mrsmorris* (all lower case).

While you're waiting for the next, and final, book of The Cassie Black Trilogy 2.0, if you enjoyed *The Unbearable Inspector Oberlin* please be sure to recommend it to someone else who loves comic fantasy whodunits or ask your local library to carry it for others to enjoy.

Finally, if you have a minute or two, leaving a review* on your favorite book retailer, Goodreads, and/or Bookbub would be extra fabulous!

One last tidbit… I know the history buffs out there will have been shouting at me that, while Mary Queen of Scots and her supporters did plot her escape, she was NEVER imprisoned at the Tower of London. She was, in fact, imprisoned in various manor houses and castles, but just to keep things fictionally tidy, I decided to throw her in the Tower.

—Tammie Painter, October 2024

ALSO BY TAMMIE PAINTER

The Humorous stuff

THE CIRCUS OF UNUSUAL CREATURES

Hoard It All Before, Tipping the Scales, Fangs a Million, Beast or Famine

It's not every day you meet an amateur sleuth with fangs.
If you like comic fantasy whodunits that mix in laughs in with murderous mayhem and mythical beasts, you'll love The Circus of Unusual Creatures.

THE CASSIE BLACK TRILOGY

The Undead Mr. Tenpenny, The Uncanny Raven Winston, The Untangled Cassie Black, The Unusual Mayor Marheart

Work at a funeral home can be mundane. Until you accidentally start bringing the dead to life.

THE UNWANTED INHERITANCE OF THE BOOKMAN BROTHERS

A novella celebrating the magic of books. Wills often come with unexpected surprises. This one especially so.

THE GREAT ESCAPE

Peculiar pet shops. Troublesome dream homes. And robot vacuums that just want to be free Looking for a captivating (and quick) escape from reality? These fifteen tales of humor, myth, magic provide just that.